THE PROPHET'S GRIEF

Pamela Gordon Hoad

Pamela Gordon Hoad

Also by Pamela Gordon Hoad in the Harry Somers series

The Devil's Stain

The Angel's Wing

The Cherub's Smile

The Martyr's Scorn

*****

First published 2019 by Silver Quill Publishing

www.silverquillpublishing.com

Typeset in Georgia

ISBN: 978-1-912513-62-8

Silver Quill Publishing

For Margaret Pegg, with love and gratitude for a lifetime of friendship, good counsel and support

Acknowledgements

I should like to record thanks to the friends who have supported me during the process of writing and preparing *The Prophet's Grief* for publication. As with my previous books, I owe a particular debt of gratitude to my son, James, who raised many useful points on the draft, both as proof-reader and historian, and to Oliver Eade, who advised on innumerable matters, technical and literary.

I am very grateful to readers of my earlier books in this series – *The Devil's Stain, The Angel's Wing, The Cherub's Smile* and *The Martyr's Scorn* – who have expressed their enjoyment of those stories and encouraged me to continue the tale of Harry Somers.

My thanks, as always, go to my husband, Peter Hoad, for his support and patience, especially during the period of his ill health, happily now behind us.

Any errors are of course my own.

CONTENTS

Principal characters in order of appearance

Harry Somers, *physician*
Kate Somers, *Harry's wife*
Judith, *Kate's attendant*
Rendell Tonks, *soldier, formerly serving the late Duke of Suffolk, William de la Pole*
Sir Hugh de Grey of Danson, Kent
Lady Blanche de Grey, *Sir Hugh's wife*
Mistress Ash, *wife to Sir Hugh de Grey's woodman*
Allan Ash, *her younger son*
Gilbert Iffley, Baron Glasbury
A man lacking upper front teeth, *serving Baron Glasbury*
Adam Ash, *Sir Hugh de Grey's woodman*
Hubert de Grey, *son to Sir Hugh and Lady Blanche*
*Jack Cade, also known as Edmund Mortimer
*William Stanlaw, *squire to Jack Cade*
Piers Ford, *wheelwright from Dartford, Kent*
Georgie Antey, *younger son of George Antey, carter*
John Toft, *carter from near Maidstone, Kent*
Leone, *physician, once Harry's assistant*
Thomas Chope, *master carpenter in the City of London*
Grizel, *wife to Thomas Chope and sister to Rendell Tonks*
Hal, Dickon, Tom and Margery Chope, *Thomas and Grizel's children*
Master John Webber, *apothecary in the City of London*
Stephen Boice, *merchant, uncle to Kate Somers*
Master Antey, *Georgie Antey's elder brother, carter*
*Sir Roger Chamberlayne, *Keeper of Queenborough Castle*
Sir Nicholas Chamberlayne, *Sir Roger's younger brother, factotum to the Duke of Somerset*
*The Dowager Duchess of Suffolk, *widow of Duke William*
Father Wilfred, *Chaplain at Wingfield Castle, Suffolk*
Perkin, *steward at the manor of Worthwaite, Suffolk*
Dame Elizabeth, *Perkin's wife*
The Prioress of St. Michael's Priory, Stamford
Robin Willoughby, *bailiff to Lord Fitzvaughan at Hartham Manor, Norfolk*
Bess Willoughby, *Robin's wife*

Anne and Rob Willoughby, *Robin and Bess's children*
Lady Eleanor Fitzvaughan
Gaston de la Tour, Lord Fitzvaughan, *Eleanor's husband*
Lady Maud, Dowager Lady Fitzvaughan, *Eleanor's mother*
Walter, *Lord and Lady Fitzvaughan's elder son and heir*
*Edmund Beaufort, 2nd Duke of Somerset
Roger Egremont, Earl of Stanwick
Lady Joan Chamberlayne, *Sir Nicholas's wife*
Mistress Ursula Bateby, *widow*
*William Waynflete Bishop of Winchester
*Richard Plantagenet, 3rd Duke of York
*King Henry VI of England
*Queen Margaret, *wife to King Henry*
The high constable for Harrow and Headstone, Middlesex

*Historical characters recorded in the annals

Part 1 Kent and London 1450

Chapter 1

I woke from the dream trembling and in a sweat. I breathed deeply to quieten my thumping heart but the vivid image was fixed in my mind and it terrified me. I had seen it before. Years before, in the states of northern Italy, I thought: a bronze panel on a church door. Somehow it had lodged in my memory and come to haunt me in a nightmare. I could recall it in detail: the cleric on the left restraining the girl while the saint on the other side put his hand on her arm, to give his healing touch and cast out the evil infesting her soul. The girl's contorted body evidenced her agony and from her mouth a fiendish figure had emerged, cloven-hoofed and horned, gesticulating in fury at being ejected from its chosen home. The artist must have been familiar with the writhing of the possessed. The victim's legs were askew, her torso twisted backwards in ungainly distress – just as my wife appeared when she threw herself about, unable to bear her demons any longer.

Kate lay peacefully at my side, still sedated by the draught I had given her to ensure we both had rest that night. Our journey was exhausting but I must get her to a place where people I trusted could care for her, where she might regain a semblance of sanity. No devil had erupted from Kate's mouth but from time to time she screamed devilish abusive words which tore at my entrails and constricted my throat with a sob. Despite the teachings of Holy Church I was unpersuaded by the concept of demonic possession but I readily admitted that medical knowledge offered little by way of remedies for those afflicted in their minds.

It was already daybreak. Soon the bell of the abbey would summon the monks to the service of Prime and we must be on our way. I had made a generous donation to secure the small garret room where we slept while our companions made do with the common dormitories in the

1

guest house. It was essential to protect Kate from curious eyes and give her respite from her cruel imaginings. God knew there was enough horror in what she had seen and suffered in recent weeks without exciting the false fancies to which she was prone. For years her uncle, Stephen Boice, had exploited his influence over her, undermining her fragile confidence, tilting the balance of her already troubled mind. Earlier in the year he had persuaded her to leave me. Then he consigned her to the care of a medical charlatan who tortured and raped her.

I rose from the pallet and flung my physician's gown over my crumpled jerkin, brushing mud splatters from the hem where it was soiled from the previous day's damp ride. I knelt beside Kate to stroke her cheek and she moaned, as she did every morning, as if in protest at the need to regain consciousness and re-join the quotidian torment of her life.

A light tap at the door signalled that Judith had come to help her mistress get ready for another day on horseback and once again I was grateful for the cheerful care she gave my wife. She had been a maid-servant at Dover Castle, where we stayed for two weeks after the dreadful events on the shore at the foot of the cliffs, but she had been permitted to accompany us to London and I suspected she might choose not to return to her previous service. The girl had a taste for adventure and her imperturbable spirit fitted her well for coping with a volatile invalid. The only drawback to the arrangement was the way she and Rendell riled each other, but he would leave us and determine his own future when we reached the City.

I went out into the yard where my young friend was saddling our horses. I had known Rendell since he was a cheeky, snotty-nosed imp and he had lost none of his wily intelligence but, as a trained and bloodied soldier, he had acquired skills for which I had reason to be thankful. Unfortunately, toleration for a feisty but homely featured girl of his own age, ready to challenge his judgement and knowledge, was not among his attributes and our progress across Kent had been punctuated with complaints and expletives exchanged between the pair of them while Judith rode pillion behind him.

'There's more of them men on the road, like we saw yesterday,' he said as I joined him. 'Mostly husbandmen from the farms, I'd guess, but there are soldiers returned from the defeat in Normandy and some more well-to-do, yeomen and merchants with small retinues. It can't be by accident. Something's up.'

'I wonder where they're going.'

Rendell tapped his nose. 'Made enquiries. They're gathering on Blackheath. You know: the common land up the hill from Greenwich.'

We both knew the location well as we had spent our early years serving the late Humphrey, Duke of Gloucester, in his palace by the River Thames at Greenwich, a few miles east from the City of London. 'That's a highly symbolic rallying point.'

Rendell cocked an eyebrow, not understanding my allusion, so I explained. 'In our grandfathers' day a great crowd of rebels congregated there and the young King at the time rode out to listen to their complaints and promise redress. Later, despite the King's sweet words, at a meeting in the City fighting broke out and the rebel leader, Wat Tyler, was killed. Blackheath will be remembered by the disaffected as the place to make a show of strength and set out demands, perhaps even as the place to rally before marching on London. Do you know who has summoned the men travelling there now?'

'The fellow I spoke to said their leader was called Mortimer.'

'Mortimer!'

The Prioress of St. Michael's Convent in Stamford, whose wisdom and knowledge I esteemed, had warned me to beware if I ever heard rumours of a Mortimer stirring up dissent and I had reason to suspect such a person might be the Duke of York's catspaw. I was certain that, not three

3

weeks previously, Richard of York's acolytes had been complicit in the murder of the Duke of Suffolk, whose household I served as physician, and one of them had taunted me with the prospect that the whole county of Kent would soon be ablaze with men's fury. It was all too probable that an apparently spontaneous rally on Blackheath had been carefully contrived.

'I don't like the sound of this. We'll need to keep clear of Blackheath.'

'Difficult when our road crosses it. Oh Christ, here comes the Queen of Sheba.'

Judith had her arm round Kate and led her to my side. 'Mistress Somers is inclined to be tearful this morning, Doctor,' she said, ignoring Rendell. 'Something's preying on her mind.'

It could be so many things – that she had suffered or seen, or inflicted on herself. I scrambled onto the saddle and lifted Kate's feather-light weight so she could sit in front of me.

'You mounting or not?' Rendell held his horse steady but neglected to offer Judith his hand.

'Thought you might whisk me up beside you, like Doctor Somers lifted his wife.'

'Likely dislocate my shoulder if I tried. Might as well have a sack of turnips behind me.'

'Fine courteous warrior you are.' She hauled herself up unaided. 'Worked as a scullion once, I've heard. Should have stayed in the kitchen emptying the slops. All you're good for.'

Rendell's rejoinder was drowned by the arrival of our escort, clattering out from the stables: two armed men from Dover Castle. They served the titular Warden there, James Fiennes, Baron Saye and Sele, and were lent to us for protection on the road. I bit my lip when I saw them.

'Rendell tells me there could be trouble brewing – discontented men on the march. It might be wise to hide your livery. Your master's not well loved in Kent.'

They nodded and drew their cloaks across their chests as we set off, soon coming alongside and overtaking a column of labourers and seamen who looked askance at us but did not impede our progress. Ignorant of how far the rally had advanced, I hoped we were gaining ground on the foot-slogging dissidents and would be able to cross Blackheath safely before they congregated there.

If all went well, we should reach the walls of the City within two days. I could lodge Kate there with Rendell's sister, Grizel, and her husband, Thomas, while I ascertained if my services were still required at the Manor of the Rose. I suspected that the late Duke of Suffolk's London house would not be occupied by his widow and eight-year-old heir until the Duchess was sure they would be safe in the City where the Duke had been deeply unpopular. She would most probably prefer to remain in their stronghold at Wingfield in the County of Suffolk and reduce the complement of servants in the London house. The position of household physician at the Manor of the Rose might no longer be needed.

When the sun was at its zenith we took a short rest by a pool under trees so riders and horses could refresh themselves. Kate had seemed in a daze all morning and I was thankful she was not attracting the attention of others on the road with the weird exclamations she sometimes emitted. She drank some of the small beer we carried but, as usual, scarcely nibbled the freshly baked bread from the abbey where we had spent the night. Judith ate heartily and then led her mistress to a hollow behind some bushes where they could relieve themselves unobserved. I stood, stretched myself and rubbed my left ankle which had been injured in a boyhood accident and gave me a jerky gait. Rendell stowed our empty flasks in the paniers the packhorse carried. Suddenly, we were both startled by Kate's scream and I hurtled down the slope, with awkward speed, to see what had frightened her. Three or four rooks rose with a chorus of squawks as I neared the depression shadowed by gorse and broom.

5

No third person had disturbed them but Judith was holding my wife's arms, restraining her wild attempts to break free with her skirts still in disarray. Kate's face was ashen, her huge green eyes full of terror, and she wrenched one wrist from her maid's grasp to point at an untidy mess in the mud a few feet from where we stood. She began to wail. 'It's a baby's leg. Look! A baby's leg. The birds were eating a baby's leg.'

I crouched beside the bloody heap of torn flesh and rose to hold Kate close against my chest. 'No, sweet, no. It's all right. It's a rabbit's leg, stripped of its skin and ripped from the rest of the carcase. It's not from a human child.'

Kate stared at me, deaf to my words, refusing to be comforted, and I understood why she was distressed. The tiny mutilated limb reminded her of the miscarriage she had procured in irrational panic at the prospect of giving birth, fearing she would bear a deformed infant as a relative of hers had done. She was beyond reason at that moment and all we could do was try to calm her until the frenzy had passed.

Unfortunately, other wayfarers had heard her cries and a band of four or five men hurried towards us despite the efforts of Rendell and our escort to prevent them. I was aware of a tussle by the roadside but I concentrated on those descending the incline, trying to dissuade them from troubling my wife further.

'I'm a physician,' I said, patting the gown which distinguished my profession. 'The lady is in my charge. Her mind is afflicted and I'm taking her where she can be cared for. She's had a fright but the source of her fear is imaginary. No cause for concern. Her maid is with her.'

I indicated Judith who bustled forward and flapped her arms to disperse the spectators as we began to climb uphill. The men let us pass, murmuring sympathy, and I thanked them for their compassion. Kate had subsided into broken sobs, nestled against me, and I hoped her grief would be fleeting but our ascent was interrupted by shouts above us.

'These here are James Fiennes's men! Villains!'

'They're spies, sent to keep an eye on us.'

'Planning to disrupt our assembly. Let's teach them a lesson.'

I took in the scene with dismay. A member of our escort had been pulled from his horse, his cloak slashed and the crest on his jerkin was clearly visible. He had drawn his sword and was fending off a trio carrying pitchforks and clubs who taunted him. His colleague, still in the saddle, had turned his horse and he thundered towards the confrontation but the men who had come down the slope were racing back to join the mêlée and they hurled stones at the rider. Only when Rendell erupted into the fray, twirling a mace with murderous intent, and slicing a man's sleeve with his dagger, was their enthusiasm blunted. The would-be aggressors fell back and the brief hiatus in their attack allowed us to mount and ride off at a gallop. A hail of missiles followed us but by good fortune we evaded our pursuers.

Even so, as new streams of travellers joined the throng a mile or two in front of us, we could not maintain our speed along the highroad without arousing curiosity and provoking more antagonism. We were forced to slow down. Most of the men debouching from side-tracks and meadows were on foot but there were some ox-drawn wagons and hand-carts which blocked progress and were difficult to overtake. When we slowed to a walk, I feared others would recognise the livery of Baron Saye and Sele, inadequately concealed by a torn cloak. I sensed the latent anger which drove these men onwards to their objective – an objective which must bode ill for those they identified as foes. If there was the slightest doubt, it was dispelled when a fellow started to chant mocking words about the King's advisers and others joined a chilling chorus.

'Let all true Englishmen be bold:
Ask God to rest the souls in peace

*Of traitors false who England sold
And give the Duke of Suffolk ease.'*

It was only two weeks since I witnessed Suffolk's head hacked from his body by vindictive mariners, after a travesty of judicial process, his remains flung unceremoniously onto Dover beach. The barbarity of the act demonstrated how feebly good order survived in King Henry's realm: when so powerful a noble could be done to death even while he held a safe-conduct bearing the royal seal. In a kingdom ostensibly at peace, no man, however reprehensible his deeds, should be confronted by irregular and arbitrary judgement; but aggrieved men had lost their faith in the rule of law and that appalled me.

I was under no illusions as to the flaws in Suffolk's character. From my own experience I knew he could be haughty, self-seeking and acquisitive. But he was also capable of kindness, he served his King loyally and in the last two years of his life he had treated me as a friend. I mourned him and was pained by the ridicule of scornful men aware of his reputation only through malicious hearsay. At the same time I could expect rough treatment if the angry crowd around me learned of my links to the Duke they decried. I must not indulge the regrets I felt but take thought for the safety of my party.

Kate was cuddled against me while I rode inexpertly with one hand on the reins but a few furlongs along the road she twitched and shuddered, before groaning loudly. My alarm increased that she would be seized by a violent paroxysm which I could not control while on horseback and I dreaded having to dismount. Her behaviour was already attracting sidelong glances from those near us and I risked being the object of amused, perhaps ribald, interest if observers believed I was compelling her to ride with me against her wishes. Our position had become untenable, our intended destination impracticable and I must take action to address our predicament. One alternative seemed possible and it was not one I welcomed. Yet the embarrassment it might involve could not outweigh the danger we faced among those travelling the road with us as we came ever nearer to Blackheath.

When we approached a cross-road where a faint track ran off to the right, I pulled my horse onto the verge and beckoned my companions to stop. 'We must find shelter,' I said. 'My wife is poorly and the road is dangerous. We must go to Danson. This is the edge of the estate.'

'We can get through this lot,' Rendell protested. 'You've got three swordsmen here. We can cut a path through this load of ruffians.'

'Think yourself a right Saint George, don't you?' Judith's voice was shrill. 'Well this lady won't put her safety in your hands, Master Rendell Tonks, nor allow her mistress to depend on your valour. These marching dragons mean mischief and by the time we get to this Blackheath place, there'll be thousands of them. If you insist on going on, you can put me down and I'll follow Doctor Somers on foot. Do you hear me, you arrogant prick?'

Rendell had jerked the reins as if he meant to ride on but Judith leaned to the side and grabbed his arm, pulling them to a juddering halt.

'No need for that, you interfering bitch. I'm not going to leave the Doctor. Him and me go back years. He can't manage without me. Now shut your mouth and sit still or you'll be tossed in the mud. Hey, what's that?'

Judith had extracted a bodkin from her bodice and was tickling Rendell's ear with its tip. 'Just do as you're told, warrior. What's at this Danson we're going to?'

The truthful answer was complicated but at that point irrelevant. 'Friends,' I said, 'and a manor-house where we'll be given sanctuary.'

'The lord of the manor's a lecherous bastard,' Rendell commented affably under his breath. 'But I wouldn't rate his chances with this lady fair. Ow!'

9

Judith replaced her dainty weapon in her dress and winked at nobody in particular.

*****

Sir Hugh and Lady Blanche de Grey had rendered me many services in the past but I was confident they did not consider their debt to me repaid. More than ten years ago I had kept my mouth shut about dishonourable acts for which they were responsible, seeing no benefit to anyone in revealing their misguided folly. Among their many kindnesses to me thereafter, I was profoundly grateful to them for providing my seamstress mother with a comfortable home in her declining years. I had not visited Danson since she died and when last I stayed at the manor-house I had misled my hosts about my romantic attachment to a French noblewoman they befriended. Probably they knew nothing of Kate and I feared some acute questioning about my life over the past three years. Nevertheless I accepted the inevitable – it was a price I needed to pay in order to provide us with safe lodgings.

Rendell rode ahead with Judith, far from submissive at his back, in order to announce our impending arrival. The rest of us jogged gently across the outer pastures of the de Grey demesne and beside a row of cottages on the edge of the estate I caught my breath at the sight of a small boy in a worn tunic several sizes too big for him. There was nothing surprising about a workman's lad wearing his brother's hand-me-downs but the child's face was unlike those of the bigger boys playing with him. There was a refinement in his features which they did not share and the beguiling expression in his eyes was familiar to me. Just then a woman emerged from one of the cottages and, seeing our party, she dropped a respectful curtsy before gathering her son in her arms. She was neatly dressed with a pretty cap and I had no doubt her comeliness had attracted the pressing attentions of

Danson's master. She would not be the only woman on Sir Hugh de Grey's land whom he had taken to his bed.

Soon after this incident I saw horsemen approaching us and recognised the lusty knight himself riding with Rendell who had relinquished his pillion passenger. Sir Hugh was graciousness personified, offering hospitality for as long as we needed accommodation and expressing heartfelt concern for my wife's health. Lady Blanche had taken Judith into the manor-house to prepare for her mistress's reception and was overjoyed that we were to be her guests. She had only lately risen from childbed, her eleventh delivery Sir Hugh recalled, and they were blessed to have eight living children. He indicated improvements he had made to his property, the ditches deepened, the stand of trees planted and the barns rebuilt. Afterwards, with consummate delicacy, he referred to my mother's death and repeated the commiserations he had previously put in writing.

Grooms ran to greet us and take our horses when we arrived at the house and, as he dismounted, I noted how Sir Hugh's natural sturdiness had broadened, making him look shorter than I remembered. He removed his velvet cap and ran his fingers through thinning hair before he replaced it and reached up to lift Kate to the ground. She had been peaceful for the last part of our ride, showing no interest in our host's monologue, but when she felt his hands on her arms she quivered and opened her eyes, turning those extraordinary green orbs on him. Sir Hugh looked up at me.

'By all the saints, Harry Somers, you've chosen a rare beauty. We must have good care for her and bring her to full health.'

I jumped down and he passed my wife into my arms but I did not like the smile she gave him as he bowed. To my shame I would have preferred at that moment that she had shrieked inanely, as she often did, and not behaved with cultured charm towards this flagrant lecher. By then Lady Blanche had joined us and I was pleased to see that, although she was pale, she appeared contented. Inevitably the rigour of annual birthing had taken its toll but she retained an elegance which I admired. She had no delusions about her husband's fidelity but treated it as a matter of no consequence. Whatever secret anguish she had suffered during their marriage, she maintained a dignity in public which defied anyone to pity her.

The Lady of Danson bade us welcome, kissed Kate on her unresisting forehead and waved her hand in the direction of the copse across the nearby field. 'The nursemaids have rounded up the children and are bringing them home. You must meet them all. There are two still in the nursery. I'll take you to see them as soon as you are rested, Mistress Somers.'

I wondered whether this would be wise but was reassured by my wife's placid behaviour while Judith helped her into the house by Lady Blanche's side. I started to follow them but noticed Sir Hugh was shielding his eyes against the sun as he peered at the flock of maids and children sallying from the wood. One young woman was running ahead of the others, stumbling on the uneven ground. Her hair had come loose beneath her cap and her cheeks were red with exertion.

'What is it, Jen? Is someone hurt?'

She was too far away for her voice to carry in reply so we hurried towards her until she dropped on her knees in front of us and threw her apron over her face. Sir Hugh pulled the girl to her feet, not unkindly, and insisted that she tell us what had occurred.

She gulped breath and tried to compose herself, speaking in a whisper. 'It's little Hubert, sir. He's vanished again. Please God, he's not drowned in the fishpond but there's no sign of him. We didn't know he was missing 'til we gathered everyone to come home. The boys thought he'd gone with the girls. But he's nowhere to be seen.'

Sir Hugh de Grey put his hand on my shoulder. 'Go to your wife,' he said. 'These rascals are given to hiding in the woods and the maids are inclined to panic. I'm sure

Hubert will soon emerge. Should we have need of your skills, Doctor Somers, I'll know where to find you.'

If the unfortunate child was lying injured after a fall, my medical knowledge could be of help, but I realised it was not necessarily my physician's skills that Sir Hugh had in mind when he made his jovial comment.

Chapter 2

I left Sir Hugh assembling a posse of servants to search for his missing son while I was escorted into the house and Lady Blanche welcomed me all over again, although she looked anxious.

'Dear Doctor Somers, we are so pleased you've come. Your wife is charming but she seems confused. She called me "your Grace" as if I was nobility.'

'Kate has been ill and sometimes her wits wander. She needs rest but the road from Dover has been anything but restful.'

'You were with the Duke of Suffolk when he was killed?'

I nodded. 'Until the end. He was treated barbarously. He carried the King's safe-conduct but the sailors who captured him scorned it. They constituted themselves as a court of law, a mockery of a court, and they condemned him. Then they hacked off his head.'

'No wonder Mistress Somers' wits are afflicted. We shall care for her, Harry, for as long as you wish.'

'Thank you, my lady, the respite will be valuable but I hope we can travel on to London in a day or two.' I did not attempt to explain that Kate's affliction had deeper roots than the impact of Suffolk's murder. 'There's a great congregation of folk on the road at present which impedes our progress.'

'Rustics from across the county, I'm told.' Sir Hugh had joined us. 'Up to no good. I'm glad to say no one from my domain has joined them. They'd face a horse-whipping if they did. Go and refresh yourself, Harry. Don't worry if Mistress Somers isn't able to accompany you to the hall for supper. I'll defer the pleasure of her better acquaintance until she is restored to full health.'

Lady Blanche raised her eyebrows in a show of evident exasperation.

I was relieved to find that Kate was already sleeping and Judith was well satisfied with the provision

14

made for our accommodation. She pronounced herself agreeably surprised to be among gentlefolk in a decently appointed manor-house after the less convenient resting places we had frequented on the journey. Reassured, I washed and changed into my best physician's gown.

Later, hearing much coming and going in the courtyard, I returned to the hall and found Sir Hugh frowning as a succession of men from the search party reported their lack of success in discovering young Hubert. Rendell had been helping them and he whispered in my ear.

'Looks like the little blighter's bunked off more than once but he's always been spotted up a tree or in the undergrowth. They've looked in all his usual hiding places and even dragged the fishpond. He ain't to be found anywhere this time.'

'Who saw the boy last?'

'Dunno. We'd have to ask his brothers and sisters or the maid servants who were with them.'

I was not surprised that, when he realised the situation might be more serious than at first appeared, Sir Hugh appealed to me to make enquiries, for we shared a memory of how long ago I had probed a murder which touched us both nearly. This experience led me into other investigations and gave me a reputation for solving mysteries which was only partly deserved but had become widely known. Sir Hugh summoned his two eldest sons who looked truculent when they were brought to me and I imagined they might have refused to answer my questions if he had not been standing beside them. I addressed the elder lad who bore his father's name and was ten or eleven years old.

'Was Hubert with you, Master Hugh, earlier in the afternoon?'

The boy's chin jutted defiantly, a replica of his paternal namesake when irritated. 'He should have stayed with the maids. He's only a baby. Matthew and I had our bows and were shooting at magpies. He was a nuisance.'

15

'So you sent him away?'

'To join the girls.'

'Where were they?'

We'd left them playing in the dell on the edge of the wood.'

'You didn't go with Hubert?'

'Do you take us for nursemaids?'

Sir Hugh raised his hand as if to cuff the boy but I deterred him and turned to Matthew, a year or so younger than the heir to the manor of Danson. He looked intelligent and had squirmed at his brother's rudeness. 'We're out there every day,' he said. 'Hubert knows his way around. He's five years old. He's often found his way home on his own.'

'I see. Was he upset when you sent him away?'

'He's not a cry-baby, Doctor. He's a de Grey.' Master Hugh had resumed the role of spokesman and he exuded arrogance. His father strode out of the hall at this point, whether in pride or vexation I could not tell.

I confirmed that the boys had not seen Hubert again after he trotted off, no doubt with their brotherly imprecations ringing in his ears, so I let them go and asked to speak to the young ladies. Accordingly three small girls were presented to me, along with the attendant who had accompanied them on their excursion, and I asked them to tell me when they had seen Hubert during the afternoon.

'He went off with Hugh and Matthew,' the eldest of the trio said in a tone that invited no contradiction.

'But he didn't stay with them, I understand. They sent him back.'

A head topped by a cloud of blonde curls was tossed haughtily. 'They shouldn't have done that. He's a boy and should have stayed with them.'

I had no intention of taking sides between the siblings. 'Did he actually come back to you?'

Three rosebud mouths clamped shut while I looked from one to the other until the youngest girl began to

16

whimper and she turned to her eldest sister. 'Joanie,' she said. 'He may be hurt or run off from Danson.'

'Then he's a dolt.' Seven- or eight-year-old eyes fixed their assertive gaze on me. 'He ran back to us but he didn't want to stay. I told him to go home.'

'So he went off on his own?'

'He knew the way, sir. You can see the roof of the house from the dell.' The girls' attendant had spoken and I smiled my thanks at her.

'Did you see him go there?'

The maid lowered her eyes and shook her head.

'We were playing a game, threading daisies.' Sir Hugh's eldest daughter did not hide her annoyance. 'It wasn't our task to watch him.'

Three small heads bobbed and I let my female witnesses return to the nursery, shrugging at Rendell who muttered an expletive unfitting for their ears. Almost at once he tapped his nose to indicate that one of the three had returned and, after peeping over her shoulder, the previously silent middle sister crept forward.

'Hubert didn't go home, sir. He went the other way, into the woods.'

I turned to Rendell. 'The woods have been searched thoroughly, haven't they?'

'Went through them meself, with the others. I'd swear the boy isn't there.'

I crouched down beside the girl. 'Thank you, little mistress, that's helpful. Have you any idea where Hubert might have gone? Does he have a den somewhere?'

She widened her eyes. 'He'd likely go to play with the boy at the cottages. Mama says he shouldn't but Hubert says they're friends.'

'The cottages near the edge of the estate, not far from the roadway?'

The girl inclined her head, then gathered up her skirt and ran to catch up with her sisters. Rendell tapped his nose ostentatiously.

'Them cottages we passed when we arrived?'

'Yes,' I agreed, remembering the lad who must be around Hubert's age and clearly resembled Hubert's father. 'Let's go there.'

The sun was sinking when we approached the row of cottages and the woman I had seen before emerged from one with a bucket of detritus for the midden. I hailed her, explaining our mission, and asked her name.

'I'm Mistress Ash, sir, wife to Sir Hugh's woodman.' She was trembling visibly. 'I heard Master Hubert was missing. I haven't seen him today but he does come sometimes to play with my Allan. Lady Blanche has forbidden it and I try to send him back, sir. I do truly.'

'I'm sure you do, Mistress Ash. You're not in any trouble. Is Allan home?'

'Yes, sir, he came in while the sun was still above the oak tree. I'll fetch him.'

At close quarters the boy's similarity to his overlord and his overlord's heirs was startling. He held his mother's hand but faced me without undue deference. He shook his head vigorously when I asked if he knew where Hubert was.

'I hope he's all right, sir.'

'So do I, Allan. Did you see him today? This afternoon?'

He nodded twice and glanced up at his mother. 'I was in the wood – looking for acorns for the pig. Hubert came running. He was angry. He'd been sent away, He wanted to play.'

'What did you do, Allan?'

Again the lad squinted at Mistress Ash. 'We chased each other. Threw acorns. We followed the stream down to the road.' He paused and I encouraged him to go on, delighted to see his mother patting his hand lovingly in reassurance. 'There were lots of men walking, all the same way.' He sounded nervous of contradiction.

'I saw them too, Allan, when I arrived here. What happened then?'

He hung his head for a moment as if plucking up courage. 'There were some horse-carts. They had to stop – to get across the stream – one after the other. They splashed us when we ran along by the ford.' Again he paused.

'Did Master Hubert fall in the stream, Allan?' Mistress Ash gasped in distress.

'No, no, he didn't. He climbed into one of the carts. He wanted me to do it too. But I couldn't. I was scared.'

'And the cart trundled on with Hubert in it? The driver didn't know?'

'No one saw. He waved at me. All excited. He was glad to go off.'

'Oh, Allan, you should have told me. Where can he be now?'

'Don't alarm yourself, Mistress Ash. Allan's done nothing wrong. They're just little boys. I know where the men were going so I know where to look for Master Hubert. There's no reason he should come to harm. He's just having an adventure. Allan's been very helpful. He's a bright lad.' I pressed a coin into his hand. 'There's no need for anyone else to know where I got this information. Don't worry.'

Allan beamed his thanks for his reward and his mother dropped a deep curtsy before they re-entered their cottage. Rendell gave me a broad grin. 'Blackheath then,' he said.

'Blackheath,' I repeated and could not mask my shudder.

*****

Rendell and I collected our horses and rode as quickly as we could up the long incline to the west of Danson. I sent a message to Sir Hugh, explaining we were extending the search beyond the estate, but did not suggest the direction in which we were bound. Where we were heading it would be imprudent to be accompanied by men in the livery of a local landowner. There was a reasonable chance that an anonymous physician and his colleague would not be seen as a threat by the men rallying to voice their dissatisfaction with those in authority. I could only pray that I would not encounter those unscrupulous companions of Duke Richard of York who had harmed me in the past and whom I suspected of close involvement in this demonstration of apparently unprompted popular discontent.

There were only a few streaks of light in the sky when we reached the heath and everywhere men were settling in for the night. Fires had been lit and pots of gruel were swinging over them from makeshift trivets while many weary travellers were munching the hunks of bread they had carried from home in slings on their backs. Some wayfarers were already bundled in cloaks hoping for sleep, undisturbed by the activity around them; others were quaffing ale from leather flasks. I was glad to see that most of the carts were clustered together overlooking a depression in the ground where half a dozen tents had been erected. Nearby, trestles were laid with victuals, presumably for the leaders of the assembly who were to be sheltered under canvas. Clearly a hierarchy of entitlement was to be observed even among the disgruntled populace.

If Gilbert Iffley and even his wife's brother, Stephen Boice, were present, they would certainly be with the favoured few and it was them I must avoid. Yet most of the carts were in the vicinity of the tented encampment and that posed a problem. I signed to Rendell to dismount and we led our horses behind the row of carts, peering inside them where we could but trying not to arouse suspicion. I noted that several of the carts were carrying timber and stakes were being erected round the edge of the heathland. This was not intended as a temporary resting place, it seemed, but one which might need to be defended.

Rendell kept well back from me and I had not gone far before I was challenged.

'What are you after, quack? Looking for pickings to steal from your fellow citizens, are you?'

The man was smartly turned out and would have done credit to a nobleman's retinue. He demanded respect both for his demeanour and the drawn sword he carried.

'No indeed. I'm looking for an errant child who climbed up on a cart a few miles back and may have been brought here with the driver all unwitting: a five year old boy who gave his brothers the slip. I've come to take him home.'

The sentinel rubbed his chin. 'There's no brats here. This is men's work. Jack Cade's insistent on that.'

'Jack Cade?'

'You've not heard of him, I suppose. Give us a week and all London will know his name. We'll march on the City, storm the bridge, and the men of Essex will breach the gates to the east. In a month Jack Cade's fame will have spread throughout England. I'm taking you in charge as having malicious intent so you'll have the honour of meeting him. Tether your horse here.'

Another armed guard had appeared on my right side but a quick glance told me that Rendell and his horse had melted into the shadows. 'I'll be happy to explain my mission to your leader,' I said.

'We'll frisk you first. If you've stolen anything, you'll be strung up within the hour. Jack Cade has no truck with indiscipline. He's ordered no disobedience on pain of execution.'

I held out my arms so they could search inside my gown and purse. They found no contraband but inevitably they discovered my dagger which caused the first man to whistle.

'Concealed weapon, eh? Christ, you could be an assassin. Disguised as a quack, spouting a cock and bull story about a lost child as cover.'

'Even a physician needs to carry a dagger for protection. Any man does. You know that very well. I imagine lawlessness in the land is one of your complaints.'

21

My captor bit his lip. 'I'll let Jack Cade judge that.'

'Cade'll have turned in for the night,' his companion said. 'He wants an early start. He's to make a proclamation and send messengers to the King in the morning. Best take this rogue to Baron Glasbury.'

I inhaled. Baron Glasbury was Gilbert Iffley's title.

'I'm acquainted with Baron Glasbury,' I said without enthusiasm. 'He can vouch for my identity.'

'Full of surprises, you are, mate,' the second man chuckled with a hint of admiration in his voice. 'Come along then. Baron Glasbury's just supervising a flogging – some bloke indulged in fisticuffs. Not allowed.'

Brought before the man who in the past had caused me to be tortured and threatened my life, I was in a deeply uncomfortable position. For years Iffley had tried to cajole me into joining Richard of York's coterie and had used his wife's brother, Stephen Boice, to menace me when I refused. Duke Richard himself, I believed, was a man of honour but his royal blood gave him a claim to King Henry's throne and the less principled of his followers were anxious for him to assert that claim. If our gentle, benignly pious sovereign was unable to maintain order in his kingdom and suppress rivalries between his nobles, the day might come when York would be persuaded to take up arms against his royal cousin: but that day could well be disastrous for England. My father had been killed in the wars in France which had rumbled on for many decades. To see violent dissension turn inwards and my country riven by bloody conflict was a nightmare I could not bear to contemplate. Iffley personified the prospect of that nightmare becoming real.

He was sitting at a table with papers in front of him but his attention was on a man with a whip who stood before him. He gave a roar of laughter and put something in the fellow's hand as he dismissed him: an unpleasant-looking brute lacking his upper front teeth. To my right the victim of Iffley's punishment was dragged away, his chest heaving as he tried to stifle his groans. The Baron caught

22

sight of my attendant and swivelled round towards us. At once he stood.

'Praise to the saints in heaven, can this be true? Can this really be Doctor Somers come to join our cause at last? Has this show of common men's outrage convinced you when my eloquence failed?' He flicked his fingers to dismiss the man gripping my arm.

'You mistake my intention, Baron. I have no hostility to humble men who are aggrieved by what they see as injustice and wish to make peaceful representations to the King, but I've not come to join their cause. Still less am I ready to support you in more dubious enterprises which I suspect you may be nurturing under cover of this gathering. I'm come to Blackheath in search of a small boy who climbed onto one of the carts bound here.'

Iffley curled his lip. 'You have a secret son?'

'He isn't mine – a friend's. If you have authority with these men, would you ask the carters to check their vehicles to see if a child has fallen asleep among the goods they are carrying?'

'I'm reluctant to disturb men's rest. I'll enquire in the morning.' His tone was measured as if his words concealed what he was thinking. 'You're welcome to stay the night, Harry. There's room for an extra pallet in my tent. I imagine the guard took your dagger from you? Good. I've eaten but I can offer you wine.' He sat and reached out for a flagon on the table.

'Thank you, no, but I'll accept a bed for the night if you'll send word round the camp in the morning to look out for the boy.'

He poured himself a beaker of wine. 'I surmise this child comes of distinguished lineage that you are so concerned about him?'

This was dangerous ground so I affected not to comprehend the implication. 'Just a local lad.'

Iffley gave a thin smile. 'For sure, you grew up at Greenwich palace and have various friends in the neighbourhood. Your status has changed since then.' He

23

crossed his legs and his manner became patronising. 'How is the charming lady you've married? I've heard much of her from my good-brother, Boice, – a relative of hers, to be sure. I'm desolated to learn of her affliction. To be burdened with a wife whose wits are addled is a grievous fate for an upstanding man. I gather you can have no confidence in her virtue either, for a madwoman may easily mistake another man for her lawful husband and share her favours more liberally than is seemly.'

I clenched my fists, struggling to ignore his goading, knowing he wanted to provoke me. 'I have every hope my wife can be restored to complete health.'

'And meanwhile your erstwhile mistress, the alluring Lady Maud Fitzvaughan, is become a widow. Shall you renew your acquaintance with her bed, lusty physician?'

'Lady Maud is in Norfolk and I have no plans to see her.'

'Alas, such self-control is not good for a man. What's this?'

He rose to his feet at the sound of shouting behind us and I experienced a turbulent mixture of emotions when I identified what he had seen. Two guards were escorting an unknown man with the crest of the de Greys on his tunic but in his arms, snuggled against his shoulder, was a chubby boy half-asleep. I clapped my hand to my mouth in an attempt to signal the need for discretion and the man inclined his head slightly.

'Who have we here then?' Iffley asked. 'Is this the boy you're seeking, Harry? You didn't tell me there was a larger search party. Who are you, fellow?'

'My name is Adam Ash, woodman.'

'Serving a local overlord, I presume?'

'Sir Hugh de Grey. I've come only to search for my boy, a mischievous scamp who climbed into a cart as it was passing. The Doctor was kindly helping me.'

Iffley peered closely at the slumbering child. 'He's finely arrayed for a woodman's son, Master Ash, but I

24

suppose your lord is generous.' He sniggered and poked Hubert in the ribs causing the boy to wake with a squeal and clutch desperately at the arm holding him. 'Where did your father find you, my fine fellow?'

Master Ash and I spoke simultaneously hoping to drown Hubert's puzzled denial but Iffley was not deceived. 'Well, well, I wonder: is your father Sir Hugh de Grey by any chance, sonny?'

Hubert looked at each of us, sensing something was wrong, and his mouth quivered but pride in his pedigree was bred in him. 'Of course,' he said.

Iffley smiled unpleasantly. 'Then we will be pleased to entertain you in our camp until our business is concluded, little gentleman.' He beckoned his attendants before addressing Master Ash. 'Why should you let yourself be in thrall to your master to such an extent that you lie for the sake of his brat? Open your eyes, woodman. You'd be wise to join our company. It's the interests of worthy men like you that we seek to uphold. Rally to our cause. A robust man should not be sent to look for his lord's wandering whelp – that's a task for a nursemaid.' The Baron signalled to his men to seize Ash's arms and lifted Hubert from him.

Master Ash held his head high and I admired his dignity. 'Sir Hugh did not send me here. This boy plays with my own son. It was my lad told me what had happened. I guessed where the cart was bound and followed. I didn't know this Doctor had also come to look for him. We've never met before.'

'I urge you to consider where your true interests lie, Master Ash, but in any case we're compelled to detain you here overnight.' Iffley turned to a guard. 'Treat this man with respect but keep him close until the morning. He'll be free to go when Jack Cade has made his proclamation but I hope he'll stay to make common cause with us. Meanwhile confine this infant where he can do no harm. He may prove a useful hostage to ensure the good behaviour of his father. As for you, Doctor Somers, my offer of hospitality stands.'

I started to express my indignation as the others were led away, with Master Ash cursing and Hubert bawling, when there were sounds of upheaval from the finest of the tents. A servant threw back the cloth which covered the opening and, seeing Iffley, ran directly to us.

'Jack Cade is taken sick, sir,' he panted. 'Vomiting badly. His squire is asking if there's a physician to hand?' He stared at me. 'The Lord God be praised. He's sent you to help us.'

Iffley guffawed and grasped my shoulder. 'Sent from heaven indeed, Harry. I've seen young Mortimer given to puking on one or two occasions, whatever name he's using, but he's entitled to a physician's attention and you cannot deny a sick man your care. It would be against your solemn oath, would it not? Welcome to Jack Cade's entourage, my reluctant friend. Go now to your latest, albeit unsought, patient.'

His derisive laughter rang through the night air as I accepted the obligations of my profession. While I made my way to the largest tent, I wondered where the devil Rendell was skulking and when he would reveal himself.

Chapter 3

My first glimpse told me that it was not the first time I had seen the man now known as Jack Cade. Some two years previously, in Dublin, I had happed upon Iffley giving instruction to a young man whose name, I was told then, was Mortimer and Rendell had heard that the leader of the men assembled on Blackheath was also a Mortimer. I was quite clear that the 'Mortimer' I had encountered before and Jack Cade were one and the same person, as Iffley himself had just implied. This was reason enough for caution.

The young man was of medium height and graceful build. He was pale and looked worried but did not appear unhealthy. 'I didn't expect a physician to be found so quickly,' he said in a pleasantly mellow voice. 'I told my man I didn't need one but Stanlaw here, my squire, insisted.' Cade strode back and forth across the restricted space of the tent.

I took a quick glance at the swarthy, tight-lipped squire in the shadows and acknowledged my approval of his concern for his master.

'My name is Somers. I happened to be in the camp and was talking to Gilbert Iffley. I've known him for some years. I was informed you'd been sick. How often has this occurred?'

'Only once tonight but I spewed up twice earlier in the week.' I noticed he was shivering.

I turned to the squire, Stanlaw. 'Have you kept tonight's vomit?'

The fellow lifted the lid over a basin and handed it to me. 'This doesn't seem particularly noxious. There's no foul bile. You had a rich supper, Master Cade?'

'I suppose so. I've always been inclined to heave easily but it would be inconvenient if I puked when conducting business.'

'Which you'll be doing in the morning? When the sickness has come before, did that precede some testing occasion?'

He stood still and nodded. 'I suppose it did. I was due to speak publicly then but the sickness went away before I addressed the men.'

'I believe the same thing will happen this time. You're a young man and you carry responsibility, Master Cade. It's natural for you to be on edge. I've seen it before – the human body responds in different ways when under pressure. We can't tell why but it seems to me the contemplation of an ordeal to come causes some of us to vomit so that, when the moment of trial actually arrives, we can be calm. Does that make sense to you?'

'The best sense I've ever heard a physician speak. Must I just put up with it then?'

I liked his matter-of-fact acceptance of my diagnosis. 'I suggest you keep to a lighter diet when facing a testing time. Don't burden your stomach with rich food. That may help. And tell yourself there's nothing to be concerned about – I'm sure that's true.'

Jack Cade fixed me with his penetrating eyes. 'You're inclined to be sick yourself?'

I grinned 'You're perceptive. I have that propensity when under pressure. You come to know your own foibles as you get older. If your servant has basic herbs to hand, I'll mix you a potion to settle your digestion. Then I suggest you take some rest, Master Cade.'

He continued to look at me. 'There are those who assert that I'm a physician from Sussex – such are the curious tales that grow up around someone newly come to public notice. At all events I truthfully assert that I'm not competent to minister to my own malady.' He took a deep breath. 'Doctor Somers, I'd be obliged if you would remain at hand until I've made my proclamation in the morning.'

He was trying to sound casual but I detected the undertone of neediness. Stanlaw, at his side, jiggled his head enthusiastically to encourage my agreement.

'I'm at your service,' I said, well aware that Iffley would confine me to the camp in any case. I was also intrigued to see how this engaging young upstart, whatever his true name, would behave in public and whether he could truly control his jumpiness when put to the test.

*****

Jack Cade was resplendent in scarlet and showed no evidence of nervousness when he read out the proclamation which his messengers were taking to King Henry, currently in Leicester with most of the court. On the contrary, he spoke impressively, his delivery combining forcefulness with charm, his personality commanding attention. I stood with Gilbert Iffley and others behind the speaker's back and was amazed to see the huge crowd in front of him, every man appearing awe-struck by his presence. It might be true that Cade had been coached to play a part as Richard of York's catspaw, but he was fully capable of winning supporters on his own account and rousing them to share his fervour.

Perhaps more than ten thousand men were assembled, few of whom could hear Cade's words, but it was clear they already knew the gist of what he had to say and murmurs of approbation rippled through the multitude. His statement was forthright. It castigated the King's evil counsellors and bribery at the court, complaining about the loss of Normandy to the French and the adverse effect on England's trade. It called for the punishment of traitors and the end of extortion from the King's subjects and it renewed the old allegations that the late Duke Humphrey of Gloucester's death was the result of murder. Finally, and significantly, it urged the King to take Richard, Duke of York, as his principal adviser.

The penultimate assertion I knew to be untrue, for I had stood by Gloucester's bedside. The seizure that felled him owed nothing to human malignity but Suffolk had been blamed for it at the time and I was presumed to have acted as Suffolk's agent. Suffolk was too nervous of his own position to save me when accusations were made and I escaped imprisonment, and probable execution, only through the assistance of friends until, many months later, he felt secure enough to reinstate me as physician in his service. It was consequently disconcerting for me to hear Cade resurrect the false version of Gloucester's death and stir the pot of dangerous supposition about those responsible. Furthermore, the naming of Richard of York, without acknowledging any prior link between Cade and the Duke's household, suggested Gilbert Iffley's devious methods and pernicious influence. Although I had sympathy with many of the complaints Cade voiced on behalf of his followers, I could not be comfortable in this assembly and I longed to return to Danson.

After the messengers departed, Cade entertained his closest advisers and their attendants to food and drink and he insisted I was one of the company. He was jocular, showing no signs of the weakness which had beset him the previous evening, but naturally he made no reference to this and he was gracious towards me. Iffley eyed me with cynical amusement but his toothless henchman scowled at me, although this could have been his normal expression. For my part I was furious to learn that the Baron had not yet released either Adam Ash or little Hubert and I was perturbed that there was still no news of Rendell. I was ill at ease when, at the end of the celebration, Jack Cade drew Iffley and me aside, along with his squire, Stanlaw, who looked less affable than on the previous occasion I met him.

'Doctor Somers,' Cade said in a pleasantly relaxed tone, 'I'd be happy to engage your services as physician to myself and our assembly. Would you contemplate accepting such a commission?'

I swallowed hard while Iffley smirked and I was surprised by my own hesitation, as I weighed a number of considerations. 'Master Cade,' I said at length, 'this would not be in your interests. Your followers may think my allegiances suspect. I served Suffolk until his death.'

He gave an artless smile 'I make my offer in full knowledge of that fact. I've learned something of your circumstances from good Baron Glasbury. I understand your reluctance to commit yourself to our enterprise and that you may not wish to leave your ailing wife. Nevertheless I surmise you're not hostile to our objectives so perhaps you'll spend a day or two in our encampment to help those who have need of your services. I'd also be grateful for your help in one other respect. I'm told you're friend to a notable landowner in the neighbourhood so perhaps you would make clear to Sir Hugh de Grey that he must take no action to interfere in our affairs. It would be reassuring to know we ran no risk of attack on our flank. Are you willing to do this?'

I turned to Iffley and looked him in the eye. 'I'm acquainted with the way you do business, Baron, and imagine you have a threat to add cogency to this request.'

'Dear Harry, always so percipient. I have no interest in detaining Master Ash here if he wishes to return to Danson, much as we would value his adherence to our cause. He's free to leave.'

'And the child, Hubert de Grey?'

'Oh, come now, Harry, don't be naïve. He must remain here as surety for his father's deeds.'

'Then I must decline Master Cade's demands.'

Stanlaw leered at me but Jack Cade intervened with obvious annoyance. 'What's all this? Do you mean you're holding Sir Hugh's son, Baron? Is this the reason you came here, Doctor? I didn't know. Iffley, you're to let the child return home. This Ash can take him. We must have no truck with abducting children to hold them hostage. Our intention is to show we have more regard for the concept of honour than the great men we criticise. Will you stay a few days, Doctor Somers, on these conditions?'

Unwisely gratified by this rebuke to Iffley, I inclined my head, while wondering whether I had taken

31

leave of my senses. 'On those conditions, Master Cade, yes, I agree and will write to Sir Hugh.'

Gilbert Iffley mastered intense annoyance and accompanied me to a table where writing materials were laid out so I could send news to my friends at Danson. He gave me a supercilious smile as he ushered me to a stool. 'Master Cade is a persuasive young fellow, isn't he? I'm full of admiration that he has overcome your adamantine refusal in the past to ally yourself with any cause, however worthy.'

'I've agreed to fill a physician's role, not to commit myself beyond that.'

'Indeed. But you're unmistakably charmed by the young fellow, as all are when they meet him. It's only a week since I encountered him and I confess myself delighted.'

I marked the bland expression on that deceitful face and was not willing to give credence to his fiction. 'Let's be clear, Baron. I'm well aware you were coaching Cade in the history of the royal line of Mortimers when I happened to see you two years ago in Dublin, at a time you were both in the household of Richard of York.'

His lips tightened as the flush spread across his cheeks. 'I advise you not to repeat that falsehood, Harry Somers. I met our young leader a week ago. I have no idea whether he has ever been in Dublin. To my knowledge he has no connection with the Duke of York. It is a mere rumour.'

I did not drop my gaze. 'I hear what you say Baron, but I know what I saw.'

'Then you will keep silent, or it will be the worse for you and your friends.'

Crowds of men were milling around us and Iffley was reluctant to raise his voice or threaten me more openly. He turned on his heel and marched towards his tent, beckoning Stanlaw to attend him. He had delivered an unmistakable warning.

I wrote letters to Kate and Sir Hugh, suspecting that my afflicted wife might appreciate my motives better than her host, recognising my need for diversion after the painful events of recent weeks. Nonetheless I did not wholly comprehend why I had made my perverse choice, after years of refusing Iffley's blandishments to throw in my lot with his companions. I could only explain it as a physician's temptation to study an intriguing young man for a little longer and add to my store of knowledge concerning the variety of humankind.

Master Ash had climbed the hill on foot when he came to look for Hubert so I gave him my horse to take the child home. I could arrange for it to be fetched when I was ready to return to the de Grey house. I waved them on their way through the wooden palisade at the edge of the camp, satisfied I had procured their safety. The beaten earth of the track beyond the fence and the surrounding grass was trampled to right and left by hooves and cartwheels but in one place I noticed the impression of horseshoes wheeling about and seeming to return downhill in the direction from which they had come. It caused me to wonder if Rendell had made off, back to Danson, when he realised I had been intercepted the previous day. Was he hoping to persuade Sir Hugh to send a rescue party? That could be disastrous. I must trust that Adam Ash's return, with the child, would deter any foolish heroics against the enormous host of potential insurgents rallied to Jack Cade's cause.

I returned to the cluster of tents but finding a meeting in noisy progress in the principal pavilion I stepped aside to avoid overhearing what did not concern me. At that moment however, the flap across the opening was thrown back and a tall gangly man stormed out, stumbling in an effort not to crash into me. He sat on the ground heavily.

'Pardon, physician, pardon. Did I alarm you?'

'It was a surprise but I'm quite unhurt. Are you all right?'

He heaved himself upright, towering above me and jerking his lanky arms and legs. 'Not in need of your professional services.' He smiled. 'If I'd stayed in there it might have been another who called for your help, for I'd have torn him to pieces.'

I was amused by his genial look while he expressed such vicious sentiments. 'Oh dear, is there dissension?'

'Among men who should be brothers: it's sad. But that bleeding Baron has no business telling us what to do. He's pursuing his own interests, not ours.'

'Baron Glasbury?'

'You know him? Have I spoken out of turn? Put it down to my short temper.'

'Don't worry. I've had my own disagreements with Gilbert Iffley over the years. Are you one of Jack Cade's advisers? Or captains, should I call them?'

'You've put your finger on the very point at issue, Doctor – Somers, isn't it? Jack mentioned you. Piers Ford, journeyman wheelwright of Dartford, pleased to meet you. Are we petitioners or rebels? Men of peace or violence? That's the crux of it. You obviously know this blasted Glasbury fellow and the dubious company he keeps. He's urging us to march on London, gather followers as we go, rally the working folk in the City to support us, dare the authorities to attack and be prepared to fight if they do.'

'That would be risky. I know the City well. You would find supporters there but the merchants and guildsmen will fear for their property and livelihoods. They'll see your company as a rabble to be put down with all the force at their disposal. Haven't you sent a petition to the King with your complaints? Won't you wait to see his response?'

Piers Ford gave a roar of glee. 'Just what I've been telling them. Exactly my argument. You must come and join the discussion.' He threw a sinewy arm around my shoulders and tried to pull me back to Cade's tent.

'No, really, I've no part in your campaign. You must excuse me.'

'But you're not unfriendly. You understand our grievances. I can tell. I'd hazard a guess you're not of gentle birth yourself.'

I laughed. 'You're astute, Master Ford, but I owe my advancement to the patronage of noblemen. You could say I straddle the classes of men, which is a good position for a physician who serves everyone needing his help.'

'You're fortunate. But don't you question acceptance of those classes or do you think they are ordained by God? Do you know the expressive rhyme which captures the conundrum?'

'*When Adam delved and Evé span*
Who was then the gentleman?'

I quoted it with ease and Master Ford clapped his hands. 'You're acquainted with John Ball?'

I gave him a searching look. 'I know there were disaffected preachers in the past like John Ball and Wycliffe's Lollards who wanted to overturn the established order of things. I remember Ball was involved with the rebels who collected on Blackheath around seventy years ago and he suffered for it.'

Piers Ford pinched my shoulder with an exclamation of delight. 'But you don't call them villains for seeking liberties and justice for the poor. I learned of them at my grandfather's knee and they are my inspiration, as I hope they are the inspiration for all the common men here. But, don't you see, we have to be wary of self-seeking interlopers like Baron Glasbury? He'd subvert our honest concerns to suit himself. Come and speak to Jack Cade on our behalf. Urge him to act prudently.'

He yanked my arm and I was not optimistic about my chances of squirming out of his grasp. He was an interesting fellow whom I would be happy to get to know but I must avoid involvement beyond my physician's calling. To my initial relief we were both distracted by banging and shouts, over to our right where a number of two-wheeled carts were assembled. I could see men struggling to release a whinnying horse from the shafts of one cart which had fallen on its side.

'Someone's hurt,' I said with more expectation than certainty. 'I must go to them.' Ford's fingers restrained me for a moment but as the cries continued he changed his mind and came with me to the scene of the commotion.

The situation was worse than I imagined and I quickly realised that I could offer little of benefit to the wretched victim crushed half-under the fallen cart. His ribcage was smashed and his belly torn open by wooden stakes which had been displaced from inside the cart. His eyes rolled as I knelt by him and his mouth gaped but he was incapable of speech. Piers Ford lowered himself to crouch beside me, staring with rapt attention while the colour drained from his cheeks. He rose to his feet swiftly, his long legs tottering as he righted himself, and he turned away, clamping his hand to his mouth and retching. It is not unusual for the heartiest of mankind to quail at the sight of guts spilling from a mortal wound.

A lad around twelve years old came running through the crowd of onlookers and flung himself down by the dying man who managed a faint grunt of recognition before he breathed his last. I checked for the absence of a pulse and closed the man's eyelids. The whole episode had taken no more than a few minutes.

'Are you his son?' I asked and the boy nodded as another carter joined us and patted his arm.

'Must be brave, Georgie,' the man said before turning to me 'We're near neighbours, sir, out Maidstone way. We'd brought in timber for the defences yesterday and today we were taking the stakes where needed. Can't understand how George's cart fell over. The ground's not that uneven though this horse was always inclined to be frisky.'

Other men murmured their agreement but none of them had actually seen the cart overturn. Accidents did happen, they commented with mournful acquiescence in their lot, and sensibly they concentrated on comforting young Georgie. They led the boy and the frightened horse away and threw a cloth over the victim until he could be removed. Piers Ford wiped his sleeve across his mouth and gave a rueful shrug, master of himself and not embarrassed by his moment of weakness. He and I were left alone with the corpse and we exchanged questioning looks.

'A damned freak mishap,' he said with a quizzical flick of his eyebrows and knelt by the shattered cart.

'You think there could be more to it?'

'A well-made wheel shouldn't buckle like this.' He wrenched up the cart and pulled the wheel loose, examining it with a craftsman's eye. 'Dear Christ!'

I sank down beside him and quickly grasped what he had found, for the peg which fixed the wheel to the axle had snapped, half of it still embedded in the spindle. This must have thrown the cart off balance, dislodged the driver and tilted the spiked timber to spear his stomach.

'How could a solid peg break like that?' I asked.

'Easy enough,' the wheelwright replied, 'if it's been sawn through so only a sliver of wood was holding it. These ruts in the ground would have been enough to wrench it apart. This was done intentionally.'

'Sawn through intentionally?'

'Looks like it.' Ford stood up. 'Poor sod must have had enemies.'

I ran my finger over the sawn peg. 'Not the most certain method of killing a man. You couldn't be sure where or when the peg would snap or exactly how the cart would fall. The driver could have been thrown clear, maybe broken an arm or leg but not necessarily killed. It was a chance movement that caused the stake to pierce his belly.'

'Someone just wanted to teach him a lesson for some reason and it turned out badly?'

I felt an inexplicable tingling down my spine and peered around us. 'Or perhaps it was merely a distraction

37

to divert attention from elsewhere. I suppose that's far-fetched. It couldn't have been timed exactly.'

Disregarding my last comment, Ford shot a glance towards the tents. 'Some bastard trying to stop me returning to Cade's canvas counsel-chamber? I'd best go there at once. I hope we'll meet again, physician.'

He left me, his long limbs striding with ungainly speed, but I thought it improbable his explanation could be accurate. This accident had been carefully contrived, whether or not it was intended to be lethal, but it could not have been organised during the short time Ford and I were talking after he fumed out of Cade's tent. I made my way to where the victim's neighbour from the Maidstone area was waiting, with a group of bystanders, his hand still on the shoulder of the bereaved son.

'Looks like something worked loose on the wheel,' I said. 'Had you and George come far this morning?'

'No, we were just carting extra stakes round the edge of the heath from where they'd been sharpened after wagons brought them up the hill.'

'Did you load the stakes yourselves?'

'Why, no, we didn't. Some bloke offered us bread to break our fast and said he'd get the carts loaded while we took our rest. Christ Almighty, was he responsible for George's death? Did he load the wood so badly it shifted the weight? If I find that fucking scoundrel I'll give him what-for.'

'It was an accident,' I said lamely, feeling awkward, and I returned to the scene of the fatality where men had arrived to carry away the body. With no precise aim in view I decided I would make a tour round the edge of the heath to see where the wood was being loaded. A sense of foreboding was gnawing at my mind with no convincing justification.

Work on the erection of the palisade was now well advanced but fresh supplies of timber were still being fetched up the hill, to the east of the camp, and decanted from large wagons by the verge of the heath, where piles of

38

tree trunks and sturdy branches were lying on the ground. Workmen sat cross-legged, whittling the ends of the logs into sharp points and a succession of small carts collected the prepared stakes for delivery round the perimeter of the encampment. There was a great bustle of men coming and going and I could imagine how difficult it would be to check the whereabouts of any individual earlier in the morning. At the same time it seemed impossible that anyone could have tampered with a cart-wheel in that place without being spotted. Decidedly discouraged, I sat on a stump regarding the scene.

I had not been there more than a few minutes when I heard shouts from one of the approaching wagons and saw the driver rein in his horses to speak to the whittler nearest the road. The wagoner was extremely angry.

'You lot'll ruin everything if you're seen to be vindictive. I thought Jack Cade promised good discipline. That's why I'm helping his cause. If you let louts loose to kill locals uncontrolled, you'll forfeit the support of good men. They'll think you no more than a load of vagabonds.'

I hurried over to the wagon and asked what had happened. The man looked approvingly at my physician's garb before answering and evidently assumed I held some position of authority.

'A bad business, Doctor, not such as a man like you would condone, I'm sure. We went over to a pond at the bottom of the hill. The horses were thirsty and I could see this water glistening beyond a stand of trees. Got more than I bargained for, I'm sorry to say. There's a body there, flat on the muddy bank. Foul play. An arrow through his chest. Some ruffian must have had a shot at him because he wore the livery of a local landowner. That won't win Cade friends.'

I masked my horror so as to appear business-like and sympathetic to the wagoner's concern. Then, with all the gravitas I could muster, I required him to convey me in his wagon to the spot where he found the murdered man. While we juddered down the hill and across the open

39

ground beyond it, which led towards the Danson estate, I had a fearful premonition and, as soon as I glimpsed what he had seen beside the pond, I knew the dread I experienced was entirely justified.

Adam Ash was slumped on his back with the arrow protruding between his ribs; his face was contorted with pain. His lifeblood had seeped and congealed over the sedges and grass near the water's edge and it was far too late for any human agency to assist him. My horse had disappeared and of Hubert de Grey there was no sign.

Chapter 4

Remembering Iffley's thunderous expression when his intentions were countermanded by Cade, I never doubted who was responsible for this outrage. I swore silently the woodman's murder would be avenged but my first duty was to carry the dire news to Danson. I found Sir Hugh and his attendants ready mounted to set out for Blackheath, because my horse had found its way back to the stables without a rider and they had concluded I was in trouble. My distraught appearance alerted them to the fact that, although I was unharmed, my tidings were grievous and they listened with growing fury to my account. Two serving women were sent to comfort Mistress Ash in her bereavement and I promised I would call on her to give all the information I possessed about her husband's murder. Before I could undertake that task, however, I needed to deter Sir Hugh from precipitate action.

'There must be ten thousand men assembled on the heath and inevitably some of them are hotheads. If you came in arms to their camp, they wouldn't wait to hear your reasons; they'd see you as enemies to be destroyed. Your party would have no chance.'

Sir Hugh rounded on me. 'Are you suggesting I allow them to carry off my child and kill my faithful woodman with impunity?'

'Of course not, but I don't want more needless slaughter. Their leader, Jack Cade, will disown this barbaric behaviour. It's in direct contradiction to his orders. He personally instructed that Master Ash and Hubert should be allowed to return home. He'll be enraged and ready to punish those responsible but he'll want proof of guilt.'

'You put your trust in the honour of rebels?'

'I believe Cade intends to proclaim their grievances peaceably and he insists they conduct themselves with discipline. But, even if you think me gullible, don't endanger more lives. Let me speak to him first and seek

41

redress. Remember little Hubert may be in danger, a pawn his captors hold. But if those responsible make threats, they'll have to declare their hand and that could help identify them.'

Lady Blanche had come to her husband's side and she took his hand. 'Harry is speaking sense,' she said. 'Let him see what he can do before you engage in heroics. For Hubert's sake, I beg you.'

Sir Hugh turned away, fighting his anger and his need for action, before giving grudging consent. 'Do what you can. I'll have the pond dragged in case my poor boy lies drowned beneath the water. But, Harry, if you find Cade's men are responsible for this atrocity and Hubert is not safely home within hours, it will not be only the men from Danson who storm the heath. I shall raise the whole district.'

He must have known as he made this threat that it was meaningless against so vast a horde. Nevertheless, it was as much as I could hope for and I accepted his terms. 'I'll send news of Cade's response as soon as I've spoken to him.'

Lady Blanche took my arm. 'Come to greet Kate before you go. She seems calmer for a day's rest but I know she misses you.'

I let the lady of Danson lead me into the house. I did not want to distress my wife by telling her of insurgents and atrocities but poor Adam Ash had been unable to deliver my letter so she was ignorant of my intentions. I explained as gently as I could that I had undertaken to remain at Blackheath for a short while and then we would travel on to London. 'It won't be a long delay and you can regain your strength while you're here, my sweet. Judith and Lady Blanche will have good care of you.'

She looked at me closely and I was happy to see in her wonderful green eyes a gleam of contentment which had been absent for so long. 'They are kind to me,' she said, 'and sometimes I'm more at ease, but dreams burden my sleep and I can't escape the terrors they bring.'

'As you grow stronger, I believe the dreams will fade. I'll give Judith a potion to help you sleep. Get well again, Kate, and then we can be together unencumbered by past agonies. We'll make a new start, free from the trickery of evil men.'

She smiled at me with such guileless joy that I felt tears prick my eyes at this small indication of her recovery. My thwarted hope for a home and family, blessed by mutual love and stability, might yet be within reach. I kissed her lips and held her close before we parted.

*****

I was uneasy at learning that Rendell had not been seen since he and I left Danson for the heath. He was canny and competent but if he had been assaulted by overwhelming numbers of opponents, his body might also have been left to moulder beside a pond or in a ditch. I tried to push away the thought and avoided Judith's eye when she suggested tartly that the 'young warrior', as she called him, could have met with his just deserts. I did not want to think badly of the young woman who was caring for my wife so diligently.

I went to visit to Mistress Ash and she received me with dignity, accompanied by her two sons – the elder, whom I had not met before, so like his dead father.

'I didn't know Master Ash would venture to find Hubert de Grey and put himself at risk. I wish I could have prevented it.' My words sounded lame as I spoke them.

'Adam believed it was his duty and he knew Master Hubert was our Allan's friend. He'd no idea he'd be walking into danger. Are they monsters, these men gathered on Blackheath? Do they wish to create havoc in the lives of humble folk?'

'Most of them are well disposed and want to help their fellow men but in any large group there will be rogues who are less biddable and seek to subvert an honest campaign for ignoble purposes.'

Mistress Ash sighed. 'I must accept God's will.'

'Well, I will not, mother.' The elder boy glared at me. 'I shall avenge my father's death, Doctor Somers. I shall go to Blackheath.'

'I beg you not to, young master. There are thousands of men there and we cannot be certain any of them was involved in your father's murder. I promise you I shall pursue the matter and I'll report back to you. Stay with your mother while I do what I can.'

Tears of frustration filled the boy's eyes but he inclined his head.

'Will Hubert be all right?' Allan's round face was white and I was uncomfortably aware how like the missing boy his playfellow was.

'I believe so, Allan, but we must be careful not to make a false move which might put him in peril.' I glanced at the elder boy and he tilted his jaw rebelliously but I knew he understood the message was for him, not just his brother.

I left the grieving family and set out again on horseback to climb the hill but I had scarcely covered a hundred yards when I saw a rider in the distance approaching the Danson lands by a track on the lower ground to the north. In a burst of excited relief I pulled on the reins to change direction and gallop towards the newcomer.

'Rendell, Rendell,' I greeted him when he was within earshot. 'Where've you been? I feared you'd been taken prisoner.'

'No chance. I've been to the City.' Inevitably he tapped his nose with pride. 'When the guard on the heath collared you, I heard him say they was going to storm London Bridge and fellows from Essex would attack the other gates. I reckoned the Lord Mayor ought to know about this and as you were about to be taken to meet your old mate, Baron Glasbury, the best thing I could do was head to the Guildhall. So I did and then I was taken to the Tower to give my account to the Governor, Lord Scales, and Lord Saye and Sele who was with him. Hobnobbing with nobility, I've been.'

I acknowledged I was impressed and summarised the events since Rendell left Blackheath. 'I'd wager Gilbert Iffley is responsible for the woodman's murder and the boy being carried off. He resisted freeing them. But I need to get Jack Cade to investigate what happened and bring Iffley to heel.'

'You reckon he could?'

'I do. Cade's an intriguing man. He may be a mountebank but he's playing the part of the upright leader with imposing authority. I think he'd like me to serve his company as physician.'

'Christ! Reckon you wouldn't last long in that role.' Rendell puffed his cheeks and exhaled. 'London's preparing a fierce reception for Cade's load of rebels. Mind you're not seen as one of them. D'you want me to come with you?'

I shook my head. 'You'd be more use on the outside – given the powerful contacts you've made in the City. It might be useful if we can keep in touch.'

'Right you are. Messages to Danson will find me. I'll arrange it.'

He was bursting with self-satisfaction and I could not resist a wry comment. 'If I send a written note you can always get Judith to read it out for you.'

I ducked the blow aimed half-playfully at my chin by the capable warrior who had only ever achieved limited mastery over his letters.

*****

Jack Cade was in exuberant mood when I returned to Blackheath in the early evening. He was in conference with his closest henchmen, a dozen or more surrounding him, but he summoned me to join them in his tent and slapped me on the shoulder with enthusiasm.

'Good news, Doctor Somers, good news. The King is coming to treat with us. He's already on the road from Leicester and in a few days' time we shall meet face to face. He learned of our assembly here and has chosen to come to greet us. He'll listen to his subjects' petition and when he appreciates their grievances, I've no doubt he'll take action to root out evil counsellors. He wouldn't come in person otherwise.'

'I trust you're right, Master Cade. He's a man of peace by all accounts but isn't there a danger he'll bring an army with him?'

I wondered if I was speaking out of turn, dampening Cade's elation, and Stanlaw glowered at me as if I had committed some solecism. By contrast two or three of his companions murmured assent and I suspected they had expressed similar worries before I arrived. I noticed that Baron Glasbury was not among them and, although I welcomed his absence from the discussion, I feared it might be linked to Hubert's abduction. Probably he was arranging for the boy to be held in some secure and secret place while he bargained for Sir Hugh's acquiescence.

'Doctor Somers has endorsed what I said before he came. We must put our trust in the King. They say he's a good man, even a holy one. Surely he'll remedy our complaints.'

Piers Ford, towering above his colleagues, his eyes glowing, spoke with conviction and it was clear that his arguments had persuaded Jack Cade to adopt this approach. I wanted to believe their optimism was justified.

Soon afterwards the conference ended and the men dispersed so I could inform Cade privately of Master Ash's murder. As I expected he was appalled but reluctant to believe Iffley could have been involved.

He spoke judiciously. 'If one of my followers, even Baron Glasbury, was responsible for the crime, defying my authority, I shall impose the ultimate penalty. But I need

46

proof, Doctor Somers, not supposition. Just because Gilbert opposed freeing Ash and the child it doesn't equate with commissioning murder and abduction.'

'I accept that. I'll do what I can to find evidence, perhaps identify the bowman. Iffley won't have loosed the arrow himself. If we can find the murderer, we may be able to get a confession incriminating the Baron. It wouldn't be the first time he paid villains to use underhand means.' The toothless flogger was in my mind.

'I perceive he's a man who operates outside conventional bounds. He's an invaluable supporter and it's expedient to overlook unscrupulous conduct in such a man if it upholds our cause. But I will not have my express orders disobeyed.'

I was struck by the emphasis placed on his final words. 'He's not in attendance on you today?'

'He has family business in the City. He's gone to his house there. He'll be back before the week is out and he'll have gleaned information about the King's progress from Leicester.'

I had not been aware that Iffley had a residence in the City but then I remembered the house on Cheapside where his wife had lived with her first husband, Andrew Cawfield. After Cawfield died, I believed by unlawful means, Mistress Jane inherited the property and when, with indecent haste, she married Baron Glasbury it would have become part of his estate. It offered a convenient place to hide a small boy held for whatever devious purposes the loathsome Baron conceived.

'Then I propose to call on him at his house and see how he reacts to straight questioning.'

'Very well. But you will return to our encampment?'

I gave him my word and left the tent to collect my horse and set out for the City but I was pleased to see Piers Ford lolling on the ground nearby. I guessed he was waiting for me and he rose to his knees when I greeted him, his eyes almost level with mine.

'I'm glad your arguments held sway with Cade but I wouldn't be sanguine that the King will acknowledge your complaints and grant redress.'

Ford smiled. 'You think me naïve, I'm sure. I do recognise the King may play us false but it's best Jack stays calm and cheerful until we know otherwise.'

I grinned. The wheelwright's common sense was impeccable. 'You benefitted from Gilbert Iffley's absence in putting your argument but I need to see the Baron. I'm heading for the City.' Then I drew Ford aside, described Adam Ash's murder and explained my intention to confront Iffley with my suspicions. 'You could help me,' I added. 'If you keep your ears open in the camp you might pick up something to suggest who the bowman was – he may have fled so it would be useful to check if anyone's left Blackheath unexpectedly.'

'Not easy but I'll do what I can. Do you reckon that poor carter's death was something to do with this – a distraction as you suggested?' When I gave a shrug he spat into the grass. 'Bastards! Undermining the reputation of wheelwrights, making it look like there was shoddy work on the broken peg. They mustn't get away with it. It's up to us, Doctor Somers, it's up to us.'

Rather, I realised with a start, it was up to me: for, as I pondered Gilbert Iffley's actions, I came to the conclusion that his purpose could well concern me directly. The little boy might not be held hostage simply to secure his father's compliance but to compel me to stay silent about what I knew. In that case, Hubert de Grey's fate was quite possibly in my hands.

*****

Once before I had made a foolhardy visit to the house in Cheapside and suffered in my bruised person and battered self-esteem as a result. It required some doggedness on my part to rap on that door again, grateful there was no sign of the inquisitive neighbour who observed my humiliation on the previous occasion. My very presence on the doorstep augured further humiliation to come but I had thought through what motive Gilbert Iffley could have for kidnapping Hubert de Grey and the most cogent reason necessitated my attendance on him.

A flunky came quickly to answer my knock and advised me that Baron Glasbury was absent from the City, paying a short visit to his wife in the country. He eyed my physician's garb and spoke respectfully.

'We expect him here in three days' time before he travels into Kent. Would you wish to see him at the house?'

'I would. He knows me. My name is Harry Somers.'

'The Baron has mentioned you, Doctor Somers. Would you please call on Thursday around noon.'

I agreed and went on my way, unnerved by knowing that my visit was hardly a surprise. It confirmed my reasoning about Iffley's intentions and what I must do to counter them. Nevertheless the delay proved useful by giving me time to compose my thoughts and prepare myself for our confrontation. I had learned from misjudged impulsiveness in the past that it was wise, when possible, to beware precipitate action.

I decided I would not return to Blackheath until I had seen the Baron and I welcomed the opportunity to make other more cordial calls in the City. I ventured to the late Duke of Suffolk's Manor of the Rose where I had lived and worked over several years and where I first met Kate. I knew the Dowager Duchess and her son, now the youthful Duke, were ensconced a hundred miles away in their castle at Wingfield but the steward at the London house was an old friend and he greeted me with enthusiasm. So too did another former colleague whom I had not expected to see in the City.

'Leone! I flung my arms round the young Italian, now a fully-fledged physician, who had left his position as my assistant to accompany the army fighting in Normandy which vainly attempted to recover King Henry's land taken by the French. 'I didn't know you were back. Are you well?'

'Unharmed in body but troubled in spirit by what I saw on battlefields across the Narrow Sea – and by ingratitude meted out to men who fought for their King. They are returned, scarred and threadbare, to receive no reward and see cowards prosper.'

Leone's anger was that of a mature man and did him credit. I described Jack Cade's assembly and his bill of complaints to the King, hoping this would give my fellow physician some reassurance, but Leone already knew about the gathering on Blackheath and was pessimistic as to its outcome.

'I foresee more misery for common folk,' he said, 'while nobles squabble. I want nothing to do with affairs of state. Medicine is my calling and to practise medicine is all I wish to do. I have no means of my own so I must seek a post as physician, serving some great house. Pray God, I find a master I can esteem.'

This was distressing and I turned to the steward of the Manor of the Rose. 'Has the young Duke or Duchess Alice given any indication of the provision they require at the City house?'

He gave me a knowing look. 'One post of physician will suffice to care for this household. The Duchess believes it will be some while before she feels safe to set foot here. She told me you were likely to leave her service; she mentioned the provision the late Duke made for you, the grant of the manor of Worthwaite and other bequests. She thought you might wish to set up independently as a physician in the City.'

'Duchess Alice is an accomplished mind-reader. It is what I should like to do. If I resign my post at the Manor of the Rose, would you be free to engage Leone in my place?'

'Duchess Alice suggested it, if Doctor Leone is agreeable.'

'Mia madre, Madonna grazie.' Leone crossed himself and then he held out his hand to me. 'You're sure, Doctor Somers, you're not just trying to help me?'

'It's long been my objective to work in the City, offering services to as many as I can. The late Duke knew this and wanted to make it possible. God rest his soul.'

I arranged to stay at the Manor of the Rose while I was in London and the three of us celebrated late into the evening, relaxing in conviviality after the trials we had faced in recent months. Deaths of soldiers on the battlefield and the summary execution of a master we respected had touched us deeply and changed all our prospects.

I did not share with my companions the hurdle I had yet to overcome in achieving my ambition: for Kate, when in reasonable health, had been bitterly opposed to me offering to treat all and sundry for derisory fees. As she saw it, I would be no better than a tradesman, setting up shop alongside purveyors of fish and haberdashery, demeaning her superior lineage. I hoped that now I could present myself as a man of property as well as one with a profession, she would relent. Most of all, in my heart I longed for her to be well enough to engage in a vigorous discussion of how best we might rebuild our life together.

*****

Next morning I walked by the riverside, past wharves and storehouses, weaving my way round groups of gesticulating merchants, ducking below enormous bundles balanced on the heads of burly dockhands, sidestepping to avoid barrows full of kegs. I watched vessels from Flanders and Aquitaine unloading their cargoes of woven cloth and wine and I heard snatches of nervy conversation about the rabble on Blackheath. The City was conducting its normal frenetic business but there were overtones of disquiet.

Eventually I reached the massive bastion of the Tower. Three months earlier I had lodged within its walls while Suffolk was held prisoner there, albeit in comfortable estate; eight years before that, I had been the

51

captive, charged with treason and in fear of execution. The fortress intimidated me and I hurried into the side streets which would take me to the premises of my old friend, Thomas Chope, master carpenter and dedicated family man. In the Chope home I would always receive a welcome and probably some shrewd, if not entirely congenial, advice.

Thomas was in conference with a customer but as soon as I appeared Grizel dragged me into her kitchen and thrust a wriggling infant into my arms while she attended to a fraternal brawl.

'Hold Margery a moment, Harry, there's a dear. Hal, Dickon, stop that at once. Put the broom down. It's not a pike and little Tom is not a Frenchman to be speared.' She lifted a wailing toddler into her arms and clapped her hands to send the two older boys scurrying into the yard. 'Sweet Mother of God, grant me patience. At least Margery's not much trouble – yet. But who'd have three boys...' Her cheeks flushed scarlet as she remembered the miscarriage my wife had suffered. 'Oh, Harry, I'm sorry. I shouldn't have said that. How's Kate?'

'Not well. She's fragile after all she's been through but she's in good hands. I believe she will recover. I'm hoping to establish her in our own house soon, in the City. I've left the Suffolk household.'

Thomas and Grizel knew of my aspirations and, when he joined us, he promised to help by seeking out a suitable dwelling for a respectable physician. We shared news and he was particularly interested to hear that I had met Jack Cade, although what he said on the subject of the assembly on Blackheath was not encouraging and reflected what I had overheard beside the Thames.

'I was at a meeting of the guild last evening,' he said with a self-deprecating grin, mindful of his advancement as a master craftsman. 'The King will arrive in Clerkenwell within the week. He's collected a vast army and they're to camp in the fields outside the City walls. It's thought he's sending a go-between to meet this Cade fellow: a draper, name of Cooke. It's all a ruse, if you ask me. Sooner or later Cade's followers will be proclaimed rebels and sent about their business – or to the gallows.'

'I hope they'll do nothing precipitate. I believe Cade is a man of peace. He wants to show how disciplined his men are. Their complaints to the King are understandable, you know. If they're given a fair hearing, no harm need come of their action.'

'Pigs might fly. Don't get mixed up with them, Harry. They're troublemakers. Stick to your trade. Mend bodies and, if you want diversion, solve the odd murder.'

I laughed and changed the subject, all too conscious that I was already involved with the dissidents, not least by reason of the murder I was in fact investigating. I did not intend to burden Thomas with this information.

Before long a din broke out in the yard as a new arrival made his way into the house, beset by youthful nephews grasping his boots and attempting to climb his legs. Rendell swept the youngest assailant into his arms and guffawed when he saw me. I was staring at the unfamiliar livery he was wearing.

'Yeah,' he said proudly, slapping his chest. 'This is the crest of Lord Scales, Governor of the Tower, no less. Told you I met him, didn't I? He were impressed by my enterprising nature. Offered me a position in the guard there, now Suffolk's dead. Doing all right, I reckon.'

I could not contradict him and gave my congratulations but I felt uncomfortable. The Governor of the Tower was likely to be suspect in the eyes of Cade's followers – possibly even a supporter of the hated Lord Saye and Sele.

We moved on to less controversial topics and I was inveigled into joining a boisterous game with the children, their father and their uncle, which involved chasing round the piles of planks stacked in the outhouse and stuffing sawdust down each other's necks. I was glad to see that carpenters' saws and chisels were stored out of reach of eager, scrabbling, small fingers. I enjoyed the light-hearted amusement which demanded all my concentration to avoid injury but was aware that, before I left this contented family, I must say something to Thomas fitting ill with the jovial atmosphere.

My opportunity came later when, sensing my need to speak to him privately, he took me into his workshop on the pretext of showing me some panelling.

'The sort of thing which might suit a physician's study,' he said loudly as we left the others. Then, when we had shut the door and seated ourselves on workbenches, he spoke again in a different one. 'Well, what is it, Harry? Can I help?'

'I just need to tell you something, in case it all goes wrong. I may be forced to act against my better judgement. If that happens, I could be reviled and held guilty of crimes. I want you to understand that what I have to do is in order to protect an innocent child. It's not that I'm turned traitor to everything I believe. I wouldn't want you and Grizel to think badly of me.'

Thomas's mouth narrowed and he watched me in silence. 'You're not going to tell me anything more.'

'Only that I have to see Gilbert Iffley.'

'Oh, Christ, Harry! Be careful. You're playing with fire, after all that's happened in the past.'

'Perhaps, but it has to be done.'

He nodded, never doubting my statement. It was immensely heartening to have his support, whatever might result, but if I was honest, I was not wholly certain of my own motivation.

Chapter 5

When I presented myself once more at the door to the house in Cheapside I was untroubled by memories of former indignities. My mind was filled with trepidation about what was to come but my resolution held firm. I was conducted at once to join Baron Glasbury in his study where he greeted me with affected charm and silky insincerity. He was tastefully dressed in a high-collared robe of fine wool, topped by heavy chains supporting medallions, with an elaborate, if somewhat old-fashioned, turban pulled down on his forehead. He was a picture of cultivated decorum and there was no sign of any brutish underlings. He smiled sardonically as I entered the room.

'Doctor Somers, this is a delight I have long desired: to receive you in my home. Can it be that you have revised your opinions? Has the engaging young Mortimer – or Cade as we must call him for the moment – won you over to favour the cause we serve?'

'That's not the reason I've come. But I am prepared to do business with you.'

One eyebrow shot up into the shadow of his headdress. 'Business? Whatever can you mean?'

'I think you know very well. You've snatched the small boy in order to have a hold over me – a pawn to bargain with – to make me comply with your demands: to keep silent on a certain matter. It's your latest trick to bring me to heel. I've resisted your blandishments and menaces in the past but this time you've succeeded. It's a vile device, holding a child captive as surety for my compliance but you've cornered me. What are your terms for returning the boy unharmed to his parents?'

Gilbert Iffley sat back in his cushioned chair and crossed one leg over the other. He exhaled noisily. 'I've heard of the woodman's death but you surpass yourself, Harry. Your imagination is remarkable. If only I had thought of such a thing. Was this what was required to render you amenable? You've shown me the method I hadn't discovered. I feel quite inadequate beside your ingenuity – and your perception of your own importance.'

I tried not to show my exasperation. He was intent on playing me like a lad tickling a trout. 'I suppose I must tolerate your self-congratulation but I'd like to bring our exchange to a conclusion. Tell me what you want of me in order to obtain your assurance that Hubert will return to Danson unscathed. Will my promise to keep silent on your earlier contact with Cade satisfy you? You may revel in my submission as much as you wish once the boy is safe.'

'Oh, Harry you tempt me. Such open-ended possibilities! You would go so far as to offer me your adherence to Richard of York's service, even if it involves acting as my minion? Am I interpreting your words aright?'

I suppressed my distaste. 'If that is the required ransom.'

In a flurry of swirling robe and clanking medallions, Iffley rose. 'A moment for me to savour undeniably.' He sighed and moved to the window, staring out at the street in silence so I could hear the tramp of many feet on the roadway below. Then, abruptly, he drove his fist into the woodwork of the frame. 'Unfortunately there is a flaw, a fundamental flaw, in the argument.'

His voice had deepened and his annoyance seemed genuine.

'What do you mean? Has the child been slaughtered? Were your men too rough with him? Did they treat him the same way they dealt with Adam Ash? By God, Iffley, if you've killed the boy, you'll reap your reward for barbarity.'

His lip curled as he taunted me again. 'Ash was probably done to death by some local antagonist, nothing to do with the men on Blackheath. And why are you so concerned about this brat? Is it truly a whelp of your own, passed off as Hugh de Grey's? Is the Lady Blanche another titled woman whom you've tupped?'

I clenched my fists, digging my nails into my palms. 'No, Baron Glasbury. I told you, the child is not mine. His parents are old friends who cared for my mother in her last years. Tell me your terms and let us end this farce.'

He snarled his response. 'There are no terms. I cannot claim the benefit of your acquiescence. It mortifies me to admit it but the ploy is not one I contemplated. If I accepted your surrender I could not deliver what you want in return. I do not have the child. I never had the child.'

I gulped. I did not trust anything Iffley said but I could think of no reason why he should refute my allegation. 'Are you denying you had any role in Adam Ash's death and Hubert's disappearance?'

He sighed ostentatiously. 'Alas, yes, Harry. I am compelled to refuse your offer because you would expect me to deliver the boy and I cannot. I have no more idea than you of his whereabouts. I suspect he ran away when Master Ash was felled. In all probability the wretched infant stumbled into the pond and drowned.'

'His father will have had the pond dragged by now and the countryside will have been combed for a little body. I've received no message to say one has been found.'

Iffley shrugged. 'Then I've no further suggestions. You must extend your enquiries elsewhere and, with my deepest regrets, I must let you go without accepting the total capitulation you implied. I'm fascinated, nonetheless, that you were willing to renounce all the avowals you've made in the past. I shall remember what I've learned from this unexpected conversation and try to profit from it.'

'I've no doubt you will. I too have learned from our encounter.' I tried not to show how foolish I felt.

'There remains the need for your silence about our young friend, Cade. So, unless you give me your pledge, I shall be bound to threaten retribution if you speak unwisely.'

'I'll take my chance on that, Iffley. I see no reason to speak out on the issue but the mere fact it seems so important to you makes me cautious and I shall give you no pledge.'

'So be it.' He spoke as if he had the taste of rotten fruit in his mouth.'

I subdued my nausea when I left that inauspicious house, cursing the twist of fate which had exposed my vulnerability, leaving Glasbury free to exploit what he would see as my sentimental weakness. I had handed him a weapon for future coercion. Moreover it had all been for nothing. I was no nearer solving what had happened to Hubert and the possibilities were indisputably disturbing.

*****

I was soon distracted from my miserable thoughts when I noticed that Cheapside was full of citizens striding purposefully towards Newgate. On enquiring the reason, I learned that the King had arrived in Clerkenwell Fields and his loyal subjects were rallying to welcome him. Perhaps more especially, they were welcoming, the considerable army which had come with him to defend their trade, their property and the well-being of their families. It was rumoured the King was to rest at the Priory of St. John that night and ride into the City on the morrow when he would declare his intentions with regard to the Kentish rebels. My informant, from appearances and aroma a prosperous fishmonger, expressed the wish that the villainous insurgents should be strung up on gibbets across the county from which they came.

'I've heard there's a huge number of them gathered on Blackheath,' I said cautiously.

'You haven't got the latest information, physician. They've left the heath. It's to be hoped they're dispersing. Their leader and the core of his followers have made off south into Kent but we can expect the more lukewarm of the discontented to run home now the soldiers are here. Ignorant cowards, most of them are.'

This was troubling news, if true, for I needed Jack Cade's support in order to identify Adam Ash's killer and establish what had happened to Hubert. It was essential to find where the murderer had gone and pursue him: not only in order to bring him to justice but to obtain some clue as to the boy's fate.

Given the commitment to his cause Cade had displayed, I did not believe he had forsaken his quest without even receiving the King's response to the bill of complaints, but I suspected his men were regrouping to employ some different tactic. Maybe, in Baron Glasbury's absence, Piers Ford had persuaded him that a confrontation with the royal army on Blackheath would be unwise and a more subtle approach might be productive. That thought was encouraging.

I excused myself from the company of the fishmonger, turning south to return to the Manor of the Rose and collect my travelling bundle. As I hurried through the crowds coming in the opposite direction I wondered if there was any significance in the fact that Gilbert Iffley had said nothing of the withdrawal from Blackheath, for he must surely have been aware of it. I surmised he had left me to make my own discovery, probably wasting time in the process, and this strengthened my misgivings about the denials he had voiced. It still seemed most probable that he was responsible for organising murder and abduction. I could not fathom why he had chosen to reject my submission but it was in character for him to taunt me to the utmost. Doubtless, in his own good time, he would announce what extra degradation he required from me before admitting he was holding Hubert de Grey hostage.

I rode to Blackheath and saw the remnants of the abandoned camp, surrounded by a well-built palisade and ditches dug for extra defence on more exposed stretches at the top of the hill. The swarms of men and carts had gone, their rubbish strewn everywhere, but it was clear the encampment could be re-occupied very easily. This reinforced my suspicion that Cade had ordered a tactical retreat designed to mislead his opponents.

I observed a small group of husbandmen sitting on the ground playing dice on the far side of the heath and at first I judged it prudent to avoid them. Then one of them hailed me in friendly fashion and I realised I had seen him previously in the vicinity of Cade's tent. This gave me confidence so I rode across and enquired where their leaders had gone, implying I was intent on joining them.

'Towards Seven Oaks, mate. Jack Cade left us here to send on stragglers. That bastard, Lord Saye and Sele, has his mansion of Knowle near to Seven Oaks. Reckon they'll sack it. Better hurry if you're after some of the pickings. Lucky you're on horseback.'

I waved my thanks and urged my horse down the hill but, when I was out of sight of the dice players, I left the highway, instead cutting across open ground to the edge of the Danson estate. I had formed an idea, a scheme which might establish Iffley's guilt, but it required the participation of others and was an unreasonable imposition on a bereaved family. Shamed by the audacity of my request, I nonetheless called on Mistress Ash.

I was humbled by the widow's willingness to assist me and I promised to send a posse of armed men to escort her to the appropriate place as soon as I could. I rode away from her cottage, heading for the de Grey manor-house, when shouts behind me caused me to turn and I recognised Sir Hugh riding furiously towards me, backed by a cluster of riders in his livery. As he neared me his face was contorted with anger and grief and I stiffened with foreboding.

'They're butchers, Harry, vile, depraved butchers, barbarians, savages. We must slaughter them all. They lack all decency. Oh, God, my little son... How can I tell Blanche?'

I dropped from my saddle and went to Hugh's side as he reined his horse to a standstill. 'Hubert?' I asked needlessly.

'They have him...,' he flapped his hand towards the riders behind him. 'We found his new dug grave. It wasn't there when we searched before. We combed the land near the pond where Ash was killed. One of my fellows spotted the disturbed earth this afternoon and we uncovered him... By Christ, Harry, I shall demand retribution against these demons. I'll have their entrails ripped from their bellies while they still live. Monsters, monsters. My little son...'

Tears streamed down Sir Hugh's face as I gripped his icy hand. His attendants had caught up with us and one of them clasped a shrouded bundle in his arms. 'May I see the child?' I asked and the distraught father stifled a sob as he nodded.

The servant handed me the diminutive body and I unrolled the cloth covering it, expecting to see the jagged wound made by an arrow in soft infant flesh. What in fact I saw was even more appalling and I heaved as I understood the fate which Hubert had suffered. The marks of a garrotte around the boy's throat made it likely he had ultimately been strangled. But the bruising and torn flesh of his lower body gave evidence of how, before death granted him respite, after perhaps several days of abuse, he had been made to serve the perverted lust of a vicious degenerate.

I swallowed the bile in my mouth for I was needed to support Hubert's anguished father and must assume my dispassionate role as physician but outrage thundered in my heart. To lose a child is cruel for a parent in any circumstances but the horror of knowing how the infant had been brutalised before he died was unimaginable.

*****

'Try to protect my wife from the details of Hubert's death if you can. They are deeply distressing for us all but it's difficult to tell what effect they might have on Kate.'

Judith looked me straight in the eye. 'She's had strange fancies about the boy's disappearance, Doctor

61

Somers. Worked herself into a frenzy, almost an unnatural frenzy, writhing – and so forth.'

The girl blushed and compressed her mouth, compounding my embarrassment.

'It happens sometimes with those afflicted in their minds. It's part of what some consider possession by the Devil. I'm sorry you've witnessed it. It has no deeper meaning.'

Judith did not flinch. 'Maybe I shouldn't say – but you're a physician not merely her husband. She speaks as if others have had her in the past, forced her...'

'She's been cruelly misused – in more than one way – by those who should have cared for her. It's worsened her state of mind. That's why she shouldn't know too much about Hubert's fate. I didn't realise she spoke of what she's endured.'

'She rambles sometimes and in the night she has bad dreams. Can she recover?'

Judith eyed me doubtfully and I saw there was no point in pretence. 'I don't know. We're ignorant of how to treat maladies of the mind, except by balancing the humours, as with any ailment. All I'm sure of is that I'll do my utmost to help her.'

'You still love her, Doctor? Oh! I shouldn't have...' Her face was scarlet and I patted her arm.

'You serve her well and I'm not offended. Yes, I love her. I'm leaving Danson again for a difficult assignment so it comforts me to know she's in good hands. I trust it won't be long until we have our own home and life can be more serene. That'll be the best setting for Kate's recovery.'

As I rode off, I reflected on my words to Judith. The final wish I expressed to her was completely true. I longed more than anything for Kate to be restored to health, but had I been truthful to say I still loved my wife? I did not know. Our relationship had been so battered by her illness and those who had taken advantage of her that I could not be sure what I felt. Yet I resolved I must not dwell on my own ambiguous sentiments. I had a mission to accomplish, to bring a villain to justice and provide some semblance of solace to the frantic, almost deranged, parents of the murdered boy.

Above all, one reservation resounded in my mind. Could Gilbert Iffley have stooped so low as to allow his infant captive to be tortured and raped by some pervert among his servants? Was it unthinkable that the Baron himself could be capable of such bestial behaviour?

*****

In the grief-stricken household at Danson, news that, when he rode through the City the King had ordered the dispersal of the rebels without responding to their complaints, incited no comment. I questioned whether the royal intentions had been conveyed in advance to Jack Cade, probably by the draper, Thomas Cooke, the go-between, and this had occasioned the rapid departure from Blackheath. At all events I was able to establish the exact location where Cade and his followers were now encamped, near the village of Solefields, outside Seven Oaks, and I visited him there, barely containing my fury at Hubert's murder. To his credit he had paled at my description of the boy's treatment and swore that if I could demonstrate one of his men was guilty, he would condemn the villain to death.

Two days later the necessary arrangements were in place and I was once more on the road to Solefields. The idea I had devised to trap Iffley into admitting he was holding Hubert had been developed into a plan to catch a double murderer. I was accompanied by Sir Hugh and his band of mounted retainers, together with a covered litter and its sorrowful occupants who were now called on to play parts in a more gruesome masque than I had at first contemplated. The participants in our journey could expect a testing time and they were pledged to preserve a calm demeanour, even in the face of considerable provocation. This would be crucial and I prayed silently that all involved would fulfil their roles effectively.

I would face the devil of a challenge to maintain my own peace of mind for, in spite of Judith's best efforts, Kate had learned of Hubert's fate and she thrashed about in wild disorder, screaming at me as if I bore responsibility for the child's death. I could not foretell her behaviour from one hour to the next but her distress was so extreme that I feared her condition would deteriorate. When I left Danson my physician's instruments were in my saddle-bag in case I had need of them, but also because I feared Kate might do herself injury if she found them

Jack Cade proved as good as his word. Despite rumours that armed men from the King's court were intent on attacking the camp at Solefields, he had assembled his principal advisers and attendants in the largest tent to receive our deputation. I breathed more easily when I saw Gilbert Iffley among Cade's lieutenants, now simply dressed in fustian rather than his finery when I called at his City house. He was backed by several rough-looking attendants. He shook his head at me as much to say I was wasting my time with whatever gambit I had devised. Well and good, I thought: we shall see. I regretted the apparent absence of Piers Ford, whose balanced views I respected, and I wondered if he had abandoned Cade's supporters when they withdrew from Blackheath.

I presented Sir Hugh to the company, impressed by his dignity and restraint as he stated the circumstances of his son's death. It did not make comfortable listening and I noted shuffling feet and downcast eyes as well as grunts of outrage but, when the bereaved father went on to allege that one of Cade's followers was responsible, there were angry exclamations and denials.

'You have my deepest sympathy, Sir Hugh.' Cade spoke with exquisite refinement. 'I cannot imagine how any father can bear the horror that has enveloped you. Yet I must have proof if any of my men are to be arraigned. Evidence is required in any court of law and one of our strongest demands to King Henry is that the law be impartially upheld.'

I stood forward and acknowledged the truth of Cade's assertion. 'As an aid to finding the proof that we all crave, I ask permission to introduce two others who have been harmed by the tragedy and may in their persons prompt some recollection among the observers.'

'Certainly, Doctor Somers,' Cade folded his hands. 'Pray proceed.'

Out of the corner of my eye I glimpsed Iffley's shrug of impatience but the flap covering the tent opening had been drawn back and all eyes turned to view the woman, veiled in mourning, who entered holding a small boy by the hand. A group of Danson retainers followed her into the tent and stood by the entrance as she walked slowly towards Cade. Several in the crowd of bystanders murmured, pronouncing the new arrivals to be Hubert's mother and brother, and they coughed awkwardly to hide their embarrassment. One or two, more accurately informed, gave gasps of disbelief and, among them, I watched Iffley who was frowning. He stood stock still, biting his lip, before he looked at me directly and raised his eyebrows, not in derision or alarm but in evident puzzlement. His toothless attendant gave a bored shrug.

I was so perturbed to see the Baron's commonplace reaction that for a moment I missed the movement towards the back of the tent, but the carefully positioned Danson men did not. When a fellow pushed his way towards the entrance, trying to slip past these sentinels, they seized him and dragged him forward. His face was distorted and his body twitching with a paroxysm of terror but I identified the squire, Stanlaw, and I held my breath.

At my signal Mistress Ash, unrecognisable beneath her veils, stepped towards him and lifted young Allan into her arms, boldly confronting the wretched man. As she came closer to him Stanlaw shrieked, struggling violently to escape his captors, and fell to his knees.

65

Allan tucked his face into his mother's shoulder but his shrill voice was audible to all. 'Mama, I don't like nasty man.' It was the instinctive response of a frightened child and its effect was perfect. A murmur of appalled consternation rippled through the onlookers.

'He thinks the child is a phantasm, an apparition resembling the boy he abused and killed.'

'But the boy is the image of the one found in the cart on Blackheath. I saw him. Baron Glasbury said he was Sir Hugh's son. I don't understand.'

'God has resurrected the boy to bring retribution to his attacker. May the Lord have mercy on us.'

'Divine intervention! Glory to God.'

'There might be another explanation.'

'Could they be twins?'

Hearing these exchanges, Stanlaw ceased to twitch and when he addressed Cade it was clear he had mastered his panic. 'This is a trick,' he said, 'to frighten the tender-hearted. You see, sir, the child is living. He isn't in the grave at all. My senses are awry. Forgive my foolishness. I was greatly distressed by Sir Hugh's story.'

Cade stared at him but said nothing. It was Hugh de Grey's voice which cut across a bevy of muttered inferences. 'What grave, you filthy bastard? Who spoke of a grave?'

Stanlaw stammered something about assuming there was a grave but Cade cut him short. 'Answer me, squire, and answer me truly. You are a skilled bowman. Did you kill the woodman, Adam Ash? Answer me.'

Stanlaw grasped what he must have seen as an opportunity to win support and extricate himself from involvement in Hubert's death. His voice became wheedling. 'I feared you were too lenient, sir,' he said. 'It wasn't right to let the woodman go. 'The man could have betrayed us. He'd seen our camp. I thought the child old enough to run home in safety but Master Ash was a danger. I disposed of him for all our sakes.'

There were some murmurs of approval from the assembly but Cade held up his hand for silence and I observed the tension in his jaw. 'And did you sodomize that child for all our sakes? You did not flout my merciful judgement because you disagreed with it. You killed Ash in order to kidnap the child and satisfy your disgusting lust. You base, inhuman animal.'

Cade had become agitated, his eyes blazing, his face scarlet, and he loomed above his grovelling henchman with hands rigid as claws ready to tear the villain to pieces. It was the first time I had seen the young man near to losing self-control and it worried me all the more when I realised what angered him most. His words were howled, as from a creature in pain.

'You disobeyed me. You presumed to defy my decree. I gave the woodman permission to leave the camp. I took responsibility to release him. How dare you oppose my will? I find you guilty of gross insubordination, of murder and the foulest abominations. I condemn you to immediate execution.' Cade beckoned one of his sergeants. 'Take him outside and strike the head from his body. Let all present understand how I shall deal with transgressors in our midst. My discipline recognises no exceptions and I shall have obedience.'

I was startled by the savagery in his voice and the speed of his judgement. I did not doubt Stanlaw's guilt but he had hardly been granted a proper trial and even the vilest rogue should be given time to repent before he is despatched to stand in the presence of God. I may have been alone in my compassion. Cade's underlings leapt forward to carry out his decree and most of the company hustled their way from the tent behind them. Very soon afterwards a blood-curdling scream was followed by cheers and catcalls, confirming that the sentence had been fulfilled. I had gone to Cade, anxious to pacify him, but he brushed me aside, turning to my companion with blazing eyes.

'Sir Hugh, I hope you are content with Mortimer's justice,' he said, pride creeping into his voice. 'We are sworn to root out evil-doers and punish them according to their deserts. It is abominable that we have nurtured a pederast and a murderer within our cohort but there are filthy villains in any assembly. I trust your party will return to Danson knowing you have been granted justice.'

Sir Hugh bowed his head in acknowledgement, choking back inadequate words. He was plainly shaken by the rapidity with which events had moved after Cade's peremptory verdict and sentence but he was satisfied that the guilty man had been identified and punished. He rallied his party to leave but when I indicated that I would accompany them, Cade intervened to prevent me.

'Stay with me, physician,' he urged. 'I may have need of your services.' He clutched his belly and it seemed all too probable that he would suffer an attack of nausea when the extremities of emotion had passed. I could not rebuff him. Sir Hugh understood and nodded thanks to me as he departed.

When the others had gone, Gilbert Iffley sidled across to join me. His sneer was ingratiating. 'A clever stratagem, Harry: I congratulate you. Reptiles like Stanlaw deserve to be castrated but it's interesting how the most fiendish scoundrels are cowards when presented with a whiff of the supernatural. A more sophisticated man would have held his nerve and wriggled out of your trap.'

What was he telling me? I could not dismiss the idea that he, who held his nerve with superlative ease, had instigated Stanlaw's crimes but I had no basis for this theory and no time to reflect on it. Shouts from outside the tent summoned us to hear news a begrimed messenger had brought, which Cade ordered him to repeat.

'The King has denounced us as rebels and sent an armed party to lay us low. Led by two noblemen, they say, Sir Humphrey Stafford and his brother. They're heading for Solefields. They're only a few miles away.'

'By God, they shall regret it.' Cade's face was flushed with excitement. 'Does the King dismiss the grievances of his subjects so lightly? Has he been toying with us, sending a fair-mouthed agent to delude us while he assembled his army? It's time to show our strength. Get the men to their stations on the slopes in the wood above the track: archers at the front with bows at the ready. We'll ambush the bastards before they reach our camp. We went in peace to Blackheath and this is how they respond. Well, the gauntlet is thrown down and we shall thrust it in their maw. My orders are that we give no quarter: slaughter every man of them.'

The spasm of colic which troubled him a few minutes earlier was forgotten. Cade was invigorated and avid for violent action, utterly changed from the simulacrum of a peaceful leader seeking to gain King Henry's ear by negotiation. Stanlaw's severed body had been removed from sight but I was convinced the episode which led to the squire's death had profoundly impacted on his master's state of mind. I did not believe it was sudden bloodlust alone which now impelled Cade towards ferocity. It could even be a mark of his insecurity and innate nervousness. His rage had been fanned by his follower's disobedience and what he sought, to alleviate his chagrin, was a triumphant demonstration of his ability to command. While men scurried to obey his will, he glowed with the intoxication of power.

Cade was granted his wish. His dutiful men fell upon the hapless Staffords without mercy, almost annihilating the force sent to disperse them. Inevitably there was much exultation at this success but, when I knelt beside the stripped bodies of the Stafford brothers, amidst the widely strewn corpses of their adherents, I speculated what the implications of that day might prove to be: for Cade, the conqueror, might unleash horrors in King Henry's realm which I dared not envisage. It was as if, with the judgement he had pronounced and the execution of his squire, he had shed the veneer of peaceful diplomacy.

69

Now, as he laid claim publicly to the name of Mortimer, he was fired by a desire to slaughter all who disobeyed his will or tried to thwart his objectives – and he had confidence that he would succeed.

Chapter 6

I was unsurprised to find that Baron Glasbury had withdrawn from the camp at Solefields with his immediate followers before the massacre began. He was accomplished at evading responsibility for deeds he had helped provoke but on this occasion I could not blame him. As Cade's former tutor, Iffley probably knew his pupil's nature better than most and he may have foreseen the explosion of violence and arrogance which Stanlaw's fate heralded.

When dawn broke over the scene of carnage, with the victors still engaged in stripping the bodies of their victims, I decided it would be wise to absent myself in future from this band of insurgents. Now they had tasted blood and defied the King's decree, there was no knowing where their actions might lead. I had been accused, unjustly, of treason in the past and could expect no mercy if I was deemed to be part of a rebellion against the crown. Cade was sleeping peacefully and had no need of my services so I was free to go and I raised myself into the saddle with relief.

I was loath to intrude further on the grieving families at Danson until more time had elapsed and I needed to provide a home elsewhere for Kate to find peace and dignity. I must concentrate my thoughts on securing our future so I resolved to return to London, to the Manor of the Rose, and to write to Perkin, the steward at my manor of Worthwaite in Suffolk which the late Duke had conferred on me. My mind was occupied in pondering how soon I would need to visit the manor in person and confront the confusion of joyful and desolate memories it would evoke, so I paid scant attention to the land I was traversing. Without thinking, I took the same route that Cade's band had followed and by afternoon I was approaching Blackheath once more. The defensive paling remained in place and extra ditches had been dug since I was there a few days previously, while a gaggle of workmen was visible outside new makeshift cabins. It would be easy to reoccupy the site and the presence of these custodians suggested this was indeed the intention.

I urged my horse across the heath, hoping I would not be spotted, and was disconcerted when a fellow ran towards me waving his arms. Then I recognised him as the neighbour of the dead carter whom I had questioned after the fatal mishap.

'Doctor Somers, sir. Please stop. God's bounty be praised for sending you!'

Puzzled by this animated greeting, I reined my horse to a standstill. 'I hadn't expected to find you here,' I said cautiously. 'Master...?'

'John Toft, sir. Sent to keep guard, we are. But that's not the issue. I didn't dare hope you'd appear again. Your mate needs your testimony, urgent like.'

'My mate?' I thought of Rendell but it made no sense.

'The wheelwright, Master Ford. He's accused of George's murder. Baron Glasbury sent men to arrest him and drag him before Jack Cade. Lucky for him, he got away. He must be in hiding, lying low. I know he didn't tamper with the wheel of George's cart – he couldn't have done it, he wasn't there at the right time. But Glasbury's men wouldn't listen to me. You know though, Doctor: you were with him, weren't you? You came together when George's cart fell over.'

'We'd been chatting and before that he was inside Jack Cade's tent with his principal colleagues, including Glasbury. The accusation's absurd.' I spoke slowly, working through in my mind what this extraordinary development could mean. 'When did Piers Ford hear of it?'

'Two days ago, Glasbury's men came. By good fortune, Ford had gone down to Greenwich to collect tackle we needed from a timber merchant. We managed to get word to him and he slipped off. Hope to God he hasn't gone home to Dartford. Glasbury's sergeant knew where he came from and was set on going there.'

'Piers Ford and Glasbury were at odds in their advice to Cade. It all smacks of the Baron scheming to rid himself of an annoying rival. If Piers hasn't gone to Dartford, where might he be hiding?'

John Toft creased his brow in concentration. 'Guess the City might be a good place. If he knows anyone there to shelter him. I wouldn't fancy it. Give me the fresh Kentish air. You will help him, Doctor, won't you?'

'Of course. I'll swear a statement about his whereabouts at the time of George's murder and send it to Cade.'

'The sergeant said it was Glasbury who needed convincing. He said if you turned up I should ask you to go to the Baron. He mentioned you, particular like. That's how I know your name, Doctor Somers.'

I heard myself sigh as it all fell into place. My misguided visit to his house on Cheapside had led me to expose my weakness. I had offered to acquiesce with the Baron's wishes in exchange for Hubert's safe return. That was not possible, beyond even Gilbert Iffley's contrivances, but my submissiveness then gave him the lever which he had long been seeking. Now he intended to barter Piers Ford's safety in exchange for my compliance.

Except that he had failed to capture Piers.

'I'll do what's necessary, don't worry. If you hear from Piers or need to contact me, a message to the master carpenter, Thomas Chope, near the Tower of London, will find me.' I paused. 'How is young Georgie and his family, do you know?'

Toft moistened his lips. 'Georgie's older brother will run the business; he worked with his father. They'll manage. Mind you, if they find out someone interfered with George Antey's cart I'd guess they'll be after a life for a life. I could tell them it wasn't Piers Ford but Glasbury's men were set on visiting the family and I reckon they'll pour poison in their ears, so they might be persuaded.'

This double-pronged attack to put Ford's life at hazard was a typical manoeuvre by Gilbert Iffley. If the

King's justice did not send the wheelwright to the gallows, a vengeful bereaved son might cut his throat – all threats, I suspected, in order to secure my acquiescence. It was imperative that I find Piers before Glasbury did and make sure he was in a place of safety. This was an extra burden I could have done without.

*****

Thomas listened to me patiently and rubbed his chin. 'I'll make enquiries but if this wheelwright has gone to ground it'll be like looking for one small chip among all the wood shavings under a carpenter's bench. Does he have contacts in the City?'

I had to acknowledge I did not know but Thomas's face had darkened and he was anxious to raise another subject. 'I've been asking round about premises in the City for you to take, where you could practice as a physician, but it's not promising.'

'Surely there are some possibilities?'

'There might be in the shabbier areas but I didn't think you'd want scruffy lodgings.'

'Kate wouldn't like that, certainly. But I noticed a mercer's house near Cornhill where they've built a new wing with a lean-to for displaying their fabrics. I thought they might have rooms to spare behind their yard. I'll go and enquire.'

Thomas put a hand on my arm. 'It's no good, Harry. I started there. It'd be perfect for you but Master Frewin won't consider the idea.'

I stared blankly until a glimmer of comprehension came. 'Because...?'

'Because you were Suffolk's physician. Because you still have links to the Manor of the Rose.'

'So I'm branded as an enemy to the City?'

'People are nervous. Especially with this Mortimer fellow making his demands. Mind you, there's sympathy for him in the City and some say he's one of Richard of

York's relations. The Common Council are dithering about inviting him to enter the gates. They dismissed an Alderman known to be a friend of the royal court – it's meant as a gesture to the rebels that there's a fund of goodwill towards them if they behave decently.'

It was clear Thomas was more comfortable talking about public affairs rather than my dubious reputation among his fellow guildsmen. What he said was interesting but I wanted to drag him back to my concerns. 'That's ironic but I could call on Jack Cade to vouch for me. He seems to have confidence in my good faith and I've just written to him to clear Piers Ford's name. Maybe I should wait until he enters the City. Is that really likely?'

Thomas grinned. 'They say the King has fled. The murder of the Stafford brothers terrified the Queen and she begged him to go north to Kenilworth where he's certain of support. If that's true and he's seen as deserting his subjects in London, it'll be a matter of days before the City gates are flung open. It's not just the Kentish horde either – there's a band of Essex men waiting at Mile End to join forces with Mortimer or whatever you call him. The Aldermen will admit them through the gates too. Best bide your time and see what happens.'

It was good advice but I felt frustrated by the difficulty of running Piers Ford to earth and the delay in resolving my own domestic requirements. The City was always friendly to Duke Richard of York and if the Common Council believed he favoured the uprising, they would be encouraged to give it their backing. The Duke, however, was far away and some of his agents, like Glasbury, were deeply unreliable. Although I did not explain my misgivings to Thomas, I was not confident that all would go peaceably if Cade was admitted to the City; I could not forget the wild, exultant look in his eyes when Sir Humphrey Stafford's men were massacred.

As if to validate my anxieties, news was brought within days of rioting in other cities of the realm and, most shockingly, it was reported that William Ayscough, Bishop of Salisbury, had been dragged from a church in Wiltshire and hacked to death by members of his congregation. Was it a coincidence that Ayscough had solemnised the vows between King Henry and Queen Margaret after she arrived from France five years earlier? The Queen's increasing assertiveness, counteracting her husband's mild disposition, was highly unpopular and the Bishop may have borne the brunt of widespread hostility to the loathed Frenchwoman and the – as yet – barren royal marriage. If this was true, opposition was creeping dangerously close to the crown itself.

We gained further evidence of the panic caused by the insurgency when Rendell brought us news that Lord Saye and Sele, the unpopular target of Kentish wrath, had been sent to lodge at the Tower on the King's orders. His arrest might be portrayed publicly as a move to placate the rebels but royal orders to the Governor of the Tower made it clear the arrangement was intended to protect the prisoner from his foes. It was all too familiar, the precedent dismal, because the late Duke of Suffolk had been accommodated in the fortress at the King's behest, for his own safety, but the device proved of temporary effectiveness. Suffolk had been done to death despite the King's favour and I did not doubt the same fate might await Lord Saye and Sele if he could be prised from the security of comfortable internment.

On St. Peter's Day we heard that Jack Cade and his growing band of dissidents had re-occupied the camp at Blackheath, which was no surprise to me, and the Common Council sent the draper, Cooke, to negotiate with him once more. It was the same day that I received a letter from the Prioress of St. Michael's Convent in Stamford, with whom I had corresponded for several years, one among many of her informants who kept her abreast of events elsewhere, not least in the City and the court. I learned from her how widely unrest had spread in other parts of the country and I paused with concern reading one passage.

I hear that there have been recent disturbances in Norfolk and the residence near Attleborough of the new-made Lord Fitzvaughan and his family has come under attack. The bailiff at Hartham Manor was slightly injured although I understand the rioters were beaten off. As this family is known to you, I thought you would wish to be aware of their travail. The Norman, Gaston de la Tour, who now holds the title and Fitzvaughan lands by virtue of his wife's inheritance, has not won the hearts of his tenants. This would have been of small significance to me except that, as you are well aware, sweet little Eleanor, who spent her childhood in the care of St. Michael's, brought him the title with their marriage. Her shameful mother, the Dowager Lady Maud, remains in their household but relations are said to be strained.

News of these people I had known for a decade jolted me. Their histories had been tangled with mine in a complicated sequence of friendship and mistrust which still put claims on me, but I was ill-placed to respond to their plight. Young Lady Eleanor I esteemed sincerely but her husband had tried to have me killed on more than one occasion, when he deemed me an inconvenience, and his attitude to me now was at best ambivalent. As for Lady Maud, the beautiful, capricious, misused woman whose fortunes had been as wretched as her resilience was impressive.... Lady Maud had been my mistress occasionally over many years and at one time for several months – before I met Kate. I could not repudiate any cry for help she addressed to me, now she was widowed and dependent on the unreliable protection of her son-in-law. Yet there was no possibility that I might go to the Fitzvaughan manor of Hartham near Attleborough until my own future and that of my wife had been secured. In the meantime it would be useless to dwell on their troubles when I could do nothing to help them and worries about my own position pre-occupied me.

Before I set aside my concerns for the Fitzvaughans, I reflected on one other implication of the

Prioress's information. Rioters at Hartham Manor were beaten off, as had happened once previously, but his lordship's bailiff, Robin Willoughby, had suffered injury. Robin's devoted wife was my own first, chaste love, Bess, from whom long ago, when we were both free, I had been parted by adverse circumstances. I wanted nothing but happiness for Bess and her husband and prayed Robin would make a complete recovery.

Feeling unsettled and reluctant to burden Thomas further with my affairs, I left the Manor of the Rose to tramp the streets of the City and wandered towards the vicinity of Newgate where the apothecary I had patronised for years had his business. Master John Webber received me courteously and eagerly agreed to supply the herbs and mixtures I would need when I established my own practice in the City but he shared Thomas's unease about the likelihood of me finding suitable premises while there was such uncertainty about the outcome of Cade's insurrection.

'There's a rumour the protesters are set on moving into Southwark, ready to advance across London Bridge into the City. It puts the Lord Mayor on the spot – does he order the central drawbridge to be raised and the gates barred, risking an assault and maybe bloodshed, or does he invite the unruly masses onto the streets of London? The Common Council is to meet on St. Thomas's Day to decide.'

'An auspicious day for doubters to make up their minds,' I said with an attempt at wry humour. 'Cade will want to reassure the City fathers. He'll insist his men observe good discipline. He's shown he's not afraid to take stern action against malefactors.'

Master Webber interlaced his fingers. 'It'll all come down to business in the end. This is the City. The shrewd Lombards have already seen advantage in agreeing to supply the man they're calling Mortimer with horses and battle-axes. Remember, Richard of York has Mortimer blood and he's popular among the merchants. He'd impose law and order if only the King would call on him to take his proper place beside the throne.' He paused and gave a thin smile. 'They say this Mortimer is an Irishman.'

'I believe he has been in Ireland.' I rose to take my leave, resisting the temptation to give details of how I had first glimpsed the young fellow in York's household when I visited Dublin. I was troubled by what Master Webber told me and he corroborated Thomas's view of my unhelpful reputation in the City.

The streets were busy as I made my way back to the Manor of the Rose and I could sense volatility in the mood of whispering, nervy citizens who looked over their shoulders and dropped their voices when a stranger passed. Even the lad sweeping ordure from the gutter outside one of the finer houses screwed up his face, regarding me with a baleful stare as if, without knowing me, he concluded I was untrustworthy. It reminded me of the time, quite recently, when the Duke of Suffolk's star was fading and hostility towards him built to bursting point. I knew how easily the City could become an acutely dangerous place.

I was not surprised to find the Suffolk steward in a state of agitation at the Manor of the Rose, alarmed by the prospect of Cade's entry into the City. He had already sent many of the servants, including my young colleague, Doctor Leone, to the Duke's residences in East Anglia and he proposed to shut up the London house until the risk of attack had passed. He urged me to find other lodgings and only then remembered, with a sniff of disapproval, that a character of dubious aspect was waiting to see me. I promised to leave the house, with those possessions I had left there months earlier, as soon as I had dealt with my visitor and I bade the faithful old retainer farewell with genuine good wishes for his welfare. Then I climbed the stairs to the small chamber I had been using for the past few days.

I recognised John Toft at once, the man from near Maidstone I had last spoken to on Blackheath, and he told me he had called at Thomas Chope's workshop, looking for me, and been redirected to the Manor.

'I've been sent ahead with one or two others to reconnoitre in the City,' he said. 'Slipped in through the gates, we did, like any honest men. Reckon we'll all be welcome here from what I've seen. Got to get back to report to Mortimer but I thought you'd want to know I found out something about where Piers Ford might have gone. He's got a married sister in Essex, village called Hornchurch. One of the other men from Dartford knew. Don't worry, he didn't tell Glasbury's snoopers.'

I grinned. 'That's hopeful. Have you any idea if Jack Cade received my letter on Piers' behalf?'

'Have to call him Edmund Mortimer, not Cade: order sent round. He said he'd heard from you but I don't think he's convinced by what you said. Baron Glasbury was with him when I saw him.'

I thanked Master Toft and gave him something for his trouble. Then I collected my bundle of possessions and left the Manor of the Rose, hoping to lodge for a short while with Thomas and Grizel, although I was not confident they would appreciate a controversial guest in their bustling household for more than a single night. I need not have worried on that score, however, for my old friends were resolute that I should stay with them as long as I needed a roof over my head in the City.

While I trudged towards the Tower, I thought through what John Toft had told me. I was intrigued that Cade was laying claim to the full name, Edmund Mortimer. The surname associated him with the Duke of York's branch of the royal house but the Christian name, Edmund, appeared to link him with a nobleman of that family who was long dead. Was 'Edmund' intended to strengthen the implication that Cade had royal antecedents or was he even pretending to be a highborn claimant to the throne, miraculously resurrected?

Of more immediate concern, I hoped that Piers Ford was truly safe in his sister's home. Nonetheless, when

80

I remembered the strength of the wheelwright's commitment to the protesters' cause, I wondered whether he would be content to skulk anonymously in Hornchurch while the rebels neared their objective at the City gates. I explained my reasoning to Thomas, out of Grizel's hearing, and his eyes lit up with pleasure.

'Fancy a stroll out to Mile End, do you? There's two hours of daylight yet. I'll come with you. Griz will be glad to be rid of us while she's getting the boys to their bed. They clamour for stories and sweetmeats and she's firmer than I am in refusing their pleas. We can have a beaker of ale when we get back past the gates. Haven't been to our old watering place together for an age, have we?'

I was pleased to have his company but urged Thomas to wear his working clothes, rather than an outfit which marked him out as the master tradesman he was, and I wore my shabbiest travelling gown. Then we set out past the Abbey of St. Clare and through the Aldgate, along the highway to the east. Within two miles we sighted the informal camp spread across the fields beside the track. It looked like an untidier version of Cade's base on Blackheath but, before we had approached much nearer, we were stopped and required to account for ourselves. I gave my name, claimed acquaintance with Edmund Mortimer and, boldly asked to speak with Piers Ford, wheelwright. It was encouraging that there was no instantaneous denial of Piers' presence but we were placed firmly under guard while the spokesman went to find someone with greater authority to deal with my request. Two burly labourers with pitchforks positioned themselves each side of us and scowled as we attempted to look at ease.

'Come from Mortimer, have you?' one of them asked. 'About time he let us know what's happening. Been here for days. Men'll go home if they can't get into the City. Got our dander up, we have, ready to slice them nobles in two, but if them Kentish louts reckon we'll wait on their pleasure, they'll have another think coming.'

He spat noisily at my feet and I forced myself not to recoil. I pondered whether Jack Cade, as I still thought of him, was aware how belligerent his Essex colleagues seemed to be and whether he would succeed in imposing discipline over their actions. Thomas, looking entirely relaxed and adopting a rough London accent, indicated that he at least came from the City where there was some sympathy with the uprising, provided householders could be sure their property was not at risk. This was provocative and our guard became red in the face and swore but we were saved from an explosion of his wrath by a most welcome sound.

'Doctor Somers, by all the saints, it is truly you! Have you been sent by Mortimer or Baron Glasbury?'

Piers Ford loped through the assembled crowd with arms outstretched and came to an unsteady halt just in front of me. 'Neither,' I laughed as he regained control over his flailing limbs. 'I wouldn't want either of them to know you're here until I'm sure certain accusations have been dropped.'

His expression became serious. 'You tracked me down out of friendship. I'm humbled.' He flung an arm round me and drew me aside, leaving Thomas and our erstwhile guards glowering at each other while I explained what had happened in Kent during his absence. As I surmised, he was ignorant of little Hubert's fate and he listened to my description of the child's abuse and murder with stunned revulsion. I described how Stanlaw had been induced to betray himself and Piers patted my arm in appreciation of my ruse but he was troubled by Mortimer's peremptory justice.

'I always feared Jack's head might be turned if he was successful. Drunk on power, they call it, don't they? I tried to stop it happening, calm him down with reasoning. Glasbury knows his nature. He probably blamed me for the carter's death just to get me out of the way.'

'There's another possible explanation – or knowing Gilbert Iffley's deviousness, both reasons are likely to apply.' I explained my idea that the Baron was seeking to put pressure on me by threatening Ford.

His eyes grew round. 'So I could be a pawn and Glasbury is relying on your decency to save me from conviction as a murderer by agreeing to do what he wants? He's putting a high price on winning your support.'

I shrugged. 'I know I sound arrogant but he's persistent and doesn't like to be thwarted. Besides, he'd be ridding himself of a thorn in his flesh by eliminating you as well.'

Piers Ford chuckled. 'It's in character, I can't deny it. So you're less than pleased to find me here? You'd rather I was lying low?' I nodded. 'But you guessed I wouldn't be in hiding. You scarcely know me but you read me aright. I can't walk away from the struggle we've begun. There's justice and fairness and good governance at stake. You know that. You have my undying gratitude, Doctor Somers, but you're to put my safety out of your reckoning. Stick to your principles and send Glasbury about his business if he threatens to do me harm. Our poor men's cause is bigger than one gangling wheelwright's future. I'm needed here to quieten some of the wilder spirits. There's a danger they'll run out of control if they get into the City and see all the fine houses full of possible booty. That mustn't happen. So I'll do what I have to and take my chances with the likes of Glasbury. When the time comes, I pray God it'll be him and his like who'll be subject to the law and called to account for their misdeeds, not only the greater overlords. Mark what I say. I mean every word.'

A wave of emotion swept over me at this out-pouring of sincerity and I blinked back moisture in my eyes. 'I believe you, Master Ford. It's a noble objective. I'll do what I can to get the charge against you dismissed. I wrote to Mortimer but I've heard nothing so I propose to visit him in person. At any rate it'll be a relief to know I have your blessing to resist Glasbury.'

83

'Blessing! Would you make me into a hedge priest rousing his listeners to riot and pillage? My way is more peaceful but you have all my goodwill and gratitude. I hope we'll meet again, Doctor, in happy circumstances.'

I echoed his hope and told him I could be contacted through Thomas, whom I introduced to him, pleased to recognise the mutual respect with which the two skilled craftsmen instinctively greeted each other. Piers hugged me as we parted and Thomas and I retraced our steps towards the City.

'That's a singular chap,' my carpenter friend said cautiously after we left Mile End. 'Did he give you the answer that you wanted?'

'It wasn't what I came for, not at all, but, yes, it was very much what I wanted. I'm free now to act as I think right. May Heaven aid me – and keep the City safe.'

I did not then grasp how easily my free agency and the City's safety could be compromised.

Chapter 7

On the following morning it was confirmed that Edmund Mortimer was now lodging in Southwark at the sign of the White Hart. The Common Council was to meet in the Guildhall to make a final decision on admitting him through the City gates and Thomas departed, wearing his guildsman's gown, to listen to the debate. He assured me that agreement would be given because the troops at the Lord Mayor's disposal were insufficient to withstand a determined attack and the rebels were becoming increasingly belligerent.

All attention was on the Guildhall, with crowds gathered outside to whisper supposed accounts of the arguments exchanged in the council chamber. I took the opportunity to present myself at the gate on London Bridge where I sought permission, as a physician intent on attending an ailing patient, to cross the Thames into Southwark. There was no open access to the City from the south that day but I posed no threat, walking on my own in the other direction, so the central drawbridge was briefly lowered, flanked by armed guards. Thus I was allowed to go forward onto the southern half of the bridge, making my way across the river between the crowded buildings on each side of the narrow roadway. I could not prevent a shiver passing down my spine as the drawbridge was raised again behind me and I was cut off from the protection of the City.

Southwark was known throughout London as a place of ill-repute, where ne'er-do-wells lurked and dark deeds were carried out with impunity. Honest citizens only ventured there with strong escorts or inconspicuously, as I hoped I appeared in my shabby gown and carrying my physician's bag. I received a knowing look when I enquired the way to the White Hart and I needed to state my name and profession three times to sentries before I was admitted to the substantial premises of the tavern. Then I was required to wait in a vestibule while a succession of underlings tramped up and down the staircase to the upper floor until at last Jack Cade's own voice summoned me to join him.

'Now I'm prepared to believe Heaven favours our enterprise!' The young leader's sprightliness belied his next words. 'I have great need of you, Doctor Somers, and beg you to mix me the potion which steadied my stomach when we first met on Blackheath. I expect to be admitted to the City before the day is out and must play my part to perfection.'

A servant was ready with a bowl of herbs and I took the pestle from him to pound them, adding a little of the liquid I had carried with me to give the mixture extra bite. 'The City seems generally well-favoured towards you, provided you can keep your men from breaking ranks and threatening property. If you maintain discipline, they'll give your grievances a fair hearing. It'll be a testing time for you and I'm glad I can be of help with my potion but that wasn't why I've come. Did you see the statement I swore concerning Piers Ford?'

'I passed it to Glasbury. He's dealing with it.' His tone was airy.

'But he made the accusation against the wheelwright!'

Mortimer looked impatient but spooned some of my physic into his mouth. He frowned at the bitter taste. 'Are you suggesting Glasbury can't act impartially on my behalf?'

'I thought you would see the roles of accuser and judge as distinct from each other. But you must know yourself it isn't possible Piers Ford caused the death of the carter. He was in conference with you and Glasbury at the time someone must have tampered with the man's cart.'

My patient turned to me with a bland, ingenuous expression and raised his eyebrows. 'How can I possibly know that? I kept no record of the hour and we lacked even a glass or dial to show us how long we spent in discussion. If Piers comes before me, I shall listen to his

86

pleas and pass my judgement. Let that satisfy you or do you doubt my dispassion?'

I bowed my head but he detected I was far from satisfied and became irritated. 'You saw how I weighed the evidence in the case of my own squire, a man I had known for many years: a follower Glasbury introduced to me when I was still a youth. Don't you think I have demonstrated my even-handedness?'

I wanted to protest at this inappropriate analogy and question him further on its implications but we were interrupted by shouts and running feet as attendants brought news that the City gates were to be opened within the hour for Mortimer and his men to enter. There was no possibility he would give additional thought to Ford's predicament in these circumstances so I moved to withdraw from the room, but he held up his hand imperiously to delay me.

'Fetch me Sir Humphrey Stafford's armour and apparel,' he shouted to his body-servant. 'I shall make a fitting entry to this self-important town. Come, Doctor Somers, you must ride in my train, my personal physician. You shall observe how Mortimer is worthy of respect and adulation. This is our moment and we shall not fail.'

My heart sank but I was bound to comply. Something Jack Cade had said seemed significant but in the bustle of preparations I did not register what it was and it slipped my mind.

*****

It was a remarkable occasion. As we traversed London Bridge and rode towards the Tower, I grew excited to witness this momentous event at close hand. Shrouded in my inconspicuous gown amid so many horsemen, I hoped I would not be recognised and, as the reception by the crowd greeting us was undeniably cordial, I began to think that my presence in the cavalcade could only advantage me. Hundreds had come out to see this commander of peasants, disrupter of the City's peace and, just possibly, sincere spokesman for the poor and saviour of the realm from lawlessness and corruption. Merchants huddled in the doorways of their premises or peeped from upstairs windows but, among the onlookers swarming by the roadway, it was possible to identify chandlers and fishmongers, porters and shoe-makers, masons and hawkers, apprentices and schoolboys. There were women too and they smiled on the good-looking young fellow who would make a presentable husband, son or beau and might bring prosperity to their families. Faces glowed with enthusiasm, caps were tossed in the air and even sober City officials scratched their chins in sympathetic meditation on what might come to be.

The man now calling himself Mortimer was resplendent in dead Stafford's clothes, with gilt spurs and helmet sparkling in the sunlight and a pristine gown of blue velvet from which every bloody stain had been removed. Cade revelled in his role, playing the sage and reasonable leader faultlessly. At the Church of St. Magnus just beyond the bridge and again at Leadenhall, he declared himself a loyal supporter of King Henry, intent on serving the crown's interests and those of its humble subjects which had been prejudiced by supercilious and acquisitive noblemen. He wished no harm to any well-intentioned man or woman and he promised that London's citizens and their possessions would be safeguarded by his followers. The least attempt at plunder would be punished by execution. He would brook no indiscipline and had made sure his men were in no doubt of this. He had already demonstrated he was as good as his word. Nervous cheers increased in volume as his listeners heard what they wanted to hear and gained the re-assurance they were desperate to have. Our progress became a victory procession.

We advanced along Candlewick Street and approached the City's focal point, where the Stone of London was sited, almost sacred in the estimation of its residents. The Stone's origins were lost in legend but, since anyone could remember, it had been accepted as the physical manifestation of London's glory, before which each transitory ruler must pay homage. It offered an opportunity for both humility and showmanship and the rebels' leader did not disappoint in his choice of response. In the presence of the Lord Mayor, Sir Thomas Charlton, and the assembled Aldermen, Jack Cade jumped from his horse, his armour glittering, and seized the ceremonial sword from the bearer who preceded him. Brandishing the weapon above his head, he struck the auspicious Stone with resounding force and his voice echoed in the sudden stillness as the crowd fell silent.

'Now is Mortimer lord of this City,' he proclaimed with pride and certainty, defying contradiction. And indeed none dared challenge him.

His assertion was repeated by hoarse and awed voices until it reached the back of the throng, where some could not hear his words, until it was lost in the groundswell of acclamation. This upstart braggart, this nobody with an assumed name and no history, had been accepted as conqueror within London's hallowed walls, acknowledged as master beside its revered Stone, with only his engaging personality to commend him. How greatly his audience must long for change, I thought, that they responded with such blind faith to his words. Yet whether the occasion would prove to be as momentous as it seemed, would depend on what followed: on Jack Cade's capacity to control the wilder elements in his train, on the willingness of thousands of individuals to submerge their personal grudges in pursuit of the common good.

The immediate indications were encouraging. Cade conferred with the Lord Mayor and secured agreement that his men would be free to come and go across the Thames into the City. Then, with the majority of the rebels, he withdrew to spend the night back in Southwark at the sign of the White Hart. A small contingent was left within the walls of London to ferret out known enemies but their activities were narrowly focused, their discipline rigorous and their behaviour unexceptionable. When I returned to my lodgings in the Chope household I found Thomas and his neighbours cautiously re-assured that their families could sleep in their homes without fear of violence perpetrated against their persons or property. I did not dispute the grounds for their optimism but felt uneasy that it might be short-lived.

I was at least encouraged by the fact that I had seen nothing of Baron Glasbury during the entry into the City.

*****

I awoke from fitful sleep before daybreak, plagued by fears that I could not adequately shield Piers Ford from Gilbert Iffley. Shortly afterwards I set out to walk the streets, anxious to establish whether there had been disorder during the night and if possible to allay the inchoate fears churning in my mind. I turned first towards the Tower but when I saw it looming, to all appearances impregnable and forbidding, reminding me of past injustices, I hurried to the riverside. I decided to walk along by the wharves to London Bridge and see if all was peaceful there. Just east of the Custom House I noted that, even at that early hour, goods were being unloaded from a vessel moored alongside the quay used by the Italians and I conjectured whether the hefty bundles contained leather goods or casks of wine and oil. They looked too bulky and unwieldy for bales of silk or lace. As I indulged in innocent speculation an elegantly robed man stepped from the warehouse to my right and at the sight of him I felt my heart flutter and my head throb.

'Can it be true? Doctor Somers in person? My good-brother, Glasbury, told me you had been on Blackheath but I didn't know you were now in the City. Is my unfortunate niece here too? Are her wits still as sadly disturbed as when I last saw her?'

I curbed conflicting instincts – to plunge my dagger into his villainous body or take to my heels and evade a confrontation I dreaded. Instead I stood erect and faced him with icy civility. 'Master Boice, I wonder that you have the effrontery to ask after the woman you have harmed so gravely, aggravating her affliction. I've nothing to say to you. You're well aware of my reasons.'

He shrugged his fur-clad shoulders. 'Can you guess what these good fellows are bringing ashore?' he asked affably. 'Protective harness for horses, swords and axes; the Lombards never miss an opportunity to do profitable business. I enjoy trading with them.'

'I thought you traded in wool and woollen cloth.'

He ignored the sarcasm in my voice. 'So I do. We are standing right beside the wharf where bales of wool are loaded to ship to our markets across the Narrow Sea. I know it well. But English merchants are alert for bargains just as much as the Lombards and I'm prepared to trade with them in other goods – to our mutual benefit.'

'And you have a market for your warlike purchases, I imagine.'

He chuckled. 'I read the signs and act accordingly. My foresight yields good returns and my business grows. But you haven't told me if my niece's health has improved. I wish her no harm.'

'I'm not here to bandy words with you, Boice. My wife is recovering in the country with friends and I trust she will never set eyes on you again. I too have business to conduct and must be on my way.'

'Towards London Bridge – and perhaps over it to Southwark? Is it really possible young Mortimer has won you to support his cause when all the efforts Glasbury and I expended to gain your allegiance have been thwarted by your pig-headedness?'

'I am a physician and serve my patients irrespective of allegiances. Good day.'

To my relief he did not attempt to detain me and I hurried on my way but the encounter was troubling. At a personal level, Boice deserved my hatred and it rankled that I must mask the abhorrence I felt while I was impotent to act against him. More worrying at that moment was the knowledge that he was importing arms into the City with every intention, I felt sure, of supplying them to Jack Cade's ostensibly peaceful supporters. My nebulous fear of menacing portents had assumed physical form.

The insurgents were pouring into the City across the undefended bridge by the time I reached it, marshalled by their own sergeants and seemingly in good humour. Yet they were coming in their thousands, numbers difficult to control if their mood should change. I stood for a moment watching them until I saw a party of horsemen approaching and recognised Cade himself at their head. I acknowledged his wave and he hailed me.

'Doctor Somers, good morning. Come with me through the City. I have in mind to free men from Newgate who've been imprisoned for spurious reasons. It's an act of charity you should approve – prisoners incarcerated at the whim of brutal overlords.'

I was embarrassed to be singled out for Cade's attention. 'Excuse me. I'm on foot.'

He flicked his fingers summoning an attendant and ordered him to lend me his horse. 'You can examine the wretched captives on their release. That's a proper function for a physician. I shall be moving on from Newgate to dine with Sir Philip Malpas in St. Mary Pattens. Am I not honoured? A City Alderman, King Henry's friend, invites me to dine in his home!'

I mounted and joined the parade, accepting the role thrust upon me and grateful for the purse of coins Cade gave to buy medicine for the sick. Nevertheless I felt self-conscious as we made our way through gawping crowds. The onlookers were not antagonistic but neither did they show the enthusiasm that had greeted Mortimer the previous day. They were wary and I shared that wariness.

I was glad to leave Cade's entourage and sent a boy to fetch Master Webber, my apothecary friend who lived nearby, so I could minister to the poor fellows set free from captivity and offer them salves and potions. Some had been shut away for several years and were weak from hunger, scabby with diseased flesh or wandering in their wits. I did not concern myself with the reasons for their imprisonment, their alleged crimes or imputed guilt, and I was relieved to be filling my proper role. Master Webber worked tirelessly by my side and, when we had finished, he insisted that I return to his house for food. It was well into the afternoon before I made my way back across the City.

I had not walked far when I realised the mood on the streets had changed since the morning – changed profoundly and in an intimidating manner. Householders were battening their doors and fastening their shutters while groups of Cade's protesters taunted them and flaunted their weapons. Citizens still out of doors scurried along the centre of the roadway, eyes fixed ahead, splashing through puddles of foul water which they would have avoided in less stressful times. Among the restless insurgents I sensed growing frustration and was not surprised when stone-throwing broke out in one of the side-streets. Whether because I was recognised as an acquaintance of Cade's, respected as a physician or the beneficiary of sheer good luck, I was not molested but I felt afraid, for myself and for my friends in the City. I wondered if some particular event had sparked a deterioration in trust between ordinary Londoners and these unreliable guests they had invited into their midst.

I buffeted a passage along Cheapside, overrun with Cade's followers, and reached Cornhill where I caught sight of scoundrels struggling with armfuls of napery, feather bedding and tapestries, causing my stomach to churn. What I feared had begun. Envy, greed, insubordination and raw hatred were proving victorious, although as yet there was no serious violence against the owners of the pillaged property. I tried to hurry past but a familiar face beamed at me over a roll of woollen cloth topped by a silver platter and I came to a halt.

'Master Toft?'

The carter from Maidstone gripped his booty more tightly. 'Mortimer invited us into the mansion, after he dined there. Told us to sack the place. Good pickings, there are.'

'Sir Philip Malpas's house? Where Mortimer had been entertained?'

'Yes, that's right. It seems he discovered the Alderman had a pile of jewels belonging to the Duke of York. Malpas said they were the pledge for a loan but Mortimer was furious – he admires the Duke. So he took the jewels and invited us in to help ourselves. We shoved Malpas and his family into the cellar while we had the run of the house.'

I appreciated the significance of Mortimer's anger on behalf of Richard of York. 'Is Mortimer still there?'

'Don't think so. I heard he went to the Tower, to demand that Lord Saye and Sele be handed over. We already caught his lordship's sodding son-in-law, William Crowmer, Sheriff of Kent, no less. Mortimer's got him in chains, going to put him on trial.' John Toft shifted the weight of his bundle from one arm to the other.

'Best get on your way,' I said. 'It's useful to know what happened.' It was not the moment to tell him I had found Piers Ford.

I stared after Master Toft as he staggered along the road, then I lifted the skirt of my gown and hurried as fast as my halting gait allowed towards the Tower.

*****

I edged through the host of rebels gathered outside London's ancient fortress and tried to establish what was happening there. I was told Mortimer's representatives were still inside the Tower, negotiating with the Governor, but he himself had gone straight on to the Aldgate, dragging his prisoner, William Crowmer, with him. My informant supposed Mortimer intended to meet up with the Essex men camped at Mile End.

Other bystanders were keen to embellish this account.

'They ain't got many guns at the Tower. They'll only fire if we attack.'

'One of the sentries told us they're under orders not to sally forth.'

'Governor don't trust his own guards. We know some of them support us.'

I thought about Rendell at his post somewhere within the walls of the bastion and suspected he might have divided loyalties, even though the Governor was his paymaster.

'Reckon we could get them gates open if we charged. There's that many of us.'

'That's what they'll be telling the Governor. Mortimer wants Lord Saye and Sele. If the bugger's handed over, we won't attack – that's the bargain. There's two Archbishops cowering in the Tower along with his lordship so the Governor's got to weigh up his choices.'

There was movement at the back of the crowd and shouting broke out around us as a path was cleared for a band of horsemen advancing towards the Tower. Mortimer and his immediate followers were returning from the Aldgate, unencumbered, it seemed, by prisoners in their train. I ducked down, hoping Cade would not see me, and evaded notice, pleased that once again there was no sign of Gilbert Iffley but too pre-occupied to question whether his absence was carefully contrived.

One of Cade's entourage stopped to greet a man to whom I had been speaking, and he gave a roar of laughter when he was asked where William Crowmer had been confined.

'Got a vacancy for a bloody Sheriff of Kent, we have now, mate. Put him on trial out at Mile End, we did. Then we cut off his head in a field outside the Aldgate. His father-in-law'll be next.'

'Have the Essex men entered the City?' I asked, worrying on Piers Ford's account.

'Couldn't tell you. They were dithering. Mortimer wanted Crowmer executed in front of them to beef up their spirit. Bit lily-livered, they are, if you ask me.'

Or paying attention to those who advocated peaceful methods, I speculated silently.

The horseman moved on and very soon cheering broke out far in front of us, outside the gates of the Tower: cheering that quickly merged with jeering. The explanation flowed through the throng, accompanied by hoots of delight, bawdy commentary and rancorous mockery. Lord Saye and Sele had been released into Mortimer's custody, to be taken to the Guildhall for trial. Within moments, and as one, the surging onlookers turned on their heels and followed their leader, along with his mounted escort and chained captive, while excitement and disorder spread with uncontrollable speed.

Some yards away from where I was pushed forward, two young lads fell and were trampled before I could struggle to their side. I forced a path but had great difficulty in making space to treat my patients until the uncle of one of them used fisticuffs to divert the stream of frenzied rebels from causing more damage. Both boys were badly bruised and one had fractured a rib but they were fortunate not to have been killed by the reckless swarm of humanity. I applied balsam from a pot I had carried with me from Newgate, used belts as temporary strapping and handed the lads into the charge of their relatives, with instructions for the care of their injuries. By then the concourse had emptied and I had no stomach to re-join the vengeful pack and view another unlawful but inevitable execution.

I turned into the nearby lane and within minutes was back in Grizel Chope's kitchen where domestic life was blessedly undisturbed. Thomas was not at home but a quartet of infants squealed with mirth as the older ones clambered over me.

Grizel hid her anxiety well but her pallor grew as I described the events of the day and her husband did not return. She sent one of the apprentices to look for him at the meeting-hall of the carpenters' guild but the youth returned without finding him, much alarmed by aggressive rioting in the streets. The candles had already been lit when at last Thomas arrived, unwilling to converse until he had re-checked the bars on windows and doors and he ordered that buckets of water be brought from the yard in case of fire-raising. No male adult in the house would sleep that night, he declared.

At last Thomas sat down with me in the upper room overlooking the roadway and told me what he had witnessed. He had been leaving the Guildhall when Mortimer's multitudes appeared and he sheltered with other tradesmen in All Hallows Church where reports were brought to them of activity outside. He knew little of how the trial progressed in the Guildhall, except that Lord Saye and Sele had been charged with many crimes including the murder three years previously of the Duke of Gloucester – an allegation I knew to be untrue. Thomas could hear the hubbub of the crowd increasing, as time went on and its patience worn thin, until a terrified priest rushed into the church with news that the Guildhall had been stormed by the mob and the trial disrupted. At this point my friend had scrambled with others to peer through a window and he saw the abject defendant hauled from the building by his rag-tag accusers, humiliated and beaten.

Thomas brushed the back of his hand across his mouth. 'They lugged him to the Standard on Cheapside,' he said, 'and struck off his head without ceremony. He died unshriven with all his sins, whatever they were, upon him.'

I crossed myself. 'God grant him mercy. Cade didn't try to stop this execution?'

'Don't think he could have if he'd wanted to. He showed clemency to some other poor fool who'd tried to resist the rebels – a man of small account whose pretty wife came to plead with this jumped-up Mortimer. Then he just went back to Southwark for the night.'

'Have his men gone too?'

'Some. Not all. They'll cause havoc in the City under cover of darkness. They've been howling the names of other men they'd like to put on trial – friends of the King, like Bishop Waynflete of Winchester. He's fled to sanctuary at the Priory of Holywell outside the walls: sensible fellow.'

I was glad to hear the Bishop was safe for, although he was not popular, he had been supportive to me when I encountered him three years earlier. Thomas cleared his throat and continued his account.

'Even while I was scampering home, when the hordes were dispersing, I saw some vile things, shopkeepers struck down and their goods raided, flaming torches flung onto roofs.' He broke off and gave a sob. 'There were too many of them. There was nothing I could do. I was thumped and forced back into a doorway while they went past, armed ruffians with a girl, a maid servant. They pulled her into an alley. I heard her screams.' He put his face in his hands.

'Don't blame yourself, Thomas. No single man can withstand the flood of evil loosed on the City today. Our task is to defend your family.'

He nodded and rallied himself. 'There's something you should know, Harry. When I was at the Guildhall, before Mortimer's men came there, the Aldermen had been discussing what to do if things turned violent. Contingencies, they called it. They were still hoping everything could be handled peacefully, but in case it couldn't they were making plans.'

He paused. 'Very sensible,' I said, puzzled by his tone.

'They've drawn up a list of the ringleaders: in case they decide to have them arrested.'

He paused and I held my breath, knowing what he was going to say.

'Your name's on the list, Harry.'

Chapter 8

The following day was Sunday and Cade made it known he would hear Mass in Southwark, portraying himself as a devout Christian who would countenance no violence during a holy day. His piety may have been genuine or he may have hoped that the excesses of the previous twenty-four hours would have terrorised the City fathers into rallying behind the rebels. Either way, he miscalculated, underestimating the fury of those prominent citizens who had been robbed – and their deviousness, holy day or not. Thomas soon learned that the Lord Mayor, Aldermen and Councillors were conferring with the Governor of the Tower and no one suggested they were discussing terms for surrender.

Thomas reported this to me after his neighbour had called to pass on the information. He was bleary-eyed, as I was, after our wakeful night and he brushed aside my insistence that I must leave his house at once in order to safeguard his family.

'You may be wise to make yourself scarce for a while but take some rest first. The City guard won't be looking to round up those on the Guildhall's list at this stage. They'll want to see Cade's bastards beaten back first. Meanwhile I'll do what I can to persuade the Mayoral officials that you're simply a blameless physician who tends all who need medical help. God knows though, Harry, your past record doesn't suggest innocent dedication to your profession to the exclusion of all shady dealings. You have a knack for being in the wrong place.'

'Gross calumny! But I accept perceptions are not always positive. I'd welcome a little sleep; then I'll leave.'

'Best wait until evening. Get a boat across Deptford then hire a horse. You'll go to Danson?'

'I had hoped to bring Kate to a new home in the City but that will have to wait. I'll see how she is before I decide what to do.'

I slept soundly on an apprentice's pallet at the back of the workshop, while the Chope family attended Mass, and I concluded that Thomas's robust physique fitted him to withstand the loss of sleep better than I could. I was woken in the early afternoon because Rendell had been granted permission for a brief visit to his sister's family, after escorting the Lord Mayor's party back to the Guildhall. He drew Thomas into the workshop to rouse me, shutting the door on Grizel and the children. With his habitual skill he had succeeded in gleaning a good deal about the discussions in the Tower that morning and he tapped his nose to indicate the importance of what he had to say.

'Lord Scales agreed to send some of his men from the Tower under Matthew Gough to defend the City. Hope I'll be one of them – I could do with a bit of action. Gough's a tough bird, just come home from years under arms in Normandy. There's a company of royal archers quartered in Fleet Street and they'll slip along to meet us, together with all the able-bodied citizens we can muster. Them rebels ain't getting over the bridge again, I can tell you.'

'You mean it'll be blockaded in the morning?'

Rendell tapped his nose again, this time to denote the naïveté of my assumption. He put his finger to his lips. 'Tonight. They'll gather at the bridge at dusk and attack the sentries Cade's posted there. Reckon we'll take them by surprise. Got to go now, ready to volunteer with Gough. Wish me luck.'

Thomas whistled as his brother-in-law made for the door. 'God help us all. Could be a bloodbath. It'll provide cover for your escape anyway, Harry. Find a ferryman near the Tower and head downstream before the fighting starts. That'll keep you out of harm's way. I'll walk down to the wharf with you before going to the bridge. I'll send the apprentices ahead of me.'

'You don't intend to keep out of harm's way?'

'I'm a householder and Guildsman. Grizel will understand I must do my duty.'

The eldest Chope boy put his head round the door and we fell silent. 'Pa, there's a funny man outside, keeps on looking at the house and walking up and down, nearly falling over his feet.'

The description did not sound like an officer sent to arrest me but I could think of one man it would fit, so we sidled to the shuttered window to peep through a crack. Thomas had no problem recognising the man he had met at Mile End.

'It's that wheelwright, Ford, isn't it? Bring him into the house quickly.'

I hurried to fetch him but Piers protested that it would put my friends in danger if he entered their premises. 'I saw a soldier coming out of the door. Was he looking for me here?'

'Not at all. He's an old colleague, Thomas's brother-in-law. You're in more danger out in the road if you're worried someone's searching for you.'

I had never seen Piers so fidgety and he could hardly contain what he wanted to say, so at last, after gazing apprehensively to right and left, he agreed to go into the carpenter's workshop to speak privately to me, away from the Chope family. While Thomas tactfully withdrew Piers clutched me in a bony embrace.

'The Saints be praised, I've found you, Doctor Somers. It's crucial you mustn't do any more on my behalf. I'm a lost man. An old mate ran into me up by the Tower and told me I must get out of the City. Mortimer's ordered my execution as soon as I'm caught.'

I must have looked aghast. 'But there's no evidence. I gave him my sworn statement.'

'Mortimer's wielding the sword of justice against all evil-doers – his words. He beheaded a thief this morning. He finds the role of avenger gratifying.'

'Does he know you're in the City?'

102

Piers shook his head. 'I'm not sure but I may have been seen at Mile End with the Essex men. The important thing is that you keep out of it or it might rebound on you.'

'That's sheer nonsense, Piers. Cade must be brought to accept the truth.' In my indignation the words tumbled out of me without reflection. 'The best way would be to find the fellow who really did for the carter, even if inadvertently.'

'How on earth could we do that?'

'George Antey must have had an enemy. Someone will know. How long could that sawn peg have held? We were concentrating on the idea that the wheel was damaged on Blackheath. Could it have been tampered with earlier?'

Piers ran his finger over his thumb as if testing the faulty peg. 'It probably could. I didn't look closely enough to judge if the pin weakened gradually before snapping.'

'We need to start with a visit to Maidstone. The chances are we can find out something from his family or neighbours. I'm leaving the City tonight – I've made myself unpopular with the authorities here so it's prudent to disappear for a bit. Come with me across the river and we'll find George's village and ask a few questions.'

The wheelwright pressed a knuckle to his bottom lip. 'I've always wanted to go to Maidstone,' he said softly, as if talking to himself. Then he shrugged. 'No one's going to confess to murder when there's no evidence against him, just guesswork.'

'We can accept it wasn't meant to lead to murder, just cause an accident, to act as a warning. We'll have to hope whoever was responsible wouldn't want to see you executed for what you didn't do. The common man is by nature honourable, isn't he?'

Piers grimaced at my inept humour but he nodded.

*****

Thomas came with us to the quayside and wished us God-speed before joining the flow of armed citizens making their way to St. Magnus Church where they were to congregate. Piers and I found a boatman easily enough, content to row across the river and deposit us well away from the southern approach roads to the bridge, but he was unwilling to travel further downstream. It was good enough. As dusk was falling, we began to trudge through the marshy ground bordering the Thames on the Southwark side, intent on skirting the common land where Cade's followers were encamped and the stews where many were disporting themselves. Once on the open road we would find an inn where we could hire horses and speed our way into Kent. Whether we would call at Danson on our way to Maidstone, I had not decided.

We had only gone a few paces when we heard distant shouting and, although we knew perfectly well what it portended, we paused to look round towards the far side of the bridge. The City's attack had succeeded in surprising Cade's sentries. In the fading rays of the sun, heightened by the gleam of torches, we could distinguish the surge of citizens towards the drawbridge until, on the main part of the bridge, they were obscured by the buildings each side of the road. On the south side where the bridge debouched onto the main road through Southwark, running figures were silhouetted as they fled for safety from the aggressors.

'If Cade's men all take to their heels, we're at risk of getting caught up in the stampede. We'd better strike off to the east.'

Piers' suggestion was sensible but it meant plodding for longer in deep mud which I did not relish. My awkward bundle of clothes and instruments, slung on one shoulder, unbalanced me and, with my weak ankle, I risked stumbling into the morass. I hesitated, staring towards the swirl of figures at each end of the bridge where they became hazy in the encroaching darkness.

'The City men seem to have come to a halt. They've crossed the bridge, maybe as far as the bulwark on the Southwark side. There's a flash of armour now and then. But they don't appear to be advancing beyond the piling. They've won control of the bridge. Perhaps they'll wait until daybreak to drive onward. Matthew Gough, the man in charge of the Londoners, is said to be experienced.'

'But he doesn't know Cade.' The wheelwright's voice sounded bleak in the gloom. 'Jack will be furious they've been attacked on a holy day. He'll see it as a perfidious trick. It'll release him from any intention of acting honourably. He won't lie quiet waiting for the dawn. Dear God, I should be at his side, to urge moderation, to caution against uncontrolled violence.'

'It's not your fault you're not there.'

'But I can't just stand by and let slaughter take place.'

'There's nothing you can do.' The words echoed in my mind as I spoke.

A shrill cry rang out, soaring above the muted din a few hundred yards away, and I sensed Piers' shudder. 'There's one skewered or clubbed,' he said. 'There'll be hundreds more soon.'

I took my friend's wrist. 'You must go on, Piers. Cade has rebuffed you and you must save yourself. But I'm a physician. I have a duty. I'll see what I can do to help the wounded. I'm going to the bridge.'

Long sinewy arms encircled me. 'I'm loath to fight and injure my fellow men and what use would I be, among so many? But I could act as a physician's dogsbody, if you'll have me?'

I did not try to argue with him so we lurched forward, side by side, while the clamour ahead of us intensified. As we neared the roadway, a troop of mounted men with Cade at their head thundered past towards the bridge, helmets on their heads, drawn weapons in their fists and massacre in their hearts. We followed in their wake and took up position under the lean-to, in front of a

105

house at the Southwark end of the river-crossing. Almost at once there was work for me.

I had never served as physician on a battlefield, as young Leone, my former assistant, had chosen to do during the fighting in Normandy. Of course I had treated wounds, staunching blood, applying tourniquets, and, in the absence of a surgeon, stitching ripped flesh, but these had been individual cases. Now I was confronted with injured men in their dozens: some were content to fight on despite serious contusions and slashed faces, but others could scarcely drag themselves to my inadequate field-post. Piers performed heroic deeds, swooping into the mêlée to scoop up victims felled by swords and pitchforks alike, but many were outside my power to assist. In the absence of a priest, I muttered prayers over spilling entrails and sliced craniums while concentrating my efforts on those who, with help, might survive. In my bundle I had a small amount of elm bark which made good dressing but I had no honey or red wine to hasten healing. Above all, with no access to flame or scalding metal I could do nothing to sear gaping lacerations. At one point, Piers tried to seize a flaming torch from a rider, for me to use, but he was pushed back against the wall and a whip lashed his shoulder.

Cade's counter-attack gained ground and the core of the battle swept forward past us but then came a new onslaught from the City and the rebels were forced back. Several times this pattern was repeated and I found myself treating mercers and goldsmiths in addition to herdsmen and hawkers. The noise was indescribable: the hooves of rearing, whinnying horses suddenly required to change direction in the cramped roadway, bludgeoned men tussling on foot, often kicking comrades rather than foes but their screams were impossible to distinguish. Some of the more lavishly equipped warriors, in heavy armour, suffered for their preparedness and ostentation when they were flung into the river, weighed down by their defensive carapaces – and left to drown. In the churn of activity we had no opportunity to take thought for ourselves and we were lucky to receive no more than glancing blows to backs and arms but I soon exhausted my meagre supplies which could offer some relief from pain.

I was aware that Cade's men were gaining ground when Piers struggled to my side carrying a fellow whose foot was cruelly mangled, in all probability by an axe or mace. I had already shredded the clean shirt in my bundle of clothes and I tightened a strip above the man's ankle in an attempt to check the flow of blood. I glanced at my friend's face, smudged with dirt and etched with worry.

'I can't save the foot. It'll putrefy and kill him if it's left. This isn't a physician's role but there's no surgeon here. He might have a chance if I strike off the foot right away. He's a sturdy lad. He might survive.'

'Can you do it?'

'With God's help, I'll try but the ordeal may prove fatal. Hold him down as firmly as you can.'

I extracted a small saw from my bag of instruments to perform an operation I had never attempted before but had heard described when I was studying in Padua. I thanked heaven for Piers' strong arms, keeping the man's leg rigid, but the victim's scream as I set about my task was gruesome and it was a mercy for us all that he quickly lost consciousness. I rejoiced that my serrated blade was sharp and it severed the shattered foot more easily than I dared hope. I could see that my patient was still breathing but I feared for him, when I had no means to cauterise the jagged ends of the cleavage, and I knew the lethal effects of shock might come later. We laid him against the wall, wrapped in Piers' cape, while I turned my attention to other unpleasant but less critical injuries.

I observed the first lightening of the sky in the east and thought how tired all these men must be who had striven throughout the night to secure advantage. I wondered fleetingly how Thomas and Rendell were faring but had no time to dwell on the fortunes of my friends when I needed to extract an arrow from an upper arm

107

without causing additional harm. Suddenly, just ahead of us on the bridge, a shout rang out in a voice and tone I recognised and feared. I glanced up to see Jack Cade, his filthy face streaming sweat below his raised visor, his eyes screwed into fiendish slits, brandishing his sword and yelling outlandish instructions to his followers.

'Light bundles of straw. Fire the houses!'

'Oh God, no,' I murmured, understanding exactly what he had in mind, but my prayer was in vain. All night long, residents of the houses on the bridge had cowered in their homes, terrified by the carnage taking place outside their closed shutters. Now their own innocent lives were put at hazard, probably seen by Cade as a means to impel his enemies to yield. Within moments, panic-stricken women and children rushed into the fray, some with hair or clothes alight, fleeing the growing inferno in the buildings each side of the road. Whether Cade hoped to use them as hostages to secure the City's surrender, I could not tell, but the chaotic situation on the bridge meant he had no control over their fate. I saw two women speared by weapons wielded by their own countrymen, while others flung themselves into the Thames, among burning brands which singed them until the sizzling waters gave release from all suffering.

Although my hands were busy binding a wound, I was sobbing at the sight of such maddened inhumanity, conscious how little we could do to moderate its effects. Piers had dashed forward using his jerkin to beat back flames and haul one or two victims to safety. He reached my side supporting an old man who reeled away from us, speechless and blank-eyed with horror, while the wheelwright thrust a spluttering batten into my hand.

'Can you use it to sear the lad's leg?'

'It's better than nothing when we've got no metal.'

I applied the charred end of the slat to the suppurating edges of my amputation and my insensible patient groaned, which I took to be an encouraging sign. I moistened his brow and tucked the cape more tightly round him. Then I turned to Piers and grasped his bony arm.

'Your hand, it's scorched.'

'It's nothing,' he said putting his other hand over the scalded skin.

'Here, I've a little oil left. It may assist healing.'

I tipped the remains of a small flask onto his wrist and worked the fluid gently over the burn. Although not yet full daylight it was now possible to see along the bridge, so we crouched together, looking at where the fiercest fighting had moved towards, and perhaps through, the City gate. The Londoners had been driven back further than before and, remarkably, Cade had reinforcements to call on, who were pounding past us to strengthen the rebels' offensive. It seemed probable that the City fathers might be compelled to sue for a truce.

A booming sound and a huge splash downstream alerted us to the guns of the Tower, as they began to bombard the enemy, now it was light enough to direct their fire at the heart of the battle. Their effectiveness was limited against close-hand fighting. Both sides were equally exposed and many cannon-balls fell short into the river, causing tidal waves to engulf low-lying boats moored nearby but failing to inflict worse damage. Despite their limitations, the guns seemed to hearten the Londoners who were facing defeat and the fighting surged back towards Southwark once again. Much later we learned that Matthew Gough, the veteran from Normandy, had urged his weary civilian army to make a final onslaught against the insurgents, leading them in a desperate sortie and, although the doughty old warrior was killed in the attempt, his tactic succeeded.

What we witnessed was this renewed swell of movement with Cade's men retreating towards us until, in the centre of the bridge, they re-formed under orders from their commander and took decisive action. A fresh burst of flame shot into the air.

'They've fired the drawbridge,' Piers said in awe. 'The two sides will be separated.'

'Not quite. Not at once.'

I could make out small groups of Londoners to the south of the conflagration and there were no doubt rebels cut off from their comrades on the other side of the flames. Cade's men gave no quarter but fell on the outnumbered foes trapped in their midst, hurling their carcases into the abyss previously straddled by the drawbridge. Blazing planks hissed as they fell into the water and the struts which had held the structure in place for so long rasped and sagged before they too descended into the steaming Thames. A few arrows were loosed from either side but, for the most part, across the horrifying chasm, exhausted, battered men stared at each other, impotent to carry on the fight.

'Stalemate,' Piers said.

Men limped towards us from the centre of the bridge, nursing wounds they had managed to ignore while under arms but now needing my help, so I was soon busily employed once more, doing what little I could with scanty resources. Others had been more fortunate in avoiding injury and I was grateful when two able-bodied fellows carried off the patient on whom I had operated. I gave them what advice I could to improve his chances of survival and urged them to find a surgeon to inspect and perhaps improve my handiwork, but I never knew the outcome of my efforts.

Meanwhile white flags were waved on each side of the divide and it was agreed in shouted negotiations that a truce would be observed, on condition that neither force attempted to cross the gap or launched an attack by boat. The awful spectacle of Englishmen viciously destroying each other had achieved nothing, but to bring misery to families bereaved and men left maimed and disfigured. For myself, I had been bloodied in a physician's role during warfare and the appalling things I had seen would remain with me to haunt my mind sleeping and waking. I

110

could tell Piers was similarly overcome and we hugged each other as we turned from the devastated bridge.

'With the bridge broken, you're safe from the City authorities at any rate,' he said. 'What will you do?'

I gave a rueful smile. I could not contemplate burdening Kate with my presence while my own mental pain was so raw. 'I thought we'd decided that before we were interrupted, Piers. We have unfinished business. We're going to Maidstone.'

If I was exhausted and distracted by the grim events we had witnessed that night on London Bridge, Piers was even more anguished. Not only had he viewed the same savagery, which was heart-wrenching enough for any onlooker to recall, but he had seen principles he held dear trampled in the gore and guts of battle between fellow countrymen. We set out on foot afresh, too overwhelmed to speak, and we did not converse until we had hired horses and were riding towards the line of hills in the north of Kent. By then we had outpaced the straggle of Mortimer's men who had deserted the battle but occasional horses passed us at speed: messengers who would carry news of the encounter on the bridge far and wide. It would be known in Maidstone well before we arrived there.

'It shouldn't have been like this. I thought we'd make our grievances known peaceably.' Piers sighed. 'The City street vendors and meat porters are our brothers but they fought against us. They thought we were a threat. We hadn't explained our case properly. They didn't realise our struggle was for them. Our interests are theirs.'

'They didn't see it in those terms. When Cade allowed the City to be plundered, he squandered the goodwill he might have won. Street vendors and meat porters earn their living in the City and they depend on the prosperity of its citizens.'

'But good rule – law and order – would benefit everyone and we were all created alike...' His voice tailed away. 'Is it all a fantasy?'

I drew on the reins to slow our speed. 'We need your dreams to inspire us but not everyone has your perception. The trouble is, ideals get distorted by scoundrels with their own objectives to pursue.'

'Like Baron Glasbury?'

'Exactly. We must concentrate on thwarting his plans – at least as far as they are aimed at silencing you.'

I grinned and tried to divert Piers from mournful subjects by asking him whether he had family other than his married sister at Hornchurch. This proved to be a mistake.

He grunted and swallowed before answering. 'A year past I buried my wife and two young children, a boy and a girl. The pox came to our village. Yet some it didn't touch. I'd have willingly gone in their place. I was about to set up as master wheelwright on my own account but there's no sense in that now. I've stayed a journeyman. There's little purpose in my life.'

'But you still stand up for what you believe is right? That encourages others.'

'It's the only thing I can do.'

I did not press him further and we urged our horses into a gallop along the highway but we could not keep up the pace and it was clear we must rest overnight before completing our journey.

We found lodgings in the guesthouse of a priory, grateful to wash miscellaneous filth from our faces and arms before throwing ourselves on pallets to sleep soundly until dawn. Despite our ablutions, in the early sunlight we saw how unkempt we looked and tidied our dress as best we could. I dabbed at stains on my linen shirt and brushed dried blood from my gown but it would be obvious to all that we had been involved in the fighting. We could only hope this would recommend us to the people we needed to meet.

Piers sank down on his haunches, watching me. 'Maybe there's no reason to go on to Maidstone now. If Cade can't impose his judgement against me, Baron Glasbury's accusation may be worthless.'

'Cade wasn't defeated. He fired the drawbridge to bring the battle to a close but neither side had the victory. If peace is agreed the terms will reflect that deadlock. In any case I wouldn't put it past Glasbury to have denounced you to the authorities in Kent and the City, not just to so-called Mortimer. We'd be unwise to leave Iffley with any missiles to loose against you whenever he thinks fit.' I paused and looked Piers straight in the eye. 'Especially if it's all a ruse to trap me as well as you.'

*****

It had been lax of me not to obtain more precise directions to where the dead carter, and indeed John Toft, lived. 'The Maidstone area' was a loose description and the two men might well have come from different, although neighbouring, villages, so it seemed best to start our enquiries in the town itself. We rode down the hill to cross the bridge towards the main cluster of buildings dominated by a fine palace used by the Archbishops of Canterbury as a resting place when travelling to London. We passed the complex and began to look round for a carter's yard where the tradesmen would know their competitors in the locality. We did not find one until we had followed the River Len from where it joined the larger Medway to just beyond a mill, but the workman we spoke to, loading a large wagon there, justified my hunch that this was where to ask about George Antey and John Toft.

'Wouldn't say they were mates,' he said, resting his elbow on the wagon. 'George Antey was a tricky character, God rest him: short tempered and could be underhand. His son's easier to deal with. You'll find him on the Aylesford road, mile or two on from town. Johnny Toft runs this yard but his main place is further out from here, village of Leeds, near the castle. I was apprenticed to him as a boy and I've served him ever since – he's as canny as they come. Not sure if he's back there yet.'

I thanked our informant but when we had turned the corner I winked at Piers. 'As neat a summary of neighbourly esteem as you'd get anywhere. Not necessarily helpful though: if Master Antey was generally unpopular.'

'There could be several contestants for teaching him a lesson?'

'Let's hope there's something more specific to explain why someone risked such a dangerous lesson. The son may be able to suggest a name. But as we're on the road to the south, let's call at John Toft's headquarters first. Mind you, we don't know what's happened to him. He could have been killed or injured in the City. We'll play the innocents.'

We found the village of Leeds huddled beside a lake in the middle of which stood an impressive castle. John Toft's premises were situated near the bridge to the fortress and they looked unexpectedly prosperous. Nearly a dozen wagons of varying sizes were lined up under a lean-to roof and grooms were attending to as many horses in the stable block. Other stalls were empty but supplied with hay and I imagined the occupants were expected to return shortly. It was necessary for me to reappraise my view of Johnny Toft as a humble carter of modest means.

I hailed the man wearing a leather apron who appeared to be in charge, and asked for news of his master.

'Have you heard anything? I last saw him in the City and don't know how he fared in the fighting. I had to leave to travel into Kent,' I said by way of explanation.

'He's thriving, seemingly. He sent word by a messenger who came yesterday. He's on his way back from London with the wagons, hopes to arrive tomorrow, and he's carrying a deal of stuff, he says, which'll bring us wealth.'

I remembered Toft's part in the sacking of Sir Philip Malpas's mansion and wondered how much more booty he had acquired. 'That's good news. I may meet him on the road in the morning. He's got a flourishing business here, quite grand.'

The man smirked. 'Principal carter over a wide area, John Toft is. He has the trade from the castle and most of the craftsmen in the district use his wagons. Other yards round here do work for us when we're busy.'

'Ah, yes. When I first met him on Blackheath, he had a fellow carter called George Antey with him. I heard the poor fellow had an accident.'

Toft's assistant spat. 'Nasty bit of goods he was. We used him sometimes but he ran a pathetic yard.'

'Not a rival then?'

He gave a guffaw. 'Beneath contempt. His son may make a better go of it but Johnny Toft will buy him out if it's worth his while.'

This was interesting but I must not appear too curious. 'Did the messenger bring you other news?'

'Yes. Three churchmen were to wait on Edmund Mortimer this morning to negotiate peace: a Cardinal, an Archbishop and a Bishop. What do you think of that? That's giving the man his due.'

I was easily able to add names to Cardinal Kemp and Archbishop Stafford. Could the Bishop be William Waynflete of Winchester? I was still grateful for his help in the past but he was deeply unpopular. If Jack Cade had accepted Waynflete as one of the negotiators, it showed how desperate the rebels must be to end their uprising. The carter was thinking along divergent lines.

'Reckon the City folk are frantic for peace. The messenger said they know now there's no royal army coming to relieve them. Left to their fate, they are. Cade's men could retake London with a flick of his wrist.'

I doubted this but did not say so.

We set off once more, retracing our route into the town, with a visit to make along the Aylesford road. Our mission had serious implications for Piers – and perhaps for me – but, compared with the torment of mind we endured on London Bridge, we threw ourselves into the quest with an almost merry air. We had agreed the account we would give to explain our presence and it did not take long to find the Antey yard, a pokey place compared with John Toft's premises but the ground was swept and tidy.

A well-built young fellow of no more than eighteen years was supervising an older man whose cart was ready

116

to set out on a delivery. We waited until the man had gone and then hailed his superior. 'Master Antey, is it? Could we have a word?'

He stared at us, evaluating whether we were reputable and likely to be bringing him business. 'You have the advantage of me. Can I help you?'

I moved forward. 'I'm a physician who was in attendance on Blackheath and had the sad duty of closing your father's eyes after his accident. My affairs take me south through Kent so I thought to call, to give my sympathy and ask how the lad is, your young brother I believe, who had the misfortune to witness the event.'

Master Antey looked commendably cautious while observing the proprieties. 'That's a kind thought, sir. Georgie has borne up well, as have we all. He's off on an errand. Can I offer you refreshment? A sup of ale?'

I accepted and he led us to a cottage across the yard where we were greeted by his widowed mother, a tired-looking woman but resilient and not incapacitated by grief. They were, I reflected, hard-working people who needed to sustain their livelihood, whatever adversity was thrown at them, but I noticed how Mistress Antey trembled when I was introduced. She busied herself fetching ale before she withdrew into an inner room. While she was present her son's conversation was stilted.

'My mother is upset,' he said after she left us. 'We'd not expected others from Blackheath to call. After the men came to tell us there could have been foul play.'

I needed to think quickly. 'Foul play? Who told you that? Several bystanders witnessed the accident. When I attended your father he was dying and all I saw of his injuries was consistent with what they described.'

'The men who came a week ago suggested the cart had been damaged intentionally. Some Baron sent them to tell us we would have a case to bring against a wheelwright, name of Ford.'

Piers had kept in the background in the guise of my well-mannered serving man and I did not look at him. 'Dear me, how unexpected. What will you do?'

Master Antey took a draught of ale. 'Nothing. I've never heard of this wheelwright but father did pick quarrels sometimes. We've no means to go to law and I don't have faith a charge would be upheld. I wasn't there and I don't want Georgie dragged before the justices to give evidence. Carts overturn and carters risk injury, specially when they're carrying a load of sharpened stakes. We accept God's will.'

'You say your father picked quarrels – could he have had an enemy or rival malicious enough to cause him harm?'

'He may have done – he was a difficult man. But they wouldn't have planned to kill him in such a chancy way. At worst it would have been a trick to put him out of action for a day or two, which went wrong.'

'You didn't go to Blackheath?'

'I went with Father and John Toft a good part of the way but I had a cartload of timber for the great hall at Eltham, so I left them the day before the accident. I made my delivery and returned home directly. Father's cart was trundling along without a problem when I last saw him.'

Throughout our exchange Master Antey had remained unruffled, almost casual, while his analysis fitted exactly with mine. I could not fault his logic so I simply nodded and set down my empty cup, preparing to wish him well and leave the premises, but at that moment the outer door flew open and the boy I recognised ran into the room. He was bursting with excitement.

'I met Nan and she said to say... Why, you're the doctor on Blackheath.'

'Hello, Georgie. I was passing nearby and I came to see how you were.'

'We're ever so well, it's much better since...'

'That's enough, Georgie.' Mistress Antey erupted into the room, white faced. She had clearly been listening to all that was said. She put her arm round her younger son. 'These gentlemen have been kind to call but we must let them go on their way now.'

'What did Nan say?' The young man was twisting his hands in impatience.

Georgie slipped from his mother's embrace and gave his brother an impudent grin. 'She'll be along by the meadow at sundown. Thought you might want to know.'

Master Antey flushed crimson and beamed with delight.

'They're to be hand-fasted,' Georgie said. 'Father wouldn't have it but now...'

His mother hustled him into the other room while I tried not to show any excessive interest as I congratulated the promised bridegroom. He was embarrassed but felt compelled to correct any unfortunate impression Georgie had given. He had become as tense as a drawn bowstring.

'My father was a harsh man, doctor. God forbid I should speak ill of him now he's dead but he didn't favour my courtship. Nan's family are poor. Her father was wounded in the French wars and he earns what he can selling baskets. I'm free to wed her now and mother is content she'll make a good helpmate. I hope you don't think badly of me.'

I assured Master Antey that he had my good wishes and we bade him farewell. Piers and I rode slowly back towards the town and it was several minutes before we were ready to speak about our illuminating visit.

'Not a household in deep mourning,' I said.

'Could the son have sawn through the peg? He's benefitted from his father's death and he was with them the day before the wood snapped.'

'He doesn't strike me as either brutal or calculating. Anyway there can't have been an intention to kill. I could be wrong. He was certainly on edge. That could have been guilt. On the other hand Glasbury's men may have threatened nasty consequences if he didn't comply with

119

their wishes and have you arraigned. Good job he didn't know what Piers Ford looked like.'

'That was a nasty moment when he named me. What about the mother? She wasn't sorrowful to lose her husband either, I'm thinking. Could she have put her son up to it? Or got someone else to weaken the peg?'

'Not impossible and she was shaking when she met us. But the key thing is they don't intend taking action. That might be because more could come out if a Justice looked into the matter, or it might be they're simply glad to leave things as they are and not tempt fate.'

'That's cheering right enough but Glasbury's vindictiveness isn't; and if the Anteys weren't involved, someone else must have been. The son and heir didn't want to name names.'

'I'd guess he didn't want to put blame on someone who in effect did him a favour. I don't know where we'd start in order to make enquiries elsewhere. Let's hope the negotiations in London bring the uprising to an end and Glasbury no longer has anything to gain by trying to discredit you. If that happens he won't be able to use you as a lever to manipulate me.'

Piers laughed. 'Charming! I think you're enjoying this charade, Harry Somers.'

'It's entirely serious but it takes my mind off what we saw on the bridge. I won't forget that barbarism easily.'

I did not add that it also distracted me from the need to consider my own future and how my wife's uncertain condition might constrain the choices open to us. We rode in silence until we regained the centre of the town, making for a hostelry we had noticed earlier, when Piers flung up his arm and gave a cry of pleasure.

'See over there, beyond the palace, that stone building with small windows! That must be the prison my grandfather told me about – where John Ball was imprisoned before the rebels freed him. My grandfather used to tell me the story. He was only a boy at the time but he never forgot what he heard about the priest who fired up his audience with incredible words. He said the dungeon was beside the palace in Maidstone. I never thought I'd see it. It should be a place of pilgrimage.'

I enjoyed seeing Piers show renewed enthusiasm for his cause and began to quote, as I had when we first met: '*When Adam delved...*'

'Not simply the old rhyme, Harry. Think of it. Ball said that from the beginning of time all men by nature were created alike and our bondage and servitude came from the unjust oppression of wicked men. That's an awe-inspiring idea – more than enough to spark rebellion.'

'If I remember aright, Ball paid for it with his life and his hacked-off head was displayed on London Bridge. Don't follow him too closely, Piers.'

'He said we could cast off bondage and recover liberty. Don't you believe that's possible?'

'One day perhaps, Piers, although I'm not sure what it would really mean. But not yet, I fear.'

'He was a prophet. He should be our inspiration.'

We turned into the courtyard of the inn and an ostler ambled across to take our horses. 'We'll drink to John Ball,' I said as we entered the hostelry, 'to mark our visit to such an auspicious town. But he found, as others have, that wicked men exist in every walk of life and undermine the aspirations of the virtuous. He was a prophet who came to grief, remember.'

Piers sighed. 'I'll have that drink. There's much I'd rather forget.'

There was also much I would rather forget, for after that evening's respite I was bound to return to Danson. I had done my duty as a physician, treating the wounded, and I had tried to extricate Piers and myself from Iffley's malignant clutches. Now I could no longer shirk my personal obligations and must abandon indecision, I feared provoking a crisis and dreaded the truths I must confront and the invidious choices I must make. Even so, I had no inkling how testing a time awaited me and where its consequences might lead.

Part 2 Kent, Stamford, East Anglia and London 1450-51

Chapter 10

Piers woke next morning clear-headed and resolved on what he would do. I had suggested that he accompany me to Danson, to shelter there until we were certain the rebellion was over and the allegations against him discarded, but he decided he would go home to Dartford.

'I'll be cautious and speak to friends: check whether there's any sign of Baron Glasbury. If it seems dangerous, I'll come on directly and find you at Sir Hugh de Grey's house. Otherwise, if the master I was working for will take me back, I'll stay in Dartford.'

I wished him well when we parted company, expressing hopes for his safety and regrets that our acquaintance had been short. Privately I thought it might be best that he should not encounter Kate until I was confident she had regained a placid frame of mind – if that could ever be. There were issues I must face alone.

I rode on with dour concentration, keeping a regular pace, until I saw several carts approaching and I pulled over to let them pass me where the highway narrowed between hedgerows. I paid the drivers only slight attention, noticing their top-heavy loads rather than the men holding the reins, but the leading wagoner was more observant.

'Doctor Somers, by Heaven! I rejoice to see you whole. We heard nothing of you and feared you'd perished in the fighting. This is the road to Maidstone. Is that where you've been?'

'Master Toft, of course, I learned yesterday you were returning home. Yes, I went to Maidstone to speak with young Master Antey and I met some of your own carters on the way.'

'Piers Ford isn't with you?'

I felt under no obligation to explain the details of my journey to John Toft and decided to be circumspect. I shook my head. 'Is Glasbury still looking for him, do you think?'

'He may have other concerns. I haven't seen him since we rode into London. Have you heard the news?'

'That there have been negotiations? Has anything been settled?'

John Toft gave a self-satisfied gurgle. 'Oh aye, most accommodating those prelates were. They read through Mortimer's proclamation of complaints and they accepted them in return for him disbanding his followers. There was a bit of argy-bargy, it seems, about how that was to be done and then the clerical gentlemen agreed that charters of pardon will be granted by name to all participants, on condition they lay down their arms. Mortimer's handed over his muster rolls so the pardons can be prepared.'

I had no idea whether my name would feature on that roll but "Piers Ford" certainly should. Strictly speaking, a pardon for rebellion might not cover an alleged crime against a fellow rebel but it might make prosecution less likely. This was helpful.

'You're not required to give up any goods you've gained during the insurgency?' I asked with cheeky insouciance.

John Toft winked. 'Form of recompense for our pains. You should see what Mortimer is sending downstream by river to keep for himself: barge-loads of booty, gold, jewels, leatherwork, silks, you name it. There've been a few arguments over ownership so he's taking no chances and getting it all clear of London. He'll be on the road by now, tracking it to Rochester. He's got a contingent with him, who weren't on the muster roll, prisoners we freed from Newgate and the like. They may not be given named pardons so I suppose they'll be looking to get across the Narrow Sea to live in safety with their newly acquired wealth – and Mortimer with them, I guess.'

'Which road will he be taking? Not this one?'

'No.no: the road following the river from Deptford to Dartford, then on to Rochester. You'll not come across them.'

I thanked him for his news and rode on quickly, intent on sending a messenger to Piers as soon as I reached Danson. I hoped Mortimer's plans were already known in Dartford so my friend could be forewarned but I would take no chances in case Gilbert Iffley was with the troop riding to Rochester. Although there might be no good reason for the Baron to pursue Piers, now the uprising was over, I knew from experience that Iffley was malevolent and if he still had a grudge against the wheelwright, he would look for an opportunity to harm him.

I reflected more generally on the terms agreed between the King's representatives and Mortimer, surprised at the ease with which an accord had been achieved, meeting both sides' objectives. I could only conclude that both Mortimer's exhausted warriors and the terrified citizens of London were desperate to prevent a repetition of the horrific hostilities they had witnessed on the bridge. I regretted that slaughter had been necessary to achieve a reasonable conclusion and marvelled that this conclusion even included acceptance of the rebels' original complaints. At the same time it seemed possible that this outcome was too neat, too perfect, and I wondered how far the good faith of the negotiators might extend.

*****

I entered Sir Hugh's lands by the track which passed the woodman's cottage and, as I drew alongside it, Mistress Ash hurried out and, curtsying, begged me to stop. Her face was lined with worry and for a moment I feared one of her sons had suffered some misadventure.

'Doctor Somers, the blessed saints be praised, it may be you can help me.'

I slipped from my saddle and led her to sit on a fallen tree trunk. 'What is it, Mistress?'

She put her face in her hands before composing herself to answer my question. 'We have to leave the cottage, sir. We've nowhere to go. My Adie is too young to take his father's place as woodman for a year or two and I suppose some other woodman may need to live here but we're forbidden to find shelter anywhere else on the estate.'

'Sir Hugh is making you move out without giving you another cottage?' I could not hide my astonishment and anger.

'No, sir.' She spoke in a whisper. 'Not Sir Hugh. It's Lady Blanche. She insists we're gone from Danson within the week.'

In spite of all that Lady Blanche had tolerated in her husband's behaviour during more than ten years of marriage, she had never seemed vindictive. Unquestionably it would hurt her to see Mistress Ash around the estate with the child she must know to be Sir Hugh's, who so resembled her own murdered son. Yet to make the widow and two children homeless was not an act that sat well with her nature for, although she had shown herself capable of forceful action in the past, she had not acted spitefully.

'Does Sir Hugh know of Lady Blanche's decree?'

Mistress Ash shrank back from me, her eyes lowered. 'It may be he doesn't. My Lady came this morning to give me her orders in person. I haven't seen Sir Hugh. Perhaps he's from home.' She lifted her head and her eyes were full of tears but she spoke with dignity. 'I would never ask him for help, Doctor Somers.'

'I understand, Mistress, but, if necessary, I will. They've suffered terrible grief, as you have, and grief can distort reason. I'll speak to them both. Lady Blanche is not cruel and Sir Hugh has obligations. We'll find a solution.'

Through falling tears, she thanked me and I remounted, saddened by this needless episode.

I rode on towards the manor-house and recognised the three little de Grey girls with their nursemaid on the edge of the wood. I assumed they did not notice me as they scampered under the cover of the trees but by then I was aware of something more disturbing. A figure in unaccustomed disarray dashed from the front door and ran, stumbling, across the rough ground between bends in the track, to catch me before I reached the entrance. The sight of Judith in such disorder froze my blood and I reined my horse to a standstill, awaiting the dire news she must be bringing, preparing myself for tragedy.

'My wife is...?' I stammered, unable to voice the fatal thought.

'Mistress Somers is in bodily health but...'

It was Judith's turn to choke on her words and I dismounted while she regained her self-possession. It was evidently not the news for which I had instantly steadied myself and I felt shame for the momentary, instinctive regret that I felt. 'What has happened?'

Judith blew her nose on a kerchief and dabbed below her eyes. 'I'm no tell-tale, sir, but you have to know. Lady Blanche will wish to speak to you but it's best you hear it from me first.'

It was enough for the premonition to assume monstrous form. 'Lady Blanche? What has my wife done?'

Judith tucked her kerchief in her sleeve and faced me, dry-eyed. 'I can't pretend she had no part in prompting what took place but to take advantage of a troubled lady was despicable. Sir Hugh de Grey is a vile rake.'

I clenched my fists, my heart pounding, and felt myself sway. 'He has forced my wife, raped her?'

In response to my shouted question Judith dropped her voice. 'No, sir. You couldn't call it rape. It happened last evening. She invited him, urged him to take her, even before they dismissed me from the room. For the past few days she'd entertained him in her chamber with intimate attentions, while I was present, and I begged her

126

to go no further. Lady Blanche had locked herself away, grieving for her son. Sir Hugh was grieving too, I don't doubt it, but he looked for the release Mistress Somers offered.'

'He took his pleasure with an afflicted woman. He is the foulest lecher.' I heard myself speaking in shaky outrage but my mind was blank except for the determination to leave Danson within the hour and never return. I was no fighter but if I was to encounter the man I had helped in the past I might attack him with my bare hands. 'Lady Blanche knows of this? How? Where is Sir Hugh?'

Judith answered the easiest question. 'Sir Hugh left this morning for the hunt. He hasn't yet returned.'

'Who told Lady Blanche? Did you?'

'No, sir, I'm loyal to Mistress Somers but you engaged me to care for her. You have the right to know I've failed. I would tell no one else. She flaunted her shame to Lady Blanche herself, hammering on the door and screaming in triumph that she'd coupled with Sir Hugh. She seemed to think it was an achievement worthy of admiration. The poor lady couldn't believe what she heard and opened the door, thinking to calm Mistress Somers' delusions. Her face is scored with scratches for her pains.'

'My wife attacked her?'

'First with her nails and then she hurled platters and ewers at whoever approached her.'

'Where is Kate now?'

'In your room, sir, under restraint, trussed like...'

'Like the mad woman she is. Don't blame yourself, Judith. Her condition is worse than I feared and I shouldn't have left her for so long. I had hopes she was improving when I last saw her.'

'That was before we were led to believe you were likely dead, Doctor. When her uncle called and told her...'

'What? Her uncle? Stephen Boice? He came here? Oh God! Oh God!'

I dropped to my knees, remembering how, when I met him beside the Thames, I had told him she was resting in the country with friends. I should have known that, with Gilbert Iffley's sources of information to probe, he would identify the haven at Danson where I thought I had left her in safety. 'He's abhorrent. He's compelled her to do his evil bidding in the past. No doubt he encouraged her wayward desires, her yen to lie with Hugh de Grey. He'll have had his reasons – to destroy both her and me.'

Judith listened to my outpouring with increasing horror and clapped her hand over her mouth until I paused. 'I was in the room with Mistress Somers and her uncle all the time they were together but I couldn't hear everything that was said between them. I'd no idea it was other than a cordial family visit.'

I stood. 'Of course not. I believed he had finished with her. I should have known better. He's a fiend. He told Kate I was dead?'

'He suggested it was likely. Mistress Somers was desolate when he'd gone, weeping for you, imagining your body hacked and riven. But it was after that she began to smile on Sir Hugh with more familiarity than was apt. All her moods were extravagant. It was as if she rebounded from desperate misery to base lewdness.'

'I must go into the house now. Is Kate chafing at her constraints? Will I find her distraught?'

Judith pursed her lips. 'No, sir, with God's mercy she'll be sleeping. I gave her some of the potion you left in case she was greatly disturbed.'

'Thank you. You've served your mistress staunchly. I'm truly sorry you've had to witness the depths of her degradation. We'll be journeying far from here but you're free to leave us if you wish. I shall understand if that is your decision.'

She set her mouth in a thin determined line. 'I'd like to stay with Mistress Somers, sir. Sinful men have harmed her, haven't they? I'd like to help thwart their wickedness.'

128

'Then I'm grateful beyond words. Please go and prepare Kate's things for departure. I shall call on Lady Blanche and conclude our arrangements.'

A hint of mischief curled Judith's mouth. 'God keep you, Doctor, that lady's no docile dupe herself. Badly used she's been without doubt, but she's a rare virago when riled.'

I wished a silent blessing on Judith for enabling me to enter the manor-house with the flicker of a smile on my face. Yet I knew the ice in my heart would withstand all attempts to melt it, frozen as it was with despair and loathing.

*****

Despite my words to Judith I went first to peep at Kate and confirmed that she was peacefully asleep before I asked to see Lady Blanche, a request granted immediately. The mistress of Danson's face was puffy with weeping and there were vivid abrasions etched on her cheeks but she held out her hands to me as one who shared her pain.

'Oh, Harry, if only we'd known you were living. I think it would not have happened.'

'If only I'd advised you that her uncle should never be given access to her. I had no idea he would seek to renew his influence over her.'

'She is mad, depraved in her madness, her mind possessed by devils.' I said nothing and Lady Blanche gave a sob. 'You know Hugh's nature.'

'I do. I need no explanation. I'll take Kate from here within the hour. I pray Sir Hugh won't return until we've gone.'

'Where will you go? She's in no condition to travel.'

'Lesnes Abbey is just a short distance from here. They will have a guest-house where Kate can rest while I make arrangements to take her by sea to East Anglia. We will go to my manor at Worthwaite.'

'Won't you put her away? She must be confined securely. Her affliction has made her a danger to all around her.'

'I don't know,' I said truthfully. 'I need time to consider. But I'm profoundly sorry you've suffered violence at her hands besides the insult to your honour.'

'Honour?' she echoed and put her fingers on my wrist. 'Harry, you have a right to demand redress from Hugh. He has shamed you, offended against your honour.'

I stepped aside, staring through the window at the untroubled orchard, heavy with blossom, beyond the curtilage of the house. 'Rest assured: I shall take no action at law against your husband. I would scarcely want an account of my wife's malady recited before a Justice. Nor, I imagine, would you wish to allege assault against your person publicly?'

She hunched her shoulders. 'It's best that you should both leave as you propose.'

'I make one condition, Lady Blanche, and my appeal is to you, not Sir Hugh.'

The lady looked perplexed and she spoke with an arrogance missing from her earlier words. 'By what right do you seek to impose a condition after your wife's abhorrent behaviour?'

I gritted my teeth, resolved not to be distracted by her insinuation. 'My Lady, in the past I favoured you and Sir Hugh with my silence when your deeds had been seriously reprehensible. You then gave my mother a home and I was grateful. Now there must be a parting of the ways between us but I believe the scales are tipped sufficiently for me to beg one act of generosity from you to settle the account.'

'You are still our friend, Harry.' She faltered.

'Then I beg you to rescind the order you have given for Mistress Ash and her family to leave their cottage.'

'Ah!' She twirled across the room, angry at first but controlling her passion. 'She's been my husband's whore.'

'I imagine he took her when it pleased him as he has taken many serving women over the years. I'd swear she is no whore. I think you vented your fury on her, as a proxy victim, when you learned what Sir Hugh had done with Kate, knowing he would be in no position, at the moment, to defy your decree.'

She tossed her head but her lips quivered. 'I am his chattel and have no power.'

'Don't punish Mistress Ash to disparage him. Don't vent your anger, which belongs elsewhere, on her. It isn't your nature to be so callous.'

She sank onto a stool. 'You're the most honourable man I know, master physician. It's my lot to share a lecher's bed with any that take his fancy and to bear his children year after year. It's small surprise I relished the chance to make another suffer: but you're right and my instinct was ignoble. I'll send word that Mistress Ash can stay – provided Sir Hugh is never told of my attempt to expel her.'

'My Lady, I thank you and agree your terms, as I'm sure Mistress Ash will. I wish you well and shall think of you with kindness. You and I are both bound to live in domestic situations we would not have chosen. Let us at least keep our integrity.'

I bowed and left her in order to commandeer horses and a litter for the short journey to the abbey. Half an hour later I carried Kate to the conveyance and settled her and Judith among cushions and blankets. Then we set off but as we approached the woodman's cottage Mistress Ash rushed out to grasp my reins and tearfully whisper her gratitude. I stopped to greet her, but while we were speaking I became aware of a horseman approaching in the distance and tensed with fear in case it was Sir Hugh.

Only as he drew nearer did I appreciate this rider was no landed knight, but one inelegantly astride a workaday horse and unaccompanied by huntsmen or servitors. I hailed him with pleasure and relief.

'Piers! You turned back from Dartford?'

'Mortimer and his entourage were making there on the road to Rochester.'

'I heard and wanted to warn you – but I've been occupied with my own troubles. My wife is much disturbed in her mind. We need to leave Danson.'

There was no obvious link between my two last statements but Piers was sensitive enough not to enquire further. He acknowledged Mistress Ash courteously when I introduced her, sympathising with her bereavement, and he referred to the loss of his own wife in an expression of fellow-feeling.

Piers fell in beside me as we rode the short distance to the abbey, so I explained my intention to seek passage by ship to Ipswich and then to travel by land to Worthwaite.

He gave me a sly grin. 'I didn't know you were landed gentry.'

'I'm not but the late Duke of Suffolk gifted me this little manor. My wife needs the quiet rest it can offer. I can't plan beyond that, until I can judge whether she will recover sufficiently to live a normal life with me while I practise as physician.'

Piers stared at me in silence for a moment. 'Bide at the abbey with your wife tomorrow and I'll find you a ship at Deptford ready to go to Ipswich. If you'll allow it, I'll come with you. I dare say there'll be work somewhere for an itinerant wheelwright who has taken up his indentures. There's nothing to keep me in Kent.'

His assistance in arranging our journey would be invaluable and I felt confident his presence would in no way irk Mistress Judith. Indeed she soon remarked to me on his civility, contrasting this favourably with Rendell's crassness. I took comfort from the hope that with the support of these faithful friends, I might bring Kate safely to Worthwaite and put behind me all dealings with Hugh de Grey, Gilbert Iffley, Stephen Boice and Jack Cade.

Not for the first time, events were to prove rather more complicated than that.

Chapter 11

Good fortune favoured us and we were able to take ship from Deptford next day on a vessel sailing to Harwich on the east coast. Its master was content to accept recompense for extending his voyage beyond that destination, along the estuary of the River Orwell to Ipswich, and he placed his cabin at the disposal of my wife. Before we gained the open sea, he needed to fulfil one other obligation, turning from the Thames into the mouth of the Medway, because he was committed to deliver rolls of gunny and fustian, with other anonymous but heavy bundles, to the Keeper of Queenborough Castle. I had no problem with these requirements and welcomed my temporary confinement within the creaking timbers of the ship, isolated from the wider troubles of King Henry's realm.

Judith had never been aboard ship before and she was excited to watch the vistas on either side of the river as we passed, so I encouraged her to remain on deck with Piers while I stayed with my wife who was sleeping on the master's narrow bunk. I sat at the cramped desk in his cabin, writing a letter to send ahead of us when we arrived at Ipswich, but as we rounded the curve of the Greenwich peninsula the motion of the tide sweeping us forward woke Kate. She gave a cry and scrambled onto her knees, staring about her in alarm, until she fixed her eyes on me and wailed. I rushed to hold her and soothe her fears but she believed she was still dreaming and recoiled from me. She was the prey of wild and awful aberrations.

'Harry! Am I in Hell? Are you sent to persecute me for all eternity? I didn't know that I was dead.' Her luminous green eyes were filled with terror.

'No, no, Kate, neither of us is dead. You were cruelly misinformed. I should have come to you before but there were duties I needed to fulfil and I didn't know how ill you were... that your Uncle Boice...'

'Ah! It is true! You are real.' Her voice became shrill as she grew more impassioned and I dared not interrupt her. 'I guessed you'd spurned me and found another doxy. He told me how you took women to your bed whenever I wasn't with you. He said you'd cast me off before you were killed, that you'd never return to me and I should find another mate. And, merciful Heaven, I had the itch for a man's cock. It grew on me as my mind cleared and I became a lusty woman once more. Oh God, when Hugh put his hand between my legs... how long ago was it since I'd been pleasured? Weeks, months? So long you'd neglected me. Now you've come back to your faithless wife, to beat me and make me submit to your will. You're a heartless husband to make me suffer so, to deny me your attentions and chastise me for finding comfort... I hate you, Harry Somers. I hate you.' She gave a screech of laughter. 'You took me, husband, you took me as your bed-mate but you never satisfied me with your feeble fucking...'

She hurled herself at me, clawing my face as she had clawed Lady Blanche, and screamed obscenities which tore at my heart more painfully than her nails slashed my cheeks. All the wit and merriment she had once possessed were smothered in a torrent of filthy abuse. I pushed her away but she came at me again, pressing herself against me for a moment, as if to be reconciled, but I realised she was eying the small dagger in my belt. I was ready when she tried to snatch it and swivelled from her, drawing my gown tightly over my jerkin.

'Boice told you lies, Kate. I've never lain with another woman since I met you. He's poisoned your mind, just when you were recovering. He's vile...'

I jumped to the side as she sprang forward, snarling, but in the narrow space I could not hope to evade her indefinitely. She seemed fired by unnatural energy and sooner or later I would be compelled to use coercion. I wrenched her arm and forced her to the ground, pulling the lacing from my shirt to bind her wrists, all the time trying to avoid her vicious teeth and nails. Then I shouted

134

for Judith to come and bring me rope so that I could strap the woman I loved to the bunk while I stuffed a gag into her mouth to prevent her biting her tongue in her frenzy.

With Judith beside her, Kate quietened and I slunk from the cabin, clutching my bundle of possessions and trembling in every limb. Piers took one glance at me and let me pass without a word. I stood alone in the bow of the ship, buffeted by the increasing wind, imagining the barren future which awaited me and mourning the destruction of the clever, vibrant woman who had fascinated me. I doubted now that Kate would ever recover her right mind and I was bound to her for the rest of our earthly lives. I could not weep and, although my external parts were shaking, inside I felt numb, prematurely dead. One day, I thought, when all hope is gone, perhaps the seething waters of the sea will offer the only sure means of respite I can find.

*****

Queenborough Castle dominated a bleak area of mudflats, but was strategically placed on a knoll, overlooking the point where the River Medway joined the Swale. We arrived offshore from its landing area the following morning, after I had spent the night on deck, rolled in a blanket, gazing vacantly at the firmament of stars. Piers had remained near me and I fancied he might have read my mind with its vague fancies of self-destruction. Judith sent word from the cabin that she had coaxed Kate to drink some of the potion which helped her sleep and she respectfully suggested I might refrain from visiting them, unless invited to call. It was advice I readily accepted.

I was puzzled why we did not make landfall as soon as we arrived off Queenborough and lowered our mainsail. Then I observed a rowing boat pulling alongside and the master engaged in conversation with an official-looking fellow seated in its stern. Although they were shouting, the

135

wind carried their words away but I gathered there was some complication to be overcome. At length the rowing boat turned and headed for the castle but we had dropped our anchor and were not making for the shore. The master of our ship came to join me at the rail.

'Looks impregnable, doesn't it? Hasn't stopped attackers chancing their luck. Three months ago French ships bombarded it from the sea. Some of the cargo we're delivering will be of use if that raid were repeated – ammunition for the cannon on the sea-walls. Yet, would you believe it, only twenty-four hours past, some fools tried to force entry from the land? They were easily repelled and took to their heels. It seems this Edmund Mortimer, who's caused such a to-do, sent a stack of booty by river to the Keeper of the castle. He reckoned the Keeper would look after it for him but, when he arrived to claim it, Sir Roger Chamberlayne refused to release what he called stolen goods. Got his comeuppance that time, did Mortimer.'

'Is Mortimer still here?'

'No, they think he bunked off to Rochester but there's a posse on his tail. However, this little affair has made the Keeper wary and before we can put ashore he wanted to check our business. When his marshal heard I was carrying passengers he asked for their names. So I told him. He's gone back to the Keeper for further instructions.'

I nodded. There was nothing else the man could do.

The rowing boat soon returned, along with a larger vessel, and our seamen began to unload packages into this second craft. I concluded that our ship was not to be allowed to approach nearer the land and hoped this meant we would soon be on our way again but a moment later I saw the master coming towards me and his expression was grave.

'I'm sorry, Doctor Somers. I did my best but the Keeper's insistent. He wants you ashore. Your name's on some list and he's chary of letting you pass unchecked. I reckon he's fearful of getting into trouble with the King's

Council, worried he shouldn't have taken custody of Mortimer's ill-gotten goods in the first place.'

'Can everyone else go on their way?'

'Yes, I can sail on freely once the unloading's done. It's only you he wants to see. I can't afford to hang about, Doctor. I've lost time already, waiting here. I'm due in Harwich as soon as may be.'

'Then of course I'll comply and you must sail on.'

I asked Piers to fetch Judith and outlined the position to them, handing over the letter I'd written the previous day.

'Once you get to Ipswich, send word to Perkin, my steward at Worthwaite. Give the messenger this letter and tell him to explain I've been delayed. Ask Perkin to send a guide and a litter to take you all to the manor. Dame Elizabeth, his wife, will provide for Kate when you get there – you'll like her, Judith, she's capable and honest. I'll join you as soon as I can.'

I noted Ford's twitch of anxiety and signalled silently that he should not speak his worries. 'I'm forever in your debt, Piers, if you'll take my wife safely to Worthwaite. You're welcome to stay at the house as long as you wish but there's a wheelwright in Diss, which isn't far away, if you want to seek employment. God be with you.'

Long, bony fingers pressed my hand for a moment while Judith murmured a wish for my safety. Then I picked up my bundle and swung myself, inexpertly, over the side of the ship to descend the rope ladder which swayed precariously against the hull. A brawny mariner half-lifted me into the rowing boat and confiscated my dagger. Immediately I was seated, the oarsmen took up their stroke, driving us purposefully towards the Kentish shore. I did not look back. I was beyond fretting about the fate which might await me.

*****

On arrival in the castle, I was taken to the Keeper's study where Sir Roger Chamberlayne was seated at his desk: a stout man with heavy jowls and a rough demeanour. He sealed a letter and gave it to a servant with instructions which I could not hear and then summoned me to stand in front of him. He looked me up and down as if evaluating my worth.

'The men who carried out their idiotic assault on the castle yesterday have forfeited their pardons,' he said without any preamble. 'When caught, they will be executed. As will the principal prisoners we took in the encounter. There's a reward of one thousand marks offered for the capture of Cade and five marks for each of his followers in the attack who're still at liberty.' He paused, flicking up his tufted eyebrows as he appraised me. 'Where do you fit into the picture, Doctor Somers? Did Cade send you to take on board your vessel the goods he hoped I would surrender to him?'

I tried to focus on this unexpected suggestion. 'No sir, I've seen nothing of Cade for the past week, nor have I heard from him. I'm not a member of his entourage and know nothing of his intentions. I'd secured passage on a boat going to Suffolk in order to take my sick wife to the manor that I hold at Worthwaite. The master explained he had goods to deliver to Queenborough Castle on the way and that was the first time I'd ever heard of the place.'

'So it's a coincidence that you chance to be in the mouth of the Medway at this time?' He did not disguise his incredulity.

'Entirely.'

'You fought alongside Cade in London?'

'No. I'm a physician. I did not fight. I treated some of the wounded on London Bridge – men fighting on both sides.'

'You'd been with Cade on Blackheath.'

It was not a question and I was startled to realise how well informed he was. 'I went there initially on a mission of charity and then provided medical services

138

which were needed.' I hoped he would not know of my involvement in other enquiries involving murder.

The Keeper stood and irony rang through his next statement. 'I take notice of your account but to my mind it hardly justifies your inclusion on the list of men pardoned for their participation in Cade's rebellion. If your role was completely benign, why should you need a pardon?'

'Perhaps for the avoidance of doubt,' I said. 'In case my professional role was misinterpreted.'

Sir Roger's face darkened. 'Don't make light of your situation, Doctor Somers. I've sent a boat to the City on the in-coming tide asking the authorities to clarify your status. If what you say is confirmed, you will be free to travel on where you will. If you are found still to be in league with Cade, your pardon will be forfeit. You will be accommodated in the castle until I receive a reply.'

'I understand.' I wondered whom exactly he was consulting and how reliable his sources of information would be, at a time when there could be continuing panic and confusion in the City.

'I suppose your name really is "Somers"?'

'Why, yes, certainly.' His question bemused me.

He gave an unpleasant chortle. 'There's a precedent, physician. At the command of the King's negotiators the principal pardon was made out to one Edmund Mortimer. Only there's no such person, you see. There was no pardon for a Jack Cade. He was forfeit, even without his foolish sortie against the castle.'

Sir Roger dismissed me and I was conducted to my lodging for the next few days: not, I was glad to see, a noisome cell but a simply furnished, passably clean room with a door securely bolted on the outside. At least my ambiguous standing would protect me from harsher imprisonment for the time being and, after the painful scene with Kate, I did not shy away from a period alone. I reflected on the trick played on Cade in the matter of his pardon – at the command of a Cardinal, an Archbishop and a Bishop. It was always unwise to take at face value the benevolent intentions of such princes of the church. Gilbert Iffley would know that, but I suspected Gilbert Iffley had long since abandoned his protégé, although I was uncertain quite what had lain behind the whole affair so far as Baron Glasbury was concerned. At all events, whatever the name of Mortimer was intended to convey, it had proved a disaster for the man who claimed it.

*****

Before Sir Roger received a reply from the City of London, news reached Queenborough Castle from Sussex and I was taken to his study so he could inform me in person of issues which gave him great pleasure.

'Such an ignominious ending,' he said by way of greeting. 'Slain in a quiet Sussex village, half-starved and clawing at grass for sustenance, would you believe it? Taken in charge by his pursuers in a gentleman's garden, mortally wounded but not quite expired. A life's progress from Blackheath to Heathfield – it has a certain ring about it, don't you think?'

I understood perfectly what he was telling me but his manner was irritating. I remembered Jack Cade had told me of a rumour that he was a physician from Sussex and, while dismissing the idea of him as a doctor, I wondered whether there was an element of truth in the tale and he had fled to an area he knew well from his childhood.

'Cade is dead?'

'Or Mortimer, if you prefer: both now deceased, stripped naked and his body set on an open cart for conveyance to London. The City is not to be deprived of its vengeance. The corpse is to be beheaded at King's Bench Prison; then trundled through the streets with the head sitting neatly on his belly. It seems the bridge has been repaired sufficiently to permit this triumphant entry across the Thames.' Chamberlayne paused but I felt no desire to comment and he continued with acerbic satisfaction. 'Two of his principal followers captured earlier are to be beheaded – in the normal way.'

It was incumbent on me to say something. 'I appreciate you letting me know the position.'

My assumed indifference annoyed him and he dismissed me but I was not unmoved. I recalled the engaging young fellow I first met on Blackheath, touting a list of reasonable demands on behalf of his fellow men, and I regretted that a taste of power had twisted his nature and played into the hands of his enemies. Perhaps, if I was realistic, the uprising had been doomed to reach this conclusion.

Cade's death had more encouraging implications too. It reduced the value of my knowledge regarding his presence in Richard of York's household, under the tutelage of Gilbert Iffley. Now the mysterious young man could not pass comment, there would inevitably be a range of rumours about his origins and upbringing: probably none could be proved or refuted with certainty. An alleged link with the Duke of York or his associates would simply be denied and, if I chose to declare publicly what I knew to be true, I could be derided as mistaken and fanciful. Baron Glasbury would understand this very well and conclude that he had nothing to gain now by threatening my family and friends in order to secure my silence. That was some comfort.

*****

It was not until the fourth day of my captivity that I was summoned back to appear before Sir Roger. A second man was standing behind him in the study, younger than the Keeper, expensively dressed and with a refined air but the line of his jaw and prominent nose suggested a familial link to Chamberlayne. As was his custom the older man glared at me and spoke without exchanging courtesies.

'You are vouched for, Doctor Somers. Two respected City men have stood surety for you – a master carpenter and an apothecary, I believe.'

I could not suppress a smile, thanking the saints for Thomas Chope and John Webber. 'I'm grateful. Am I free to go?'

The Keeper obviously did not share my delight. 'I pray God you will not disenchant these worthy citizens by your future activities. I should be failing in my duty if I did not caution you to show more prudence in the company you frequent and the patients you engage to treat.'

It was not the moment to take issue with his attitude and I compressed my lips but I was saved from responding by a cough from the gentleman in the background. Sir Roger smothered his irritation and became obsequious.

'You are free to leave Queenborough but first Sir Nicholas wishes to speak with you. I shall leave you to discourse privately. I trust you will pay heed to his advice.'

I bowed as the Keeper left the room and prepared myself for more smug criticism of my actions. 'I don't think we've met, Sir Nicholas?'

An elegant arm motioned me to a chair. 'Nicholas Chamberlayne; Sir Roger is my elder brother. I know something of you from acquaintances who've met you or were friends of William de la Pole. You served as physician to the late Duke of Suffolk's household. For my part I am factotum to the Duke of Somerset.'

I concentrated more intensely on what this gentleman might have to say and spoke cautiously. 'I haven't had the honour of meeting Duke Edmund.'

'But you attended his late uncle, Cardinal Beaufort, in his dying days. The Cardinal's successor as Bishop of Winchester, William Waynflete, speaks highly of your skill and your integrity.'

'He's most gracious.'

Sir Nicholas gave a genial shrug. Clearly my comments were superfluous. 'Bishop Waynflete is an

142

influential adviser to the King. He contributed significantly to the negotiations with this Cade. My Lord, Duke Edmund, esteems him, as do I. The Duke will be returning to England shortly, from across the Narrow Sea, and he will assume his place among the King's chief advisers. He will establish his household in London at Blackfriars and I know he would be glad if in due course you would offer him and his attendants the services you previously undertook for Suffolk at the Manor of the Rose.'

My mouth fell open in astonishment. 'I'm deeply honoured. But I'm unprepared and don't know when I might return to London. I have personal duties – a sick wife to accommodate in safety...'

'Ah, yes, the unfortunate Mistress Somers, I've heard of her affliction. Certainly you must provide for her as is best for her recovery but the Duke doesn't need your immediate attendance. Perhaps to begin with a looser connection will serve you both. He would like to think of you as an ally.'

The inflection of his speech as much as the words he spoke alerted me to the true meaning of this proposal. 'It's not simply the practice of medicine that he seeks from me?'

Sir Nicholas smiled with enchanting naturalness which could only be false. 'Bishop Waynflete said you were astute. Let me be frank. You are acquainted with Gilbert Iffley, Baron Glasbury, and his wife's brother, Stephen Boice.' I nodded, holding my breath. 'I think you've been disgracefully treated by these acolytes of Richard of York. I make so bold to say they are your foes.'

'That sounds stark but I can't deny it.' I could not bring myself to say more and he evidently knew many details of my past dealings with these men.

'What I propose, on behalf of the Duke, is that we do not publicise your attachment to his interests until – unless – at some future date you are able to take up a position as physician in his household. But in the meantime you will lend your wider talents to furthering a plan to expose the machinations of Glasbury and Boice and lay them low. Would you object to that?'

I did not answer at once. It might be reckless to give an absolute assurance but the desolation I faced in my personal life encouraged rashness. It offered a tempting diversion. 'I can't see what part I can play in your devices but I don't object in principle to what you suggest.'

'Cautious, measured – excellent! I'm most gratified and will enjoy working more closely with you, Doctor Somers. I assume you wish to proceed to your manor of Worthwaite forthwith. The vessel which brought me from London is at your disposal to take you to Ipswich. I shall stay with my dear brother until it returns here. I'll communicate with you regularly. This is my seal. You will recognise it.'

He pressed his ring onto the wax the Keeper had left on his desk and handed me a scrap of parchment with the impression of his complicated Arms. 'You'll perceive that on my mother's side I am related to the illustrious Percys. As, of course, is the formidable Prioress of St. Michael's, Stamford, with whom you are acquainted. She intimated to me recently that she would appreciate a visit from you if you were able to afford the time to make the journey.'

The final piece in this pattern of connections fell into place. It was all I needed to persuade me of the enormity of this proffered alliance and the potential peril into which I was straying.

'I'm sure I can arrange to go to Stamford after I've called at Worthwaite,' I said. 'At this time of year when the waterways are clear, it isn't difficult.'

'I recommend you make this journey, Doctor Somers. The Prioress will be delighted to renew her acquaintance with you and explain the background to your new commission.'

His manner was suave, the undercurrent of his proposal incendiary and my stultified vitals tingled with excitement.

144

Chapter 12

It was on my route from Ipswich to Worthwaite, so I called at the great castle of Wingfield to pay my respects to the Dowager Duchess and her young son, the new Duke of Suffolk. They were in deep mourning but Duchess Alice received me gladly and welcomed my intention to spend some time at my nearby manor. She had already learned of Kate's arrival and proposed to invite my wife, who had been one of her attendants, to visit Wingfield. Expectation of such a courtesy was one of the reasons I was calling on the Dowager.

'Your Grace, Kate is not well. She's suffered in the last few months and her mind is gravely distressed. I trust the peace of Worthwaite will help her recover but I can't tell if that will be possible. In the meantime her behaviour is unpredictable.'

The Duchess was full of compassion. 'My family is not the only one torn apart by violent events, I know that. Kate was always impulsive, volatile – it was part of her charm – but perhaps she lacks the serene resignation, as well as the resolution, women need to survive the burdens of a hostile world. Let me know how she progresses. I shall pray for her.'

I secured a brief word with my old assistant, Leone, while he was on his way to the bakehouse where a maid had been scalded lifting a tray of bread from the oven. He eyed me nervously at first and I guessed he thought I might seek my old position in the Suffolk household but, when I assured him this was not the case, he relaxed and beamed at me.

'It suits me well,' he said, 'this life in the castle, away from the turmoil of the City – a bear-garden it is there, you call it a bear-garden, no?'

'A good description. Nevertheless, I hope to return one day and practise there as a physician. I can't do that at present but I don't know how long I'll be at Worthwaite. I shall have to travel a bit. My wife is sick in her mind and if she suffers a relapse when I'm away from the manor, my steward, Perkin, may ask the Duchess for your help. I don't believe there's any treatment that can help Kate other than peace and quiet and use of potions which sedate the senses. I wouldn't want her subjected to rougher remedies which some physicians employ but she can become very agitated and it has been necessary to restrain her. It'll reassure me to know you are aware of her condition.'

His dark eyes were moist. 'I am so sorry, Doctor Somers. If I am needed, I will do what I can. You have my word I will not use barbarous chastisements as if I was an ignorant quack. Like you, I learned my medicine at Padua.'

I slapped him on the back in gratitude and let him go on his way to the bakehouse. He gave a wink as he passed me.

'She is most pretty, the scorched maid,' he said. 'I think she put her hand too far into the fire so I must come.'

He had gained in self-confidence from the lovesick lad who had been heart-broken all too often in years gone by, when his admiration for a girl had not been reciprocated. He was only a few years younger than me but nowadays I felt old beside him.

There was another person at Wingfield I wanted to see and I found him as he was leaving the chapel. The Duke's chaplain had helped me previously in moments of devastating grief and I valued his counsel, so I was warmed by his kindly greeting. He had heard of my marriage, which he referred to as joyful news, and he knew that Kate had arrived at my manor. Beaming with unimpeachable sincerity, he said he hoped to meet her.

'I hope you will do so in happy circumstances.' I took a deep breath. 'But she's afflicted in her mind at present. There may be those who advocate the ministrations of the church to help her.'

'You mean she is... she is possessed of a devil?'

'We cannot tell. We don't understand the workings of the mind. If a man is consumed by a wasting in his belly, we may say a devil is eating his guts but if he is opened up

146

we find nothing but a foul growth, not an identifiable devil. We cannot do that for the mind but it may be no different.'

Father Wilfred clasped his hands on his chest. 'You are telling me this because some may think exorcism appropriate?'

It was essential to choose my words carefully. 'I honour Holy Church and don't doubt the blessed relief which sacramental intervention may bring to some disturbed minds but I'm not convinced it is always beneficial. I've never witnessed an exorcism but I believe it's a powerful and frightening experience. When a patient is terrified, even violent, suffering from deluded fantasies they cannot explain, I find it improbable that exposing them to new terrors, new forms of violence, could cure them of their affliction.'

The chaplain did not respond at once and I regretted the hint of belligerence in my voice. I did not want to lose his friendship. At length he spread his hands wide and bowed his head.

'May the saints assist you, Doctor Somers. I have never conducted an exorcism and would seek Heaven's guidance before agreeing to do so. You are the lady's husband and if you forbid such an occurrence, I would not presume to act against your wishes. As for your medical opinion, I cannot comment but I respect your secular learning. Yet, surely there is a priest nearer to Worthwaite: in the town of Diss. If you are fearful of an intervention by the Church, he would be the cleric to be approached, not me.'

I pulled up my gown on my shoulders, taking my time. 'While I am with Kate at Worthwaite, the occasion will not arise but if I have to leave her in the care of attendants, I shall instruct them that should her condition deteriorate so profoundly that some other remedy must be sought, you are the priest I wish to be consulted. If you consent, that is.'

He chuckled. 'You are designing and devious, physician. Our Lord said that, in their generation, the

147

children of this world are wiser than the children of light. So it proves. I counsel you to beware that the Foul Fiend does not entrap you in your own ingenuity. But I am willing to accept the charge with which you honour me. If I am called upon, I will offer spiritual comfort to your sad lady but I will not attempt to drive out her demons with salt and Holy water unless you grant permission.'

I gave him my heartfelt thanks and dropped to my knees for his blessing. I had done all I could to safeguard Kate in the uncertain future facing us. Now I must brace myself to encounter her once more in person.

*****

I crossed the ditch which marked the boundary of my land and looked around at the stand of trees by the riverside and, to my left, the higher ground cropped by sheep. These were my trees and my sheep but it felt unreal to accept the fact. I had not accustomed myself to owning a manor and all that went with it, leaving its management in the hands of my excellent steward. I would need to listen to his recital of high-quality fleeces traded, wool spun and woven locally, then sold to merchants who organised fulling and dyeing before shipping fine woollen cloth across the sea. The operation of the wool and cloth markets was interesting but in an abstract sense; I found it difficult to relate it to my life, even though it provided a modest income to support my household.

A letter was waiting for me at Worthwaite, from the Prioress at Stamford. It was not unexpected and I was glad it gave substance to my hope of moving on in the next few days. I recognised this was not a laudable intention but I welcomed other calls on my time, for both the past and the present were oppressive within the walls of the manor-house and in the locality. It was at least some consolation that there had been no repetition of the frenzy which seized Kate when we were on board ship in the Thames estuary.

I pushed aside the memories which threatened to deflect me from my current duties and I trusted that Perkin and Dame Elizabeth, his wife, would not refer to my visits to Worthwaite years earlier, which had been in different circumstances. They were wholly dependable and, although Kate's presence must have burdened them with extra responsibilities, they made no complaint when they greeted me. Plainly much of this was due to Judith, who had already won Dame Elizabeth's approval and bore the brunt of caring for her mistress. It was pleasing to see the mutual respect between two practical women, each recognising the other's intelligence and competence. If only Kate could be restored sufficiently to share enjoyment of their company.

Judith reported that my wife seemed satisfied with her chamber at Worthwaite and, for the moment at least, was less restive than she had become at Danson. She was still eating little, visibly losing weight, and her sleep was troubled by menacing visions but Judith saw grounds for optimism.

'It could have been much worse, sir,' she said and when I looked at her uncertainly she became more explicit. 'She's not with child, Doctor, may the blessed saints be praised.'

The danger had oppressed my mind but I had not dared to enquire. 'Amen. Will the sight of me cause her condition to deteriorate, do you think?'

'Only one way to find out. I'll wait by the door. Call for me if you...' She put her hand to her face. 'Forgive me, Doctor Somers, I shouldn't be telling you how to behave.'

'Indeed, you should. You are with Kate night and day. It's from attendants like you that we medical men might learn how better to treat distortions of the mind.'

Judith grinned and did not disagree.

Kate was staring through the window at a line of small ducklings, a late brood, following their mother across the sward beside the fishpond. She did not move when I entered the room and I walked slowly for fear of alarming her but she could probably see my reflection in the bubbled glass of the window-pane.

'One of the babies has fallen behind,' she said. 'The smallest one: pecking under a bush. Will the mother miss it? Surely she won't – there are so many.' She turned her head and I was horrified by the blankness in her huge eyes. 'You've come to cast me off. Where will they put me?'

'This is your home, Kate, and I hope you'll be content to live here while you recover from your illness. I can't stay with you all the time but I'm not casting you off. You are my wife.'

She rose and her expression darkened. 'You will go to your whore. Uncle Boice told me of the titled lady who has shared your bed in the past. And the woman here told me this Maud is living not many miles from the manor. Is that why you've put me here, so you can pretend to care for me while you consort with your trollop?'

I had to play the part of the physician, not the husband; I had to remain composed. Dame Elizabeth must have mentioned the Fitzvaughans as people I knew, living less than twenty miles from Worthwaite. She would have been unaware of my earlier entanglement with Lady Maud.

'No, Kate, you have my word. The Dowager Lady Fitzvaughan is nothing to me. My sole interest is that you regain your health.'

'So will you bed me, husband? Will you take me in carnal knowledge, even after I have soiled your honour?'

I shut my eyes momentarily, telling myself that Kate's conversation was entirely rational; she had never been afraid of speaking salaciously. 'When you're well enough I shall delight to play the husband's part. I long for it. But you must regain your strength. Look, the laggard little duckling has reached the water to join his brothers and sisters.'

I thought my observation would cheer her but her eyes half-closed. 'They will peck it to death,' she said and I shivered.

*****

I stayed a week at Worthwaite before travelling to Stamford, reassured that my household would be well ordered in my absence. I had emphasised that there were friends at Wingfield who could be consulted if the need arose and I gave instructions that under no circumstances was Stephen Boice to be admitted to the house, if he called, whatever claims of hospitality he might invoke.

Kate was undeniably calmer than she had been since leaving Danson, although she was often in tears, consumed by an inner melancholy. I could only hope this was a stage in her recovery. Judith and Dame Elizabeth relished each other's company and Piers had obtained occasional work at the wheelwright's in Diss. He spoke of seeking a permanent position further afield, in a larger town like Saint Edmundsbury, but I impressed on him that he could stay at my manor-house for as long as he wanted. I set off from Worthwaite with a lighter heart than I had thought possible when I arrived there.

It was less than a year since I last crossed the fenland, journeying by water and low causeways, but it seemed I had suffered a lifetime of sorrow since then. Yet the places I passed through had not changed and, when I came to Stamford, the streets, the Raven Inn and the looming wall of St. Michael's Convent were all as I remembered and this was heartening. Next morning the gatekeeper admitted me without a quibble to the familiar guest-parlour beside the entrance and I settled on the window bench to wait for the service of Tierce in the convent chapel to conclude. I reminded myself that when I last saw the Prioress she was recovering from an illness, appearing older and more bodily frail than she had been, but still indomitable in her mental powers.

I heard the key in the lock of the door from the cloister and I stood, readying myself for whatever deterioration the past months might have wrought in her

151

health. She moved into the room with deliberate steps and fixed those all-seeing eyes on me, causing a tremor to run down my spine as they always did. She still used a stick to lean on but I suspected she could wield it as a bludgeon should the need arise. She was slightly bent in her posture but drew herself upright while she appraised me, her hawk-like nose twitching as if I had imported some unpleasant stench into the room.

'Reverend Mother.' I dropped to my knees.

'Doctor Somers: may the Lord bless you and pardon your transgressions.' She eased herself onto the bench I had vacated. 'I trust He will, in His great mercy. I would have more difficulty in overlooking your extreme foolishness. I suppose He might account your loyalty to the late Duke of Suffolk a virtue. I recall advising you to quit his service. You are fortunate not to have earned a worse recompense for your devotion to the man.'

I bowed my head. No reply seemed necessary.

'Since then you have been cavorting with that false claimant to the blood of Mortimer. What possessed you to involve yourself with that escapade?'

I attempted a reasoned explanation. 'The complaints he addressed to the King on behalf of the common people were not unreasonable and he impressed me with his manner when I first met him, but my involvement was merely in my role as physician.'

'Did you study medicine or hair-splitting sophistry at the university? You have been self-indulgent, Doctor Somers. I had some part in assisting you, through Holy Church, when you were in difficulty some years back; you repay our efforts with ridiculous day-dreaming, impracticable whims. You are a full-grown man and should be ashamed of yourself. And what of the woman you rashly married?'

'Kate is ill. I'll accept your criticism of my own behaviour. It's proper for you to berate me as you think fit. But Kate is afflicted in a way we do not understand.'

'Possessed by devils?'

'I don't believe that description but her mind is deeply troubled.'

'Humph!' The Prioress fingered the rosary at her waist. 'The woman has Neville blood. I am kin to the Percys, sworn rivals of the Nevilles in the north of the country.'

'Despite that, when we last met you said you'd heard nothing to her discredit. You knew she was high-spirited.'

'And I recommended you to take her away from the court to live quietly as your wife.'

'I wanted to but events prevented it. She is now at my manor of Worthwaite and I trust her peaceful life there will help her recover. She is my wife and I will fulfil my duty to her.'

The Prioress slapped her knee. 'That's better. I feared you'd become a milksop. She's not the wife I'd have chosen for you but you're right to recognise the obligations of the Sacrament of Marriage. Now, to business: are you still wary of Richard of York? He remains in Dublin, I'm told.'

'I'm wary of his henchmen, Gilbert Iffley and Stephen Boice. They continue to threaten and harm me. Iffley was determined I shouldn't disclose what I knew of his contact with Cade years ago in Richard of York's household. Cade's death should have diluted that concern but I can't be sure and Boice always acts with malign intent towards me.'

I did not wish to explain the part Kate's uncle played in acerbating her mental turmoil and was glad the Prioress ignored my reference to him. What she focused on was in any case mind-boggling enough.

'I divine that Iffley is an astute student of men's frailties. He knew Cade well when he trained him to act as a stalking horse for Duke Richard. The uprising was a test to see how much support a future intervention by one with a genuine claim to Mortimer blood – and to the throne – might glean. If it had achieved longer-lasting success York

153

could have ridden on the crest of its wave. As it was, Iffley undoubtedly knew Cade's weaknesses and the probability that power and the prospect of wealth would go to his head. He was always expendable if he failed to stay true to the principles he advocated and ceased to be useful to his paymaster. Iffley looks into men's souls and explores their flaws. Then he exploits them for his own ends – and of course Richard of York's.'

The Prioress's analysis of the thwarted rebellion was insightful but it was her final comment which caused me to remember something Cade had said to me, the importance of which I should never have disregarded. In my head I heard his melodious voice referring to the wretched squire he had executed – Stanlaw: *'a man I had known for many years: a follower Glasbury introduced to me when I was still a youth.'*

Iffley had known Stanlaw longer than he had known Cade and if he was so skilful at identifying men's inner compulsions, which I believed he was, he would have been aware that the man was a pederast and a potential killer. I had entertained instinctive suspicions that Iffley had a hand in the deaths of Adam Ash and Hubert de Grey; now I was certain he had procured them. He had not needed to instruct Stanlaw to seize the child, only to provide the villain with an opportunity to act according to his foul nature.

'What are you staring at, physician?' The Prioress banged her stick on the floor to divert my attention from self-absorption. 'Do you disagree with my summary?'

'Forgive me, Reverend Mother. I agree entirely. Your words reminded me of something.'

'Something to Iffley's discredit? Good. Because we are now coming to what can be done to undermine the Baron once and for all – and with him neuter Richard of York's ambitions. With Suffolk's death there is a vacancy.'

'A vacancy? I don't follow.'

154

'For a counterweight to York. For a man with the King's ear and the Queen's trust, to lead the court party. That is why Somerset is returning to England.'

'Won't he be out of favour because of the military defeats he suffered – the loss of Normandy?'

'The King will not rate that highly. He has such an abomination of fighting; he never liked renewing the war with France. Somerset is a congenial fellow, I'm told: fair-featured and unquestionably loyal. My kinsman, Sir Nicholas Chamberlayne, and Bishop Waynflete think he will fill the position of chief counsellor admirably. A suitable foil to Richard of York, you understand? A provocation too.'

I dipped my head, understanding a great deal. 'It's been suggested I might serve Somerset's household in London as physician although I'm not in a position to accept.'

'I know and I trust it will not be too long before you can. Think of the lure you would offer Iffley. He will be enchanted to see you at Somerset's side. He'll approach you on his master's behalf, seeking to suborn you. It may well provide the chance necessary to undermine York himself.'

I was familiar with the scenario she proposed. Boice had used threats to induce me to harm Suffolk when I was in his service and it was Kate who had suffered when I refused. 'I would prefer to slip away completely from public affairs and live an obscure but useful life as a doctor.'

She smiled thinly as if indulging a recalcitrant and stupid child. 'A passing fancy and not your destiny. In any case you can hardly expect to achieve your aim while skulking in your manor at Worthwaite where you are neither one thing, nor the other: neither a landed squire nor a professional man of medicine. But I have no concerns. You will come to your senses and comply. Your reckoning with Iffley is incomplete.'

155

She fell silent but did not rise and I was perplexed as to whether the interview was at an end. I stood awkwardly, shuffling my feet, while she tilted her head on one side so that her heavy wimple flapped at her left cheek. 'These matters of state are of fundamental significance but they are not the principal reason that I wished to see you.'

I must have looked bewildered and she laughed. 'Come now, Doctor Somers, you should know what to expect from me. I am a woman of dedication and determination but I have my weakness. Only one of my former charges at St. Michael's can tug at my heart so forcibly but sweet little Eleanor does. Lady Fitzvaughan, I should call her now, heiress of vast lands in her own right and mother of the infant who will inherit all that has been bestowed on her and her ungodly husband. I wish you to visit her before you return to London, to give assurance that she is well provided for, in health and honour. As I informed you, there was unrest on the estate during the disturbances and I should be glad to know there has been no lasting harm affecting Eleanor.'

I tried to conceal my dismay but could not quickly invent an excuse for declining her request. Only, of course, it was not a request but an instruction.

'Hartham Manor is not far from Worthwaite, as I recall.'

'No, indeed. I could certainly go there.'

'Then why the hesitation? Can it be that you don't trust yourself to reject the favours which Eleanor's wayward mother will inevitably offer you?

I felt the flush spreading over my face. 'Not at all. I'll go there if you wish it, Reverend Mother.'

The Prioress rose. 'Thank you, Doctor Somers. Lady Maud must abominate her dependence on her son-in-law – her late husband's erstwhile bedfellow. It's a situation full of interest, is it not? Keep me informed on all the points we have discussed.'

She turned at the door, hand on latch, and nodded approvingly at me. 'The Abbot of Peterborough remembers

156

you with warmth and has told me how highly Bishop Waynflete regards you. These connections bode well for your future advancement. Don't let your misguided marriage hamper your prospects. There are worthy houses of my Order where the sisters care for those whose minds are possessed. Remember that. Not here; as you know, our vocation at St. Michael's is to nurture the young. Others embrace even more challenging duties. Bear this in mind. May God guide you in the paths of wisdom and virtue.'

Chapter 13

Little had changed when I returned to Worthwaite. Kate's face was thinner, her eyes enormous and their frightened expression reflected her confusion. She was tearful but subdued and it was possible to consider this a tiny step forward in the progress of her illness. I was desperate to find grounds for encouragement in her condition and rejoiced that she received my return calmly, seeming unperturbed when I greeted her in person.

Within a week of my arrival, news was sent from Wingfield Castle that the Duke of Somerset had arrived at court and been made welcome by the King. This was very likely to antagonise Richard of York but, despite the aspirations of others on my behalf, I wished never to be drawn into the vortex of their rivalry. Nearer at hand there were reasons to be cheerful. Perkin reported good prospects for the harvest on my land and Judith could be heard singing contentedly as she went about her duties.

What might seem joyful was not straightforward, however, and Dame Elizabeth was anxious to acquaint me with her interpretation of this latter development which she feared might have regrettable consequences.

'Master Ford is well enough as a tradesman, I suppose,' she said without preamble when she drew me aside to inspect the contents of the pantry. 'But Judith is a treasure we would be ill-equipped to lose.'

'Lose her? That would be appalling. She sounds happy surely?'

Dame Elizabeth gave a superior smile. 'That's just it, Doctor. I note that Master Ford is courteous to her. It may be they have an understanding.'

'Good heavens, I never thought of such a thing.'

'You men are not observant of the nuances women notice. Judith deserves true happiness but, if she were to leave Mistress Somers, I don't know what might happen. Besides, Master Ford is still only a journeyman: albeit, he may enhance his status when he goes to Hartham Manor.'

I nearly dropped the jar of preserves I was sniffing. 'Hartham Manor?'

'I understand Lord Fitzvaughan has offered him employment on his estate. But I shouldn't speak out of turn. No doubt he'll tell you himself.'

Piers did just that when I saw him later. He had made it known in the neighbourhood that he was seeking a position and the temporary work he undertook in Diss had earned commendations. Within a few days an invitation to call at Hartham Manor had come from Gaston de la Tour's bailiff who explained that the sudden death of the estate's wheelwright left them with only an inexperienced apprentice who needed a master. 'I've arranged to go next week. It's a rare piece of luck,' Piers said.

I agreed but my mind had wandered to think of Robin Willoughby, the bailiff at Hartham Manor, who had married Bess, my first love. He was an excellent fellow in all respects and I had no doubt that, if he had heard Piers had accompanied me to Worthwaite, he would have taken it as a recommendation in the wheelwright's favour.

'I'm due to pay a courtesy visit to the Fitzvaughans. I've known the family for years. Let's ride there together.' Then I remembered Dame Elizabeth's anxieties. They now seemed more immediate but I did not know how to broach the subject. 'You'll set up as a master with your own yard?'

'That's the offer. It'll give me a new start. It's what I need. There'll be new opportunities, new interests.'

'Will you think of marrying again?'

Piers looked taken aback by my blurted question. 'Oh, I didn't mean that. I'm not ready. One day perhaps but I'll need to find someone to have me.'

'I surmised you might think Judith suitable.'

He roared with laughter. 'Dame Elizabeth has put that idea in your head, I'll be bound. She's already tried to sound out my intentions when I've done no more than exchange pleasantries with Mistress Somers' attendant. Judith will make the right man a superlative wife but I'm too old for her and I fancy she's settled her heart elsewhere.'

'Really? I'm sorry, Piers, I shouldn't pry but when you mentioned new interests I thought it fitted with Dame Elizabeth's notion.'

He lowered his voice. 'I meant something different. There've been disturbances in the district around Hartham Manor and there must be men in the area who share the grievances we set out on Blackheath. I'd welcome involvement in furthering their cause – by peaceful means.'

'The new Lord Fitzvaughan may not be the most amenable overlord to persuade with their complaints. But I've met the bailiff and Robin Willoughby strikes me as a reasonable man so I suggest you put your arguments to him in the first place.'

'Don't worry, I won't cause havoc. I'm too conscious of my good fortune. And I won't carry off Judith either. She's happy here and she knows her own mind. Don't let Dame Elizabeth inveigle you into match-making on Judith's behalf.'

'Heaven forbid!'

Relief swept aside the foolishness I felt at interrogating Piers in such a ham-fisted manner and, not for the first time, I considered myself ingenuous beside his greater maturity.

I felt slightly guilty about leaving Worthwaite again, so soon after my return, but a visit to Hartham Manor would take no more than two days and offer a distraction from the conundrum the Prioress had identified. This had plagued my thoughts since seeing her and I recognised the anomalous position I was in at my manor: neither landed gentry nor practising physician.

*****

Hartham Manor was a large and prosperous estate. Its flocks of sheep grazing on the ridge which ran along, above the centre of the demesne, were several times bigger than those on my humble holding. It employed craftsmen in half a dozen trades as well as a bevy of outdoor labourers and a multitude of house-servants. This was a lordship befitting a nobleman. Worthwaite shrank into insignificance by comparison, which moderated my feeling of incongruity at possessing my own manor.

We stopped at the bailiff's house near the cluster of woods on the Fitzvaughan estate so Piers could report to Robin Willoughby. The complex of tradesmen's quarters, with the wheelwright's yard, the smithy and the labourers' cottages, lay further on, nearer the manor-house and its domestic buildings which were sheltered within a walled enclosure. I was bound for Lord Fitzvaughan's inner sanctum but I was glad to break my journey and greet his bailiff and Mistress Willoughby. Robin looked none the worse for the injury he had received in the fracas earlier in the year and that was cause for pleasure.

We were offered refreshment which was taken hastily because it was obvious the bailiff wished to show Piers the wheelwright's yard. Robin urged me to linger over my ale and he asked Bess to fetch their children so I could admire how they had grown since I saw last them. Anne was an inquisitive three-year-old who immediately demanded to know why I had come and what the birthmark on my face denoted.

She ignored her mother's attempt to hush her and rested a chubby finger on a chubbier chin as if considering an erudite question. 'Your cheek's like a squashed bramble-berry.'

'That's a good description. I was born like it. Some people have these dark patches – not always on the face. They don't mean anything. Look, I've brought something for you, Anne. Something my friend the new wheelwright made. See.'

I held out a miniature wooden figure Piers had carved and the child seized it. 'What's his name?'

'He hasn't got one yet. You must name him.'

161

'Anne, you must thank Doctor Somers and say sorry for being rude about the mark on his face.'

The child bobbed her head towards me and ran off, talking fiercely to the newly designated 'Woody'. I caught her mother's eye. 'She meant no harm, Mistress Willoughby. I've heard much less pleasing descriptions of my face.'

'She's too pert but I hope she'll grow to learn discretion. Rob is quieter than she ever was at his age but he can get himself about on the floor fast enough.'

She set down the infant she was holding and, as if to demonstrate his prowess, he manoeuvred himself by a mixture of crawling and sideways bouncing to reach a ball lying by the side wall. Bess smiled at him proudly and then looked at me. 'I'm blessed,' she said. 'And you...?' She sounded embarrassed.

'My wife is ill. I hope one day, when she is better...' For a moment we held each other's gaze and I remembered when I had first met Bess more than ten years previously and started timidly to court her, before a series of mishaps intervened and kept us apart. 'I must be on my way to the manor-house.'

'Of course, they'll be glad to see you. Will you call at the dower-house also?'

The Willoughbys had lived in the dower-house until the late Lord Fitzvaughan was killed in battle in the spring. Now the Dowager, Lady Maud, resided there, as was her right. Bess's enquiry was not made in innocence.

'Lady Maud will still be in mourning but I wouldn't wish to be impolite. I'll enquire whether she would receive me.'

Bess gave a mischievous grin. 'You know full well, she'll ask to see you, Doctor Somers. You'll likely be treated to a stream of grumbles about her son-in-law.'

'I can imagine it isn't the smoothest of relationships. Do you see her, Mistress Willoughby?'

'Yes, now and then. Since she was widowed, she has asked me to visit her. You'll remember I used to serve as her attendant years ago, before I married.'

'She shows great sense in renewing the contact. I'm sure your company is good for her.'

Bess blushed and scooped Rob into her arms, gently removing the handful of rushes he had gathered from the floor and was attempting to thrust into his mouth. 'You shouldn't pay me compliments, Doctor Somers. I think you'll find Lady Maud is becoming bored with her widowhood.'

In spite of myself I grinned. 'I appreciate the warning.' Then I bowed and left the bailiff's house.

I was uncertain how much Bess knew of my dalliance over the years with Maud Fitzvaughan but it seemed probable she had learned a good deal and this made me acutely uncomfortable.

*****

It was the young Dame de la Tour who was waiting in the vestibule to greet me when I arrived at the manor-house. She was now also properly known as Lady Eleanor Fitzvaughan, as a result of the inheritance she received from her late step-father and the honour conferred on her husband when he was granted the vacant title. She was approaching her sixteenth birthday but was already the mother of a son a few weeks younger than Bess Willoughby's boy. At the behest of both his parents, Eleanor's infant had been named Walter to preserve the memory of the late Lord Fitzvaughan whose lands in Norfolk he would inherit.

Little Walter de la Tour was also heir to the estate of Ravensmoor in the north of Yorkshire which had been held by the late Earl of Stanwick, Eleanor's natural father. Earl Ralph's marriage had been childless and he had secured royal consent to endow his bastard daughter with his extensive lands, which were now likewise held in

163

Eleanor's name by her husband, Gaston de la Tour, the new Lord Fitzvaughan. The Stanwick title could not be passed on with the estate and the earldom was now held by a distant cousin, Roger Egremont, a violent man I did not wish to remember.

Lady Eleanor was delighted to welcome me and played the part of chatelaine with charm and confidence. I was overjoyed to see how she glowed with good health and contentment, while marvelling that her unlikely marriage continued to please her. I would have no problem in giving the Prioress all the assurances she would wish to have regarding her favourite protégée.

'Walter is with his wet-nurse but you shall meet him later. He's teething at present and dribbles over everything so be careful if you lift him on your shoulder or your physician's robe will be streaked with drool. You'll want to refresh yourself and there's food and drink in your room. Gaston is occupied with papers in his study but would be glad if you'd join him in an hour or so.'

I caught the difference in tone as she spoke of her husband. 'How is he?'

She sighed. 'He's still grieving for his friend – as are we all of course but the loss hits Gaston most cruelly. He was badly injured himself and was only able to travel here from Normandy two months ago. He may not tell you himself but he suffers lingering pain from his wounds. You may be able to help him.'

'I'll do what I can. I imagine he's proud of his son.'

'Infinitely and I bask in the glory of having borne him. Gaston is the sweetest man and I'm richly blessed.'

Gaston's sweet nature was not something I had experienced when he organised attempts on my life but I was happy for Eleanor. 'How is your mother coping with her widowhood?'

Eleanor crinkled her nose. 'She's restless and bad-tempered. She quarrels with Gaston whenever they encounter each other – a situation I endeavour to prevent. You'd better call on her, though I don't think there's any physic would benefit her. She'll invite you into her bed – that might be good for her.'

The young mother had acquired a new directness and understanding of her mother's passions. 'I shall disappoint her if she does and remind her I'm a married man.'

'Since when has that acted as a deterrent to the generality of men? I've heard your wife is stricken with some ailment. If you wish to renew your familiarity with Lady Maud, it may be good for you both. Don't tell her I said so – she considers me boringly virtuous and moral. I would not wish her to think otherwise.'

She laughed but I was uncertain how to interpret Eleanor's jest. To be invited by her daughter to accept Maud's illicit favours was disconcerting.

When I was shown into Gaston's study later in the afternoon, I was grateful Eleanor had alerted me to his condition. His face was pale and drawn, his appearance that of a much older man, and his manner lacking in the arrogance I associated with his usual behaviour. He reached out a hand to grip mine as if we were old friends reunited.

I'm glad you've come, Doctor Somers. It's timely. You may be able to assist me.'

Remembering Eleanor's caution in mentioning her husband's injuries, I was surprised but took my chance. 'The wounds you suffered still trouble you?'

He gave a brief chuckle. 'Well, actually they do. If you can alleviate the throbbing it would be a benefit. That wasn't what I meant but...' He stretched his arm to pick up a document and flinched.

'Where were you wounded?'

He grunted then shrugged. 'The back of my shoulder is the worst. The blade sliced between the plates of my armour. That's what inconveniences me most.'

'May I see?'

He removed his short robe and loosened the tapes of his shirt, slipping it from his left shoulder so I could inspect the long, jagged scar.

'I'd have wished the sewing done more tidily but it isn't infected. The flesh needs to gain more flexibility. You should exercise your arm, without straining, to help it regain strength but you may also find some balsam useful to ease the skin. I have a mixture which an apothecary taught me how to make years ago. William de la Pole found it helpful for his back.'

'I'd be grateful to try it, Harry. I need to recover my energy. It has been difficult enough...' His voice tailed away.

'The loss of Walter Fitzvaughan was a tragedy.'

Gaston nodded. 'He died by my side on the battlefield. I believed I would be joining him shortly afterwards but they hauled me away and patched me up. I wasn't appreciative of their actions at the time. Yet now I'm ennobled and have a son, as well as an amiable, complaisant little wife who adores me. I have reasons to live and Walter would wish me to care for my family.'

'That's good...'

He cut me off. 'Yes, but I need to recapture the vigour and resilience I had. I'm not ready to deal with tiresome issues. I can't brush them aside as I once would have done.'

'There's something in particular?'

'A silly thing has happened. I know it may be nothing, a trivial trick to upset me but there could be more to it. I can't ignore it as I should. It's preying on my mind.'

By this time I had worked out that it was not my medical knowledge he wished to call on, but other experience. 'You'd better tell me what this is about, my Lord.'

He curled his lip at my courtesy. 'That may be the cause of it,' he said, 'this lordship. 'I've been taunted and threatened many times in the past for what I am and I've grown used to vulgar slights. Now there's more fodder for

166

those who hate me to feed on. I'm seen as gaining unmerited profit from my friendship with Walter – from being his bedfellow – and that's more than the bigoted can stomach. Walter was respected as an honest man and his reputation shielded me. My foes are less inhibited now he's gone. Besides, I'm a stranger here, a Norman and therefore suspect.'

'You've received abuse – a threat?'

'A tangible one. This came four days ago.' He held out the letter he had picked up from his desk. 'Read it.'

The message was concise. *Scum, villain, you will receive your quittance. What you treasure, you will lose.*

'How was this delivered to you?'

'With papers brought to me from the Duke of Norfolk's castle at Framlingham. A small packet slipped in between legal covenants for me to sign.'

'Was it sealed?'

'Yes, with a worn seal, difficult to decipher: a kind of bird, I think. Not a crest I recognise. I ought to shrug it off as malice, nothing more.'

'Do you know of anyone at Framlingham who would wish you ill?'

'I've been in dispute with the Duke of Norfolk, John Mowbray, – over a land transaction. But the papers which came with this note settled that matter.'

'Perhaps one of the Duke's adherents was irritated on his behalf by a newcomer seen as an unworthy upstart?'

'Perhaps. I've learned the Duke himself had a reputation for wildness in his youth and still nurtures bitter enmities. He hated the late Duke of Suffolk. The only noble he seems to respect is Richard of York. He's recently held a gathering of like-minded cronies at Framlingham.'

'Ah!' My exclamation was involuntary. 'I understand your alarm but I'd guess your instinct to dismiss it is correct. It's probably just mummery, not a real menace. Maybe John Mowbray is aiming to stir up opposition to the court and trying to put pressure on neighbouring nobles in East Anglia so they'll support him.

167

You may receive an explicit request to join his cause, in return for withdrawal of the threat.'

'That's plausible but I want nothing to do with these rivalries. Walter was always true to King Henry. That's good enough for me.'

'Wait and see if you receive an approach from Norfolk or any other menacing communications.'

'I'd be reassured to know I could call on you for advice, Harry, if the need arose. I feel isolated in my newly acquired domain.

'My manor is less than seven leagues from here and I expect to be there for some time. I'm at your service.'

I had never before seen Gaston de la Tour so genuinely worried and humble in his neediness. He evoked my sympathy and, unprecedentedly, I warmed to him.

*****

My visit to Lady Maud was brief but intensely unsettling. She was richly adorned, more than would be deemed apt for a dowager, and she had lost none of her allure. I estimated she must now be about thirty years old but her face was unblemished, her teeth intact and, if her hair had acquired a deeper shade of gold than it had in her youth, this suited her well. Of course her hair should have been fully covered by her widow's veil but Maud had contrived that her headdress allowed several tresses to escape and frame her immaculate pale cheeks. She summoned me into her chamber with an imperious gesture and indicated the presence of her attendant, Marian, who had served her faithfully for many years – a servant afflicted with profound deafness which had often proved a boon to her wayward mistress.

'So, Doctor Somers, you deign to visit me. I thought you scorned to come to the dower-house as if I exhaled the miasma of a foul disease.'

'My Lady, I hesitate to intrude on your mourning. I come as a physician, in case you are unwell.'

She sauntered forward to stand an arm's length from me. 'Oh tush, Harry, don't be ridiculous. You wished to avoid me in case I seduced you. Sweet Heaven, if you knew how bored I am! I would welcome five minutes intelligent conversation, let alone more intimate exchanges: albeit I would not repulse you if you embraced me.'

'I'm happy to offer five minutes' conversation. You must decide whether it is intelligent. I'm sorry you are discontented.'

'What did you expect? Am I made for widowhood? Fretting away the months in solitude, pretending grief for a husband who had no time for me? I sustain this pretence for Eleanor's sake only, so she will not be disgraced by her wanton mother. But I shall become demented if I'm forced to endure another day of this misery after the year of mourning is concluded. Won't you offer me a little comfort to relieve my desolation in the meantime?'

She took a step forward and put her hand on my disfigured cheek, stroking it gently.

'You know I can't offer more than conversation.'

She swirled away from me. 'I think I am not so demented as your wife. Do you still lie with her?'

'Kate is my consecrated wife. Nothing can change that.'

'And you were my unconsecrated paramour while my husband lived. Nothing can change that.'

'That time is past, Maud. You must look to the future. You're free to marry again.'

'I will not delude another man into thinking I might bear a child. You are a physician and I've told you my past. You know I am now barren.'

'There would be many men happy to wed you without needing an heir.'

'Old wizened freaks with shrivelled pricks? Gaston has already suggested such a monster. He would be glad to be rid of me from Hartham Manor.'

'You can hardly complain of that when you are equally eager to be rid of him.'

'Oh, you base, insolent quack!' She hurled herself at me and I was forced to steady her with my arms. She tilted her head and I kissed her lightly. Then I disengaged myself from her and bowed. In struggling against temptation I had become a pompous bore.

'I cannot resume my visits, my Lady. I beg you to understand. If I can be of help, with physic or advice, you may send word but otherwise I must desist from seeing you.'

'Because you lust for me as much as you ever did. Very well, Harry, you may leave me. Go to your addle-headed wife. Get her with child if you can but with such a frenzied, flagrant maniac, will you be certain that any brat in her womb is yours?'

On my lonely pallet, for many weeks to come, I remembered Maud's heartless words and they echoed in my mind with their bitter truth.

Chapter 14

In the middle of September news came to Worthwaite of two ominous occurrences. Edmund Beaufort, Duke of Somerset, had been appointed Constable of England by the King and Richard of York had abandoned Ireland to his deputy and landed at Beaumaris on the island of Anglesey off the Welsh coast. It was assumed he intended to march to London. Taken together, these developments afforded a prescription for turmoil. Summons had been sent out for Parliament to meet in London and that meeting was likely to provide the occasion for animosities to come to a head.

I registered the significance of this renewed rivalry between royal cousins but pushed it from my thoughts. It seemed far removed from my constricted world, centred on Worthwaite and its neighbourhood. I could not say with honesty that I was happy. Chiefly this related to Kate's continuing indisposition but I was also frustrated by my inability to practise my profession, other than in the most limited way. The handful of retainers who served my manor were reasonably healthy and, although I let it be known in the small town of Diss that I could be called on to perform a physician's duties, I was seldom contacted for this purpose. I missed the hurly-burly of the City or a noble's bustling household but I told myself sternly that I must concentrate on my duties and the exigencies arising day by day.

For the first few weeks after my return from Hartham Manor Kate was withdrawn and dejected, seemingly oblivious of my attempts to cheer her, even of my presence. Then Judith told me she had begun to prick the inside of her wrists with a sewing needle and it became necessary to try reasoning with her about this harmful habit. I did not disclose that I was forewarned but, sitting by her side her one evening, I fondled her hand and slid back the cuff of her tight sleeve.

'What are these tiny dots of dried blood, Kate?'

171

She stared at them as if she did not recognise the marks. 'A rash?' she asked as if uncertain.

'I think not, they've been inflicted from outside. They are tiny punctures of the skin. I don't believe anyone has done this to you. Why have you hurt yourself?'

My question annoyed her and she pulled her hand away from me. 'It's nothing. I'll thank you not to pry.'

'Kate, I only want to help you. Why do you want to hurt yourself?'

She squirmed in her chair and shouted her reply. 'So that I know I am living. The pain confirms it.'

Her answer horrified me but the fact that she could articulate her reason was encouraging. 'How can you doubt you are living?'

She clutched herself. 'Sometimes I am locked so tightly in my head and cannot escape. The demons speak to me in my head.'

Mention of demons was unhelpful so I bent towards her and brushed her forehead with my lips. 'Would you feel that you were living if I kissed you?'

She looked startled, baffled, but she pursed her lips and we exchanged a chaste embrace. She did not shriek or push me from her and this seemed a momentous victory.

In the days after the season of Michaelmas, Kate began to walk with me beside the little River Waveney, clasping my arm and noting the changing colours of the trees. It was a simple but unmitigated joy to stand together in glorious autumn sunshine, shining low through the branches, to admire the russets and golds of fluttering leaves which shimmered against the glimmering water. The banks of that modest stream were made magical by the glitter of dew on the sodden grass and the magic was reflected in the clear brilliance of my wife's remarkable eyes. I discovered new hope during those miniature expeditions around my manor and sitting with Kate at table, elated to watch a gradual improvement in her appetite. I wanted no interruption in this fragile continuum of recovery but knew some intrusion by the wider world was inevitable. Fortunately the first such incursion was benign.

I was alarmed when Perkin announced a visitor had arrived to see me and begged a night's accommodation to break his journey, together with his small entourage, but I was delighted when I heard the visitor's name. I gave appropriate directions as hospitality demanded before hurrying to our parlour to greet the knight I had met at Queenborough Castle, Sir Nicholas Chamberlayne.

'I'm honoured to welcome you here. Are you travelling far?' I poured a beaker of wine and held it out to him.

'To Lynn. I've been at Wingfield and it seemed churlish not to call on you when I was so near. You'll not have heard the latest news.' I shook my head and after sipping his wine he continued. 'Richard of York has been processing in regal splendour across the country, accompanied by more than three thousand men. He's sent protestations of his loyalty to the King but they've been accompanied by complaints that his landing on Anglesey was opposed by armed soldiers. Be that as it may, while on the road he arranged to meet William Tresham, lately Speaker of the Parliament, but when William set out to meet him, villains attacked his party. Tresham was killed and his possessions stolen. York's attitude to this outrage may have been equivocal but when the Duke arrived at Westminster he behaved like a lunatic.'

Chamberlayne paused for effect and drank more deeply. 'He would not wait to be shown to the presence of the King but pushed his way into the royal chamber and laid hands on Henry, as if to shake sense into a refractory tradesman. This was an intolerable affront to the King's dignity.'

'Was York arrested?'

'No, our beneficent sovereign overlooked the solecism and accepted his cousin's assertions of loyalty, while York denied that he had any intention of challenging Henry for the throne. All is now harmonious and Richard

173

has retired to Ludlow to await the opening of Parliament in November. Nonetheless, the King is said to favour proclaiming Somerset Captain of Calais, in addition to his other honours, which would be a provocation to York so it may be supposed that the moment of confrontation between the noble rivals is merely postponed.'

I murmured a word of regret while Chamberlayne put the beaker to his lips again. 'My Lord of Somerset would be glad to welcome you to his house at Blackfriars when he resides there for the duration of the Parliament.'

I hesitated. 'That's gracious of him. My wife's health has improved but I'd be wary of bringing her to the City yet.'

'Perhaps you could pay a short visit without her. Think about it. But there's something else I want to ask you. What do you know of the Duke of Norfolk?'

'Very little. He's said to have been wild in his youth and his seat is at Framlingham.'

'Where he held an assembly of gentlemen, mainly from Norfolk, during the summer.'

'I heard something of that.'

'Did you hear the names of any who attended?' I shook my head and Sir Nicholas gave a mischievous smile. 'The names of Boice and Glasbury appear on the list I've seen.'

'I was told the Duke favoured Richard of York so perhaps that's not surprising.'

'He swithers in his allegiance but has no time for Somerset. Ostensibly the meeting at Framlingham was concerned with imposing order in the county of Norfolk where there's been unrest in recent months. I'm not aware that Glasbury has any interest in that county, although Boice may have, so there could have been other issues to discuss – maybe the subject was how to foster further unrest rather than curtail it.'

'York sees benefit in encouraging disorder?'

'He promotes himself as the champion of good order and the rule of law. I fancy he is looking for an opportunity to show he's capable of imposing both.'

'You mean his cohorts provoke unrest he could quell? A neat stratagem! One thing puzzles me. If the Duke of Somerset has the King's ear, won't he be able to pre-empt York by upholding law and order himself?'

Chamberlayne spread his hands on his knees and leaned back in his chair. 'My Lord, Edmund Beaufort, is charming and congenial as a companion and courtier. He has great and appealing talents but they are not limitless.'

I grinned at his tactful but informative reply and thereafter we spoke of more domestic matters. I took the risk of asking Kate to join us at table when we dined and was immensely encouraged to see how naturally she conducted herself, at ease with our guest. She seemed a little shy and seldom spoke but what she said was cogent and interesting. I felt we had taken a huge step forward in her recuperation.

When he left Worthwaite next morning and thanked me for the hospitality his party had received, Sir Nicholas referred respectfully to Mistress Somers as a delightful hostess. I could have hugged him for his courteous words, an independent endorsement of Kate's improved health. He slapped me on the shoulder as if I were an old friend and leant forward from his saddle to whisper in my ear.

'Do your best to come to London next month. Somerset would be pleased to meet you. Don't let yourself be viewed as tied to your wife's apron-strings in bucolic tranquillity, however alluring the prospect. You have a reputation as a physician – and more. Don't let it go to waste.'

*****

I had not resolved whether it would be possible to accede to Somerset's request when other events

175

intervened. The signs for a more stable domestic life had seemed promising but unfortunately I was so cheered by Kate's progress that I became foolhardy and her relapse was due to my own unthinking action. As days passed and she remained calm, I began to caress my wife as I had done in the early months of our marriage when our harmony was complete and she seemed happy with my attentions. Perhaps I should have waited longer, understood how frail her stability of mind was bound to be, given her more time to settle into the conjugal companionship I longed to share with her. My yearning to restore our loving relationship made me hasty and one night, when she responded passionately to my embraces as we sat together in her chamber, I lifted her and carried her to the bed where, since our arrival in Worthwaite, she had slept alone.

She loosened the laces of her stomacher so my hands could stray freely and lifted her skirt so I could stroke her thighs. In retrospect I know I should have gone no further but waited for another encounter when she had become used to the renewed intimacy between us. I should have recognised how closely the physical act was linked to the horrors which obsessed her mind. It is easy to be wise in retrospect. One moment she was holding me close and returning my kisses but the next, when I drew back and exposed my member, she screamed and hurled herself from the bed, seizing a small knife from its sheath hidden beneath her pillow.

Her eyes blazed with emerald brilliance while I covered myself and shrank away from her. 'Forgive me, Kate. I misunderstood...'

'You want me to bear your child! That's what you want of me. I won't, I won't. If you try to force me I'll kill myself.' Her voice soared into a frightening screech.

'No, Kate, no, I'd never force you. I beg you to trust me. I love you... please, put the knife down. I won't touch you unless you wish me to.'

Her eyes narrowed and she scowled at me. 'You want me to bear a child. You seek my recovery so you can thrust your seed into my womb.'

'I want you well for your own sake. It's in God's hands if we are to have children. I want us to share our love as we did in the past but not until you are ready.'

My words did not pacify her and I did not dare to reach for her knife. 'Go to your whore at Hartham Manor. Get her with child. Do you sleep with the whore's daughter too? Lady Eleanor? She's wed to a sodomite, I hear. Is the child she bore yours?'

I struggled to contain my anger. 'Certainly not. That's a gross slander on a virtuous young woman. And my association with Lady Maud is all in the past. I've never been with her since I met you. I promise you...'

I faltered, seeing her eyes glaze over as if she was looking past me into another time or place. She licked her lips and the moisture on them glistened in the candlelight. 'Sir Hugh de Grey's cock is larger than yours.'

My self-restraint snapped. 'Didn't you fear he would give you a child?'

She flung back her head and cackled, gesturing vulgarly. 'He had more finesse. Like others who have taken me. You're so prissy: you'd believe it against God's Holy law to penetrate elsewhere...'

'Stop it, stop it, Kate, you don't know what you're saying. You're overwrought. You must rest. I'll send Judith to you.'

'She'd open her legs for you if you asked. She lusts for you. Why don't you make her your concubine? That would satisfy us all. That's it! Fuck Judith – I give her to you!'

As Kate's voice grew louder the door opened a crack and I realised Judith had heard every word. She strode past me with determined steps and took the knife from her mistress's hand without provoking any resistance. Her face was flushed and, as she held out the weapon for me to take, her hand trembled.

'I didn't know she'd hidden the knife,' Judith said. 'I try to keep it from her. I'm sorry.'

I began to mutter something, deeply embarrassed, and missed Kate's sudden movement as she hurtled forward and wrenched the knife from Judith's fingers. My wife slashed at her own wrist and, although I snatched the blade from her, blood was pouring from her arm when she began to scream. While Judith held her, I bound the wound and gave her the potion which sedated her. After Kate slipped into sleep, I laid her decorously on her bed.

'It's lucky the knife sliced that side of her wrist, not the main blood vessel. I hope she'll be quieter when she wakes. Call me if I'm needed but it may be best for me to keep away from her.'

Judith looked up at me and nodded, business-like but now pale. 'I blame myself for not realising the knife was there.'

'It's not your fault. I shouldn't have upset her. I believed she was more fully recovered than she is – perhaps than she ever will be.'

Judith lowered her eyes. 'God's will be done. Leave her with me, Doctor. And whatever she said, don't take it to heart. It may not be demons put those thoughts in her head but her sickness is evil.'

I reeled from the room, numbed with anguish, unable to sob or think straight. For an hour I sat silently in the darkened hall until Perkin lit a sconce and placed a flagon of ale at my elbow. The dreadful scene with Kate was known to everyone within earshot in the house and there was no way of concealing its implications from them. They all appreciated that my wife's brittle state of mind led her to speak wildly but I regretted she had implied Judith would be willing to grant me her favours. Moreover Judith had overheard this. An appalling thought came to me as I remembered Piers' assertion that the young woman had settled her heart on someone other than him. What if that person was me? It would be mortifying for both of us if she were to declare herself. With all the problems facing me, this would be a complication I could not handle. I poured ale into a goblet and, in solitary misery, began to drink.

*****

The opening of Parliament at Westminster was due in just over a week and I resolved that it would be best for everyone at Worthwaite if I set off to attend Somerset as invited. I would return by the Feast of the Nativity at the latest. On the eve of my departure, however, a messenger arrived from Gaston de la Tour imploring me to go to Hartham Manor without delay because he believed his family was in danger. I told Perkin and Judith my changed plans but did not share them with Kate and set out, as if for London but striking across country to the north-east rather than heading directly south.

As soon as he learned I had entered the curtilage of his manor-house, Gaston rushed out to greet me and led me to his study without giving me the opportunity to greet his wife or mother-in-law. He looked in better health than when I had seen him some weeks previously but his brow was furrowed with worry. He handed me a goblet of wine, waved me to a chair and began to speak.

'Thank you, Harry, thank you for coming so speedily. I need your advice. Perhaps it's only Mowbray or some cowardly prankster harassing me because of my reputation or because I'm from Normandy: but I can't take the risk. It's become more serious, much more serious, than when we spoke before.'

His hand was shaking and he seemed to find it difficult to explain fully but it was clear where his concerns lay. 'Have you received a second message?'

'Not simply a written one this time: it's more ominous. Yesterday morning my favourite hound was discovered in the wood with his throat cut. An arrow to his flank had brought him down; then he'd been slashed across the gullet. I treasured him and now I'm afraid what – who – will be targeted next.'

179

'Can you be sure this incident is linked to the message you received before? Couldn't your hound have disturbed a poacher after your gamebirds?'

'In other circumstances, yes, but a poacher wouldn't have needed to finish off my dog when he'd already incapacitated the poor creature. In any case, a blood-soaked note lay under his paw. See.'

The edge of the sheet was stiff with dried gore but the words were legible. *Scum, villain, your quittance is approaching. This is but the first loss you will suffer. Your audacity will reap its reward.*

I remembered Sir Nicholas Chamberlayne's suspicion that adherents of Richard of York were fomenting trouble in Norfolk but I could see no link to the slaughter of Gaston's hound. 'It's certainly consistent with the first message. Do you think it came from someone on your estate? Surely an outsider wouldn't know which was your favourite hound, or where he might be, in order to do him injury?'

'A carefully concealed observer might note that the dogs were usually allowed to run loose beside the wood in the early morning. He might even have seen me with the hound on the leash when going to the hunt.'

I understood his reluctance to accept that one of his own servitors might nurture a dangerous grudge against him. 'Has there been any sign that your accession to the Fitzvaughan title is resented here?'

'Only by Lady Maud.'

'It's hardly likely her Ladyship would harm her daughter or grandson, if that's what you fear.'

Gaston shrugged. 'I accept that. I believe Lady Maud is capable of malice but she loves Eleanor and Walter and the threat has no meaning if it's not aimed at their safety.'

'Has any attempt been made to force you to comply with specific demands? Has Mowbray demanded your support?"

'No, the threat is not contingent. As I understand the message, I am considered to have earned the promised quittance without hope of mitigation.'

I agreed with his interpretation but could not dismiss the probability that the note came from someone at Hartham Manor. I lowered my voice. 'Is there no one who serves you with ill grace? No one you sense dislikes you? Can you trust all your followers equally?'

'I have no reason to suspect anyone who serves me.'

The words stuck in my throat but I forced them out. 'Do you believe Robin Willoughby is beyond doubt? As your bailiff he would have knowledge and opportunity to kill your hound.'

'I'd take my oath Robin Willoughby is an honest man. He is no dissembler.'

I smiled with relief. 'I think you're right.'

'Don't forget the first message came with correspondence from Framlingham but I suppose it could have been inserted into the messenger's pouch after he arrived here.'

'I don't think we can discount any possibility but there've been several weeks between the two missives. I wonder why that was.'

'No one has been absent from my estate during that time. Don't you think it points more strongly to someone from outside the demesne? I spoke of a concealed observer – such a person might have been in the vicinity for a few days. It would be possible to make enquiries in case a loiterer has been seen. At the moment Robin Willoughby and his men are looking for signs of a poacher. I don't want to alarm the household by suggesting it's a more dangerous scoundrel.'

'I suggest you confide more fully in Willoughby. He's sensible and is best placed to help if someone at the manor is involved. But it's true we can't discount a link to Framlingham and it needs to be pursued. I'm on my way to London, at the request of the Duke of Somerset. I could

181

journey there by way of Framlingham and make what enquiries I can about the people there. It's a long shot but it's the best I can suggest at present. Keep a strong guard around your family meanwhile.'

Gaston grasped my wrist. 'I will and I'll follow your advice and speak to Willoughby. God keep you, Harry. I'll be forever in your debt if you can solve this riddle and safeguard my family.'

These were not sentiments I had ever expected to hear Gaston de la Tour express.

*****

I dined with Gaston and Lady Eleanor and admired young Walter, their heir, who was an attractively sturdy infant. Lady Maud did not join us at table but sent a message asking me to call at the dower-house before I left Hartham Manor. She contrived that I received her invitation in the others' company so it would have been obvious if I shirked the demands of courtesy and failed to visit her. Gaston refrained from comment while looking exasperated but Eleanor rolled her eyes at me and grinned. After the meal I duly crossed the courtyard to the house where Bess and Robin had once lived and which I still found difficult to associate with Maud. In fact I found it even more difficult to think of Maud as a mourning dowager, not yet twelve months since her bereavement.

On this occasion she had not attempted in any way to reflect her status in her dress, flouting every convention. She wore a low-cut stomacher with a vivid yellow skirt and her golden hair was loose, cascading over her shoulders, with a curl straying provocatively over the swell of her bosom into the recess of her bodice. Deaf Marian hovered at the far end of the chamber, head lowered over intricate needlework.

I bowed with mannered civility. 'I'm pleased to see you looking in radiant good health, my Lady.'

182

'Tush, Harry. You know quite well why I've taken trouble with my appearance. I cannot stand this isolation, unable to entertain the most aged, menial male alone in my solar. Do you know I have even tried to seduce the Fitzvaughan bailiff, Master Willoughby? He's a well set-up fellow and I'd have overlooked the difference in our positions if he'd have taken me. But he's a boor, tied to the apron-strings of that pious girl who used to be my tiring-maid. Can you imagine the chagrin I endured when he repulsed me?'

'My Lady, you are incorrigible but I suspect you embroider the circumstances.'

'Oh, you are tiresome, Harry, you always see through my artifice. I wouldn't dare try to seduce Robin Willoughby, however enticing the prospect. Not only would he repulse me but he'd inform Gaston de la Tour of my transgression.'

It was a relief to laugh whole-heartedly after so many days of painful solemnity. 'Is there no news of an acceptable husband to content you?'

She flounced across the room. 'No, there is not. Perhaps in time I shall weaken so far as to accept one of the shrunken ancients Gaston offers but for the present I refuse them all. How is the incomparable Mistress Somers?'

Her question, coming abruptly, unnerved me and I stammered my reply. 'She's had a relapse. She isn't well.'

'Ah, you're really sorrowful, Harry. I can tell and I'm sorry. You truly care for that pathetic woman.'

Her unexpected perception took me by surprise and the sympathy in her eyes led me to express fears I kept guarded from others. 'I begin to dread that she may never completely recover. It's terrifying to see her when the madness overcomes her and she says cruel, hurtful things. She's a danger to herself and others.'

Maud swept to my side and I did not resist when she held me, smoothing my disordered hair. 'My poor Harry, it's wicked that you should suffer such a fate –

perhaps in its way as harsh as my own. We both had such capacity for love, did we not? And we are both condemned to make what we can of our lonely existences.'

Her lips pressed against my distorted cheek, then moved to my mouth and I returned her caress, gradually yielding to the urge to accept her comfort. After the months when I had espoused abstinence as the proper, patient, desired response to Kate's incapacity, my inhibitions melted away while Maud soothed and then roused me. I noticed the flick of her fingers directed towards the back of the room when she dismissed Marian and I did not protest. On the contrary, I let her lead me to a curtained recess which concealed her bed and I lifted her onto the counterpane.

Night had fallen by the time I departed from the dower-house and by then I had betrayed my marriage vows with grateful abandon. I knew I would suffer the pangs of remorse when the elation had passed but for the moment I embraced Maud with delight. 'I'm in your debt for your generosity but I should not come to you again,' I said with half-hearted rectitude as I left her.

'Nonsense,' her ladyship replied. 'I'm happy to resume my position as your occasional mistress. Since our youth you've been a serviceable lover and it gives me pleasure to excite your juices. Come as often as you can and save me from the nauseating tedium of propriety.'

It was a characteristically two-edged invitation guaranteed to tantalise me.

Chapter 15

Before I left Hartham Manor for Framlingham Castle I called on Piers Ford in his wheelwright's yard and was pleased to find him well settled. He was full of praise for the kindness of the Willoughbys and in particular mentioned that Mistress Bess reminded him of his own dead wife, which I found strangely upsetting. I asked him if he had heard about Lord Fitzvaughan's slaughtered hound as I was anxious to know what gossip there might have been on the subject among the workforce on the estate. He was reticent in his reply.

'Nasty business. I don't hold with killing dogs because their master's unpopular.'

'And Gaston de la Tour is unpopular?'

'Too strong a word probably: he's an incomer who's married well and lacks the common touch in dealings with his followers.'

'I think he feels awkward about his position himself.'

'You won't get labourers and skivvies appreciating their lord's finer feelings.'

'But would any of them mount a campaign of harassment – killing his dog as some kind of threat?'

'I don't think so. It was a lovely hound. Are you looking into its death for his lordship?' When I nodded, he looked round and then continued.

'On the day before the attack I saw a fellow in a strange livery lurking by the edge of the wood. He wasn't doing any harm but when he caught sight of me he scarpered back towards the trackway.'

'Could you make out the crest on the livery?'

'Not clearly. Some sort of dark bird, I'd say.'

It fitted with the impression of the worn seal on the first missive Gaston had received and I thanked Piers for his information, not expecting that he had anything to add.

'There've been troublemakers from further afield nosing round the place looking to stir up hostility against

Lord Fitzvaughan, not because of who he is but as if they were followers of Jack Cade hoping their wider complaints would be addressed.'

'Don't they know how Jack Cade ended?'

Piers laughed. 'They've heard but the lesson hasn't stuck. There's been an uprising here before, I gather.'

'More than one. Do you know where these troublemakers come from?'

'All over: town called Swaffham mostly.'

'They talk to you?'

Piers rubbed the back of his hand across his mouth. 'They know I've sympathy with their views but don't like violence.'

'Could these men have killed the dog?'

'I doubt it. It's not their style to be subtle and they're not aiming at Lord Fitzvaughan personally.'

'They don't wear the livery with a bird on it?'

'They don't wear livery at all. Worn tunics and tattered aprons are their working clothes and probably all they have.'

'It'll be helpful if you keep your eyes open for what's going on, Piers, but don't put yourself at risk.'

'I certainly won't, not on Lord Fitzvaughan's behalf. I'm not giving up the principles my grandfather taught me if there are well-meaning men I can help. Don't worry, Harry, I won't go out of my way to cause bother for your friends in the manor-house.'

I knew it was as much comfort as he would give me. I was glad to escape before he enquired after the dependants I had left at Worthwaite. I had locked my anguish for Kate in the deepest corner of my heart but I was already suffering paroxysms of guilt for betraying her.

*****

Framlingham Castle was a vast and impressive fortress from which John Mowbray, Duke of Norfolk, had for years harried his neighbours and fomented disorder.

He had been a sometimes violent opponent of my late overlord, William de la Pole and, when I arrived at his principal seat just as the light was fading, I was relieved to find he was not in residence. It was to be expected that all comers to the castle would be accorded hospitality and this lone physician travelling south was given the customary courtesies without question. I did not expect to know anyone in the household and it seemed ambitious to assume I would elicit any information relevant to the threats Gaston had received. Nevertheless I had to make the attempt.

I began by trying to converse with the serving man summoned to show me to the guest-chamber. I asked generally about the provision made for wayfarers seeking an overnight resting place.

'There'll be a pallet for you in the common hall,' he said, mistaking the reason for my curiosity. 'You've only got three companions so far, though others may arrive. Distinguished guests have separate accommodation.'

We squeezed past a group of well-dressed gentlemen in earnest conversation, blocking the corridor. 'I've heard you had many such guests at the castle in the summer.'

'And we still...'

His rejoinder was lost as one of the gentlemen swivelled round and grasped my shoulder with a cry of surprise. 'Harry Somers, by all the saints! What brings you here?'

I summoned my disorientated wits and bowed stiffly. 'Baron Glasbury, an unexpected encounter. I'm merely a traveller seeking a bed for the night.'

'Unlikely, I'd say, especially when you express an interest in previous guests at the castle.' He turned to the servant. 'Doctor Somers will share my chamber tonight. Have a good bed-frame and linen supplied there. He is by no means an ordinary wayfarer and I'd stake my supper I shall benefit from his conversation during the evening.'

There was no escape and, as the serving man hurried off, I was compelled to let Gilbert Iffley escort me to the lavishly furnished room placed at his disposal in one of the towers. To find him installed at Framlingham was unnerving but also intriguing and it gave me an opportunity I must not ignore. I suspected he would also have questions to put to me and, during the communal meal and entertainment in the great hall, I turned over in my mind the answers I must give. I was mindful of the Prioress's perceptive comment that I might offer a lure to catch Iffley but I also remembered how I had been willing to place myself in his power in a misconceived effort to save Hubert de Grey.

The occasion for our inevitable discussion arose after we returned to the Baron's room to share a jug of wine and he opened the proceedings in his familiar, ingratiating manner.

'You're commendably bold, Harry, to venture into John Mowbray's domain. He's set on hunting down Suffolk's former allies, among whom you would certainly be counted. Or dare I hope that you are reconsidering your reluctance to commit yourself to Richard of York's cause? Mowbray is his closest supporter.'

'I never thought I was making a declaration of allegiance by seeking a night's lodging in a hospitable castle. I'm simply pausing in my journey.'

'That's unconvincing from you, Harry. You rarely do anything without a hidden motive. I take it you want to know about Norfolk's visitors in the summer?'

'I was making idle conversation when you overheard me. There'd been talk of a gathering here and I thought it interesting. Should I enquire why you are at Framlingham?'

'No mystery there: I often have business with Mowbray's people, on behalf of Duke Richard. Framlingham's hardly on your route from Worthwaite to anywhere you'd be likely to visit.'

'You presume to comprehend my travelling plans? As it happens, I haven't come from Worthwaite.'

'Ah! Forgive me, I wasn't seeking to pry. How is Mistress Somers' health?'

'Indifferent, but she's in good hands. I'm free to journey when I wish.' I was bored with this polite parrying and decided to face him with a direct accusation. 'I can't pretend I'm comfortable to meet you, Baron. Since we crossed paths during Cade's uprising, I've become convinced that you had some responsibility for the deaths of both Adam Ash and little Hubert de Grey. You knew Stanlaw's propensities and you procured him the chance to act according to his foul nature.'

Iffley gave an extravagant sigh. 'Still harking on about those trivial incidents? Sometimes I despair of you, Harry. You have such potential to make a significant mark on the affairs of men but you allow yourself to be distracted by incidental affairs of small concern to the generality of mankind.'

'It is not the generality of mankind that concerns me in this case but the fates of two particular people. I suggest you surrender to the despair you speak of and abandon your attempts to win me to your way of thinking. We have nothing in common.'

'There I disagree. Why are you going to London?'

I was proud that I did not hesitate in my reply. 'I never said I was. Were you present at the gathering here in the summer?'

'Good. As I hoped, you're willing to trade. That's what I prefer. Are you sent for by someone attending the Parliament?'

'Not sent for: invited to call. I've accepted no commitments.'

'Somerset?'

Curse the man, he was far too astute but he had confirmed his interest in my movements. I had no alternative but to exploit the situation. 'I've been recommended to him as physician but my family obligations make it improbable that I can accept his offer.'

Iffley smiled with vulpine cunning.

'Oh, but you should, Harry. You could be an invaluable contact for me, in the heart of Somerset's household.'

'You and Stephen Boice tried to use that ploy with me when I served Suffolk and you did not succeed in bending me to your will.'

'Times and personalities have changed. Somerset lacks William de la Pole's intelligence. You won't warm to him in the same way. Think about this, when you've met him, and see if you might willingly become a channel to Richard of York, reporting on what you learn while serving Edmund Beaufort. But trade is trade, you've answered my enquiry. I might offer something in return. Why are you interested in the summer meeting here?'

'Someone at Framlingham around that time sent a vile message to the new Lord Fitzvaughan at Hartham Manor and it's been followed up with unpleasant action. I want to know who did this and whether it's designed to put pressure on his lordship to support Richard of York or if there's some more personal motivation.'

Iffley sank back in his chair and stretched out his legs. 'Well, well, you're acting for Gaston de la Tour; I am surprised. There were so many men here who might have reason to dislike the fellow.'

'Did you send a note to him, Baron, using another's seal? Or did Stephen Boice? I'm sure you'd know if he did.'

'I'm certain he did not and neither did I.' He paused and twirled the wine in his goblet, smiling slyly. 'But I'd fancy you were right in surmising it might have been done through personal spite. I'd hazard a guess who might have done it. He was here again until a few days ago.'

It was too circumstantial to ignore. I was trapped. 'What's your price?' I knew the answer.

'That you accept Somerset's offer and keep in contact with me.'

'I refuse to act as your spy.'

'That isn't what I asked. My words are to be taken literally. Do you want me to share my hunch or not?'

'My wife's health may compel me to return to Worthwaite.'

'Understood.'

'I won't betray any specific confidence I'm given.'

'Understood.'

'If I merely report information which you could glean from elsewhere, what use will that be to you?'

'That's for me to judge but what I expect is that you will be able to report something not available from outside the household. Gossip.'

'Gossip?

'Exactly: the gossip of servants about their superiors. That's all I'm asking. I don't deny the occasion might arise when I need to put a more specific request to you but, at such a time, you would be free to accept or refuse my request.'

There was inevitably a hidden motive for this superficially facile request but I could not identify it. I pretended to consider the alternatives before replying. 'Very well, on those assumptions, I accept your terms.'

He pushed the jug towards me with a self-satisfied smirk. 'Roger Egremont, titular Earl of Stanwick, has become an habitué at Framlingham although he's on his way to the Parliament at present. Don't you think he might have a grudge against sweet Gaston? He bears an empty title while Gaston's fertile little wife has conferred on her husband all the Stanwick lands her father left her.'

I was dumbstruck by my stupidity. Why had I not thought of the possibility? Roger Egremont was a violent, resentful fellow who was known as one of Richard of York's adherents. He had sought to marry Lady Eleanor and thereby reunite the Stanwick lands at Ravensmoor in Yorkshire with the title he bore: Ravensmoor which accounted for a raven in his crest. He must hate Gaston de la Tour who thwarted these aspirations. Moreover, his animosity was not confined to the new Lord Fitzvaughan. In a fracas earlier in the year he had tried to kill me and been badly injured himself. I swallowed hard.

'I'm obliged to you, Baron.'

Gilbert Iffley roared with laughter. 'How it stuck in your maw to admit that, Harry Somers. I shall treasure the memory. I take it that your concern to resolve Fitzvaughan's difficulties signifies that you've taken his mother-in-law, the redoubtable Lady Maud, to your bed again? How truly delightful! And how still more welcome is your commitment to serve Richard of York by providing information – gossip – from within Somerset's household. Your affectionate nature was bound to be your undoing one day. This time we have you, physician, this time we have you.'

I feared what he said was true although I could not detect his purpose. At least he was unaware that I was also pledged to inform on his activities to the Prioress of St. Michael's and her associates. It was a small consolation in my hazardous double role.

*****

I left the chamber before Baron Glasbury was awake and was pleased to join a large contingent of travellers riding from the castle to London, thereby offering protection from the dangers of the road. Many men wore Mowbray's colours and were to swell their lord's entourage when he attended Parliament. Others had completed the business which took them to Framlingham and were returning home to the City. At the back of our column a number of wagons trundled along and our progress was punctuated by cries of the drivers urging their carthorses to keep pace with the rearmost riders. I was happy to be among the slowest of these, my mind somewhat hazy from an excess of wine and sleep disturbed by remembrance of my conversation with Iffley. I had not yet sent a message to Gaston de la Tour, naming Roger, Earl of Stanwick, because I did not trust the integrity of any messenger service operated on behalf of John Mowbray, so I passed the time composing in my head the letter which I would send when I found a reliable emissary.

We made a stop on open ground to eat the provisions brought with us from Framlingham and, despite the covering of wet leaves blown on the trampled earth, I stretched out to relieve the ache in my lower back provoked by too long in the saddle. I closed my eyes but opened them instantly as a voice I recognised hailed me.

'By all that's holy, I do believe it's Doctor Somers. I'd not have credited the evidence of my own eyes but I heard you'd spent the night at the castle.'

I had no forewarning so my surprise was greater than his but I tried not to show it. 'Master Toft, you've ventured far from Maidstone.'

He squatted on his haunches beside me. 'I made a bit of money from our adventures in London so I've been able to expand into other areas where I do business. Had a consignment of goods to deliver to the Duke of Norfolk's chamberlain. Baron Glasbury and his family hire my carts from time to time to convey such loads. Didn't expect to see you among John Mowbray's entourage.'

'I'm merely travelling with the group for convenience. I had a trifling commission to fulfil at Framlingham.' I was annoyed that I felt it necessary to account for my visit and preferred not to think of the ill-gotten gains which had funded Toft's prosperity.

'Strange bedfellows we have these days, Doctor.'

What did he mean by that? I was already wary of the carter and his acknowledged link to Gilbert Iffley made me doubly cautious. If that connection was long-standing, I might need to reconsider Toft's role at Blackheath. He had purported to be supportive of Piers Ford, assisting the wheelwright's avoidance of Baron Glasbury's men, letting me know the fugitive might be in Essex, emphasising that

193

he knew Piers was innocent of George Antey's murder. Could this have been artifice intended to deceive me? Could it in fact have been Toft who was responsible for his colleague's death? How close was he to Iffley? Was Toft part of the network which served the Baron? If so, why was he now drawing my attention to the possibility?

'I would hope rivals might be reconciled and legitimate grievances remedied.' I spoke guardedly.

Toft made a face. 'They tell me there are tales of horses which flew in years gone by. As likely, I'd say, as your hopes being realised. You'd best keep away from Framlingham when the Duke returns. He's sworn to do for every man who favoured Suffolk.' He made a slashing action with his hand across his throat.

Then he winked and what he said next undermined the earlier impression he had fostered of a casual meeting. 'If you've a message for the Baron when you're in London, pass it to Ned Bartlett, one of Somerset's grooms. He'll make sure it reaches Glasbury.'

Before I could comment, Toft had turned back towards the carts and hailed another driver.

It was a disturbing encounter, carefully crafted and loaded with ambiguous meaning.

Chapter 16

On my arrival in the City I went first to call on Thomas and Grizel who offered me stability in an unpredictable world. I would also be able to glean from them something of the situation in London, now Parliament was sitting. Thomas was busy in his workshop but I found Rendell in his sister's kitchen, boots off and jerkin flung aside, nephews scrambling on his shoulders. He swung the youngest boy round onto his knee and hooted with laughter.

'The country yokel's come to town and he wants to know what's happening in the big city. Listen to this then: one of York's mates is appointed Speaker but Parliament won't handle any business until the Duke returns from Ludlow, next week they say. Then the fun'll begin.'

Grizel wiped floury hands on a cloth. 'Somerset's lodging at Blackfriars and his supporters are installed in their houses nearby. You can sense the tension in the streets and when Richard of York comes there's bound to be trouble. Keep out of it, Harry.'

'Why d'you think he's come to town, Griz? Can't help himself, can he? Is Somerset after your services?'

Rendell was always sharp and it was clear he was well attuned to affairs of state. He rubbed his nose. 'Get a lot of information at the Tower, we do, if we keep our ears open. The King's in a right panic, they say, at the prospect of his royal cousins facing each other down across his throne. There's no doubt he favours the affable Somerset more than austere Richard.'

Grizel wagged her finger at her brother. 'Enough of that dangerous talk! Hal and Dickon are listening and might repeat what they shouldn't hear. Off you go, you two. Take Tom and run round the yard for a bit. Give your uncle some peace but don't go out into the street.' She turned to me with a shrug. 'See what a fretful mother I've become. You'd never have expected it, would you? But there's been a child carried off two streets away and his tiny corpse dumped in a gutter. Unbelievable barbarity.'

The villainous Stanlaw was dead but he was not the only perverted abuser lying in wait for infant prey. I shuddered but Grizel did not linger on the subject. She wagged her finger at her brother a second time. 'And you'd best change the subject, Rendell.'

The royal guardsman chuckled and lifted his baby niece from the cradle with surprising gentleness. 'Nag, nag, what a harridan your mother is, little Margery.' He glanced up at me. 'And how's that other vixen, sour-faced Judith? Is she still at Worthwaite?'

'She is and she's invaluable in caring for my wife.'

Grizel probably identified the forced lightness in my tone. 'How is Kate?'

'Up and down, her health varies but she's happy with Judith. The girl has a knack for comforting her.'

'Keep her safe at Worthwaite.' Thomas had entered the room, brushing sawdust from his tunic onto his wife's tidy floor. 'The City's no place for anyone in delicate health. Good to see you, Harry, but I imagine your presence here implies trouble's afoot. It follows you around. Anyway, let's celebrate your visit. Get the jug of ale, Griz, and we'll drink a round without mention of any damned Dukes and the disruption to trade their antics cause. Confound all nobles!'

*****

Next day I presented myself at Somerset's lodgings and was received with courtesy by his steward who was fully informed about the proposal for me to become physician to the household and the problem I faced in committing myself. A room had been prepared for my use and I was soon occupied with a succession of servants who consulted me on a variety of minor ailments and a handful of more ominous symptoms. By the end of the day I was weary but experiencing deep satisfaction that I could once more practise my profession.

I wrote my letter to Gaston de la Tour and consigned it to a trusty messenger bound for East Anglia. I had done all I could to help Lord Fitzvaughan and he must now take steps to defend his family and lands against a dangerous enemy. I knew that across the country local tensions between landholders had turned to violence. In the absence of effective law enforcement there were few constraints on aggression. Roger Egremont's venomous hatred could flourish unchecked in such unruly times.

I also recalled the concern Sir Nicholas Chamberlayne had expressed about Mowbray's acolytes stirring up unrest and, although it might have been inappropriate for me to tell him of the threats Gaston had received, I wrote a short note on the subject, naming Roger Egremont. I asked Somerset's steward to forward this to Sir Nicholas wherever he was known to be.

My pleasure in my new post lasted just over a week, during which I did not meet Duke Edmund in person. This omission was unimportant as I had no expectation of forming with Somerset the personal bond I built with the late Duke of Suffolk. It would be rewarding enough to serve a large and diverse assembly of retainers and their families who presented me with a daily hotchpotch of strains, cuts, stuffed nostrils and bellyaches.

Indications that change was afoot came as soon as Richard of York entered London with a vast entourage, when the atmosphere in the streets became charged with latent antagonism. Crowds of emboldened apprentices shouted at passers-by demanding they declare their allegiance and intimidating those who gave inadequate replies. Somerset's friends needed their wits about them, concealing their identity, to avoid a thrashing from the armed bands which roamed the City flaunting York's emblem of the fetterlock. At every tavern scores of ruffians were to be found drinking deeply to fuel their belligerence. Trepidation among the populace was palpable and cautious citizens kept to their houses.

During the hours of darkness silent contests of propaganda ensued. On walls and fences badges with the fetterlock design appeared, only to be torn down and replaced by the royal coat of arms. By the following morning the process had been reversed and York's crest was dominant, before the cycle was repeated. The Lord Mayor ordered that chains be strung across the streets to thwart mass disorder but, for three days running, Richard of York and the Duke of Norfolk rode through the City with a huge company of armed men as escort, greeted by a raucous mob screaming support.

I continued to visit Thomas and Grizel when I could but in the last week of November I decided it was foolhardy to venture so far alone as I could not be confident of returning unscathed. Rendell and his colleagues at the Tower had been confined to their base, ready to be deployed in its defence, and that fact alone showed how feeble the Governor's ability to impose order had become. Without question some climax must arise: the only uncertainty was when and how.

On the first day of December the issue was resolved in a frightening manner. Somerset's own lodgings were attacked in an outburst of fury by discontented hooligans egged on by disciplined men of war. I was in the garret of the house, in the servants' quarters, at the bedside of an elderly retainer who had been taken short of breath but whose condition stabilised once he was resting. The shouting and thumping outside the house had become a familiar accompaniment to my ministrations and at first I took no notice of the cacophony but, when it intensified, I guessed a party of Somerset's followers, and perhaps the Duke himself, was attempting to enter the premises through the ranks of a cat-calling, stone-throwing throng.

I heard the clash of arms and much scuffling before the thud of the front door suggested the new arrivals had succeeded in effecting entry, but this was followed swiftly by the pounding of a ram against the exterior framework. Then, as the noise below grew louder, I was summoned to attend a wounded attendant, stabbed through the fracturing panels of the woodwork, and I hurried downstairs.

When I reached the principal floor I ran into a bevy of gentlemen, some clutching bundles of possessions, scurrying in confusion towards the back stairs. Seeing bloodied sleeves and ripped jerkins, I realised there were several potential patients for me to assist but no one was seeking medical attention in the hubbub. Flight from the house was the priority while, in the entrance hall beneath us, an actual battle had erupted and intruders were seizing goods from the ground floor rooms to carry off as loot.

The Duke's steward grabbed my shoulder and propelled me through the jostling crowd and down the narrow stairs, using his authority to demand passage ahead of inferior retainers. The postern door of the house gave direct access to the river and a barge flying the Beaufort pennant was making ready to cast off from the jetty. In an instant I was hustled onto the vessel and pushed towards the stern where an awning covered a cushioned seat on which a man was sitting with a rag pressed to his forehead.

'Your Grace, this is Doctor Somers. He will dress your injury.'

Thus it was that I first made the acquaintance of Edmund Beaufort, Duke of Somerset, of royal descent, grandson of the illustrious John of Gaunt.

The gash below the hairline was unpleasant but not serious and I cleaned it as best I could with river water while recommending that, when we had landed somewhere secure, two stitches should be inserted to encourage healing. The Duke frowned.

'Careful stitching will make it less likely a scar will be visible, your Grace.'

I had guessed correctly what was perturbing my handsome patient. He smiled and grasped my wrist. 'You guarantee that, physician?'

'No, your Grace, I can't give guarantees but I will do my best.'

He patted my hand. 'I appreciate your honesty and you've staunched the bleeding. You're welcome to my household. There are others needing your services now. Come back to me when we put in to land and sew me together.'

He sounded agreeable enough but I thought him a light-weight figure compared with the late William de la Pole. No doubt he was able to cajole gentle King Henry without alarming him and I could imagine Queen Margaret responding well to his charming blandishments. Richard of York might be a more successful warrior and skilful administrator but he lacked the graces Edmund Beaufort possessed. I wished it was possible to combine the virtues of each man and eliminate their weaknesses; ideal royal counsellors were not created to order.

The Duke of Somerset was safe but his house was ransacked, as were those of two Beaufort supporters linked, in popular opinion, to the loss of Normandy. The Duke of Norfolk's men were said to have been implicated in the violence and I wondered whether Roger Egremont, Earl of Stanwick, had been among the perpetrators. It would accord with his natural instincts.

Only one of Somerset's attackers was captured and speedily beheaded on Cheapside: a token to deter further rioting. The City Fathers, horrified by the outrage in their midst, decreed that law and order be enforced and they turned to the one champion they saw as competent to secure this: the very man in whose name the disturbances took place. Thus it was that Richard of York rode through the streets proclaiming, in the King's name, justice against thieves and rebels and receiving the plaudits of the authorities. Two days later King Henry followed suit with a parade through London accompanied by an imposing escort. Then the royal party retired to Greenwich where they remained to celebrate the Feast of the Nativity.

The scales of power had tilted and, for the moment, Somerset's glory was eclipsed. Yet how decisively the balance had shifted was unclear. Richard of York's preeminence among the King's counsellors was likely to be challenged for many among the nobility distrusted him. His actions were taken scrupulously in Henry's name, without any attempt to challenge the crown, which was admirably correct, but there was food for thought in the fact that the disorder in the City, which he sought to quell, had been instigated by his own adherents. Meanwhile, our kind-hearted sovereign, who doubtless wanted nothing more than reconciliation between his hot-tempered relatives, misguidedly fanned the flames of their rivalry. As Sir Nicholas Chamberlayne had foretold, he named Somerset Captain of Calais, perhaps in the hope that the royal favourite could withdraw safely across the Narrow Sea, but it was a position York was said to covet and the cousins' mutual loathing was not abated.

I had nothing of significance to report which was not already public knowledge, for I was privy to no confidences in Somerset's household, but I duly passed brief messages describing daily activities to Ned Bartlett, the groom, for transmission to Gilbert Iffley. I would fulfil my part of the bargain we had made but I hoped Glasbury would soon come to accept that my position in the Duke's employ was never likely to give me access to the kind of information he craved. The main burden of my reports was that Somerset was often absent from his own lodgings, in attendance at the court, which was hardly newsworthy.

I wrote an account of the attack on the Duke and his house for the Prioress in Stamford, sharing with her my own reflections on responsibility for the outrage. She would lament the breakdown of law and order in the City but ensure that the Abbot of Peterborough was informed of my report. He was a key contributor to the Church's impressive network of information and influence. Both he and the Prioress knew of my arrangement with Gilbert Iffley and she, at least, was amused by my double-dealing.

*****

I had promised to return to Worthwaite for the season of Nativity but it was a promise I did not keep. Partly this was due to the continuing need for my services in Somerset's household, which I could justify to myself professionally. If I was truthful, however, I recoiled from the risk of aggravating Kate's mental turmoil and the pain of watching as her wits fragmented. The diligent Perkin had written reporting on my wife's condition and he quoted Judith's message that *'Mistress Somers is inclined to melancholy but she is peaceful'*. I thought this improvement as much as I could hope for and dreaded a repetition of the disastrous impact my actions had on her previously.

I gladly spent time with the Chope household during the festivities and, with uneasy calm restored in the City, Rendell was allowed to join us one afternoon. My young friend joined in rumbustious games with his nephews but I could tell he was disgruntled and when an opportunity arose to speak to him alone, out in the yard, I asked what had annoyed him. He was unexpectedly frank.

'Don't want to spend the rest of my life cooped up in the Tower. Bored with standing on guard with no action, put on alert then nothing happens. I want to travel again like I did with you, Doctor: France, the Italian States, even the north of England. I'm bloody fed up with it all.'

'Why the sudden change? You seemed to relish getting inside information on affairs of state from being in the Tower.'

He spat onto the midden and stamped his foot. 'You always were too quick at knowing what was in my head better than I did. There's a girl among the laundry maids, I had her a few times and was getting sweet on her, more than I'd done before. Now she's upped and got hand-fasted to one of the gate-keepers. Told me to get lost, she did, as if I was an old glove that didn't fit any more.'

'Bad luck. It happens but that doesn't make it easier. You remember how Leone was moonstruck more than once but always seemed to be rejected in favour of someone else?'

'Yeah, I used to poke fun at him. Never thought I'd get so fixed on a floozy. Christ, women are fucking cock-teasers, nothing more.'

'Most aren't. You've been unlucky.'

'I keep seeing the whore mincing her way across the outer bailey and she's driving me mad with her airs and graces. I could throttle the bitch.'

'You must let her go, Rendell. Don't allow her to become an obsession that twists your mind. It'll be painful for a while but your life can move on if you let it.'

'I reckon it could if I got away from the Tower. Ain't got much chance while I keep seeing her.'

'Is there any possibility of the Governor sending you elsewhere?'

'Only if someone important asks. I wondered if Somerset might need an extra bodyguard. I'm a good fighter. You know that. You could vouch for me.'

Now I understood why I had been honoured with Rendell's personal confidences and I wanted to help him. 'I'll see what I can do but I've only met Somerset a couple of times. You'll have to be patient. Don't get into trouble in the meantime or the Governor won't be helpful.'

Rendell gave a broad grin. 'You've got a plan, haven't you, Doctor? I knew you'd come up with an idea.'

An idea was indeed forming in my mind but I could not at that stage see any way towards its implementation.

*****

When Parliament reconvened in January, York was riding high and the Commons offered him support by submitting to the King a list of twenty-nine persons they wanted removed from the court. Inevitably Somerset's name headed the list which included some of Suffolk's former circle, even Alice, the Dowager Duchess, safely ensconced at Wingfield. As usual King Henry sought to placate the critics without endangering his friends and he agreed to banish many of those named from his presence for the period of one year. Specifically, however, those suspended from the court did not include Somerset. Instead Henry directed that the Duke be confined in the Tower for his own safety: the same formula he had adopted previously in vain attempts to safeguard Suffolk and Lord Saye and Sele.

I was not asked to attend Somerset during his brief sojourn in the Tower. He was quickly released, at the insistence of the Queen who was aware of the unfortunate precedents and confident of her influence over the King. This was a gauntlet thrown down to York who must have been perplexed as to what more he could do to outmanoeuvre his less competent Beaufort cousin. Despite the wild cries of hired rabble-rousers in the streets, he lacked the widespread backing he needed if he was to oust Somerset as principal adviser and ensure King Henry followed his guidance. Crucially, the great nobles of the north, the Earls of Northumberland and Westmorland, were firmly opposed to him and only the impetuous Duke of Norfolk endorsed his cause, to questionable effect.

I watched these events from the comfort of Somerset's household, noting with satisfaction that there was no sign that Baron Glasbury had followed his patron to the City. This indicated to me that there was no credible plot for York to seize power, still less to assert any claim that the throne was rightfully his, for Gilbert Iffley would have found his natural place at the heart of such a conspiracy. Over the following weeks I concentrated my attention on the patients I attended, augmented in number as a virulent version of the rheum spread among Beaufort's servants.

A cryptic report from Perkin at Worthwaite suggested there might be renewed problems related to my wife's health but it gave no details and I thrust the matter aside, so it should not threaten my general sense of contentment. I appeased my conscience by obtaining Somerset's permission to absent myself from London to visit my manor during the season of Easter which was fast approaching. The hours of daylight were growing longer and, although the wind funnelled bitter chill along the City streets, it was possible to believe spring was at hand in narrow gardens behind close-packed houses. Still more would it be obvious in the countryside and I persuaded myself a journey to Worthwaite would be a pleasing proposition.

The misgivings I had at that time related to Rendell, whose temper frayed as his frustration increased. He had received a reprimand from his captain for engaging in fisticuffs with a fellow soldier at the Tower and I feared he might commit a more serious misdemeanour which could damage his prospects irreparably. I knew what I would like to arrange on his behalf but could see no way of securing it, for I had no influence with Somerset comparable to that I enjoyed with Suffolk. I seldom saw the Duke in person but, with little hope he would heed my request, I wrote a short note of supplication to him.

I was reflecting on this unfortunate situation while on my way to visit Thomas and Grizel a week before my intended departure for Worthwaite. It may have been because Rendell was in my mind that I took a longer route than usual, crossing the concourse outside the walls of the fortress in order to enter the back-street where the Chopes lived. A year previously one of the grander dwellings on Tower Hill had been occupied by Stephen Boice and others of Iffley's cronies, when they were plotting Suffolk's downfall, and I had been assaulted there. Fortunately there had been no sign of their continued use of the premises and they were far from my thoughts as I passed the entrance. I was totally unprepared when the door was flung open and two muscular ruffians set upon me and dragged me inside.

I had no opportunity to draw my small dagger and it would have been ineffective against those brawny assailants. They quickly disarmed me and, while one held my arms rigidly behind my back, the other kneed me in the groin and belaboured my face and chest with his fists. My mouth was full of blood and one eye closed before they flung me forward on the tiled floor of the entrance hall, to land at the feet of a newcomer who had joined us. With a gloved hand, this amiable fellow seized a handful of my hair and pulled up my head to face him before depositing a globule of wine-infused sputum on my cheek.

'This time, physician, you will receive your dues,' said Roger Egremont, Earl of Stanwick. 'Last time we met in arms, your disciple saved your life and nearly took mine. This time I propose to hack off your privates and then cut your throat.'

Chapter 17

I was close to losing consciousness when they hauled me into an adjoining room and strapped me to a table where I presumed the initial part of my dismemberment was to be accomplished. It was not the first time I had faced death at an enemy's hands but there was no prospect now that Rendell, who had rescued me more than once, could come to assist me. No one knew where I was or that I was in any peril. The only possible defence against the Earl of Stanwick's gruesome intentions lay in my own wits and they were befuddled by pain and scarcely functioning. He glowered over me and, seeing me close to fainting, threw a jug of ale into my face.

The rough liquid splashing into my open wounds was agonising but it brought me to my senses and I yelped. The Earl drew back to extract a thin curved knife from a case of weapons laid out on a stool and with a flourish slashed through a cushion beside it.

'Adequately sharp for my purposes,' he said. 'Imagine your balls splattering the floor like these feathers. There's no need for finesse in this surgery, eh, physician?'

I licked blood from my lips, trying to summon fluency. 'Scum, villain, so this is to be my quittance?' My voice was weak but my words were intelligible and Egremont frowned. 'Those are terms you understand, my Lord Earl; they are ones you enjoy using.'

'What are you talking about?'

'Your threats to Gaston de la Tour. He will know where to look for my killer. He's already aware who is menacing his family. He'll seek a warrant...'

My attempt at bravado was cut off by the Earl's fist. 'I have the protection of the Duke of Norfolk, you simpleton. I can do what I please in the lands where he is overlord. That upstart, so-called Lord Fitzvaughan, asked for your help, did he? I'll show him how ineffective your assistance has proved to be. Then I intend to slaughter him and his heir and carry off his widow to make her my bride, as she always should have been.'

'It's the lands of Ravensmoor you really want: the Stanwick inheritance to go with your title.' It was an effort to focus my eyes but I knew he was listening to me.

'They are rightfully mine. The girl is my late cousin's bastard. She had no claim to inherit.'

'He was free to leave the estate where he chose and Eleanor's claim was legitimised.' I spluttered but made myself continue. 'I wonder you didn't seek to negotiate with Gaston. He has no interest in Ravensmoor.'

'What do you mean?

'Now he's Lord Fitzvaughan his interests are at Hartham Manor.'

'There are sizable rents from Ravensmoor.'

'He's already rich. A castle in the north of Yorkshire, even with its farms and hunting grounds, doesn't compare with Hartham. Besides, he still has his patrimony in Normandy.'

'You can't believe he'd give me Ravensmoor.'

'He might have done if you'd approached him in a civil manner. I doubt he will now you've threatened his family and killed his hound.' I held my breath when Egremont did not immediately respond. 'But he might.'

'He might not and I'd be a laughing stock.'

'If you use force against Hartham Manor you'll become an outlaw. John Mowbray won't be able to save you if you kill Lord Fitzvaughan – Gaston's a noted hero of the French wars. Forcible marriage of an heiress is a serious offence...'

I never finished the arguments I was attempting to marshal with fading strength. Roger Egremont's patience was exhausted. I did not see him put down the knife, for my eyelids were closing, but in the next moment I felt the pummelling of his fists and then, as he toppled the table, his boots drubbing my groin as I lay on the floor. Darkness enfolded me.

*****

There were moments of lucidity during the night. Remembrance came fleetingly and I could not understand why my demise had not been accomplished in the vile manner Egremont promised. The throbbing of my battered body soon prevented rational thought. I was bruised from head to foot, especially in the nether regions, and there was no balsam to lessen the aching, no poultice of herbs to soothe the open wounds. I could not be sure whether or not a rib had been broken. Compounding insult with injury, my wrists and ankles had been fettered, even when I was incapable of standing. Yet I was alive and had been laid on a pallet, so I must view this as encouraging. I told myself sleep was restorative and let my weakness carry me into fractured rest.

In the morning, a taciturn servant gave me drink and slopped gruel between my swollen lips while ignoring my questions. When he had gone, I dragged myself into a sitting position but, although I could see where my gown was ripped and stained, I could not examine my injuries with bound hands. I shouted a few times and was ignored so I reconciled myself to waiting, for surely Egremont would come at some point to explain his change of plan and outline his revised, but probably equally distasteful, intentions? In the interval I concentrated on regaining my strength, breathing deeply and moving my constricted limbs as much as I could to test their flexibility.

The sun had moved round to shine through the small window high in the wall when I heard angry voices in the corridor: men, who stopped outside the door, arguing. The thickness of the stonework prevented me hearing their words but the tones were clear enough. A burst of protest identified Roger Egremont but the other speaker was more restrained and difficult to distinguish until the door clattered open and I realised I knew him all too well. Gilbert Iffley, Baron Glasbury, strode across to where I sat crouched on my pallet and, from his expression, I came to the astonishing conclusion that, uniquely, his presence might advantage me.

He rounded on the Earl, in no way moderating his outrage in front of me. 'You dolt, you drunken ignoramus, you've ruined my plans! It's taken me years to cajole Doctor Somers into assisting us, putting him in a position where he's honour-bound to act on Richard of York's behalf when I request it. Now, you've half killed him. If you'd gone any further you'd have rendered him useless for my purposes, just when he's started to give me invaluable information.'

'How was I to know? Somers is my enemy and his life is forfeit to me. Get someone else to do your spying. Anyway he's still alive. For the moment. I'm taking him to Hartham Manor to use as bait to catch this jumped-up Norman who styles himself Lord Fitzvaughan. This is my business, Baron Glasbury. Keep your interfering nose out of my revenge.'

'You're an idiot. You're wholly dependent on Richard of York's patronage. If you pursue this vendetta you'll lose it and have nothing.'

'I aim to have Ravensmoor. No piffling physician will stand in my way. Mowbray will help me.'

'Mowbray is Duke Richard's associate but he's unreliable and can be a dangerous liability.'

I watched in fascination as Iffley seized the front of Egremont's gown and bellowed in his face 'You will do as you are told, my Lord Earl, and set Somers free. Unlock his fetters now. Then you will send for an apothecary to treat his wounds. He's a free man. You understand? I must depart for Ludlow shortly. You will accompany me and comply with my orders. I shall ensure Somerset is informed that his physician has been set upon by vagabonds and is recovering in the care of friends. If you try to defy me, I shall name you as the man responsible. You understand?'

Egremont mumbled something angrily but he unlocked my shackles and Iffley addressed me for the first time. 'My profound apologies, Harry: this should not have happened.'

I was amused to hear Iffley acknowledge that there were some misadventures he could not control but it hurt to curve my lips into a grin. 'I'm glad you came, Baron, the Earl had threatened to castrate me before cutting my throat.'

'I'd already changed my mind,' Egremont objected. 'I want you to negotiate with Lord Fitzvaughan. You said yourself I should have tried negotiation.'

'You described using me as bait to trap Lord Fitzvaughan. That's not negotiation.'

The effort of speaking hurt my chest and I put my hand on my ribs, gulping, while Iffley shouted for his attendant, the man lacking front teeth I remembered from Blackheath. 'Doctor Somers needs help. We must send for another physician or an apothecary.'

'No,' I said as forcibly as I could. 'I won't stop in this house when you've gone, Baron. My friends live only a stone's throw from here. If your man can help me to get there, I'll be in safe hands. I'll remember your assistance with gratitude.'

'If you're confident you can manage to walk with our shoulders to lean on, I'll attend you to their door myself. As for you, Egremont, I'm placing you under guard and I forbid you to go near Hartham Manor on pain of denunciation before the King's Council. I shall report every detail of your outrageous behaviour to Richard of York. Don't look for his patronage in future.'

He was surprisingly strong, lifting me from the pallet with ease. Then, with his man on my other side, he escorted me from the house while I bit my tongue to prevent crying out in agony at the movement. Behind us, Roger Egremont could be heard babbling incoherently in frustration and fury. This at least was satisfying.

*****

A small boy playing with a top screamed in terror when we entered the yard of the Chope house but Grizel was soon in control of the situation. She dismissed my escort with courteous words of thanks and directed an apprentice to fetch the nearest apothecary. A servant helped her strip off my tattered clothes and bathed my excruciatingly tender body. This enabled me to examine my injuries for the first time: a patchwork of inflammation, which would turn to discoloured bruises, with here and there black concentrations of clotted blood beneath the skin. In some places, including on my head, there was swelling and, where I had been kicked, there were also cuts, some unpleasantly deep but not, I judged, needing to be stitched.

The apothecary came quickly and brought salves, with a tincture of columbine, for my bruises. He peered doubtfully at a jagged wound on my inner thigh, where a heavy boot had broken the skin, and suggested I check it regularly. Thomas hurried in to see me on his return from visiting a client's house where he was to install panelling in the principal rooms. He blanched at the sight of me but I assured him I was beginning to feel better than I looked. At my request he sent an apprentice to Somerset's lodgings to fetch fresh clothing and deliver a short note in which I explained that, after my misadventure, I proposed to leave for Worthwaite a little earlier than planned in order to recuperate there.

'You're not fit to travel,' Thomas said. 'You need rest and care, physician. You must stay here.'

'For a day or two, that would be welcome but I mustn't linger. It's not just Worthwaite I must visit but Hartham Manor where my friends may be in danger.' Thomas started to protest but I interrupted him to give, in confidence, an abbreviated account of Earl Stanwick's assault and Iffley's intervention. 'I don't trust Egremont to stay clear of Norfolk,' I concluded.

Thomas whistled between his teeth. 'This is appalling, Harry. Though why you should put yourself at risk for Gaston de la Tour I don't understand. He's shown himself your enemy time enough.'

'True but he's changed and in any case it's his wife and child I want to protect. They're innocent of wishing me harm.'

Thomas did not try again to dissuade me but he agreed to use his contacts to see if a band of merchants would be travelling into East Anglia shortly so I could join their party. In the meantime he ordered me to rest, a prescription I endorsed with relief, and under Grizel's care my recovery progressed.

There had been no sign of Rendell while I was at his sister's house, which was unusual, but at first I did not enquire because I feared he might have been confined to his quarters in the Tower for some new misdemeanour. In my weakened state I could not face further anxieties on his behalf but, before I left the City, I gritted my teeth to ask how he was.

'Oh!' Grizel was shocked. 'In all the kerfuffle we've forgotten to tell you. We meant to give you the good news when you visited but it went out of our heads. Just two days before you arrived here, all beaten about, he told us he was one of a small posse being sent with a sergeant to carry out some task he couldn't talk about. I don't think he knew the details himself but he was cock-a-hoop to be leaving the Tower. He said it was all due to you because the Governor told the sergeant the Duke of Somerset, no less, had asked for him to be given duties outside the City. Oh, I should have remembered to tell you, Harry, and thank you. It'll give Rendell a chance to make a new start.'

I was able to leave the Chope household in a more cheerful mood than I had expected, still sore in body but cheered by Somerset's action and relieved for Rendell's sake. When I set out from the City, in the company of half a dozen merchants and their attendants bound for Wingfield to do business with the Dowager Duchess of Suffolk, I hoped that I too might be able to make a new start.

*****

We travelled faster than I found comfortable but I consoled myself with the thought that this would shorten the number of days on horseback. Although my limbs ached and some bruises were aggravated by riding, in general I was much recovered. Only the cut on my inner thigh continued to be painful and I could explain that by the chafing it received from the material of my gown pressed hard against the saddle. Nevertheless by the time we were within a day's ride of Wingfield the pain had intensified to such an extent that I knew I must seek a night's rest there before journeying on to Worthwaite. In that way Leone could give me a second opinion on the suppurating wound which was refusing to heal.

My young Italian colleague embraced me on arrival and was amused at being consulted by me professionally but, when he had me climb onto a table and stretch out my leg, all the laughter left his eyes. 'This is not good, Doctor Somers. It is most inflamed.' He grimaced. 'I'd judge it should be cauterised.'

'Is it so bad? It's difficult for me to see closely. I'm stiff from the saddle. But the soreness has been getting worse.'

He helped me bend forward to have a clearer view and I was horrified how far the inflammation had spread beyond the cut itself. 'You're right. It's dangerously infected. Will you do it, Leone? With a red-hot brand?'

'It will be agonising,' he said, 'but it must be done. I have done it before. I will fetch my instruments and a man to hold you still.'

I thought of the poor wretch on London Bridge whose limb I had amputated and attempted later to cauterise. Now it was my turn to feel the torture of scalding and I told myself it was no bad thing for a physician to endure the treatment he gave to others.

214

I fainted at the moment of impact but Leone knew his business. I should have remembered the experience he gained on the battlefields of Normandy when he served as a physician with soldiers fighting for King Henry against the French. Doubtless he had learned to improvise successfully in challenging conditions. I was in the safest of hands and, when Leone attended me next morning, we could both see that the brutal operation had achieved the desired effect. The putrid material gathering in the wound had shrivelled but the area of skin scorched and blistering was no wider than necessary. I would be in pain for several days and must remain at Wingfield longer than I intended but I would recover.

Leone looked at me quizzically when he joined me on the third day of my convalescence and I feared he had noted some degeneration in my condition but he quickly reassured me that was not the case. He twisted his hands in his lap. 'There is something else I should tell you, Doctor Somers: something most awkward. Forgive me.'

I was slow to grasp his meaning and he took a deep breath. 'About six weeks ago I was called to your manor. They were concerned...'

'About my wife?

'I am afraid so. She is most ill in her wits, Doctor. I am sorry. She had behaved badly, not in her right mind. You had advised me but I was shaken to hear what had happened.'

'Tell me, Leone. Please, I need to know.'

'I think so, yes. A visitor had stayed at Worthwaite for two nights when the weather was bad, someone of your acquaintance and your steward was sure you'd wish to give him hospitality. Chamberlayne, I think was his name.'

'Sir Nicholas Chamberlayne. Certainly, he had stayed with us before.' I could not hide my shudder because I guessed what was to come. This was my fault for leaving Kate, shirking what should be my prime duty.

'Mistress Somers insisted to entertain him at supper and then...' Leone hesitated.

'She offered him more personal entertainment? Such wildness is part of her affliction. It happens from time to time. Did...?' I could not frame my question.

'I understand the gentleman was most gallant in declining her offer and left the house at dawn. It was after that Mistress Somers became violent. She smashed dishes and jugs and attacked Dame Elizabeth, the steward's wife. Then she ran into the river and flung herself down in the water as if she wished to be drowned. They dragged her out and sent for me, as you had suggested they should. I was able to give her medication and calm her, with her woman's help. She is most competent, Mistress Judith. I have returned to see them and Mistress Somers has become more placid but her peacefulness is not normal. She is acutely melancholy and I fear for her.'

I took Leone's wrist. 'I too fear for her. Thank you with all my heart for what you've done and for telling me.'

His dark eyes were brimming with tears. 'Last time I saw Mistress Somers, she asked for you, Doctor.'

My heart missed a beat and guilt enveloped me. 'Tomorrow I will go to Worthwaite. Kate shall be my charge from now on. I mustn't leave her again, not for any significant length of time. I can't tell where this mind-sickness will lead but I must accept my responsibilities.'

In that moment my decision was made. What it would mean for my future, for practising my profession, for my whole life, I could not foresee. The prospects appeared grim in all these contexts but I must no longer evade the commitments I made when I took Kate as my bride. I had sworn before God to care for her come good fortune or ill. In any case, my entanglement with the affairs of great men had hardly brought peace of mind and the recent buffeting I received put me in mortal danger. It followed that I should formally abandon my position in Somerset's household and henceforward live privately at Worthwaite. Heartrending torment in my home might test my endurance with severity comparable to anything I had suffered elsewhere but I made my choice.

Part 3 East Anglia and London 1451-52

Chapter 18

My return to Worthwaite was greeted with such obvious relief that the guilt I already felt for abandoning my household was exacerbated. Perkin and his wife voiced no criticisms but I could see from their expressions they had been racked with worry and Dame Elizabeth's face carried a scar from cheekbone to chin which had not been there before. I was ashamed to have neglected my personal responsibilities yet my appearance was enough for them to discern how physically weak I was and they voiced their concern for my health.

'My injuries will heal now they've been properly treated and I can rest from the saddle. I'd like to think my presence will be helpful to my wife.'

Dame Elizabeth puckered her brow. 'Don't cherish false hopes, Doctor. You need to talk to Judith. That girl is a saint, no less, and Mistress Somers trusts her but, so far as we can see, there's no lasting improvement – only occasional ups and bigger downs.'

Perkin shook his head as if discouraging his wife from saying more and I did not press for details. Judith was the appropriate person to give me those but I felt awkward about questioning her directly. The possibility that she held some special affection for me reasserted itself as an inhibition against shared confidences. My first step must be to see Kate and make my own assessment of her condition.

My wife was sitting serenely, staring into space as if in a trance and she did not acknowledge me. Judith was at the far end of the room but retreated into the adjoining chamber when I entered and I noted her discretion. 'Kate,' I said softly so as not to frighten her, 'I'm returned from London, Kate.'

I thought my words had passed over her but then she turned her head and looked towards me, blankly before her eyes focused on my face. 'You're hurt.'

I caught my breath. 'I was injured but I'm recovering. There's no lasting harm done.'

'No lasting harm? That has a joyful sound. I'm glad. For me there is only lasting harm.'

'You mustn't think that. You can get better. You're better now than you have sometimes been. I'm very happy to see this.' My words sounded stilted.

She sighed. 'Perhaps. Today the demons are quiet. They are not plaguing me. But I know they will return and, when they do, they drive me to do things I cannot remember.'

I was unpersuaded about the role demons might play in her illness but recoiled from challenging her explanation. I did not want to remind her of the impulse to debauchery and self-destruction which she may have forgotten. 'We must find a way to send the demons packing, once and for all.'

'They frighten me. They've always frightened me. They've always been there even before they became so venomous.'

'I don't know if that's true. You held them at bay when we first met. You never mentioned them and were contented.'

'Was I? I don't remember.' She lowered her head and trembled. 'Some days the demons are waiting for me when I wake in the morning. At other times my mind is empty.'

'Isn't there some occupation which would interest you, to keep you from thinking of the demons? I'm sure Dame Elizabeth would be happy if you wished to involve yourself with running the household.'

'Dame Elizabeth...? I don't know.'

Her capacity to hold this unremarkable conversation was heartening but I must not press her beyond what she could handle without agitation. One

218

cautious step at a time must suffice. 'Let's see if we can think of something to interest you.'

She inclined her head and I wondered if it signified agreement. 'I'm tired. Judith can sing me to sleep. Will you ask her?'

'Of course. I'll come to you again when you're rested.'

I pressed her hand lightly and she did not withdraw it, which was encouragement enough. I must be satisfied with every tiny step away from the horrifying depths where her mind plummeted beyond all comprehension.

Later I talked to Judith. Her face looked thinner and there were new vertical lines etching her brow which indicated the burden she carried in caring for Kate but I sensed she would not wish me to mention this.

'After the account Doctor Leone gave me of my wife's behaviour when Sir Nicholas Chamberlayne visited earlier in the year, I hadn't expected to find her so subdued and even cogent. How long has she been like this? Do you see grounds for hope for the longer term?'

Judith smiled sadly as she shook her head. 'I can't delude you, Doctor, it's almost as if there's a pattern. After her wild episodes, the over-excitement, when I fear for her life and the danger she might pose to others, she becomes morose and silent. Then she's tearful for days before a sort of serenity comes and she's capable of almost normal speech. As you've seen her today. But it isn't likely to last.'

'Does it need some event to change her mood, do you think?'

Judith gave a rueful laugh. 'You ask me as if I'm the physician, Doctor. I don't know. If Sir Nicholas hadn't come to Worthwaite would she have stayed quiet? Maybe; but if the mood was inside her, boiling up, it could have been some other happening which burst her mind open.'

'That's what it's like, isn't it? Everything becomes excessive and her mind bursts open. What a horrible thought. Has she ever been violent towards you?'

'Not in earnest. She's pummelled my shoulder in her distress but only before collapsing in sobs. She seems to know I'm there to support her but I'm not sure I can rely on that.'

I looked at the girl with genuine admiration. 'However did you acquire your wisdom, Judith?'

'I don't think I've got any wisdom. I've just learned what works from caring for Mistress Somers – and watching you, Doctor.'

I was suddenly nervous that our discussion had crossed a line, acutely aware that Judith might misconstrue my interest in her feelings. 'I'll spend more time with my wife now I've returned. Please take the opportunity to rest.'

Early next morning, while the dew was moist on the grass, I wandered by the riverside puzzling whether there was any pastime which might divert and absorb Kate's mind constructively. Near the house Dame Elizabeth nurtured a small bed of herbs for the kitchen and I stared at them, noting that some had medicinal as well as culinary uses. They prompted recollection of the Infirmarian's garden at the Abbey of St. Swithun in Winchester, where I had lodged for some months four years previously. I stood still, glancing round at the unkempt stretch of grass between the house and the river, with the rough hedge on its eastern side which provided a modest windbreak.

Kate had broken her fast when I entered her chamber and she greeted me with a sweet smile as I knelt beside her. 'Do you remember,' I asked tentatively, 'how you helped me by labelling the herbs in my dispensary at the Duke of Suffolk's house in London?'

Her eyes shone for a moment, luminous green, but I realised some aspects of the memory could alarm her. 'I was wondering,' I went on quickly, 'whether we might create a garden behind the house, where you could grow aromatic herbs I could use in potions but also sweet-scented-flowers to delight our eyes as well as our noses.

You could have a bower there, a trellised nook, where you could sit when you were weary, shaded from the sun but sheltered from a cold east wind.'

'Betony and mugwort, comfrey and chamomile.' Her face lit up and she touched my cheek with her fingertips. 'Oh, I should like that.'

I gasped at her recollection. 'That's splendid! Come with me and I'll show you what I have in mind. You must say how you'd like it arranged and I'll get a workman to install a stone seat while we collect seeds and plants to fill the beds.'

Her response seemed to me a fulsome reward when she kissed me lightly on the cheek. Then she took my hand and faint hope burgeoned in my heart.

*****

I had an obligation to report personally to Gaston de la Tour, following my encounter with Roger Egremont, but I was reluctant to declare this intention to Kate who might suspect my motives for visiting Hartham Manor. Now, however, I had an additional reason to explain my purpose, for I remembered the garden at the dower-house which Bess Willoughby had tended when she and Robin resided there. I determined to travel by cart, with one of the Worthwaite workmen as driver, and request supplies for our garden to augment those we were obtaining from elsewhere. As the hours of summer daylight were long, we would be able to accomplish our mission and return within one day. Kate smiled at this and raised no objections.

When we trundled towards the edge of the Fitzvaughan estate I saw that new defences had been erected and I was impressed by the measures Gaston had taken to protect his demesne. A timber palisade did not constitute a major encumbrance to effecting entry to the grounds but it was a deterrent, while the sight of an armed guard patrolling the boundary showed a seriousness of purpose not so easily dismissed. We passed a sentry-post, explained our business and were permitted to proceed to the main gate of the central complex of buildings where I was identified and admitted.

Both Lady Eleanor and Gaston came to welcome me. It was more than six months since I had seen them and I was aware of two agreeable developments since then: Lord Fitzvaughan looked in better health and his lady was once more with child. Both seemed happy. We shared refreshment, I made a request for help in establishing our new garden and later Gaston conducted me into his study to discuss matters he did not wish to raise in front of his wife for fear of alarming her.

'You've greatly increased your security,' I said. 'It'll put off the casual ne'er-do-well.'

'All to the good. I hope it'll send a message to any with evil in their hearts. I owe it all to you, Harry.'

'To me? Well, indirectly, perhaps. I hope Roger Egremont has been dissuaded from his vile intentions by Baron Glasbury and is kept under control in Richard of York's castle at Ludlow, as I wrote to you.'

'I don't trust the fellow but we'll be prepared if he attempts an attack. Actually it was your help in strengthening our defences I meant.' I indicated that I did not understand and he continued. 'It was your friend Sir Nicholas Chamberlayne who called and offered advice. He's concerned to assist potential supporters of the Duke of Somerset in this area, to counter the plans of John Mowbray of Norfolk who's caused disruption and strife in the county of his title. Sir Nicholas had identified the Fitzvaughan lands as at risk, thanks to you, so he recommended constructing extra barriers and getting trained guards to give advice. He arranged for these soldiers to help landowners at risk from Mowbray's attacks and they've been travelling round in East Anglia. A week ago they came here and their knowledge is invaluable. I can't tell you how grateful I am.'

'Chamberlayne's a shrewd operator.' I said. 'An upright man too, I believe. Not that usual a combination.'

Gaston laughed. 'You've become a cynic, Harry Somers.' He straightened his face. 'There's perhaps something else you should know. I suspect he bedded my illustrious mother-in-law while he was here.'

I spluttered. 'What? Really? Goodness!' I was completely taken by surprise.

Gaston threw back his head and roared with laughter, until he was coughing. 'That's the best joke I've been able to enjoy since before Walter died. Thank you again, Harry. Actually, I'm not sure. She certainly entertained him in the dower-house and was at her most alluring but – as you say – he's an upright man.' Gaston doubled up with mirth once more. 'Oh, I'm sorry. She was your mistress, wasn't she?'

'I've no claim on her. I'm a married man.' I sounded prudish and my words sent Gaston into renewed peals of laughter until he controlled himself.

'You'd better go in search of the plants you came for before I cause you more embarrassment. It won't surprise you that Lady Maud doesn't tend the garden at the dower-house herself but I fetched over some of my attendants from Normandy and Master Pierre has turned Mistress Willoughby's little vegetable plot into a miniature parterre. He'll be delighted to help you.'

The cart was quickly filled with specimen cuttings and bags of seeds but before we left Hartham Manor I wanted to see how Piers Ford was progressing. On the other hand, if I could avoid Lady Maud, this might be expedient, but it was not to be. Seeing me clutching an armful of lavender, she glided from the dower-house and grasped the lappets of my gown with a snarl.

'Are you trying to evade me, physician? Have you forgotten how pleasantly we spent an hour when you were last at my daughter's manor?'

I did not challenge her description of the property. 'My Lady, I must be on my way. I can pay you only minimal courtesy. Forgive me. I rejoice to see you so radiant.'

She purred. 'On this occasion I will forgive you as I have a letter to dictate. I've acquired a truly assiduous correspondent of the finest sensibility. How is the woman you were fool enough to marry?'

I concentrated on her question, not the statement intended to provoke my curiosity. 'With God's blessing, I believe her condition is improving. We're building a garden to engage her interest. I'm here to collect plants.'

'Plants?' The scorn in Maud's voice was unrivalled. 'Of course, you're a physician. Shall you grow your own herbs in future? How many apothecaries will you displace?'

'I knew you would tease me. That's why I wasn't anxious to face your mockery.'

'Ah, so sweet, poor physician! I'll let you go unchastised but when you come again I beg you will visit me unencumbered by vegetation. Have you seen the soldiers in the grounds? Are we about to be attacked? My blood races with excitement at the thought. Will the handsome Sir Nicholas return to defend my honour?'

I bit back a reply suggesting it would depend whether he had already taken her honour and bowed solemnly as I bade her goodbye. Her trill of merriment followed me across the courtyard to the entrance gate. There was no doubting her unusual good humour but I would not speculate about the reason.

*****

I arranged for the cart to join me when the hour-glass was half full and made my way to the wheelwright's workshop where Piers saw me approaching and ran out to greet me. He was bronzed and looked content, which was pleasing for I was inclined to worry that his position at Hartham Manor might not truly suit a man of his unusual talents and interests.

'Doctor Somers, this is fortunate! I'm always happy to see you again but this time, by remarkable coincidence,

I've just been hearing about your history – far more than you ever told me.'

'Why, who have you been talking to?' I thought one of the servants must have been prattling.

'Come into my cottage and you will see.' He took my arm and dragged me out of the sunlight, through the door to where I could see a shadowy figure.

'If it ain't me old buddy, Doctor Somers,' the apparition said with wry amusement and I hurried forward to embrace its sturdy form.

'Rendell! You're one of the soldiers! I heard the Governor released you from the Tower but I didn't know you were in East Anglia.'

'Christ, you make it sound as if I was imprisoned! Lord Scales said the Duke of Somerset had asked for my services so I knew it were your doing. We've been tootling round to beef up the defences of manor-houses at risk of attack by Mowbray's followers. More variety than at the Tower and I ain't having to look at that fickle baggage flaunting herself at me every day. Found a bit of other talent among the laundry maids too.'

'I suppose I should be glad you're not moping.'

'Funny thing though, meeting Piers here and working out who we were and how we both knew you. He said you might turn up at Hartham one day.'

Piers was much amused by Rendell's banter, and I suspected he welcomed the company of a street-wise visitor from London, even if this was a soldier who had served at the Tower during the disturbances. I could imagine him trying to suborn my young friend from his duties and wondered how Rendell would respond. I took a moment to ask Piers if he now felt at home in Norfolk.

'There're some good people here, without doubt, even though they're prepared to follow their lord in blind obedience, misguided as they are. Slower in their wits perhaps, than the men of Kent, but ready to help a fellow.'

'You miss Dartford?'

'I do and I mean to return there. I'll stay put through the winter but by spring my apprentice will be skilled enough to take over this wheelwright's shop. Then I'll chance my arm back in the south. I've got the King's pardon for what's past and I'll make a new start among my own folk. I've not done with struggling to help poor men but I'll do it better where there's a groundswell of support.'

'I hope there'll be no more rash enterprises like Jack Cade's. There must be a better way of making your demands known to the King.'

'If Richard of York took up our cause, there might be but he's likely to prove as self-seeking as the rest.'

Rendell's eyes were round with curiosity at our exchange and I thought it best to change the subject but I did not need to intervene because a tap at the door alerted us to the presence of a newcomer. Piers hurried to admit the visitor and there was Mistress Bess Willoughby, pink in the face and carrying a covered dish which she nearly spilled when she recognised me.

'Doctor Somers! I didn't know you were at Hartham Manor. Excuse me. I've brought Piers some broth for his supper.' She gave a puzzled glance towards Rendell as she set down the broth and I chuckled.

'Years ago, at Greenwich, you met this ferocious man at arms when he was a scruffy urchin.'

'Rendell Tonks, at your service, Mistress.' He executed a creditable bow.

Bess clapped her hands with glee. 'Oh, I remember you and I've heard reports of you since. What a remarkable gathering! I'm sorry to have intruded. Keep the broth warm, Piers, and come to eat with us tomorrow. Robin will be glad to see you at our table.'

She curtseyed and withdrew, opening the door wide so that I saw the waiting cart outside. I realised it had been standing there while the hour-glass filled completely and it was time I left my friends so I quickly made my farewells. Piers was fussing with a cloth to wrap over his bowl of broth and, although it was difficult to be sure in the shadows, his face appeared flushed. Rendell came to see me off and, as I clambered aboard the cart, I extracted a promise that he would ride over to Worthwaite before he left the neighbourhood.

'We're nearly done here and the sergeant's decent. I'll wangle a day's leave. Is that flaming termagant still there?' He had a mischievous grin.

'If you mean Judith, she's the mainstay of my wife's care and is not to be upset. Mind you, I'd back her against you any day.'

Rendell refrained from the vulgar riposte I expected but rubbed his nose with determination. He was incorrigible but it was good to see him in a contented mood. By contrast, it was the look on Piers' face when he opened the door to Mistress Willoughby that troubled me – and, or did I imagine it, the way she smiled at him.

Chapter 19

Rendell duly called a week later and joined us for our midday meal but he could spend only a short time at Worthwaite as his detachment had received orders to move on to another manor further north in the county of Norfolk. Kate was weary and did not come to table but Judith was prepared for our visitor and swept into the room with a superior gleam in her eye. She concealed any surprise when he bowed civilly.

'Knocked the rough edges off you at the Tower of London, have they?'

'Comes of calling on woodworkers, I reckon,' he countered, 'smoothing my impeccable manners still more. You're thinner.'

'I seem to remember you were insolent about my weight when I rode pillion with you. Either way, it's crass to comment.'

'Not exactly scraggy anyway, are you? I won't be offering you room on my saddle.'

'The saints be praised! I hear you've turned fence-builder by way of occupation. That what they do before they put run-down soldiers out to grass?'

'You won't be so free with your taunts when John Mowbray's troops come to harry the countryside.'

'Is that right? You'll be safe back in the Tower by then I suppose.'

'Yeah, lopping off noses of prisoners. I expect that's what you think we do?'

'If not worse.'

Before Rendell could expatiate on the possibilities, I pushed the serving platter towards him and he tore off a capon leg. I broke into the conversation and learned that he and his companions were to spend the night at Wingfield. I asked him to convey my greetings to Leone.

'He's suggested that between us we could offer services as physicians in the wider locality. He's got time to spare and I'd like to keep my hand in.'

'So you've not entirely abandoned medicine? I thought you'd turned gardener.' Rendell winked.

'If the garden helps Kate, I'll dig and delve like old Adam.'

Rendell dunked his capon leg in the sauce-bowl and took a bite from it, the juices running down his chin. 'You've spent too much time in the company of Piers Ford.'

'Ah, you recognise the words of John Ball. Has Piers won you over to his cause of justice and liberties?

He licked the grease from round his mouth. 'Not a question that should be put to a man at arms from the Tower,' he said. 'Wouldn't be courteous to suggest Piers had no powers of persuasion but if I said 'yes' it might be held seditious.'

Judith clapped her hands ostentatiously. 'Mercy on us, the barbarian's got a smidgeon of common sense.'

'Barbarian my arse!' He looked ready to hurl his chicken bones across the table but Perkin prevented Rendell's behaviour degenerating further.

'I understand the Duke of Norfolk's cronies have been making mischief along the coast, attacking a worthy knight's bastion.'

'Yeah, that's what the Duke of Somerset's men are trying to prevent by sending us here. We ain't in the area to admire the scenery, you know.'

The atmosphere became more serious and Rendell slid into the role of military sage, full of cautionary tales about ignorant country folk who failed to follow the advice given them to protect their flocks and harvests from human predators. He was an ebullient mass of contradictions, always liable to act first and reason later, but his greater maturity promised well for his future. I was sorry to see him go from Worthwaite.

*****

During the next month I supervised the construction of stone walls and timber trellises, helped

229

plant mint and columbine, comfrey, pimpernel and yarrow, pennyroyal and periwinkle; and whenever the sun shone I coaxed my wife to sit in her new arbour, reminding her of the qualities the herbs possessed, whether for medicinal use or the cook's pot. It was a joyful time for, in the scent and sight of the flowering greenery, it seemed we had found the means to hold Kate's misery at bay. Little by little she seemed more settled in her mind and she showed simple pleasure in the floral kingdom where she was undisputed queen.

Although my happiness could not approach the jubilation I felt during the early, carefree months of our marriage, after the black despondency we had endured since then, I considered it sufficient. I had written to Somerset formally withdrawing from his service, begging his forbearance with my change of plans, and he had replied graciously. Even Baron Glasbury accepted I would send him no more reports from Somerset's household and he must have recognised this was not a great loss. I had no wish to spy for him and was glad that disturbing role had ended. More fittingly, I continued to offer medical services in the locality and met Leone to discuss unusual cases which one or other of us was treating. My rustic life was not what I would have chosen in the past but it was adequately fulfilling.

News trickled through to Worthwaite of doings in the Parliament. Various lands previously granted to subjects by the Crown were to be taken back but could be redeemed on payment of a fee. This was a crafty move in order to replenish the royal coffers without increasing taxes on the general population and I wondered if the device owed anything to the complaints voiced by Jack Cade and his partisans about excessive taxation. I confess I felt relief that my title to my small manor, granted directly by the late Duke of Suffolk, held good, for I could call on no resources adequate to purchase the land I had been given.

230

Other news was carried in letters from Somerset's household and by garrulous pedlars. Both sources hinted at an attempt by one member of the Commons to bring a motion in Parliament naming Richard of York as King Henry's legal heir while the sovereign remained childless. It was said the reckless member had been confined in the Tower of London for his pains and there were also rumours of executions in the City where men had been emboldened to speak against the King. Somerset was firmly reinstated at the King's right hand and he sent a second kindly letter wishing me well and my wife restored to health.

By late summer we heard of extraordinary events in the west of the country, where one nobleman had been besieging the castle of another until Richard of York sallied forth from Ludlow, marched his men one hundred miles and imposed peace between the warring factions. York's action proved brilliantly decisive but he had in fact usurped Somerset's proper role in Somerset's nominal territory. Once again, however, Edmund Beaufort singularly failed to act and re-establish law and order on his own account, thus giving his rival the opportunity to intervene effectively. When he had completed his self-appointed task, York mildly withdrew to Ludlow and did not seek to build on his success. I could not help but conjecture what part Gilbert Iffley and Stephen Boice might have had in these occurrences and whether, yet again, they were frustrated by York's reluctance to exploit the advantage his resolute action had created.

I had last seen Boice during Cade's rebellion and I realised that more than a year had now passed since he tricked his way into Sir Hugh de Grey's manor at Danson and shattered my wife's fragile recovery from the mental turmoil his earlier machinations had provoked. Now I had nascent hopes for Kate's lasting improvement, my loathing for her uncle returned with complementary force. I prayed we would never see him again.

By the beginning of October, blustery winds were making it less comfortable for Kate to sit in her garden and most of the flowers we had planted were withered. It would be a challenge to sustain the interest she had shown in the verdant plot during the summer and I racked my brain to think of an alternative amusement for her. In the circumstances it was not surprising that she became more shut within herself, but I was desperate to prevent her falling into the melancholic state which in the past presaged a more virulent episode in her illness. When she agreed to accompany me on the short expedition to Wingfield to meet some of her former companions who served the Dowager-Duchess of Suffolk, I was overjoyed.

Kate was subdued but not noticeably troubled in her mind during the visit. Indeed, she was delighted to examine a fine Book of Hours which had been given to the young Duke, expressing appreciation of the brilliant colours the artist had employed in the illustrations, which made me happy.

We were preparing to set out on our return journey, amid a flurry of goodbyes from the other ladies, when a sweat-soaked messenger was admitted through the main gate and clattered to a halt beside us. He wore the Fitzvaughan livery, his horse was flecked with foam and he gasped for breath before speaking.

'Doctor Somers, pardon. I went first to Worthwaite and was told you were here. Hartham Manor has been attacked, barns fired, stores burned and men hurt. His Lordship was away in Norwich. He's been sent for but Lady Eleanor has asked if you could come. The assailants have withdrawn but there are injuries to dress which worry her.'

I glanced at Kate and she inclined her head. 'You must go.' Her voice was low and she began to tremble.

'I'll take you home and collect my instruments then ride at once to Hartham.' I turned back to the messenger. 'How many are injured?'

'Four or five, Robin Willoughby, the bailiff, among them. He scorched his arm, fighting the blazing straw and fleeces running with searing grease. Others have been stabbed and slashed.'

I cleared my throat. 'I'll be there by nightfall.'

*****

The hard ride left me aching in every muscle but there was no time to consider my own discomfort, for two of the injured men had lost a good deal of blood and one of them was unlikely to survive. Lady Eleanor and her women were busy swabbing and mixing sedatives. Robin Willoughby was not in immediate danger but his right arm was severely burned and it would be important to avoid the wound becoming infected through bad humours in the air. Bess Willoughby was at his side and had dissuaded him from setting off on a vain and hazardous attempt to catch up with the attackers. When I had done what I could for my patients, I joined Gaston de la Tour who had returned from Norwich and was striding around his hall in furious impotence.

'The flames could be seen from the house,' he said. 'The shock could have caused Eleanor to miscarry. Perhaps that was the aim. All my hay is destroyed and two of the farm horses had to be put down. Some of my men chased the fire-raisers and you've seen how they were treated when the villains turned on them with sword and axe. They would have known I was in Norwich. Cowards: attacking women and farm-hands! By God, Harry, if Roger Egremont is behind this I'll have him quartered while he still lives.'

'Has there been any sign that he's behind it?'

'The rogues wore no livery but one dropped a badge from his cap – a Mowbray crest. I shall make complaint against the Duke of Norfolk and his servitors.'

'They didn't get near the house at any rate.'

233

'Not this time but one of them shouted they'd be back as he skewered my woodman. It's part of the pattern, my hound, my possessions, my servants – my family.'

'If Egremont has escaped from Richard of York's duress, he's very likely to be the culprit but Mowbray's men are a law unto themselves with or without his prompting.'

'I won't bow down to this, Harry. I'll die in defence of my manor rather than yield an inch to Egremont.'

I refrained from saying Gaston's death would achieve the Earl of Stanwick's purpose. 'Can you strengthen your defences?'

'It's men we need to guard the perimeter – stop them getting near the enclosure round the house. I've asked for reinforcements from neighbours and sent word to the Duke of Somerset. That wheelwright fellow you brought here has gone after Sir Nicholas Chamberlayne. He's thought to be in Cambridge.'

'Good. You should get some rest, my Lord. I've encouraged Lady Eleanor to break off from her labours too. I'll stay with the injured. I've asked your chaplain to attend the woodman.' I paused. 'Is Lady Maud safely in the dower-house?'

Gaston curled his lip. 'She hasn't been at the manor these last few days. She's gone on some kind of pilgrimage: to a holy woman she knew long ago, I believe.'

'The Prioress of St. Michael's in Stamford. I know her and Lady Maud had dealings with her when your wife was cared for at the priory as a child. She's a most astute and reverend lady.'

'She sounds a most unlikely recipient of my mother-in-law's attentions.' Gaston gave a half-hearted laugh. 'But it's convenient Lady Maud isn't here during this trouble.'

He was correct, I thought, in both respects.

*****

234

The woodman died during the night and his death sent a tremor of horror throughout the estate. Hartham Manor had not been spared the depredations of hostile bands in the past but no serious injury had been sustained by its inhabitants. This vicious attack had been different and I sensed unease among the Fitzvaughan followers who could not be expected to feel the same loyalty to Gaston as they had to the late Lord Walter. At least it was encouraging that by morning four men at arms had been sent from neighbouring manors to help defend Hartham Manor if another assault was mounted.

I was unsure how long I should remain with the Fitzvaughans as I was anxious to return to Kate. My services were no longer essential, for the wounded were receiving appropriate care from the womenfolk, and there seemed no immediate danger of further violence. One issue concerned me and I decided I must explain it to Gaston in case it rebounded against his family in the future. I went with him to observe the repair of his barns, pleased to see Robin Willoughby directing operations although noting how the bailiff held his bandaged arm against his chest and winced whenever he moved it. Afterwards, as I walked back to the house with Gaston, I broached the subject which embarrassed me.

'There's something you should know in case Roger Egremont reappears. It's not a thing I'm proud of but I hope you'll understand the circumstances. When the Earl took me captive in London and threatened to castrate and then kill me, I made a suggestion in a desperate attempt to deflect his purpose. It was all I could think of that might interest him.'

Gaston shrugged. '*Force majeure*, we would term it. No man can be held to a suggestion made in such exigencies. What was it?'

I took a deep breath. 'That you might be willing to negotiate with him, to give him something to compensate for the way he was left landless when his late cousin made Lady Eleanor heiress to the Ravensmoor lands.'

Gaston's mouth twisted into a grimace. 'What? You offered him Ravensmoor?'

'He knew I couldn't offer anything on your behalf but he thought it worth pursuing. He was prepared to let me live for the moment on the strength of it. The idea of occupying the Stanwick lands to accompany his Stanwick title attracted him. I can only plead *force majeure* as you recognised.'

I stood still waiting for the tongue-lashing I expected but Lord Fitzvaughan gave a guffaw. 'Do you think that would truly buy him off? I'd have no objection to him occupying Ravensmoor, holding it from me as his liege, if he undertook to leave my family in peace: only for his lifetime of course. I won't alienate an acre of my son's inheritance. But Egremont has no children.'

'He might cavil at that restriction. He's widowed. He'll probably marry again.'

'I wouldn't agree to any other terms.' Gaston clamped his mouth shut and I was not surprised by his decisiveness but a few moments later his eyes shone and he slapped his thigh. 'I would have one refinement to make to the bargain you offered. Along with Ravensmoor he could take Lady Maud to wife. You wouldn't begrudge him your barren mistress, I hope.'

My throat was constricted and I coughed awkwardly, assuming he was teasing me. 'I fancy Lady Maud would have a view. She's never shown herself amenable to what doesn't please her.'

'On the contrary, my dear Harry, I think she'd be delighted. She'd love to queen it over Ravensmoor as Countess, to be free of Fitzvaughan charity, living at Hartham Manor.'

'Egremont is a callous brute.'

Gaston gave a full-throated laugh. 'You're letting your partiality for her influence your judgement. She's an unscrupulous, beguiling bitch. She's survived worse than Egremont. Ravensmoor would throb to their passionate encounters. You've fired my imagination. I almost wish the

Earl would reveal himself as Hartham's assailant so we could put the proposal to the test.'

I offered up a silent supplication that this would not happen but by suppertime Piers Ford had returned from Cambridge with a posse of Sir Nicholas Chamberlayne's men and confirmation that Roger Egremont was known to be in Swaffham, some twenty miles away. He had eluded pursuit from Ludlow and recruited a band of desperadoes eager for action and plunder. The Duke of Norfolk had given him backing and the prospect of a quiet life at Hartham Manor in the future was non-existent.

Gaston thumped his fist on the table after Piers finished his report and swung round to face me. 'I shall seize the initiative: take him by surprise, challenge him with your inventive idea. You're its originator, Harry, and I need your help. You owe me this at least, as recompense for your readiness to barter my possessions in return for your life. I'll write to Egremont requesting that he receives my agent, under safe conduct, and you will go to him to negotiate conclusion of the arrangements we've discussed. You won't deny me this?'

He was grinning as he made the outrageous request and I was never certain how serious he was. It would have been prudent to refuse and no reasonable person would have thought I owed him any service but I have always suffered pangs of guilt too readily. I had preserved my life with my wild suggestion, at Gaston's expense, and I recognised that, in consequence, he had a claim to my assistance. 'Provided the safe conduct can be relied upon,' I said, 'and I can take one witness with me, I agree.'

*****

Three days later arrangements had been agreed and I set out from Hartham Manor for the rendezvous with Egremont. At the last minute he had asked for the meeting to be in Norwich, not Swaffham, but this seemed of no significance and we presumed he was more comfortably accommodated in the Mowbray mansion, which he now named, rather than the inn in Swaffham he had mentioned previously.

By the time of my departure I had come to regret my willingness to meet the Earl, doubting the sincerity of his safe conduct, but my word had been given and it was agreed I would be accompanied by a single, unarmed witness, as I requested. There would have been good sense in taking Piers Ford as my companion for I trusted him and we had faced hazardous situations together during Cade's rebellion. It occurred to me, however, that Egremont would disdain the presence of a wheelwright and it would carry more weight to have with me one of Gaston's senior followers, known in the locality as devoted to the Fitzvaughans. For this reason I asked Robin Willoughby if he felt able to ride to Norwich with only one good arm and was content to come with me. He said he was and concurred that it would demonstrate our peaceful intentions if my witness was visibly not a fighting man.

We had reckoned without Mistress Bess Willoughby and this was remiss of us both, for it was understandable she would be concerned for her husband's well-being on the mission. I understood from Robin he led her to believe it was Gaston's command that he should go to Norwich, so her silent complaints would be directed towards their overlord without any expectation of remedy. My involvement in the expedition had not been mentioned and we planned to leave the manor by a route furthest from the bailiff's house. We were disconcerted therefore when we rode through the postern gate and found Mistress Willoughby waiting outside.

Robin drew on the reins as his wife ran across to wish him God-speed, but when she saw me she blanched.

'Doctor Somers! Is Robin attending you? Surely you don't consider it good for him to ride so far when his injury has barely started to heal? I thought he was to fulfil some commission for Lord Fitzvaughan. What rash escapade is this?'

I regretted that Mistress Bess viewed my participation in the venture with such pessimism and Robin strove to give her re-assurance. 'You should be pleased, my dear, that a physician is here to have a care for me if I tire or my arm is too troublesome.'

He spoke lightly, bending to kiss her, and she gave him her blessing but when he trotted forward Bess put her hand on my bridle. 'I pray God that is your role, Doctor Somers, and you will ensure Robin comes to no harm.'

'That's my intention, Mistress Willoughby, I accept your charge. Please don't worry on Robin's account.'

I waved cheerily as I rode off but I was rattled by Bess's mistrust and wished the encounter had not occurred.

*****

We were expected at the gates of Norwich where the guards saluted and waived collection of a toll. An escort joined us and we trundled uphill along cobbled streets, amidst the stink of ordure and rotting filth, with the cries of hawkers, shopkeepers and crossing-sweepers mingling in the strident disharmony of urban life. I felt a wave of nostalgia for London but forced it aside. It belonged to a phase of my life which was now over, while I must concentrate on the matter in hand. The correctness of that conclusion was evident when, under the shadow of a fine church spire, we entered the courtyard of a mansion and I identified the Duke of Norfolk's coat of arms prominent above the entrance. This was expected, I reminded myself, but a shiver passed down my spine for assuredly I was entering unfriendly ground.

We were received in a spacious room on the first floor of the mansion. Egremont was more tidily dressed than usual and, notably, he did not appear to have been drinking. He was accompanied by a Mowbray retainer wearing a sword and we all remained standing but the atmosphere was not aggressive. We exchanged brief courtesies, the Earl confirmed our visit was taking place under safe conduct and we would be free to leave after our meeting, then I outlined Lord Fitzvaughan's proposal, making no reference to Lady Maud. My words were received in silence but Egremont bit his lip and his eyes narrowed.

'He offers me occupation of Ravensmoor for the duration of my life, as his sworn liegeman?' His tone was measured and I had rehearsed my reply to such a question.

'The tenure is by way of form only, to legitimise the occupation in a manner conformable to common practice and recognised by law.'

'Is it? And so an Earl is to do homage to a lesser noble? A man who holds my rightful birth-right by virtue of his wife's wrongful inheritance? The wife I should have taken to the altar to reunite the lands of Ravensmoor and title of Stanwick? And I am to disinherit children of my body yet unborn in favour of a Norman sodomite's brat? Do I hear you aright?'

'You use tendentious descriptions. What Lord Fitzvaughan offers is intended to give you a landholding and castle where you can be fittingly lodged. In return he seeks to safeguard the security of his family. It's an accord designed to meet the main objectives of both parties, a compromise, as all such accords are bound to be.'

'Is that so? But he does not come in person to seal this accord as you call it?'

'If you agree the terms, my Lord, he will happily meet you and sign the necessary documents. I'm simply a messenger to outline proposals for you to consider. If you wish time to do so that will be understood.'

'Prevarication! Time is of the essence for me. Why haven't you brought the papers with his signature? How am I to believe in his good faith without proof?'

I was taken aback by his sudden desire for speed but encouraged that the proposal seemed to commend itself to him. There was the clatter of horses arriving in the courtyard outside and Egremont cast a rapid glance towards the window, momentarily distracted.

'Lord Fitzvaughan thought you would wish to consider his offer at leisure.'

'Did he? And I'm supposed to be grateful for his lordship's condescension?' The Earl's agitation grew. 'I'm supposed to listen compliantly to the arrogant proposals of a mere quack who once bargained with me for his life? This is foul humiliation you have devised for me, you and that jumped-up pervert. You don't deceive me with your platitudes, physician.'

It was clear Egremont's temper was fraying dangerously and the meeting should end so I bowed and suggested he send a messenger to Hartham Manor with his considered reply. 'Safe conduct will of course be accorded your man as you have accorded it to me.'

'Safe conduct! I give no safe conduct to a snivelling swine who is my sworn enemy. Those were John Mowbray's words and I applaud them. You are his enemy because you served Suffolk and you've always been mine. You will not leave this house alive.'

He clicked his fingers, stepping back, and in a few moments the room became a scene of appalling carnage. The Mowbray servitor leapt forward with his drawn sword driving at my chest while I twisted to the right and whipped my dagger from beneath my gown, shouting at Robin to escape.

I ducked and pivoted but Egremont seized my arms as his subordinate made at me again when, in an instant of convulsive horror, Gaston's unarmed bailiff flung himself in front of me and took the full impact of the sword-blade through his body. Insensate fury gave me strength and I wrenched myself from the Earl's grasp, thrusting my dagger into the murderer's throat before hurtling at Egremont who crashed into the window and subsided, stunned, to the floor.

I knelt beside Robin Willoughby, cupping his shredded guts in my hands, knowing there was nothing I could do. His eyes met mine for a moment, then they rolled into their sockets and it was over.

I was paralysed with grief and shame, scarcely aware of shouting in the courtyard and outside the room, heedless of everything except Robin's shattered life and my culpability. When the door was thrown open and men at arms rushed into the room, I lifted unseeing eyes towards them, ready to surrender myself gladly to immediate execution, fancying that a toothless face was leering at me.

Chapter 20

The man who burst into the room at the head of a band of soldiers stood still, taking in all that the horrific scene implied. Then he ordered that Egremont be dragged to his feet, brought to his senses and placed in confinement. He peered at the man I had killed and ordered that the body be removed, before dropping to his knees beside me, staring at my blood-soaked gown and vacant eyes. Part of my mind knew perfectly well this was Gilbert Iffley, come at a moment of crisis for the second time, but I had difficulty in processing the significance of his arrival. I also registered that the man lacking his upper front teeth was one of my rescuers and the menace I had perceived in his face on previous occasions entirely receded.

'Where are you injured, Harry?'

I forced my thoughts into some sort of order. 'Nowhere. Only a bruise or two. The blood is all Robin's. He came as my witness, unarmed, incapacitated from an earlier attack. He was my friend and I've caused his death.'

'What were you doing here?'

'Trying to negotiate a settlement with Egremont on behalf of Lord Fitzvaughan. To offer him occupation of the Ravensmoor lands...'

'Dear God, what folly! The man's a maniac. He got away from Ludlow Castle and I've been tracking him across the country. It took a day or more to find where he was heading and then I was directed to Swaffham. We reached there this morning to discover the bird had flown.'

'My meeting was arranged for Swaffham. It was shifted here only yesterday. Oh, Baron, if you'd been able to come directly to Norwich, this... could have been prevented.'

He helped me to my feet and ordered his men to prepare Robin's body for respectful conveyance to Hartham Manor. 'I shall accompany you. I come with Richard of York's authority to give Lord Fitzvaughan a pledge of friendship and a guarantee that his right to Lady Eleanor's inheritance will not be challenged – by anyone.'

'That will be welcome.' I shut my eyes and reached a hand to steady myself against the wall. 'All this... Robin's death... Mowbray's man I killed in response to it... it was all needless, achieved nothing. Sweet Christ, why did I come? What have I done?'

'Damnable bad luck, that's what it is, Harry. You've had your fair share of it. Come. Egremont will bear responsibility for all that's happened. You must put it behind you.'

Easily said, I thought, easily said; but I had to live with knowledge of my disastrous failure to protect Robin. I had to account for that failure and my broken promise to Mistress Bess Willoughby. I had ruined her life, made her a widow, rendered her children fatherless, brought them all incalculable misery. I deserved every recrimination she would heap on me.

*****

It was worse than anything I could imagine. Gentle, long-suffering, loving Bess screamed at me all the imprecations I richly merited, but it was more painful when she lowered her voice and looked at me with sheer hatred in her eyes.

'I esteemed you, Doctor Somers, from the days of our first acquaintance, but you have changed. Your arrogance killed Robin, your belief that you knew best. You decided that a humble, wounded bailiff would fit well into your make-believe in front of a heartless butcher. You disregarded the risks he would face. Did you think you could defend him? You never gave it a moment's thought. I loathe you, Harry Somers, I loathe you. I never want to see you again. Don't dare offer apologies or try to help me. I thank God there are others who will do what they can to assist me. Go now. Take your clever schemes elsewhere and I pray they bring no other family the grief you have brought mine.'

I wanted to protest, to say her strictures were unfair, to beg her forgiveness, to prostrate myself before her just anger, but firm hands grasped my shoulders and propelled me away from her.

'I never conceived that you could act so basely,' Piers Ford said. 'I'm almost ashamed to have considered you my friend. I hope you'll reflect on what you've done.'

'I'll entreat the Fitzvaughans to care for Mistress Willoughby and her children.'

'Save your breath, physician. She'll not lack for support. Others will uphold her through her hours of anguish. Not all men are as heartless or opinionated as you. But if you trespass on her sorrow with your whinging explanations and useless commiseration, you'll have me to reckon with. Do you understand?'

I understood.

Gaston and Lady Eleanor bore me no ill will and were grateful for the efforts I had made on their behalf but I left Hartham Manor resolved to journey there no more. I would carry my burden of guilt forever and I could not bear the idea of renewing its intensity by venturing near to the family I had wronged. Strangely, Gilbert Iffley seemed to comprehend my feelings. When he bade me farewell as I set off for Worthwaite, he implied I would now be free to concentrate on my most immediate and personal obligations and he gave a cryptic smile. He was always a provocative, mocking presence and I suspected no inner meaning.

*****

As I rode along the familiar route back to Worthwaite, soggy with wet leaves and autumnal dankness, I could think of nothing but Robin Willoughby's death. Why had he flung himself in front of me? It was an instinctive movement. He had no time to make a rational

245

choice. Did he regard a physician as of superior status and therefore to be protected? Did he consider that his duty to his overlord lay in saving me as Gaston's agent? Whatever intuitive concept lay behind his self-sacrifice, it was dire in its consequences. Had it been bred into him to disregard wife and children when he needed to take the ultimate action? How, before heaven, could it be justified?

I splashed across the little River Waveney to reach the edge of my manor land and I sensed wariness in the air, a feeling that I was being watched. At that moment a labourer popped up his head from behind a bush and greeted me, saying that my steward would be glad to see 'the master' returned. What new agony awaited me? Fearing for Kate, I ran into the house and met Judith descending the stairs, looking tight-lipped. She gave a start when she saw me. 'My wife,' I panted. 'How is she?'

'Doctor Somers, praise be! Mistress is in one of her melancholy moods. She has been since you left but she's quiet, causing no upsets and doing herself no harm. She's dozing by the fire at present.'

I began to express relief but Perkin had heard my voice and begged me to spare him a moment so I entered the small office where business was transacted. 'We've had to handle a difficult situation,' he said when we were both seated.

'Judith told me Mistress Somers...'

'Mistress Somers knows nothing of this, Doctor. Judith ensured she has remained unaware of the visitor who sought our hospitality and I turned away: Master Stephen Boice, sir.'

'Boice came here?' When?'

'Only yesterday. In accordance with your orders I repulsed him, rejected his request to stay the night. It was not easy – I felt ill-mannered declining the obligations of an open welcome to travellers.'

'You did right and I thank you. He has caused my wife great suffering in the past. Did he ask to see her?'

'Not at first. He said it was you he wished to meet. He was offended by my discourtesy – as indeed he had a right to be – but he's waiting in the neighbourhood for your return. He's at the inn in Diss, across the square from the church. He asked that you call on him there. He left a nosegay for Mistress Somers, with his avuncular greetings, but Judith agreed with me it should never be delivered to her.'

'I'm deeply grateful to you both.' Then with profound distaste I added, 'I'll call on the wretched man tomorrow.'

Perkin gave me correspondence delivered by messengers during my absence but only one missive among them roused my interest. I broke the seal on the Prioress's letter, wondering what she would say of Lady Maud Fitzvaughan's visit to Stamford but there was no reference to it. The date of the letter suggested the Prioress would have known it was in prospect, even if her guest had not yet arrived, but the reverend lady did not account it of sufficient significance by comparison with her commentary on Richard of York's alleged misdeeds. She expatiated with approval on the measures taken by her relative, Henry Percy, Earl of Northumberland, to make clear his opposition to the Duke. She contrasted this with the unreliability of the Nevilles, *the basest villains among the nobility*, she called them. Stephen Boice had Neville blood, but so indeed did my wife, and the Prioress's opprobrium made me uncomfortable.

When Kate was awake, I entered her room and kissed her softly on the forehead. 'I'm back, my sweet. Are you rested?'

For a moment she seemed not to know me but then she took my hand and spoke confidentially into my ear. 'The sparrow-hawk tore the ducklings to pieces, although they were full-grown. There were feathers scattered beside the pond. They won't come again.'

She folded her hands in her lap as if satisfied with this conclusion and I patted her fingers. 'I'm sorry.'

'Why should you be sorry? It was their function to die and feed the hawk. It cannot be altered.'

I shivered at her indifference but tried to convince myself that her serenity was something to be celebrated.

*****

Stephen Boice was well known in East Anglia as a prosperous merchant who traded in wool and woven cloth and, additionally when the occasion arose, other goods which promised a generous profit. At the best inn in Diss he occupied the landlord's own parlour and he gestured expansively for me to take a high-backed chair across the table from where he sat. His face was gaunt but his over-gown was of fine silk and he wore a heavy gold chain at his neck. 'I'm honoured, Doctor Somers, that you are content to come to me in person after your steward's sad blunder against the laws of hospitality. I rely on you to chastise him for his surliness.'

'My steward carried out my instructions to the letter, Boice. You can hardly be surprised. My door is barred to you for the misery you brought on your niece.'

'She's completely out of her right mind, I hear. Such a burden for you!'

'Keep your sympathy and let me know why you asked to see me. I won't spend an instant longer than necessary in your presence.'

'I shan't draw a sword on you, Harry. I'm not our dear friend, Egremont. And you don't have the companionship of a humble bailiff to drag in front of you and take a blow intended for your belly. We'd best remain at peace, had we not?'

Inevitably he knew all the details from Gilbert Iffley but I could not handle his taunting with equanimity. 'Get to the point, Boice. What do you want?'

'What have my good-brother and I ever wanted with you? Your goodwill, Harry, your support for Richard of York, even if covertly conveyed. Gilbert would like your agreement to recommence your role as his eyes and ears in London.'

'That's out of the question. Iffley accepted that Kate's health would override other obligations. When I saw him the other day he made no mention of any expectations for my help in the future. I've retired from City life.'

'The Baron has left it to me to remind you of your debt to him – a debt recently reinforced, I understand.'

'He saved my life. I acknowledge it but I must stay with Kate.'

'Why must you? Put her away, you fool, and resume your old life. She'll never be any good to you, you know that. Put her in some house of charity and forget her. She'll likely die before long if they keep her on scant rations and you can take a wife of sound mind and acquiescing body for your pleasure. In the meantime you can amuse yourself with demoiselles of high and low degree, as you did in the past. There are whores enough at court, Harry, as you well know, not just in the brothels of St Giles.'

I must not be goaded by his disgraceful suggestion or his vulgar innuendo about the noble lady who years ago had served the Queen and returned my passion. 'Kate is my wife and I stand by her. There's no point in continuing this conversation.'

'Oh, I think there is. You could be very useful. You have the goodwill of influential men – Sir Nicholas Chamberlayne for instance. He would help you re-establish yourself in Somerset's household and gain the Duke's confidence, like you did with the late lamented Duke of Suffolk. We are most anxious to learn some of Edmund Beaufort's most private secrets.'

'Even if I were willing there's no prospect I'd ever get close enough to Somerset for him to share his private secrets, whatever they may be.'

'Are you really as ignorant as you sound, Harry? Let me be frank. It is in the interests of our beloved King Henry and the whole realm of England to know if the

249

strutting peacock of Somerset has polluted the royal bed with his essence. Say our redoubtable Queen Margaret were to become with child, after so many barren years of marriage to the King, what grievous insult and affront would it be to his honour and the continuance of his line if she bore a son with Beaufort blood in his veins?'

'I know nothing about this, Boice, nor would I be likely to find out anything, even if there was an ounce of truth in your speculation.'

'An ounce of seed, more probably. Gilbert has been too mealy-mouthed in his dealings with you recently, hoping to soften you with kindness. I shall be explicit. In the fair realm of France there dwells a noble lady, a Countess no less, married to a respected and pious old gentleman. He took her to wife believing her a virtuous widow and they've lived in harmony some four years or so. He is a man of honour but somewhat narrow views. Would you like him to discover that his lady once bore a son out of wedlock, fathered by a humble English physician? The child died within a few days, did he not? But if I have heard aright the infant is buried not a stone's throw from where we sit. Consider, Doctor Somers, have you no regard remaining for the lady you once rashly aspired to marry? Would you be content for her shame to be bruited abroad in the French court, the butt of merriment and derision? How would your own afflicted wife react to your new notoriety? I have composed a vivid description of your impudent amour. A copy is already with my underling in Paris. He awaits my word to deliver it to the venerable Count. Shall I give that word?'

My limbs were quivering and my stomach heaved as I listened to this travesty of my earlier doomed love affair, years before I met Kate. I always knew that Boice had discovered the fact of my liaison with the widowed Yolande de Langeais but I believed the secret of the child she bore to be safe in his tiny grave. I trusted Father Wilfred, the chaplain at Wingfield, who had baptised and all too soon afterwards buried our infant son, but it was entirely possible he had been observed by some unknown witness and in due course Boice had pieced the story together. I knew nothing of Yolande's circumstances since her remarriage but the harm she might suffer by the exposure of our association was all too credible.

My mouth was dry but I would not capitulate without an attempt to deflect the threat. 'I don't deny I'd wish the past left in peace but I can't see what expectations you can have of me: what could I possibly do that would help Richard of York?'

He did not answer my question. 'Don't underestimate my intentions. You did that before and my niece suffered for your refusal to expedite Suffolk's sad demise, did she not?'

'You bear sole responsibility for your cruelty towards her. I'm not a murderer and, in any case, the situation doesn't arise in the case of Edmund Beaufort, if that's what you're suggesting. I've left his service and when I was briefly with his household I had only the most limited and formal contact with him.'

Boice rested his elbow on the arm of his chair and studied his finger-mails. 'Alas, it is true. You are not a murderer, you say, but you have killed, have you not?'

'In self-defence.'

'Perhaps in revenge also?' He was obviously referring to the man who slew Robin Willoughby and I did not answer. 'I'm glad to find, Harry, that you are a man of flesh and blood, not just a virtuous physician. But what I have to ask does not require you to kill anyone, at least not as a matter of necessity. My commission is different from what my good-brother discussed with you months ago. Indeed he might be somewhat disconcerted to hear my proposition. I wish you to write a letter.'

'To whom?'

'Your dear friend and assiduous correspondent, the Prioress of St. Michael's Convent in Stamford.'

I cursed inwardly. His sources of information were impressive but I doubted he would be aware of the contents of sealed letters. I said nothing and Boice continued.

'Here are writing implements. You will write to the Prioress in your own words but you will mention that you fear Sir Nicholas Chamberlayne may be playing Somerset false. You will say that you know he recently held a meeting in Cambridge with Baron Glasbury under the utmost secrecy.'

'Is that true?'

'As it happens, they did meet in Cambridge and Chamberlayne arranged an assignation as cautiously as if he was trysting with a lover. There now, you have been informed and can write what you've heard with a clear conscience.'

'Why would you wish the Prioress to be advised of this? What's the implication? The meeting could have concerned preliminary overtures of peace between King Henry and Richard of York. Chamberlayne and Iffley could have been testing each other to see if both sides were amenable.'

'It's not for you to concern yourself with motives. But I will answer your first question. The Prioress will pass on the information to the Abbot of Peterborough who, as you know, is privy to matters of state at the highest level and has the ear of several great men.'

'So you're trying to blacken Sir Nicholas's name?'

'Write your letter. Here's the ink-horn.'

'How can you be confident I won't send another letter, telling the Prioress I sent false news under duress?'

'Because you know I will find out whether the reverend lady has acted on your news and, if she does not, Countess Yolande's honour will be at risk.' He licked his lips as if savouring the prospect.

There were purposes here which I could not fathom but the subject matter seemed relatively innocuous; all would depend on the interpretation put on the circumstances. So I wrote a suitable letter, Boice read it and I affixed my seal. He gave gracious thanks and I was free to leave but I was under no illusion as to the completeness of my surrender to his will. This would be merely the first of his demands, now he possessed a means of coercion over me.

It occurred to me that his menaces differed from those Iffley employed. The Baron's threats were matters of expediency, delivered for a purpose, to achieve a particular end, but they gave him no personal pleasure. Boice gained vicious satisfaction from the pain his taunts inflicted on me and all his victims. His compulsion was to control the actions of others; his gratification came from forcing them to subject themselves to his will and he would use any foul means to achieve this.

Alongside my helplessness in the face of Kate's debility of mind, my guilt at Robin Willoughby's death and my shame when Bess reviled me, submitting to Boice's eccentric demand seemed of trivial importance. If I could protect Countess Yolande from harm it would be a small victory against the malignant fate which had trapped me. My self-respect was in tatters and it seemed improbable that time would dull the dejection I felt at my multiple failures.

Chapter 21

News percolated to Worthwaite over the next few weeks suggesting that tensions were increasing once again between York and Somerset. Outraged by the fighting in the West Country, the King had summoned York to attend him but Duke Richard simply disregarded the order and royal authority was too weak to act against a disobedient cousin. At this point King Henry's chief adviser threw down a challenge by targeting a proxy for his hated rival. The new Speaker of the Commons, Sir William Oldhall, was Duke Richard's adherent and Somerset chose, provocatively, to indict him on a charge of high treason. Oldhall had wind of the indictment and sought sanctuary in the royal chapel of St. Martin-le-Grand but Somerset's goading forced York to take action.

Not long after the season of Yule I heard that Duke Richard had issued a statement of loyalty to the King, claiming his good name was being traduced by his enemies. He tried to undermine their slanderous allegations by offering to swear his good faith on the Sacrament but when this solemn appeal was ignored he announced his intention to arraign Somerset and bring him to trial for losing the King's lands in Normandy. More ominously he began to mobilise his followers.

The Prioress wrote to tell me how York's supporters in the eastern Midlands, where the Duke owned several estates, were being rallied and asked to supply money and arms. She had heard from the Abbot of Peterborough that companies of men carrying weapons were seen marching to answer the summons and it was believed they intended to advance on London. This could have alarming repercussions but, for me, the significance of the Prioress's letter was what it omitted. It cast no doubts on what I told her about Sir Nicholas Chamberlayne in the communication Boice obliged me to send. She did not query or express surprise at the news. In such unsettled times, improbable and misleading assertions could easily gain credibility.

By the beginning of February there were reports that King Henry was marshalling his supporters in Northampton. Somerset, perhaps backed by Queen Margaret, was encouraging the King to show rigour and it seemed all too likely that there would be a confrontation between what were in effect two opposing armies. I lamented the prospect of hostilities between fellow Englishmen but these events were far removed from my immediate concerns.

Since before Yuletide, Kate's condition, while not combative or violent, had deteriorated into brooding melancholy from which it was difficult to rouse her. Sometimes tears streamed from her eyes, at others she picked at her skin or nibbled her nails, but her actions were subdued, underscoring her frailty. She seemed scarcely aware of my presence and, although she responded in silence to Judith's ministrations, she showed no comprehension of the wider world. Her misery cast a pall over the household and even Judith's resilience was tested by the gloom inside the house which paralleled the greyness of the dreary winter skies outside. My own mood seemed frozen in hopelessness.

I was checking the wood store behind the stables when I saw the rider approaching the manor and I stared for a moment in disbelief but the gangling figure of Piers Ford was unmistakeable. During the past few months Gaston had sent occasional messages to say that all was well on his estate but this was the only contact I had with Hartham Manor and I could expect no more. I rejoiced to see Piers but was anxious about what he had come to say and he was awkwardly formal when I reached him, as the groom helped him dismount.

'Doctor Somers, I'm bound for Wingfield to help them out as their wheelwright is unwell. Lord Fitzvaughan asked if I'd call here to give you the joyful news that Lady

Eleanor has borne him a second son who promises well. The lady is also in good health I understand.'

'I'm truly happy to hear this and I'll send them good wishes. Will you come and take refreshment at the house?'

I thought he was about to refuse but Judith had appeared round the corner of the stables, carrying a pile of dirty linen for the laundry-maid to wash. She was untouched by my apprehension and ran forward to welcome Piers wholeheartedly. In her company he relaxed and agreed to take a glass of ale before proceeding on his way but he emphasised that his visit must be brief. I wanted to ask how Mistress Willoughby and her children were but I did not dare to put the question immediately and was relieved that he spoke of other matters.

After Judith had left us, we talked of public happenings, safe topics we were both ready to discuss, and Piers took the lead. 'You'll have heard of the calls to arms that have been sent out. Sad days these are and no mistake. The concerns of humble men won't occupy the thoughts of noblemen preparing for battle. Those petitions we sent to the King when Jack Cade gave us hope of securing redress will be trampled underfoot when knights in plate armour clash in poor men's fields and flatten the sprouting corn.'

'I hope it won't come to that. King Henry is a peaceful man.'

'But his kin are at each other's throats. Great men are bred to delight in swordplay. They need an outlet for their warlike instincts. The only chance for peace in England may be if their energies are diverted elsewhere. Lord Fitzvaughan says there could be fighting across the Narrow Sea again. I don't wish harm towards humble Frenchmen. They're as much at their masters' command as we are but if we were at war with them again it might distract our bloodthirsty nobles from attacking each other.'

I had not heard any rumour of renewed conflict in France and the possibility of the King raising funds for ships and soldiers seemed remote. I said as much and then, as we were easier with each other, I took my chance. 'Are you still content at Hartham Manor? It's well over a year you've been there now.'

Piers fixed me with his clear grey eyes and it was obvious he understood exactly what I was really asking. 'I might have gone home to Dartford by now had events not turned out as they did.'

'You're looking out for Mistress Willoughby and her children...?' His mouth set in a thin line and I faltered, fearing my question too intrusive.

'Of course: I owe Robin Willoughby that duty. They have removed from the bailiff's house so the new man can occupy it. The Dowager Lady Fitzvaughan has taken them into the dower-house.'

My stomach somersaulted but this was pleasing news. 'Mistress Willoughby served Lady Maud many years ago. I'm glad her ladyship has remembered her debt and given the family lodgings.'

'Mistress Willoughby will do well enough at the dower-house though it must pain her to live there in such circumstances when it was once her home with Master Robin. But there's no doubt it's a proper solution to her troubles for the year of her deepest mourning.'

I could not frame the next inevitable enquiry: 'and then?' But he comprehended what I wanted to know, impertinent though it was.

'When that time is past, I shall ask her to become my wife,' he said.

It was what I presumed would happen. 'I shall beg Heaven's blessings on you both.'

His expression was grave as he faced me. 'Perhaps I was sent to Hartham Manor to bring her comfort after you caused her unutterable grief. Heaven is merciful to those men's sinfulness has hurt.'

He would spare me nothing.

*****

Only a few days later another visitor arrived at Worthwaite and, having confirmed that I was at home, begged accommodation for the night. This arrival caused me pangs of guilt, though different in nature from those Piers evoked, but Sir Nicholas Chamberlayne gave no sign of bearing me animosity, although he looked drawn, and I was sincere in wishing to renew our friendship. After we had eaten and were sitting companionably with a flagon of wine, he enquired delicately about Kate's health.

'She's in a doleful mood at present. I wish her tranquillity might presage a permanent improvement but experience shows she can relapse. I'm sorry she behaved in an embarrassing manner when you came here previously.'

'I was very sad to see her condition but I assure you I gave it no further thought. I've had my own problems to engage with recently.' He paused and I waited, not wanting to press him if he was disinclined to say more, then he sighed. 'It would be a help to share my difficulties. Indeed I came here specially to ask you one thing but I'd like to burden you with another if you don't mind.'

'Please go on.' I did not relish the idea of sharing his confidences.

'My position has changed since we first met at Queenborough, since I saw you last year in fact: just in the past few weeks, certainly since the Feast of the Nativity. I was with Somerset then and he was as confiding and affable as ever, giving me important commissions to carry out on his behalf. Yet now I'm commanded to stay in East Anglia, report to him regularly on events concerning his interests but not to join him at court. At the same time the confidential information he used to send me has ceased to come. I've been put out to grass, as if my usefulness is ended – or he no longer trusts me.'

I squirmed privately, fearing that Sir Nicholas no longer trusted me, that he was testing me, in the knowledge that I had informed against him with malicious

258

lies about his loyalty. 'Do you have any idea how this could have happened?'

'I've racked my brains but I can't think of anything. My actions have been dictated by the remit Somerset has given me. I've always had a free hand to act for his interests and he's never queried what I've done. He hasn't now. He's just cut me off from his confidence.'

'Have you asked for an explanation?'

'I'd rather do that face to face but I'm barred from seeing him. If I'm driven to send him a letter protesting my good faith, I'll sound like Richard of York whining incessantly to the King about his fidelity.'

'Is there anything you've done that could be misinterpreted?' I was sailing into the wind by putting that question but I owed him as much truthfulness as possible.

'If someone is dogging my footsteps, checking those I meet, putting false constructions on my actions, of course there are incidents that could be presented as dubious. But that's always been the case: it was the essence of what Somerset wanted from me. He expected me to act covertly, to ferret around to discover secrets, to speak to men who are his enemies when necessary.'

'Secret assignations?' I purposely employed Boice's description.

Chamberlayne chuckled. 'Hardly the word I'd use. Assignations have a hint of loose living, trysts with lady-loves. I've had no trysts to cause Somerset any qualms. Undeniably, I've met those I dislike in the path of duty: John Mowbray and his minions often enough, Gilbert Iffley and that rogue Egremont who caused Lord Fitzvaughan such trouble. Somerset knows all about this.'

By now I was convinced from Sir Nicholas's manner that he did not suspect me of betraying him, nor did he have particular concerns about his contact with Gilbert Iffley. I felt both relief and remorse.

'Perhaps if Somerset has been fed lies,' I said, 'he'll soon discount them, knowing how you've served him faithfully. Maybe he's just being cautious for the moment.'

'I hope so. It is possible. But it's been helpful to put my concerns into words, see things in proportion. You're right. I should give Somerset time to reflect. He may decide it's all a mistake and revert to the old relationship, at least summon me to talk about it.' Sir Nicholas drank some wine and smiled. 'What I wanted to ask you is something quite different: a favour.'

I was overcome by a sense of obligation. 'What can I do?'

'I've never spoken to you of my family: my wife and two youngsters at my house north-west of London, at Harrow on the Hill. I've been blessed in my marriage. My wife is dear to me but she is sadly ailing: a wasting disease, they term it. I know there's little hope for her but I would wish to ease her final months. There may be medication which could aid her, reduce her pain. The physicians who have visited her are old men who mean well but I fancy they're limited in what they offer. I wondered if you would come with me to see Joan and give your opinion. It would only take a few days to ride there and return to Worthwaite. If you can safely leave Mistress Somers for that length of time, I'd be profoundly grateful.'

His request took me completely by surprise but there was no doubt how I would respond. I was flattered and pleased to be asked to play the physician's role, which was my, too often neglected, calling. Moreover, although Sir Nicholas could not know this, I wished to do whatever I could to mitigate the harm I had occasioned him.

'Kate will be well cared for,' I said. 'I can leave her for a few days. I'm at your service.'

*****

The Chamberlayne manor-house was situated high on the prominent hill at Harrow, near to the church of St. Mary's and the small village which straggled down the upper reaches of a steep slope. Farmland adjoined it, benefitting from the good soil of the ground above the

260

muddy swamp at the foot of the hill, and Sir Nicholas leased these fields and orchards from the Archbishop of Canterbury who held much of the land in the neighbourhood. The house was not fortified, as was common within a half day's journey from London, but it consisted of a tower standing separately from the range of domestic and guest accommodation within a walled enclosure.

It was a charming spot, with wide views to the south, but our visit was distressing, for Lady Joan was severely ill. I could offer little to help her except an infusion of primrose root which her regular physicians had not tried and may have given her a degree of relief. She was a lady of robust spirit, counter-balancing her physical frailty, and she was determined to resist the grasping hand of mortality until her strength was exhausted. I could see she had been a beauty until illness stole the bloom from her cheeks and flesh from her body. It was affecting to witness Sir Nicholas with her, each struggling to comfort the other while both knew they had limited time left together. The son and daughter, around twelve and thirteen years old, were clearly devoted to their mother and sat beside her bed while she slept, gazing at her as if to make a picture of her face in their minds to preserve and treasure when she was gone.

I confirmed my depressing diagnosis to Sir Nicholas but he was touchingly grateful to me for journeying to see his wife and we spent another quietly agreeable evening together. I arranged to set out on my return to Worthwaite the following morning but as dusk was falling a messenger arrived from Northampton with news that changed my plans – and in many respects my future life.

Sir Nicholas broke the seal excitedly, extracting several papers and gulping the one word "Somerset" as he did so but his expression, while he read the letter, was inscrutable. He laid down the paper when he finished and sat silently for a moment staring at his clasped hands. 'For myself there is encouraging news,' he said, 'but for our country the outlook is troubling. Somerset is on the road with the royal entourage, making south to London. He has sent me a safe conduct to enter the City so that I can join him at the court in Westminster.'

I began to express pleasure at these tidings but realised he had more to tell.

'By the King's order the gates of London have been closed to all without the authority of a safe conduct and specifically to Richard of York and his followers. It seems that the Duke has amassed a vast army and is believed to intend attacking the City. It looks dangerously probable that there will be fighting when the two armies meet.'

This bore out Piers Ford's gloomy yet prophetic words but I concentrated on the news as it affected Sir Nicholas, hoping it might alleviate my guilt. 'Does Somerset sound welcoming towards you?'

'I think so. He speaks of "these uncertain times in which misrepresentation and half-truths abound". I judge he'll listen to my denial of treachery. But this isn't all. The messenger had sought me in Suffolk before coming here and he sought you too at Worthwaite. Somerset begs that you will also attend him at Westminster. He has a commission which he believes you could undertake. See, a letter to you is enclosed in case the messenger found you in my company.'

I took the missive with a trembling hand, torn by irreconcilable emotions of eagerness, horror and shame. It used similar wording to what Sir Nicholas had read out except for the added confirmation that Her Grace, Queen Margaret, endorsed the request for me to join the court and promised she nurtured no continuing bitterness towards me for events in the past. This could only refer to the anger she had felt over my dastardly liaison with Countess Yolande. It was satisfying to have the Queen's sanction but I could not imagine what commission Somerset had in mind. I hoped fervently it would call on my physician's skills.

'There's no knowing how long I'd be needed at court,' I said. 'I've sworn not to leave Kate for more than a few days. My absences can affect her adversely.'

'And I must leave my dying wife without a second thought. I have no choice if I am to redeem my fortunes. Nor I think do you, Harry. These directives carry the royal imprimatur. We're not at liberty to refuse.'

His words put my misgivings in perspective and I acknowledged their accuracy, so shortly afterwards I took up a pen to write the necessary letters to my wife and household at Worthwaite. When great men decreed, we were all pawns.

*****

By the time we reached Westminster next day we learned that there was no immediate danger of encountering Richard of York's army. Once he was informed that the gates of London were barred to him and the citizens opposed to his arrival, because of the disruption it would cause, he had diverted from his proposed route. Instead, he crossed the Thames some dozen miles to the south-west of the City, at Kingston. It was thought he was then marching eastwards, possibly to attempt entering London over the rehabilitated bridge, nearly two years after its destruction on Jack Cade's orders. Whatever this might portend in military terms, it meant that Sir Nicholas and I could enter the precincts of the royal palace without obstruction.

It was many years since I had last ridden under the great archway marking the entry to the palace on the landward side, although I had arrived by river with Suffolk when he was taken from the Tower to appear before the King. This and other memories of my presence within the precincts were disturbing and I did not want to remember the dangers, challenges and betrayals they encompassed. I wished I had not consented to come there.

Oblivious to my disquiet, Somerset exuded charm when he received me, worryingly grateful to me for travelling to Westminster, asking earnestly after Kate's welfare and my own health following the assaults I had suffered months earlier. When he shed formality like this he was easy to speak to, but I always felt there was something superficial in his bonhomie which put me on my guard. I waited for him to explain why he had sent for me and, after many pleasantries, he did so.

'I've heard several accounts of your skill in investigating secret matters with discretion. I want to call on those services.'

Silently I groaned; this was not what I wanted but I gave a gratified smile. Somerset beamed and continued.

'I have reason to believe an attempt is being made to infiltrate a spy at court, an agent for our enemies. Does that seem possible to you?'

I cleared my throat to control my voice. 'All too possible, your Grace. The late Duke of Suffolk's household was similarly targeted and mischief caused before the culprit was identified.'

'Ah! Then it's right to be prudent especially when it is Queen Margaret's household which is beset. But, you understand, we would not wish to alert this potential spy to our suspicions. We need to be certain and perhaps to use the situation to our own advantage.'

It was not clear whether "we" included the Queen or simply indicated Somerset's own self-assumed grandeur. I was not going to enquire. 'You wish me to sound out the person concerned and form a judgement?'

'Assuredly. You grasp the position exactly.'

'What place does the fellow hold in the Queen's household?'

'It's a young woman, Mistress Ursula Bateby, a widow who was briefly an attendant to Duchess Cecily of York. The Duchess has recommended her to the Queen's service as a tiring-maid skilled in dressing hair and fashioning headdresses, sent her as a gift you might say.'

264

'If the intention is for Mistress Bateby to act as York's agent, it's rather blatant for the Duchess to recommend her, isn't it? Surely they'd know she'd be an object of distrust?'

'It could be a clever double-deception, couldn't it? So obvious, we wouldn't believe the duplicity?'

'I suppose so. But how am I to encounter one of the Queen's tiring-maids and hold a suitable interrogation?'

'That's the intriguing thing, Doctor Somers. Mistress Bateby has asked to meet you if you come to court. She has a connection with your family, it seems. Queen Margaret has agreed I should arrange an introduction.'

While inexplicable, this shone an entirely different light on a murky business and I definitely did not want to be involved. Yet it was difficult to refuse without calling into question my own loyalties. 'I'm at your service, your Grace,' I said reluctantly, 'but I don't hold out much chance of exposing her as a spy if there's a plot as devious as you suggest.'

'I'm obliged. I'll have her brought to the long gallery at sundown. The Queen's Chamberlain will introduce you. Do your best. At any rate the prospect won't be displeasing.' He gave a knowing chortle.

I understood Somerset's flippant comment when the Chamberlain conducted me to Mistress Bateby after I entered the long gallery. She was sitting in a window recess while liveried flunkies, pages and all manner of attendants bustled to and fro along one of the busiest thoroughfares in the palace. Our conversation would be noticed but not overheard and there were many rendezvous taking place in front of other windows along the wall looking onto the courtyard. At the far end of the narrow chamber I glimpsed Sir Nicholas Chamberlayne engaged in animated discourse with an attractive young woman who gazed at him with admiration. I noted his elegant gestures and thought of him as the consummate courtier.

265

I bowed as the Chamberlain withdrew and took stock of the strikingly pretty face in front of me which somehow managed to combine modesty and impudence in its expression. For one skilled in fashioning headdresses, she wore a noticeably plain and modest cap as befitted her widowed status.

'I'm indebted to you, Doctor Somers. They said you were not at court, yet here you are. I was anxious to meet you.' Her voice was mellow, richer in tone than might be expected from her slight, girlish frame. I judged her about twenty years old.

'Mistress Bateby, I'm honoured but you'll have to enlighten me as to your wish to see me.'

'Oh, I think you can surmise my purpose in being at court. You're reputed to be astute. I bring you greetings from Baron Glasbury.'

It was exactly what I feared. 'I wouldn't recommend that you refer to that gentleman while you serve Queen Margaret. He isn't in favour at Westminster.'

'Of course, but this is a tête-à-tête between two of his acolytes, is it not? We are both bound to do his bidding, under threat or promise. Don't let's pretend. Somerset has sent you to assess whether I am to be trusted. For my part I can give you my solemn assurance that I have no weapon concealed about my person and will do no one physical injury. My business is simply to observe and report, as you were once asked to do. Your new role, as the Baron described it, is to vet my honesty and swear to my integrity. There now, are you clear?'

'I understand perfectly but if I were willing to lie on your behalf, asserting your innocence of wicked intent, I would need a convincing story to back up my conclusion.'

She gave a low, rather vulgar laugh. 'I appreciate your directness, Doctor. I have a story for you and it happens to be true. I was married two years ago to a boorish soldier in Richard of York's company at his castle of Ludlow. I was however widowed when Master Bateby was killed in the fighting last autumn in the West Country.

266

He was no great loss to me but I expressed the wish to leave the scene of my married life, whereupon Lady Jane Glasbury, the Baron's wife, arranged for me to go to Fotheringhay, another of the Duke's residences where Duchess Cecily spends much of her time. This was not greatly to my liking but before long the Baron devised the plan to send me to court with the Duchess's blessing. You will not of course mention the Baron when you report to Somerset but you may recount my restless existence since my husband died, my wish for a different way of life after I was left bereft.'

'Of the husband you do not truly mourn?'

'That's impertinent, Doctor Somers, and neither here nor there. I am at court as a bystander, quite blameless in my intentions. You will not need to perjure yourself in confirming this. I will serve Queen Margaret with diligence.'

'And watch her bedchamber assiduously?'

Mistress Bateby's containment was ruffled for the first time. 'You are too knowing for your own good, physician.'

'I hear rumours, mistress, and I appreciate how valuable certain information might be to York's interests.'

'So, we need not dissemble. If I become aware of imprudence, I shall report it.' She had regained her calm demeanour. 'I hardly need to be explicit, Doctor Somers, but I assume Baron Glasbury has some hold over you that will ensure your compliance with his wishes – or maybe it is Stephen Boice who is threatening you.'

I tried to disguise my tremor. 'You're acquainted with him also? I can't applaud your choice of friends.'

She held my eyes with her own dark, unblinking orbs. 'Stephen is my lover,' she said. 'That may discredit me in your view, I imagine, but you will comprehend the importance of doing his bidding. Go now and confirm to Somerset that I am a sorrowful widow wishing to serve her sovereign lady with true devotion, glad to escape the clutches of the distasteful folk who follow Richard of

York's fortunes. I promise you I will play my part with dedication. I shall meet with you again, when I am ready to speak further.'

She reached across to touch my hand and her cool fingers burned into my skin.

Chapter 22

With a heavy heart I reported to Somerset, provisionally exonerating Mistress Bateby from malicious intent but salving my conscience to some extent by indicating I was not wholly convinced by her story. This had the inevitable effect of prolonging my stay in Somerset's household, with the prospect of meeting that disquieting young woman once more. Natural compassion told me to be sorry for her, for I was all too conscious how Boice misused the women he encountered, including his own estranged wife. The knowledge that Ursula Bateby was his mistress, forced for some reason to act as his puppet, was abhorrent. Yet she appeared self-confident and a good deal more at ease in her duplicitous role than I was. Gilbert Iffley had set up my contact with her and succeeded in enmeshing me in his coils more effectively than ever before. I was ashamed to have become his creature – and more so Boice's – but I could see no escape.

There was little time to ruminate on my situation as news came the next day that York had skirted the City to the south of the Thames and set up camp on Dartford Heath. I speculated how Piers Ford would feel about the Duke's army in such proximity to his home town. Would he yearn to return there? Would he see Duke Richard as upholding the interests of ordinary folk?

York was reported to be accompanied by nearly ten thousand men, backed by other contingents led by friendly nobles. Off-shore, seven ships rode at anchor, equipped with stores to sustain his followers and ready to sail up river, if necessary, to attack the City. The danger was clear and the King's adherents were alert to it. The royalist army, with its complement of nobles loyal to Henry, crossed London and within two days were camped on Blackheath, less than ten miles from Duke Richard's dissidents, neatly prejudicing their route to the City.

I hated returning to Blackheath in Somerset's train, for it held too many painful memories, but he urged me to go with his men to attend to their wounds if there was fighting and this seemed all too likely. I rode up the slope from Deptford and noted that some of Jack Cade's palisade was still in place although much was broken down. Probably stakes had been taken for firewood or to make fences. There were carts standing in the same area used by John Toft and his companions nearly two years earlier and I thought of the unfortunate George Antey. I wondered briefly how his family in Maidstone had fared since I met them but their concerns now seemed far removed from mine.

I was lodged in a tented pavilion with a score of others and the air inside the sheets of canvas was fetid with sweat, bad breath and body odours. As darkness fell I sat in the open, wrapped in a horse blanket against the chilly February air, leaving my return to the makeshift dormitory until exhaustion overcame me. Torches had been set in brackets between the tents and servants hurried about with smaller flaming brands so, beyond the shadows, there were occasional pools of light. Nevertheless it was the sound of a familiar voice which roused me before I made out his profile. He was shouting goodbye to a companion.

'Rendell! How good to see you.'

'Good that I'm in line to be slaughtered by some fellow Englishman? Christ, Doctor Somers, what are you doing here? Ready to stick us back together again when we've been cut in bits?' He sauntered across and sat down beside me.

'Pray God fighting can be avoided. There's to be a delegation to Richard of York tomorrow to see if peace can be upheld. Are you back with Lord Scales's men from the Tower of London?'

'No, thank the Lord! I'm part of Somerset's entourage. Sir Nicholas Chamberlayne fixed it up for me. Don't want to fight in England though. If they get an army together to cross the Narrow Sea, like they want to, I'll be off like a flash. You with Somerset too?'

I nodded. 'For the time being. I hope to get home to Worthwaite soon.' I found it difficult to say more.

'You in trouble, Doctor?' Rendell's intuition could be impressive and unnerving.

'Not for the first time, you might say.' I drew on information I had learned which might catch his attention. 'If there is fighting in France, it won't be in Normandy this time. The folk in Gascony, to the south-west, have become tired of the French King's rule and they've asked King Henry to reclaim the land which used to belong to his forefathers. If he manages to raise money to send an army, that's where it will go.'

Rendell whistled. 'You're in the know! Sounds interesting. I'm itching to get a sword in my hand and lay into some French rogues. But don't think I ain't noticed you changed the subject. If you're in need of a bodyguard, I'd happily help you out. Done so before often enough, haven't I?'

'Very true, but all I want is to get back to Kate and see how she is.'

'That Judith still with her? Christ, she'd be able to chase off a battalion of devils with a flick of her eyebrow.'

Although genuinely glad to see Rendell, as I always was, I felt relief when an attendant emerged from Somerset's tent and summoned me to attend the Duke. The double-dealing ambivalence which now permeated my life made me shamefaced in front of my old friends and, miserably, I preferred to shun them.

In the principal pavilion, Somerset was discussing arrangements for the following day's delegation with a number of notables, some of whom I recognised. The Earls of Salisbury and Warwick were Nevilles, brother and nephew respectively of York's wife, Duchess Cecily. In spite of this they were at that time loyal to King Henry and I had glimpsed them at court in the past. Two Bishops stood alongside them: one was introduced as from the See of Ely but the other needed no introduction: William Waynflete, Bishop of Winchester, whom I knew

271

personally. He greeted me in front of the assembly as if I was worthy of their notice and immediately turned to Somerset.

'It would be fitting to have a physician in our party, your Grace. Along with us clerics, the presence of a quack will convey a message of peace but also remind people that his services would be needed if the two sides come to blows. I'd be happy to have Harry beside me.'

Somerset readily agreed and I was given no option to refuse. I had mixed feelings. I always enjoyed attending key occasions, as this was to be, in order to watch how great men behaved when under pressure and attempting to outwit one another. This time, however, I would be all too aware of my two-headed nature, viewed by both sides as their servant, but I did not expect to be more than an observer.

Next morning I rode down the long hill, past the edge of Sir Hugh de Grey's lands, fighting back the vile memories the area evoked. In the distance the dull gleam of grey water reminded me that this was the pond by which Adam Ash had been killed and little Hubert de Grey abducted to suffer torture and death at the hands of the squire Stanlaw. There was enough sorrow for me in the scene without dwelling on Kate's later aberrant behaviour and the abuse she received at nearby Danson.

As we approached, my inexperienced eye could see that, despite rumours to the contrary, Richard of York's army was a good deal smaller than the royal forces arrayed at Blackheath which were blocking his way to the City. It was especially noticeable that there were few grand tents festooned with heraldic banners and served by dozens of attendants. The Duke had not succeeded in attracting many of the nobility to his cause. There was evidence of some popular support in the ranks of humble soldiers but most men's eyes were downcast, not filled with the exhilaration I had seen in Jack Cade's followers. If York had been driven by exasperation to take up arms, he had not secured the approval of the populace for disturbing the peace.

When I saw York once before, I had been struck by both his intelligence and pride. His manner on greeting the King's representatives at Dartford reinforced those impressions but my attention was distracted by the sight of Gilbert Iffley standing near his overlord, smirking at me openly. I was thankful there was no sign of Stephen Boice.

'My Lord Duke,' Bishop Waynflete began with a cordial smile, 'I am no warrior able to estimate fighting capabilities, but I deem you would be hard pressed to take the field against his Grace, the King, with any chance of winning. Not to put too fine a point on it, I surmise your position is hopeless. I need hardly mention the fact that to come in arms against your sovereign lord is treason, however virtuous your intentions. How is this sad conundrum to be solved?'

Iffley gritted his teeth with annoyance but the Duke was prepared to concede a forced withdrawal while remaining resolute in pursuing his main objective. 'I've brought armed men to defend me while I negotiate because I have too often been imperilled by my enemies' belligerence. I am no traitor and will willing swear my loyalty to our beloved King as I have often done. In return for the renewal of my oath and the dispersal of my men, I ask one thing only: that Edmund Beaufort, Duke of Somerset, be arrested and punished for his gross incompetence in losing the King's territories in Normandy and his mismanagement of this realm's government. If that is granted, so justice may prevail, I shall throw myself before my royal cousin with protestations of my allegiance and set aside my weapons.'

Bishop Waynflete clasped his hands in prayer. 'Your Grace, these are seemly sentiments. I commend them. Our dearest hope must be to uphold peace in our land, peace and the rule of law. It is troubling to men of all estates when their highest liege lords, cousins of the royal blood, cannot resolve their differences by fair exchange.

273

Compromise is always necessary between men of honour and good will. We will most gladly report your words to King Henry.'

The other members of the delegation had their say, reiterating Waynflete's sentiments in less conciliatory words. York listened patiently but whenever his guests referred to his wish that Somerset be arrested, Duke Richard gave a thin smile of satisfaction. There was no doubt he was ready to endure the humiliation of capitulating if he eliminated his hated rival.

Towards the end of the talks, refreshment was brought and small groups broke away from the main party to hold their own conversations. At that point, as I feared, Baron Glasbury bore down on me and grasped my arm. 'Dear Harry, how delightful to find you in this estimable company! A certain winsome young widow in the Queen's service is also pleased with your assistance. I give you my thanks. Is Duke Richard right to trust the good faith of the Most Reverend Bishop?'

'I'm not privy to any deviousness. The King is a man of peace so it's credible he would make concessions to keep his cousin's loyalty. Bishop Waynflete is his trusted negotiator.'

'As he was with Jack Cade – who, as I recall, was tricked by Waynflete and his cronies, given a pardon in a name which was not his?'

'It behoves both sides to pay careful attention to the words used in speech or on paper.'

'I note what you say, Harry, and in this case what has not been said.'

'Then no doubt you will advise the Duke accordingly.'

'He won't listen to doubts because he has no alternative. He knows he cannot overcome in the field at present. He has to trust their good faith. But let us be cheerful – all may indeed go well. If so, we will no longer need to impose on Mistress Bateby's ingenuity in watching her royal mistress and you will be able to return to your

274

manor and your unfortunate wife. What a happy outcome that would be!'

I could not work out whether Iffley believed this to be at all likely or was merely indulging his habitual cynicism.

*****

Back at Blackheath preparations were made to receive York's submission next day and, along with other middle-ranking attendants, I was kept away from the principal pavilions. There was no sign of Somerset and I wondered if he had already been taken in charge, or perhaps spirited away into exile before his enemies could assault him. The lesson of Suffolk's leisurely departure, albeit under the King's safe-conduct, might have been learned because that had given time for the disaffected to mount their attack and stage their outrageous execution. If Somerset had departed, I promised myself, I would set off for Worthwaite at the earliest opportunity.

When the scouts announced that Richard of York was approaching, accompanied, as had been agreed, by just forty retainers, a great body of the King's followers assembled in front of the royal pavilion and I welcomed the opportunity to be present. To my pleasure, Sir Nicholas Chamberlayne beckoned me to stand with him at the entrance of the great tent and I was relieved to confirm that Baron Glasbury was not among York's escort. After the Duke and his party had gone inside, we followed, to stand in ranks each side of the dais where the King sat in state.

Immediately we entered, we saw what York saw and understood the dastardly implications. It was not Duke Richard who was forsworn.

At the King's left side, in brazen splendour, stood Edmund Beaufort, fully at liberty and in royal favour, bathed in the smiles of Queen Margaret who sat with arrogant beauty on her husband's right. Ranged behind the trio were the clerics and nobles who had ridden to Dartford Heath the previous day and given the impression that Richard's terms were accepted. Around them an overpowering number of attendants and soldiers, not overtly bearing arms, of course, watched the proceedings with closed expressions but some could not suppress their grins.

As I took up my position with Sir Nicholas Chamberlayne, I spotted Rendell standing to attention in the back row and he winked at me. He was under no illusion as to the mischief that was afoot. I felt soiled by association with the deception which had been practised and for a moment I considered myself exonerated from guilt for the personal double-dealing in which I had become involved.

'Your Grace,' York broke out in fury after a cursory obeisance. 'This is not what was agreed. I offered my pledge of loyalty on the understanding Edmund Beaufort would be arrested and face imprisonment.'

The Queen gave a clicking sound of impatience with her teeth but King Henry needed no prompting. He was in command of the occasion. 'Cousin of York, you are presumptuous to tell us whom we may and may not have as our chief counsellor. It is for us to use our judgement with the advice of other worthy members of our Council. You are the royal kinsman who has placed our realm at hazard of disruption, not my Lord of Somerset. You came in arms against your sovereign lord, in defiance of all the laws of chivalry and obedience to your King. You hovered on the brink of treason and only our magnanimity has saved you from the dire consequences of such baseness. It is not for you to set terms for your future compliance with our will.'

Richard of York spluttered with outrage and poured out angry invective against Somerset and his friends, only managing to avoid blaming the King himself with tortuous circumlocutions. He was impotent, at the mercy of his foes and the King whose favour they had won.

He blustered and roared his complaints but forty retainers could achieve nothing on his behalf: he had no choice but to bend the knee and accept Henry's decree. In return for his imposed submission, he was to be spared no disgrace. His humiliation was to be public, swearing a solemn oath of allegiance before the high altar of St. Paul's Cathedral in the City before a massed congregation, with assembled citizens thronging the streets outside. He was to pledge never again to raise a body of soldiers, never to attempt violence against King Henry's person, always in future to obey the King's commands. Then, by the King's grace, he would be allowed to return to his castle at Ludlow, exiled effectively from the court and any exercise of power.

In accordance with the public nature of this mortifying charade, all the court and its hangers-on would be expected to witness the Duke's ceremonial surrender at St. Paul's and I knew that I would be required to attend. I accompanied Somerset to court once more, in preparation for this occasion but in fact I was saved from observing York's dishonour and, although I regretted the circumstances, I did not regret this omission. The prospect of seeing a noble of the blood-royal shamed was not to be relished.

Nevertheless I hoped the occasion would bring an end to the threats Baron Glasbury and Stephen Boice employed to force me to follow their orders. Somerset was triumphant and the King had declared his hand in supporting his chosen adviser. Surely York's cause had finally been rendered fruitless?

*****

Somerset took a sizeable entourage with him to the Palace of Westminster, flaunting his supremacy. His wife was to join him there and, after York's public disgrace, Edmund Beaufort was to accompany the King on an ambitious programme of royal progresses through the southern and middle counties of England. King Henry's

277

ascendancy was to be made visible to the disaffected, justice dispensed to the aggrieved, punishment imposed on the guilty and the impression given to all restless subjects that the King's Council, headed by Somerset, was fully in control of affairs. There was even renewed and serious talk of raising funds for an attack on the French in Gascony. York's brief assertiveness, his angry bluster and the attempt to enforce his terms on the court party had come to nothing.

I assumed my inclusion in the entourage taken to Westminster was temporary. There was no suggestion I might travel on the progresses and as soon as I was released, after the ceremony at St. Paul's, I expected to be at liberty to pursue my own interests. I intended to visit Thomas and Grizel, whom I had not seen for more than a year, and then return to Worthwaite. There I would nurture Kate's halting recovery and concentrate on building my physician's practice in the locality, which had been interrupted far too often. I had been rewarded with gold for my participation in the embassy to Duke Richard at Dartford and, although I did not consider I had done anything to merit payment, augmentation of my modest resources was welcome. Even more welcome would be confirmation that Iffley and Boice would now desist from their coercive efforts to promote Richard of York's prospects.

I should have realised I would be called on to encounter Mistress Ursula Bateby once more before I could escape the clutches of her sponsors, but I was taken by surprise when I was asked to meet her on the evening I arrived at Westminster. I was tempted to refuse but I decided that would be churlish when she might be as unwilling a pawn as I was, so I attended her in the long gallery where she was waiting in a window recess as before. Her headdress was still unadorned and her dress severe but I noticed a bloom on her cheeks of which I had been unconscious on the first occasion.

'You've comported yourself successfully,' she said as I bowed. 'You were chosen to attend the negotiations with York and, more significantly for me, you've kept my confidences. Thank you.'

'The outcome of the negotiations will have dismayed your friends.' I remained standing.

'Oh, indeed. Master Boice has left London and Baron Glasbury will keep in the shadows until this mockery at St.Paul's has been accomplished. Although I regret their discomfort it suits me well for, in the interim, I can pursue my personal interests undisturbed. My reason for seeing you this time is to put my own questions to you.'

'Your own questions, Mistress Bateby? About what?'

She would have noted my wariness but it did not disconcert her. 'I understand you were in Jack Cade's company during the insurgence? On Blackheath and at Solefields, as well as after he entered the City?'

'You're well informed, Mistress, but I was not one of Cade's followers. I simply fulfilled my role as physician.'

'That's irrelevant to what I want to know. I wish to question you about the events at Solefields. You remember them no doubt?'

I was puzzled and on my guard but I nodded. 'You mean the attack by the Staffords on Cade's men?'

For a moment she looked annoyed as if I was mocking her. 'No, Doctor Somers, I refer to events which preceded the attack. A man was executed. His name was Stanlaw. Cade sentenced him to death for atrocities.'

'Yes, Mistress, that's true.' I felt myself tremble but strove to disguise it.

'I wish to know whether Master Stanlaw – the squire Stanlaw I believe they called him – confessed to the crimes of which he was found guilty. I ask you to tell me honestly.'

'He admitted to the murder of a woodman from a nearby estate. The man was returning there with his master's little son who had ventured by accident into Jack Cade's camp at Blackheath.'

'And the little son – did Stanlaw confess to brutalising and killing the child?'

She clearly knew the whole story and I would not hide the truth from her. 'Not in so many words, Mistress. He reacted to questions put to him in a way that aroused suspicion of his guilt but he never admitted responsibility for what happened to the child. Cade gave judgement on the basis of what he saw and heard and the execution took place almost instantly.'

'Did you believe justice had been done?'

'I regretted that there hadn't been a proper trial but circumstances were not normal and I didn't doubt Stanlaw was guilty of both murders.'

She rose to her feet and tilted her pointed chin towards me. 'Bateby is my late husband's name. I was born a Stanlaw. William Stanlaw was my brother. I know he was capable of killing if he believed a man to be his enemy or a danger to his cause. But I would swear on the Host he was no child molester. Some other man committed that foul crime and went free from punishment when my brother died.'

I remembered Grizel's fear of a murderous predator in the City of London and I knew monstrous perversion was not exclusive to one evil man. I tried to remain composed and pick my words with care. 'If that's true, it would be a grievous consequence. I have no evidence that another person was involved but I didn't know Master Stanlaw at all well, as you did. I'm horrified if a villain has gone free.'

'Did Baron Glasbury witness these events?'

'He was present throughout most of the proceedings at Solefields but didn't attend the execution, I think: nor did I.' Recollection came back to me. 'He spoke to me after Cade had given judgement and seemed fully convinced of Master Stanlaw's guilt. He had known him for some years and referred to him in abusive terms. I'm sure that Iffley's views corresponded to those of others who were in attendance.'

'I don't doubt it. I believe the contrivance which you devised to catch the culprit was skilful. I've heard of it. I don't hold you blameworthy, Doctor Somers. I suspect you didn't expect it would be my brother who was found responsible – held to have incriminated himself.'

This was disconcerting. Out of my memory, Iffley's unexpected words came to me: *A more sophisticated man would have held his nerve and wriggled out of your trap.* Was it possible Iffley doubted Stanlaw's guilt but was content for him to be found culpable?

'You're correct, Mistress. I hadn't expected your brother to be involved but he confessed to the woodman's killing.'

'I don't dispute that. In a court of law he may well have been sentenced to hang. But I believe him innocent of sodomising a child and undeserving of the dishonour done to his reputation. It's not a foolish sister's partiality, I assure you, but I accept there's unlikely to be evidence to acquit him.'

'The only way would be if another could be shown to have assaulted the boy.'

'Improbable, you imply. Baron Glasbury may know more, don't you think?'

I gasped. 'Do you really...?'

She gave a throaty gurgle of delight. 'Oh I didn't mean that! Gilbert Iffley would never soil his hands but he wouldn't hesitate to use another man for vile purposes.'

'I agree with that. I admit I held him responsible for letting Master Stanlaw loose on little Hubert de Grey, imagining he was aware of the man's propensities.'

Mistress Bateby touched my wrist and gave a sweet smile. 'You were not to know. It was cleverly contrived. I suppose Glasbury wanted to protect someone who was more valuable than my brother. But you're not wholly convinced by my contention, are you?'

'No, Mistress, but I respect your opinion.'

She looked up at me through her eyelashes. 'Then you will try to find the man who really killed the child? And show how Glasbury connived with William's execution?' She had stepped close to me and I breathed in her perfume.

'I can't hold out any hope of doing this. It's nearly two years ago. Cade's followers are dispersed – some are dead.' Her head drooped and I did not like disappointing her. 'If I received the slightest hint... if an opportunity arose... then, yes, I would do what I can.'

'It is enough, Doctor Somers. I'm grateful. I will wait in patience as I have waited two years, piecing together what I could about that day at Solefields. I rejoiced when you were sent to see me, to be my warranty, to vouch for me. I shall remain at court, in the Queen's service, until Stephen Boice sends for me. You will be able to find me, if you wish. It is my hope we shall meet again. After all, there is now unfinished business between us.'

She kissed the palm of her hand and pressed it to my disfigured cheek. 'Think of me sometimes, physician.'

She moved away from me, gliding along the gallery, and she did not look back, which was as well or she would have seen the flush on my face. I was utterly bewildered by our conversation and by Mistress Bateby herself, reluctant to think of her as the scheming hussy she probably was, appalled by the thought of her in Stephen Boice's bed, fascinated by the way she had cajoled me into offering help, however remote the possibility of rendering it. I was achingly conscious of the trace of her perfume which hung in the air.

I retraced my steps to Somerset's quarters but as I approached that wing of the palace Sir Nicholas Chamberlayne rushed towards me, white of face and unusually untidy in appearance.

'Thank God, I've found you, Harry,' he said grasping my arm with painful force. 'Word has come from Harrow. My wife is on her deathbed. I beg you come with me to give what ease you can. Get your things. Somerset has given leave for us to go and the horses are being saddled.'

As we galloped north-west, I felt profound sorrow for Sir Nicholas and Lady Joan but I was relieved to be excused attendance in St. Paul's to witness York's abasement. I regretted missing the opportunity to visit Thomas and Grizel but I longed to return directly to Worthwaite when my duties at Harrow on the Hill were concluded. Yet I could not quite dismiss the memory of those searching dark eyes, the touch of cool fingers and the tantalising promise of unfinished business which I knew I must unequivocally shun. My fancies seemed innocuous for I did not consider it in the least likely that I would encounter William Stanlaw's sister again.

Chapter 23

Sir Nicholas was in time to hold his wife in his arms as she breathed her last and to comfort his children when she had gone. There was nothing I or any other physician could do to delay her demise but it was one of those deaths when a medical man feels frustrated he cannot offer more to thwart malignant fate. A loving couple had been parted too soon and young siblings forced to watch their mother's decline, day by day, until they were finally bereft. It was a heart-rending occasion when the priest officiated as Lady Joan was laid to rest.

I prepared to leave the grieving family but Sir Nicholas asked me to stay a few more days, saying my company helped him at a time of painful change in his circumstances. I was glad to offer what assistance I could and agreed to delay my departure by one week.

On the evening before I eventually set out Sir Nicholas invited me to take wine with him and we sat together in his study, each side of a crackling fire. I had come to like and respect him as a man of integrity and a pleasing companion and I hoped we would become good friends. I invited him to call at Worthwaite whenever he was in the area.

'I'll be happy to,' he said. 'My first obligation is to join Somerset on the royal progress to the West Country but later in the year I should be able to resume my role as his agent in East Anglia.'

'You'll be leaving your house soon?'

'In a week or two: when arrangements are complete for my children to go elsewhere. There've long been plans for Nicky to go as page in Somerset's household. He wanted to stay while his mother lived, but now he will ride with me to take up his position. I'll be able to see him frequently while we're on the progresses. That will be good. Young Mistress Joan is to join a lady's household where she can be with maidens of her own age. It will give her new interests. I'd like her to enjoy some time of carefree girlhood before she's betrothed.'

I smiled, approving his thoughtfulness, feeling the wine agreeably dulling my senses, but his next words made me look up in surprise.

'When the time is seemly, I shall marry again.'

Of course, I reflected vaguely, a gentleman of his status needs a helpmeet, someone to run his household while he is on business, a proxy mother for his children, even though they will be elsewhere. I mumbled something appropriate.

'She's a lady of noble blood. It'll do my prospects no harm in the eyes of the world.'

He clearly had a particular person in mind and I remembered the beautiful young woman he had conversed with in the long gallery at Westminster. I had assumed their apparent intimacy derived from nothing more than the affectation of the court. Perhaps I was wrong.

'And she'll accept you?' As I spoke, I thought my question impertinent.

'Oh Lord, yes: she agreed months ago. We knew it was only a matter of time of course. You look shocked, Harry. It's how things are done. We'll wait a decent interval naturally. But I don't mind telling you, man to man, she's as lusty a lady as I could hope to find. After such a sad period I mean to indulge myself.'

I gave congratulations and indeed I was sincere in hoping Sir Nicholas would be happy in his second marriage but I was taken aback by the timing of the arrangements. I had been called prissy in the past and perhaps I was, deeming it precipitate to organise a replacement before the wife one loved had expired. I did not like to imagine myself in his situation, a widower: Kate dead. Because her health was so precarious it seemed improper, although not inconceivable, to picture that eventuality. There was no substitute I would wish to identify to fill the void she would leave. If such a thing should happen, I would not face the pressures confronting a man of high birth and large inheritance, with children too. I felt sure that, after the pain I had suffered in my doomed relationships, I would choose to remain alone.

I shook myself out of my morose day-dreaming but Sir Nicholas had not noticed my self-absorption. His mouth was curled into a smile and he had an absent air which I did not begrudge him. He deserved all the happiness he could find.

*****

It was well into the month of March but there were crisp frosts of a morning as I returned to Worthwaite, although trails of mist cleared quickly and the days were bright. I had been away some six weeks and, despite an encouraging report on Kate's condition received ten days earlier, I never knew what I would find on arrival home. I did not call at Wingfield but urged my horse to quicken his pace as I passed the de la Pole lands until I glimpsed the edge of my manor grounds beyond a copse. Drawn up beside the track where the trees petered out were six heavily laden wagons with their drivers.

I drew on the reins instinctively, fear of ambush running through my mind, however unlikely this might be so near my house. At the same time I was reluctant to switch direction, as if alarmed, when there might be no cause. While my horse hoofed the earth reflecting my uncertainty, a youth jumped down from the leading wagon and ran towards me. His face was vaguely familiar.

'Georgie! Georgie Antey! It is you, isn't it? You've grown so tall, I wasn't sure. Is your brother here too?'

The lad shook his head and the older man now lumbering towards me was definitely not Master Antey. I had mixed feelings when I recognised him.

'Master Toft, you've ventured even further afield in East Anglia than when I met you at Framlingham. I hope your journey has been satisfactory.'

286

'Uneventful, thank you, Doctor Somers. We called here a few days back and did business with your steward: gave him a good price for the wool the women at your manor have spun. I'm taking a consignment to Ipswich to be shipped to London. He told me you were expected home shortly so we made a detour to another estate and we've just returned to wait 'til you came. I'm glad you remember young Georgie. He's with me now, learning the trade. His brother's one of my men as well but he's on business in Kent. I've something to tell you when you're at leisure.'

Given John Toft's links to Gilbert Iffley, I was sure I did not want to hear what he had to tell me but I bade the wagoner welcome and accompanied him and his companions to the manor-house where they were given refreshment. I undertook to return after I had greeted my wife and seen my steward and I hoped there would be an opportunity to question young Georgie about the well-being of his family.

Kate was sitting in her room looking into space and she did not glance at me immediately I entered. She was wretchedly thin and her cheeks were pale but there was no wildness in her eyes and, when she turned to look at me, they focused. Judith scurried forward and curtsied, watching her mistress closely as if Kate was a schoolgirl about to recite her lesson.

'Are you in good health after your journey, husband?' Her enquiry was formal and stilted but its normality touched my heart and I struggled not to tremble.

'Thank you, yes. I'm always tired after riding so far. I've never become a natural horseman. I'm glad to be home and to be with you, Kate. Summer will be here soon and we must revive your little garden.'

'I should like that. I have walked to the garden with Judith when the sun shone. There are dead leaves blown into the corners beneath the trellis and there's moss on the stonework.'

'I'll have them cleared at once.' I could not hide the catch in my throat.

'You are mud-spattered and will wish to wash and change your robe. Will you come later to take wine when you are refreshed?'

'With all my heart, sweet. I'm so happy to see you well...' She looked at me with a puzzled expression and I did not know what else it would be appropriate to say but Judith bustled to the door and held it open.

'Mistress Somers grows stronger day by day,' she said, fixing me with a meaningful gaze. 'Spring has been a laggard in coming this year but the catkins are formed and the season is settling.'

'I can't tell you how joyful that makes me. I'm so grateful'.

Once I was cleanly clad I went to see Perkin, ready to listen to his catalogue of news concerning the manor, but he was anxious to engage my attention on another matter. I noticed his voice was husky and he coughed as he spoke, yet it was not his infirmity that worried him but Dame Elizabeth's.

'We've been beset by the rheum,' he said, 'a nasty one that takes time to clear. I'm just left with phlegm in my throat but my good lady is sorely affected and can scarcely see. She's tried bathing her eyes but to no avail. Her eyelids are nearly closed with the swelling and the discharge is not wholesome, not at all.'

His description was not exaggerated. Dame Elizabeth's infection was severe and needed urgent attention to prevent it affecting the eyes themselves but I had to strain my memory at first to recall the best remedy. Fortunately there was chamomile in my small dispensary which I pounded into a paste and applied carefully along the lady's swollen lids, advising her to rest with them closed. I was gratified that the treatment gave rapid relief.

It was satisfying to practise medicine again, in however minor a way, and to recognise that I had recovered from the aimlessness which threatened to envelop me before my absence from Worthwaite. Nevertheless I was disturbed by my lapse in memory on basic herbal properties and resolved to return to my profession with all possible diligence.

By the time I was ready to join them, the carters had been given food and ale in the kitchen and I knew they would shortly be departing to continue their journey. I needed to hurry if I was to speak to them but by good fortune, as I crossed the yard, I met Georgie carrying tackle so I asked how his brother and mother were managing now he had left home.

He frowned. 'Right cosy little love nest they've got. Ned and Nan have been married a year and a few weeks back they whelped. Still lovey-dovey, they are and mother's all soppy over the baby. She and Nan are like two versions of the same tune and they chime together while Ned just does as he's told. Not that he minds: got no ambition. He didn't even mind Master Toft taking over the business. I'd have hated it if I'd been him. I want something better.'

I could not help but laugh at his enthusiasm. 'Good for you, Georgie. But people differ. So is it working out for you, being with Master Toft?'

'Oh, yes.' The lad's face glowed. 'And because I know my letters I help him with the dockets. There's a deal of records to be kept with carting on behalf of merchants – collecting wool from the farms and cloth from the weavers and fullers, taking it all to the wharves to be shipped. After we've unloaded our woollen goods at Ipswich, we're to pick up barrels of Essex beer to take to London by road. Then we'll collect rich silks from Lucca to carry back to Maidstone for the nobs who live at Leeds Castle. It needs a deal of organisation, all this does. I've learned more than I ever did when I was with father or Ned. Master Toft's a man of substance and I've a mind to become one too.'

I gave Georgie an appreciative pat on the back as we entered the kitchen. I was encouraged by his news and his eagerness, while hoping he would not become involved in more dubious activities, which I suspected Master Toft undertook on Gilbert Iffley's account. I noted the ease with which the master carter had taken over the Anteys' business and wondered if he had some hold over Georgie's brother – like knowledge of who was really responsible for the late George Antey's death. I had speculated once that John Toft himself might have had a hand in a prank which went wrong. Now it occurred to me that Toft was a wily operator, more likely to have induced young Master Antey to saw through a wheel peg and then use his knowledge to threaten disclosure.

The carter in person advanced and I did not care for the sidelong glance he gave as he drew me aside.

'I've been to pay my respects to your good lady. She's a beauty and no mistake. I'd heard she was in feeble spirits so I was glad to see her quite well.'

I was alarmed that Toft had managed to intrude himself into my household and call on Kate but fortunately no harm seemed to have been done, so I merely grunted.

Toft smiled smugly. 'I've done good business for my principal on this trip, including at Hartham Manor. Fine estate, that is. You know it well, I believe. As it happened one of the wagons needed a new wheel while we were there so it won't surprise you that we met the wheelwright. Crafty move on your part, that was, getting Piers Ford installed there.'

His tone suggested some inner meaning but it was not clear to me what it could be. Piers had received his pardon for his part in Cade's uprising and was not in hiding. It was true that during the tense days of the insurrection Gilbert Iffley had sought to muzzle the wheelwright, whose moderate approach angered him, but that had long since ceased to have any relevance. I could not believe the Baron continued to nurture a pointless grudge against an obscure workman when he had far more significant issues to engage his energies.

'I saw Piers earlier in the year. I trust he's still well.'

The corners of Toft's mouth turned down. 'Well enough, I dare say – at present. Unlike the bailiff fellow he told me about. Sad business that. Lord Fitzvaughan and his minions won't want Roger Egremont erupting on the scene again, will they?'

'I understand the Earl of Stanwick is in confinement at the Duke of York's command.'

'He has been. Whether he still is I couldn't say. When I was in Norwich, I heard the Duke of Norfolk was seeking his release. Mowbray likes his ruthlessness, finds him useful for causing havoc with troublesome neighbours.'

'From what Baron Glasbury told me when he took Egremont in charge, I'd be surprised if York agreed to set the Earl free.'

'Times change though, don't they? York's wings have been clipped for the moment but he might welcome Mowbray creating a diversion: breakdown of law and order, Somerset incapable of upholding justice, you know the sort of thing.'

Toft's words were chilling and I was unpleasantly aware how knowledgeable he was. I suspected that in the past he had intentionally downplayed both his intelligence and his role in serving Gilbert Iffley as well as, indirectly, York. I wondered why he was telling me about Mowbray and Egremont. Was it so I could warn Gaston de la Tour, because Toft's 'principal' was trading with the estate at Hartham Manor and had an interest in preserving peace there? His next words corrected my illusion.

'Mowbray is looking for retribution. You killed his man.'

'Who had just murdered my friend and aimed to skewer me.'

'Maybe, but the Duke didn't take kindly to that outcome. Just thought I'd tell you.'

'Are you suggesting Mowbray would attack Worthwaite?'

'No, I think you're safe here. It's too near Wingfield and Mowbray won't want to rouse the de la Poles. But you'd be wise to keep clear of Hartham Manor if Egremont reappears. Don't bother warning Lord Fitzvaughan, by the way. He's heard the rumour about Mowbray and the Earl of Stanwick.' Toft waved his arm to where his wagons and drivers were assembled in the yard. 'Need to be on the road. I'll call again if I'm up this far north. I'll see you somewhere I don't doubt.'

I watched the column of wagons depart while trying to make sense of what Toft had told me. Was there an inwardness I could not gauge? Could I be certain Gaston understood the continuing danger he might face? Was Toft's reference to Piers merely a means to introduce the subject of Roger Egremont? It was a tortuous approach and could be designed to confuse.

I strolled across to Perkin's office and, as he was not there, I glanced at the document lying on top of his desk, the bill of lading and receipt for the wool sold to Toft's principal. It was boldly written, in Georgie Antey's clear childish script, and it named the trader whose business had been transacted. I should have guessed what it would say but I read it with a shock: *goods accepted and paid for on the account of Stephen Boice, merchant and broker*. However indirect the contact, I felt polluted by it.

✳✳✳✳✳

To my joy I was able to set aside the uncomfortable aspects of the carter's visit and find solace in my wife's improving health. She had found a calmness that seemed more secure than the interludes of serenity she had experienced previously and she was increasingly at ease in my company. What warmed my heart most was her attempt to tease me for fumbling when I held the wool for her spindle: a sign that humour was meaningful to her after so long when the concept of affectionate mockery would have been alien and alarming.

'I trust, Doctor Somers, you aren't so cack-handed with your patients when they need gentle handling.'

'I'm smoothness itself, disentangling sinews, madam. They're a damned sight more straightforward than this confounded fluff. I'm lost in admiration for your skill in spinning it into manageable threads.'

'I never had patience for it when I was a girl. Judith has taught me to take pleasure in producing good quality whether spinning or sewing. I've been blessed to have her at my side while I was troubled in my mind. I know that now. I didn't always understand.'

'It was your ailment clouded your understanding.'

'Sometimes I couldn't think. My mind wasn't always there. I couldn't find it. Will it go from me again?'

'I pray not. We must tend you carefully, like a seedling in your garden, nurturing it while it grows strong.'

She set down her work and stood, reaching out for my hand. 'It would be right to pray, to give thanks. I should like to make a pilgrimage to give thanks.'

I thought quickly, delighted by her decisiveness. 'You'd like to go to the shrine at Walsingham?' If you were happy to ride pillion, we could be there in two days' reasonable riding. Would you really wish to go?'

Kate gave a mischievous laugh, reminding me of the time of our courtship and new-found marriage. 'I could give thanks in any holy place. It need not be at Walsingham, despite the sacred shrine there. I have a fancy to go to the reverend lady you've often spoken of, the Prioress in Stamford. I should like to meet her and give my thanks in her chapel. Will you take me there?'

'It's a longer and more arduous journey, best made partly by water. You might find it tiring. Walsingham is nearer.'

For an instant she gave an angry pout and I feared she would become agitated. 'Would you be ashamed to introduce me to the holy woman?'

'Of course not: I'm only concerned that the journey might be exhausting for you.'

293

'You think the demons will seize my mind again? That I shall disgrace you in front of the worthy Prioress?'

'No, no, not at all. If it's what you really wish we'll organise it. We could travel in short stages. Judith will come with us. I'll write and advise the Prioress to expect us. It will be a gallant expedition.'

I masked my reluctance, for I did not relish the idea of seeing the Prioress after I had given her false information and risked jeopardising Sir Nicholas Chamberlayne's career. Nonetheless a moment's thought told me there was no contest. If assisting Kate's recovery caused me embarrassment and perhaps earned me a reprimand, it was a price I must willingly pay.

*****

We made the journey at the beginning of May and, although it was tiring for Kate, she found interest in what she saw: wildfowl on the wetlands, fishermen lowering their nets, reed-cutters piling their carts with material for thatching and bestrewing floors. She gurgled with pleasure at the flights of duck which rose from the shallows, disturbed by our oars, some skimming the water in front of our boat, and she tried to catch the luminous damsel flies hovering low in the sunlight beside us. She marvelled at the statuesque heron holding its position majestically while we slipped past without interrupting its concentration on the hidden prey at its feet. She gasped with excitement when the boatman pointed out a crane rising from the bank, huge wings and sinuous neck stretched as it soared above us. She tried to scoop a tiny fish from the dyke and giggled with glee when she tipped a handful of water into her lap, drenching her skirt. I hadn't seen her so happily, healthily animated for nearly three years and I too wanted to give thanks to whatever beneficent saint had raised a protective shield over her frail being, sheltering her reason and battered intellect.

Chapter 24

I escorted Kate and Judith to the convent of St. Michael's in Stamford where they were greeted by the Prioress and the guest-mistress. They were to stay there for two nights while I was left to spend my time as I wished outside the priory walls. The Prioress promised to meet me for a longer discussion when I came to take my wife home but, as Kate was whisked through the gatehouse by the guest-mistress, I could not resist detaining the Reverend Mother to ask a question which intrigued me.

'Forgive me for my curiosity but I have wondered about Lady Maud's visit here last year. It seemed unlikely on her part. I hope it passed off successfully.'

The Prioress stared at me as if it was I who was afflicted with confusion of the wits. 'Lady Maud Fitzvaughan? The Dowager Lady Fitzvaughan? Lady Eleanor's mother? She has paid no visit to St. Michael's. Whatever gave you that idea?'

I hastily tried to cover my tracks. 'Your pardon: I thought it was strange. I must have misunderstood what I was told.'

'Lady Maud did not give you this erroneous information herself?'

'No, no. Someone else mentioned she had gone on pilgrimage and I assumed it was to Stamford. It made me inquisitive but I'd jumped to the wrong conclusion.'

'I'm glad the lady can be acquitted of falsehood and rejoice to hear she undertook a pilgrimage: Walsingham would be the obvious destination from Hartham Manor. You would do well, Doctor Somers, not to place your own interpretation on events and develop fantastic theories. It lessens the reliability of the information you supply. I shall see you again in two days' time.'

I bowed with humility, much alarmed that her criticism might refer to the fabricated story I had passed on because of Stephen Boice's menaces. There was no one but myself to blame. I had made an unjustified assumption about Maud's pilgrimage and pried into what did not concern me. Now I must prepare myself in case the Prioress was more forthright in her criticisms of me when I next saw her.

I spent the intervening day and a half at unaccustomed leisure, exploring the town and talking to fellow visitors to the Raven Inn. One merchant had come from London and reported renewed disturbances in Kent while a pedlar from the north-west also had his story to contribute.

'There's been trouble in Shropshire too,' the hawker said. 'Near Ludlow of course. It's even been rumoured York's eldest son is leading a protest about the way his father's been treated.'

'The boy can't be more than ten years old.' A local fellow with a chain of office sounded authoritative.

'Could be a figure-head for older dissidents.'

'Some are calling for Richard of York to be put on the throne.'

'Fat chance,' commented the official. 'King Henry's going to visit Shropshire himself, I've heard. On his progress – he'll impose law and order. York's got his tail between his legs.'

'Don't be too sure.' The London merchant beckoned the potman to refill our jug of ale. 'The word in Kent is that Jack Cade's still alive and coming out of hiding to lead another uprising.'

I spluttered over my mug. 'That's ludicrous. He was certified dead by those who knew him.'

'How do we know it's true? I wouldn't put anything past some people.' The sceptic was reluctant to name names but everyone suspected he meant the Duke of Somerset. It would be unwise to pursue the matter.

I had more than one conversation along these lines at the inn before it was time to meet the Prioress again and be reunited with my wife. I remained nervous about incurring the reverend lady's wrath but I resolved to apologise openly for forwarding mistaken gossip about Sir

Nicholas Chamberlayne and explain that no lasting damage to his reputation had resulted. False rumours abounded in a realm fraught by divisions. I collected myself, crossed coolly from the inn to the convent gatehouse and was admitted to the familiar parlour where visitors were received. I was not kept waiting and stood up as soon as the door from the cloister creaked open, to face that clever, penetrating, hostile gaze; then I knelt before her.

She motioned me to rise, speaking words of greeting as if by rote. 'God's blessing on you, Doctor Somers. Your lady will be with us shortly. I wanted to meet you alone first.'

I expected her to rebuke me but was not prepared for the thunderous tone of disapproval.

'This will not do, Doctor,' she said. 'This is unacceptable.'

I lowered my head and stared at the spotless tiles on which I stood.

'It is not fitting for you to be shackled to this afflicted woman. I have suggested previously that you put her away, consigning her to an order of sisters who care for those possessed by devils. For both your sakes it is imperative that you do this.'

My mouth fell open in a vain protest. 'My wife was much recovered...'

'She seemed so. Satan's minions are devious. I don't deny Mistress Somers was modest and restrained when she arrived here and yesterday morning she attended Mass in our chapel when we said prayers of gratitude for the restoration of her senses. I was myself beguiled by her behaviour but it was not maintained. By nightfall she was screaming obscenities and tore the veil from a respected sister's head.'

'Oh, sweet Heaven!' I was shuddering and had difficulty mastering my voice. 'Was Judith able to pacify her?'

'In time and with the Infirmarian's assistance. They gave her a potion. The girl Judith is a gift we should all give thanks for. If you put her mistress away, as you should, I will most happily take Judith into this house. If she will enter our noviciate, I'll warrant she'll achieve a post of seniority among our sisterhood before many moons are past.'

'If Judith acknowledged a vocation, I shouldn't stand in her way, but she's expressed no such desire to my knowledge and, while she's content, I'm most anxious to keep her in attendance on my wife. I regret Kate has suffered a relapse and caused disruption in the convent. It was a risk exposing her to different experiences but she wished to come here and I hoped it would benefit her. She positively revelled in the journey. It's perhaps too much to expect her affliction will vanish in one smooth movement as if a curtain was lifted from her mind. It's necessary to be patient and persist with her care. There's no question of putting her away as you term it.'

My words tumbled out in a rush and the Prioress looked affronted by my outburst. 'You are a stubborn man, Doctor Somers, and I fear, in this matter, a stupid one. You're hamstringing your own prospects with your pig-headedness. I foresaw an outstanding future for you at the centre of public affairs, with the ear of great men. You've already forfeited opportunities to advance your career. Come to your senses now. If you devote yourself to this tiresome woman and ignore the chances Heaven sends you to make your mark in the world, I shall wash my hands of you. You need write to me no longer. You will have nothing of interest to say.'

Her scorn was lacerating but I would not yield. 'So be it, Reverend Mother. I respect your wisdom and your virtue and will regret losing contact with you. I appreciate you mean well but I must follow the dictates of my own judgement and do what I believe is right.'

She snorted with derision. 'You've succumbed to beguiling views which may lead you into heresy.

Conscience is God's bridle to control our wayward inclinations but if we claim conscience as excuse to follow our own fancies, we are in danger. I pray God will enlighten you and show you what you must do. Clearly, the advice of his faithful daughter, dedicated to his service in this earthly but sanctified house, has been insufficient to sway you. Beware your arrogance does not lead you into irretrievable sin, physician.'

There was venom in her final word and the door to the cloister crashed as she slammed it behind her. I sank onto the bench, deeply upset. The Prioress had been for many years an anchor of good sense in my turbulent life and I regretted offending her. Moreover, if her disfavour implied I would forfeit the good will of the Church more generally, that could be a serious loss. I had reason to be grateful for clerical support in the past. Yet overriding these misgivings was my despair at Kate's regression for, despite what I said to the Prioress, I had nurtured strengthening hopes that my wife was securely set on the road to recovery. Faced with denial of those hopes I feared that my own ability to persevere would prove insufficient.

I have no idea how long I sat there sunk in dejection but at some point I heard movement in the cloister and the connecting door was again unlocked. Judith led my wife into the parlour and the unseen nun who accompanied them turned the key after they entered the room. Kate was ashen and her eyes were vacant. I suspected she was heavily sedated. I held out my arms but Judith shook her head.

'Forgive me, Doctor, but Mistress Somers is best left alone for the moment. She's hardly capable of responding to questions. I think we should journey as quickly as we can while she's quiet. Something at the convent affected her mind and we should get her away from here. If you need to pursue what happened, there'll be time enough when we're back at Worthwaite.'

I opened the inner door so they could pass through into the gatehouse. 'I'm sure you're right. The horses are waiting outside. But the Prioress suggested you might not wish to leave the convent, Judith. I told her I would not prevent you staying if it was your wish.'

Judith raised her eyebrows in exasperation. 'May the saints forgive me but that reverend lady has the guile of the devil. She's been angling to persuade me I had a holy calling since we arrived here. She insisted on showing me all the chambers and offices of the convent and gave me a fulsome description of their uses and the roles of various nuns. It was while we were making a tour of the buildings that whatever happened to Mistress Somers occurred.'

'Kate wasn't with you?'

Judith put a finger to her lips, lowering her voice to a whisper. 'We left her with a charming old nun who seemed entirely harmless. When we came back Mistress Somers was enraged and had ripped the wimple from the woman's bald head.'

'Did the Prioress ask the nun what had been said?'

'Not in my hearing but I imagine it concerned you, Doctor. Mistress was muttering about you wildly before the Infirmarian gave her some cordial to quieten her.'

Grimly I lifted Kate to sit in front of me and start our homeward journey. I cursed the optimism that had brought us to Stamford and prayed that Kate's semi-conscious state would be maintained until we reached Worthwaite, so she would be safely unaware of whose helpless, loving arm encircled her.

*****

It took more than a week for Kate to regain awareness of her surroundings after we arrived at the manor. Even then she was sunk in despondency and, whenever I approached her, she began to weep. I thought it essential to find out what had distressed her for it was clear something specific must have done so – which was not always the case when she became agitated. Judith understood my need to question Kate and one afternoon

300

she suggested the moment might be propitious as her mistress was much calmer, sitting among the flowers in the garden arbour. I asked Judith to stay with us, although it was clear she was reluctant and I noticed her blush. It alerted me to the likelihood that whatever Kate might say could be personally embarrassing.

I fashioned a small nosegay of blossoms and took it to Kate, hoping that she was feeling better, although I was never sure whether referring to her health was wise for, from day to day, it was impossible to tell how she viewed her mental turmoil. She did not repulse me and laid the posy on her lap so I was encouraged to continue.

'I was very sorry that something at St. Michael's Convent upset you. You had seemed so happy on our journey there.'

She began to tremble. 'I forget.'

'You loved the waterfowl when we were in the boat. You tried to capture a slimy fish and soaked your skirt with water.' A flicker in her eyes told me I had sparked a recollection. 'And the Prioress said you attended the service in the chapel and heard Mass.'

'Their singing was beautiful but the stone floor was cold.'

I smiled to encourage her. 'It must have been later in the day that the Prioress took Judith on a tour of the convent. She said you were talking with an elderly nun. Did something happen then which troubled you?'

'No! No! I forget. I hated the old woman. She told me things... She knew.... You deceived me!'

Kate's fingers were tearing at the nosegay and I put my hand on hers to still them but she pulled away from me. 'Your daughter! She is your daughter.'

I froze for a moment, utterly mystified, but Judith came forward and put her hand on Kate's arm. 'Will you tell us, mistress, what the nun said? There may be some mistake.'

I stood back and let Judith mollify my wife while I tried to make sense of what she implied. 'The nun had been at the convent for many years?'

'She tended her as a child. They have several children in their care. She loved the little girl. Then you came and took her away. You didn't tell me...that you had fathered a child.'

I fought to sound matter-of-fact, while appalled by this parody of the truth. 'I think the nun must have been speaking of young Mistress Eleanor who is now Lady Fitzvaughan. She is not my child, Kate. She was born years before I met her mother, Lady Maud. I must have been about thirteen years old when she was born. Her father was the late Earl of Stanwick.'

Kate pushed Judith aside and rose to her feet scattering the torn petals of my posy on the earth. 'You went to Stamford and took her away. The nun saw you. She was in the gatehouse.'

'The nun is mistaken. I did not take Eleanor from the convent. I went there first because the child had gone missing from St. Michael's and Lady Maud was frightened what had happened to her. She asked me to investigate her daughter's disappearance. It was the girl's natural father who had taken her. Later he went back to explain to the Prioress and I met him there, with Mistress Eleanor. It was the first time I met her.'

While I was speaking Kate became more and more frantic, ripping off her headdress and pulling her hair from the gilded net which held it. 'Are you lying? How can I tell? Why should the nun lie?'

'She was muddled in her memory. It must have been around eight years ago. You say the nun is elderly. I did go to the convent when Eleanor was there with her father. I remember they left before I did. I stayed to speak to the Prioress about other matters. This is the truth, Kate. I have no daughter.'

My wife's eyes were not blank with that emptiness which pained me but they were narrowed with cunning and I was jolted by their sudden spitefulness.

'Why did Lady Maud Fitzvaughan ask you to investigate the child's disappearance? Why you?'

This was a question I did not choose to answer with the whole truth. 'When we were both at the late Duke of Gloucester's palace in our younger days I investigated a death which took place there. Lady Maud remembered this and thought I had some skill in making enquiries.'

'Hah! The woman is a whore. Her daughter is a bastard.'

I held my breath, terrified that Kate would ask for more details about my relationship with Lady Maud. She knew there had been other liaisons before I met her but seemed content to let the past bury itself. I did not want to trawl over the history of Maud as my former mistress but more especially I quailed at the prospect of admitting I had more recently made love to her on one occasion, which I regretted. I dreaded what effect the truth might have on Kate's fragile temperament but I did not want to lie. There was enough dissimulation between us.

To my relief no further question came but Kate clutched Judith's arm and let herself be led back to the house. As they passed me Judith gave a smile which seemed full of commiseration and perhaps admiration. It re-awoke the old anxiety that the girl had tender feelings towards me which could result in increased awkwardness and pain for us all.

*****

The next weeks of early summer were mournful at Worthwaite. Kate was subject to the deep melancholy which rendered her passive, lost in herself, and at first I had little to absorb my interest. It was through Leone that I was given challenging work as a physician to fill that gap. He came to seek my advice and described the suffering of

303

one of the knights who served the de la Poles and rode frequently between their scattered possessions in different parts of the country.

'It's not a nice condition,' he said. 'I've seen minor cases but nothing so severe. Where there have been abscesses from riding, from pressure of the saddle, but they do not heal.'

I smiled at his delicacy. 'I think you're referring to anal fistulae, holes burrowing deep into the flesh. They're nasty. Days on a wet saddle don't help.'

'There is a treatment I remember hearing about but I have never seen it carried it out. I wondered if you had.'

'I suppose it's properly a surgical matter but I did manage to perform it myself on one of Suffolk's men a few years ago. It takes time and needs frequent cutting and cleansing of the affected area. Before it was introduced, acid was used to sear the wounds but that was dangerous and many victims died.'

'Would you come to Wingfield and help my patient? I could learn what to do.'

So I made several visits to the Suffolk castle to treat the unfortunate knight and supervise Leone as he learned the medical process. We were rewarded by success in our efforts and received generous payment as well as thanks from the de la Pole henchman but the episode brought me an extra advantage. I enjoyed conversing with a wider group of Suffolk followers, many of whom I had met in the past, and most particularly I renewed my friendship with Father Wilfred, the chaplain. This was to have consequences of significance to many people.

Usually I gossiped with the chaplain in Leone's company but on one occasion the young physician excused himself saying he must visit a patient who had sprained her ankle. Father Wilfred gave a guffaw after my colleague had gone.

'This is a maid who works in the kitchen and the bakehouse. She is rather susceptible to slight injuries – and perhaps to the physician who hurries to attend her. I think I may be called upon to bless their union at the chapel door before long.'

'That's happy news. Leone mentioned a pretty maid who'd scorched her arm. It must have been two years ago. Is it the same one?

Father Wilfred nodded. 'I imagine so. The courtship has not been rushed. Doctor Leone did not consider he was ready to marry until he was established in his post. It would be a match above her station but she seems a pleasant, sensible girl. She will support him well.'

We sipped the excellent Bordeaux wine we had been served and the chaplain swirled his glass. 'I thought at one time our young friend was taken with your wife's attendant. He spoke of her qualities in glowing terms.'

'Judith? She has natural gifts as a nurse.' I did not say that she would make an excellent doctor's wife but the thought hung in the air and I hoped the priest would not pursue it.

He sighed. 'Young men are too greatly influenced by external appearances.' He shifted position and set down his glass. 'There's something I should tell you, Harry. Maybe I should have mentioned it before now. It was last summer, a merchant visiting the district made enquiries in Diss. My friend, the rector, informed me that the fellow asked about babies buried there who had been born at Worthwaite. I fear something was disclosed that should not have been. The rector is an old man and has become forgetful.'

'I'm acquainted with the merchant and discovered that he'd learned of my son. It was unfortunate but no one is to blame.'

'That's forbearing of you and I should have let you know at the time. A sin of omission, I'm afraid. But the merchant returned here a week ago and tried to interrogate me. I must not judge but I found his manner disquieting.'

'His name is Stephen Boice. One of York's followers. He is my wife's uncle and he has occasioned us both much harm.'

'Mistress Somers' uncle? That's extraordinary.'

'What did he want to know?'

Father Wilfred cleared his throat. 'He asked if I had conducted a marriage ceremony between you and the Countess de Langeais.'

'Well that was easily answered. Despite my passionate wish for it, that mésalliance with Yolande never took place, as you very well know.'

'Exactly. But that isn't the answer Master Boice wanted. He urged me to admit I had conducted the ceremony – promised a generous donation to a religious foundation of my choice if I did. Why should he wish to render his niece an adulteress?'

'He wouldn't be concerned about causing her more harm than he already has. But I don't imagine that was the outcome he intended. He was looking for a new threat to hold over me: to make me comply with some heinous demand. It's his method. It gives him pleasure to have me at his mercy, to see me squirming on the hook of his malicious torments.'

'Heaven help us. Is this the way Richard of York operates?'

'I don't believe so. When I've seen York, he's struck me as a man of integrity: frustrated not to have King Henry's trust, perhaps capable of rash actions, but not unscrupulous. I don't know if he's aware how his minions behave. Gilbert Iffley and Stephen Boice are the ones who use menaces and intimidation to achieve their ends. Iffley has no compunction in using force to get what he wants if he judges it expedient but Boice seems to derive personal pleasure from the mere exercise of power; he delights in coercing his victims.'

Father Wilfred made the sign of the cross. 'I'll pray to the saints to defend you, Harry, and whatever inducements he offers, I shall not betray you.'

I waited for Stephen Boice's next move. I imagined he might find amusement in persecuting me while Richard of York was biding his time quietly at Ludlow, apparently resigned to the fact that he had no chance to frustrate Somerset's ascendancy. It would be cheering to think that York's quiescence might discourage attempts to force me to do something unpalatable, ostensibly on his behalf, but I had no confidence Boice would be restrained by the Duke's inactivity. Quite the contrary, if baiting me provided mischief for a bored head and idle hands. The fact that he was prepared to have my marriage declared adulterous and his niece disgraced, showed the depths he was willing to plumb.

I sometimes wondered whether Ursula Bateby had been reunited with her unwholesome lover. It was no concern of mine but I preferred to think of her attending the Queen during the King's extensive progresses around the country, looking for evidence that Somerset was making illicit visits to the royal bedchamber. It was an unsavoury commission for the young woman but, in my view, indubitably preferable to sharing Boice's embraces and possibly suffering venomous mistreatment as his plaything.

In high summer a welcome visitor came to Worthwaite. I was pleased to see Sir Nicholas Chamberlayne so spritely and contented. Although he must still be grieving, I realised he had been freed from the strain he suffered during his wife's fatal illness. Kate was poised and apparently had no recollection of her previous encounter with the man she attempted to seduce so our meal, joined by our principal followers, was a jovial occasion. Afterwards, in the late afternoon as a light breeze moderated the heat of the day, my friend and I strolled by the riverside and for a little while reverted to boyish diversions, skimming stones across the surface of the water. Then Sir Nicholas turned to me with an impish grin and leaned against the gnarled trunk of an old willow tree.

'I've just travelled here from Hartham Manor and I'll be returning there in two weeks. I'd like you to be with me then: Mistress Somers too if you think she's well enough. I have a letter here from Lord Fitzvaughan confirming the invitation. There are to be festivities and I'd be glad for you to be there at my side.'

I took the sealed letter he held out without opening it but my puckered brow signalled my surprise and he laughed. 'You didn't think I was a familiar at Lord Fitzvaughan's residence. That's true. I went there first last year. But his lordship approved of my recent visit and my intentions which will be consolidated next time.'

I struggled to puzzle out his meaning, mumbling something inarticulate and he slapped me on the shoulder.

'Oh, Harry, have you really no idea what I'm talking about? My betrothal has been formalised to the incomparable Dowager Lady Fitzvaughan. I hinted to you once before that I would remarry as soon as was seemly and in two weeks I shall. I'd be delighted if you will be my groomsman.'

'I... I'm honoured. I'd no idea it was Lady Maud you referred to. It never occurred to me. Of course I'm overjoyed for you. I didn't realise you knew her at all well. Of course you'd met her at Hartham Manor...' My voice faded as I registered this extraordinary announcement.

'Yes and I was struck with her unusual charms from the moment I met her. Happily she responded positively to my tentative advances. But you mustn't think it's the caprice of momentary infatuation. I will confess to you, Harry, although few others know it, that a year ago Maud and I spent a glorious week together when I was lodged in Cambridge. It was at the time of the attack on Hartham Manor. Our clandestine tryst was rudely interrupted by urgent messages of fire-raising and assault. We kept our secret secure nonetheless.'

He did not need to remind me that his mortally ill wife was still living at the time. 'Lady Maud let it be known she'd gone on pilgrimage. I made myself look rather foolish trying to deduce where she'd gone.'

'Pilgrimage! That's priceless. She's matchless for wit and beauty. Yet she's content to take a mere knight in wedlock. We're both of mature years but I'm proud to designate our union a love-match.'

I was uncertain whether he knew of my own intermittent liaison with the lady over a decade or more but I suspected he would have deemed it irrelevant. I could not dismiss the disagreeable idea that by consenting to be his groomsman I was rendered complicit in their furtive and premature association but that was in the past. I imagined Maud would be highly amused by my role in the nuptials; indeed it seemed to me probable she had suggested it.

*****

Sir Nicholas brought news of state affairs as well as his astonishing personal disclosure. York remained in Ludlow, sullen and ineffectual, while the royal progresses received popular acclaim across the south of the country and the Midland counties. Indeed the King seemed so heartened that he had finally consented to the despatch of a military expedition to Gascony with funds to provision it. He had given command of the troops to the veteran leader John Talbot, Earl of Shrewsbury, who had a distinguished reputation on the battlefield. Talbot's very presence would indicate to the French that this was a serious attempt to wrest back some part of the English King's former patrimony beyond the Narrow Sea. It would also mitigate the aching shame felt by many of Henry's English subjects since the loss of Normandy. I regretted the renewal of warfare with the French but hoped it would divert attention from festering divisions within our own realm.

Sir Nicholas's visit and the prospect of attending the festivities at Hartham Manor lifted Kate's spirits. With Judith's support, she urged that a new gown would be required and, through the good offices of her former colleagues at Wingfield, a roll of magnificent green silk, embroidered with tiny flowers, was delivered to Worthwaite. I would need to sell a ring the late Duke of Suffolk had given me in order to pay for the material, but if it gave my wife pleasure and diverted her from pernicious melancholy, I deemed it money well spent. A seamstress from Wingfield was sent to fashion the gown and Dame Elizabeth and Judith both stitched away at trimmings under her instruction.

I insisted that Judith should also have a new dress and Dame Elizabeth produced a robe she had worn in her youth which was in good condition but no longer fitted her. Two years earlier it would not have fitted Judith either but she had lost weight and I was told only modest alterations would be needed. I was barred from the parlour which the industrious needlewomen commandeered and set about obtaining a dark brocade jerkin for myself to wear under my best physician's gown.

We made the short journey to Hartham Manor without mishap the day before the ceremonies were due to begin. Gaston greeted me cheerily, while Lady Eleanor accompanied Kate to the room set aside for our use, and he insisted I shared wine with him before I re-joined her. He gave a wicked grin as he drank my health.

'You're not grieving over these nuptials, I hope?'

'Not at all: I trust they'll make each other happy. I take it you've no qualms either?'

'Far from it: I'm delighted to cede responsibility for the dowager. I'd tried to pass her over to a series of worthy noblemen but she'd have nothing of them. She's a difficult woman and I never imagined she'd be satisfied with a mere knight but I underestimated the lure of a lusty bedfellow. They're like youngsters half their age, hardly able to keep their hands off each other.'

310

I echoed his hearty laughter slightly ruefully. As the months passed I had come to accept my own enforced celibacy, for the sake of Kate's fragile wits, but it was not easy. I did not wish to be reminded of the peculiarities of my situation.

Gaston was unaware of my discomfort. 'I want you to meet one of my companions, newly come to my household,' he said. 'Sir Jacques d'Avranches has come from Normandy to seek his future here. I met him when I was in London a few months back and persuaded him to join my household. I value his friendship.' He did not need to be more explicit and he recognised the one implication that concerned me. 'Don't worry for Eleanor, Harry. She is the mother of my sons and, with God's blessing, will bear me a third child after the Feast of the Nativity. I shall always esteem her and treat her with honour. She will not suffer from my new attachment, I promise you.'

I inclined my head and did not say that honour and esteem might not compensate her for the lack of a husband's love. Fortunately we were distracted by the sound of horsemen entering the courtyard and Gaston moved to the window.

'The jocund bridegroom is arriving with his entourage. By all the saints, what an entourage! There are dozens of them. Our hospitality will be stretched to its limit but we need not fear assaults by John Mowbray's ruffians while this company of armed warriors is lodged here.'

I noted the undertone of seriousness in his merriment. 'Are the Duke of Norfolk's men still harassing you?'

'Pinpricks mostly: jeering and pestering my servants on the road. Enough to remind me Mowbray thinks there are scores yet to be settled. But he has many enemies and I'm not sure he rates Hartham Manor a priority for attack.'

We went out to welcome Sir Nicholas with his followers and later, while they were shown their accommodation, Gaston accompanied me, in my capacity as groomsman, to visit the dower-house and its triumphant occupant. Maud's beauty had matured but in no way diminished with the passing years and I could not deny a pang of regret when I saw her. I was quickly drawn back to uncomfortable realities when, among the women attendants ranged behind her, I glimpsed Bess Willoughby fixing me with a baleful glare. I could not face her justifiable hostility and lowered my head until Maud dismissed all the servants except deaf Marian who had so often witnessed our encounters. Gaston gave a chuckle and also left us.

'My lady, I come as groomsman for Sir Nicholas Chamberlayne to pay my formal respects,' I said pompously.

'Oh, that's sweet, Harry.' Her giggle was unhelpful. 'In days gone by the groomsman was required to drag a recalcitrant bride to the church. Will you throw me over your shoulder and deliver me to my new lord and master?'

'I have no reason to believe you're an unwilling bride, quite the contrary. I shall come to escort you to the church in the morning as convention requires but I see no need for physical constraint.'

She gave a trill of delight. 'Indeed I shall accompany you tomorrow as mild as maidenhead and decently demure. But just for the moment now, shall we pretend I am in need of forceful direction? It isn't necessary to throw me over your shoulder but you may grip my waist and bid farewell to our occasional frivolities.' She came close and put her arms around my neck. 'I'm minded to be a faithful wife to Nicholas. He pleases me and I aim to have him ennobled within a year. But you have provided pleasant diversion when I was most in need of it, Harry. For that, you have earned my last embraces.'

She put her lips to mine and I did not repulse her so we kissed eagerly and then we stepped apart. Her calm and gracious self-containment was a novelty which confirmed the joy she experienced. I was sincerely happy for her but in my own heart there was emptiness.

*****

The three days of jollity passed in a whirl of entertainments and a haze of exquisite wine. Gaston spared no cost to send his mother-in-law on her way with fitting pomp, and to indulge his newfound familiarity with the handsome Jacques d'Avranches, but amid the lavish amusements Lady Eleanor was pale and ate little. She might be lamenting the clearer appreciation she had gained of her husband's nature but in the early months of pregnancy a loss of appetite was entirely usual. I also considered this pregnancy followed undesirably close to the last, before she had regained her full strength, but that was not a subject on which I should pontificate.

Despite Eleanor's pallor she remained a competent and charming hostess, assiduous in drawing the two Chamberlayne children into the merriment of their father's precipitate remarriage. I admired her for that and for her gentle kindliness towards Kate who tended to be withdrawn, although smiling, in the midst of the gaiety. I noticed several of the bridegroom's entourage giving sidelong glances towards my wife, clad in her magnificent green gown which intensified the emerald depths of her eyes, but Kate gave no sign of responding with coquetry towards her admirers.

On the fourth day Sir Nicholas and Lady Chamberlayne left Hartham Manor with their vast combined retinue, heading for Harrow, and we formed an archway of well-wishers for them to pass through. My small party was to stay another night before returning to Worthwaite and I took the opportunity to walk out to the workmen's enclosure where Piers had his yard. Although a bevy of labourers had attended the main feast in Gaston's hall, I had not seen Piers and wondered whether he was unwell. That fancy was dispelled when I saw him lifting a heavy wheel onto the axle of a cart but I noted his drawn features.

I hailed him and he looked up with expressionless eyes, giving a brief nod, and returned to his work. 'I thought I might have seen you at the manor-house,' I said. 'I didn't want to leave without asking how you are.'

'As you see, I'm busy.'

'You're still angry with me?'

He shrugged. 'I feel nothing towards you. Our worlds are far apart.'

'That wasn't always the case, when we helped the wounded on London Bridge.'

'A different life. The dreams I had then were shattered, the prophecies I inherited from John Ball – the end of bondage and servitude – they've been trampled underfoot. There's only grief left for me and my sort.'

'You used to be more hopeful, taking a longer view. Has something happened?'

He thumped his mallet onto the peg which held the wheel in place. 'There'll be no accidents with this cart,' he said when he was satisfied with his efforts. 'But you asked whether something had happened: yes, it has. It's nearly a year now since Robin Willoughby was killed and, although in other circumstances I'd have waited a few weeks more, when I heard Lady Maud was to take her household with her when she wed, I put my proposal to Mistress Bess.' He paused and I did not interrupt him. 'She turned me down and now she's left the manor with her children, for some village close to London where Sir Nicholas has his house. My life has no meaning now she's gone.'

'Perhaps it was simply too soon for her. She may need longer to grieve.'

'I'm trying to persuade myself that's the case. Anyway, I shan't moulder here in Norfolk. I'm resolved to leave Lord Fitzvaughan's estate. I'll find my way to this Harrow place and seek employment there. I'll bide my time and approach Mistress Bess once more.'

'Well then, that's sensible. You've still got hope.'

'Maybe I shouldn't have come to Hartham Manor. I'd never have met her then. When I heard Richard of York was in Dartford months back, I regretted not being there, in my home town. I'd have joined his following. He's our best chance for getting common men's grievances addressed.'

'You'd find yourself alongside Baron Glasbury once more. Richard of York may be well-meaning but he's attracted some dubious supporters.'

'We can't all afford the luxury of your scruples, Doctor Somers. They haven't done much good, have they? They caused the death of a good man.'

Although I was expecting him to refer to my responsibility for Robin's murder I flinched. 'Whatever words of forgiveness priests speak in the confessional, I shall carry that guilt with me forever.'

He looked at me sardonically. 'Such an extravagant self-indulgence for you to nurture!'

He turned back to the cart, striking his mallet against it with resounding force, and silently I left him.

*****

When I reached the drawbridge to re-enter the manor-house, the guard's grimace alerted me to the likelihood of encountering some problem inside the walls. I hurried across the courtyard, never doubting who would be involved, although unable to imagine the circumstances, and sure enough Judith ran down the steps to meet me. Her face was as white as her bleached cap and she twisted her hands together. Her cheeks were streaked with tears.

'Thank the saints, you're back, Doctor. Mistress has taken very bad. It was like something snapped in her head all of a sudden. We were in the nursery. One minute she was holding the little boy, tracing his features with her finger, and then she ran from the room and tried to throw him down the stairs.'

315

'Dear Christ! Is the child hurt? Whose child is he?'

She shook her head, gulping. 'I managed to snatch the boy as she raised him above her head. I'd seen the look in her eyes, the look when she's possessed and can't control herself. Thank God little Walter is unharmed. He thought it was a game.'

'Walter? Lord Fitzvaughan's son? Merciful heaven!'

'Lady Eleanor fainted. They fear she may miscarry. Lord Fitzvaughan has had Mistress Somers locked in a storeroom. He wants you to take her away from Hartham today. The men are preparing the horses and a litter. I've put our baggage together. Mistress will need to be calmed, given a cordial.'

'I understand. I'll go to her. I can't thank you enough, Judith, for what you've done.' Instinctively I put my hand on her wrist and I felt her shiver.

'I'll show you the storeroom,' she said. 'There's a servant posted outside the door. He'll let you in. I'll fetch the potion.'

I was prepared for Kate to hurl herself at me when I was admitted to her cell but she remained crouched against the wall, her eyes fixed like a cornered animal. The cackle she gave on seeing me froze my blood but I forced myself to go forward and knelt beside her.

'The old woman made a mistake but you didn't correct what she said. That's as good as telling a lie. You're a false charlatan. I hate you.'

I attempted to maintain a doctor's dispassionate manner. 'What do you mean, Kate? What old woman?'

She screeched and hugged herself, rocking to and fro. 'The nun, you faithless rat, the nun. She said you'd fathered Lady Eleanor but it was her child you sired, wasn't it? Lord Fitzvaughan is a sodomite. You boarded his wife to give her a son. You've neglected my bed and usurped his. I wanted to kill your brat, both your brats. Lady Eleanor has two. You'll have me put away but that won't stop me. Uncle Boice will uphold my honour. I'll appeal to him.'

316

The horrible, ranting gobbledegook brought a sob to my throat and for a moment I could not speak while she began to laugh ferociously.

'None of this is true, Kate. It's all delusion. I've never been with Lady Eleanor, never imagined such a thing. Gaston is her children's father. Whatever his nature, he wants heirs. Put this gibberish out of your mind. It's your illness incites you to imagine nonsense and do dreadful things. Don't let it destroy you. You've never tried to harm others before, an innocent child.... Oh Kate...'

I was in hopeless, unprofessional tears when Judith brought the medicine to pacify my wife and she held Kate firmly while I forced the liquid into her mouth. Within the hour we were ready to depart, my comatose patient flopped in the litter, moaning to herself but presenting no danger. Gaston did not come to bid farewell and I could not blame him. I was saddened to think I might never again be welcome at Hartham Manor. The only scrap of consolation was that Lady Eleanor was reported to be much recovered and the fears of a miscarriage had receded. For that I gave heaven thanks.

I rode in a trance, wondering whether I must now consign my wife to the care of an enclosed community who would prevent her causing harm, except possibly to herself. Although I knew what she had said was garbled and inaccurate I could not prevent my thoughts lingering on her words: the allegations that I had neglected her bed when it was she who spurned me; that she might appeal to Stephen Boice who in the past had tormented her so cruelly that I held him responsible for the weakening of her wits. I believed the episode at Hartham Manor had brought me to the nadir of my fortunes.

That evening after the household had retired to bed, I sat in the parlour at Worthwaite with my head in my hands and might have remained like that all night, ignoring the flagon of ale at my side. A tap at the door roused me and I knew who had come to offer support at

317

whatever cost to herself. Judith sank to her knees in front of me.

'She doesn't know what she's saying, Doctor, whether it's the Devil puts ideas in her head or however you describe it. You understand that as a physician but because she's your wife you're hurt as any other man would be by her wild fancies. Don't lose hope.'

'Only your action prevented her murdering a child. This is a turning point I can't ignore.'

'I've learned how confused she is about childbirth and children. She's torn apart by wanting and hating at the same time.'

I stared at this untutored girl who had such instinctive understanding of the turmoil in an afflicted mind. 'She may become quiet again, I suppose. She has done in the past but it's not sustained. I can have no confidence what may happen.'

'Perhaps she should rest here at Worthwaite and not travel afield again, even if she seems restored in her wits. I'll stay with her, Doctor. Give her one more chance to find peace.' Judith stood up and I too raised myself from my chair.

'Why do you tie yourself to this sick woman, Judith? I could recommend your services to the highest in the land if you wished. You might have the company of young people, entertainment, freedom from the thankless task you've accepted.'

She gave a faint smile and shook her head. 'I'm useful to Mistress Somers. It's not her fault she's as she is. There's nowhere else I'd rather be, nowhere remotely possible. I don't waste time hankering after the unachievable so I make do with something else – somewhere I can be useful. Keep her at Worthwaite, Doctor Somers. I'll do everything I can to keep her safe.'

She gave a bob and turned to the door. I held out my hand to detain her but she did not look back and left the room. I thought it as near as she had ever come to admitting affection for me and it was done with dignity and propriety. She had not breached the invisible wall between us and she never would; but if she had extended her hand to me at my moment of misery, I would have undermined the foundations of our correct association and taken her in my arms.

Chapter 26

Over the next few days I pondered Judith's request and her wisdom. It might be that Kate would find peaceful equilibrium if she remained in her attendant's care, untroubled by attempts to reintroduce her to the wider world. So often the episodes of manic behaviour had been linked to encounters with other people and the incursion of their concerns into her troubled mind. This was not the conclusion for which I hoped, but it now seemed inevitable. If Judith was content to stay at Kate's side, that would be preferable to putting her away as the Prioress urged.

My thoughts drifted beyond this conclusion. All too often, when she became frenzied Kate's fury was directed against me, as if in the depths of her spirit she blamed me for everything that had happened, as if she loathed me. However unjustified and perverse her reasoning might be, perhaps I should now accept the logic of her affliction and live apart from her. I would not seek to have our marriage set aside, as might be possible with the good offices of influential clerics, but I must reconcile myself to living separately from my wife. She would remain at Worthwaite and I would return to London where I would practise as a humble physician serving any who sought my help. This lonely future was far from what I yearned for but I concluded it was now inevitable.

I talked to Perkin and Dame Elizabeth as well as to Judith and they endorsed my conclusion. I sensed sadness in the girl's response which I did not intend to enquire into but I persuaded myself she put a brave face on her disappointment.

'You've many friends in the City, Doctor. You'll welcome seeing them again.'

'I shall write to Thomas and Grizel Chope asking if I can lodge with them while I seek my own quarters. It must be a year and a half since I saw them and I trust they and their family are well. I know I can rely on their generosity to provide me with a roof in time of need.'

Judith pursed her lips. 'Mistress Chope is that insolent Rendell's sister, isn't she? If you come across him you can give him my contemptuous greetings.'

'On the last occasion I saw him he was in the Duke of Somerset's bodyguard, looking very smart and official.'

She put her hands together devoutly. 'I must pray for the noble Duke's safety if he's dependent on the like of that reprobate's services to defend him.'

'I'll quote you exactly if I see Rendell.'

'Do that. God be with you, Doctor. Will you come here sometimes?'

I nodded. 'Yes, when I can. You must let me know how my wife fares as the weeks pass. Letters to Master Chope's house will find me. You have my lasting gratitude.'

I wondered whether I imagined a tear in her eye as she curtsied.

*****

For those without access to the liveried messengers who frequent the highways on behalf of their patrons, it is necessary to use the good offices of other travellers to convey letters towards their destinations. I consigned my message for Thomas to a passing merchant who promised he would take it to the City and I accepted I must wait a week or two for a reply. In the meantime I saw Kate only occasionally but I noticed how she tensed whenever she registered my presence and this confirmed the decision I had made.

In the early autumn I was occupied by a series of visits to the small town of Diss where a fever affected some of the residents. Two of my older patients did not survive the malady but most of those I treated recovered well. I was returning from my latest visitation when I recognised the line of wagons drawn up in the courtyard of my manor and gritted my teeth to encounter Master John Toft once more.

It was young Georgie Antey I met first in the yard, carrying a bag of fodder for the horses. He had grown noticeably taller since I saw him earlier in the year and his voice had begun to deepen.

'We're grateful for your hospitality, Doctor Somers, but I've left payment with your steward for our victuals. We're on our way to Lynn but Master Toft has a letter for you. He's taken it to the house.'

This was welcome news and I was anxious to see if this was Thomas's reply but I exchanged pleasantries with Georgie before going indoors. I met John Toft in the doorway and he grinned at me in a manner which was strangely patronising.

'Doctor Somers, how pleasant to meet you in person! We can't linger so I feared I might miss you. I'd brought a packet for you. I've given it to your delightful lady.'

'To my wife?' The shock unnerved me.

The carter winked. 'Well, to her woman actually. Is it from your doxy, eh, Doctor? I reckoned it might be something a bit off the straight and narrow so I'd better be careful who saw it. But your lady's looking sprightly; better than when I saw her months back. God bless her.'

I thanked him, made my excuses and hurtled to Kate's room, hugely relieved when Judith answered my knock. She slipped out onto the landing and thrust a letter in Thomas's careful script into my hand, obviously reading my mind. 'Don't worry, I haven't shown it to Mistress Somers in case she tried to destroy it. She was a little overwrought earlier today.'

'Did John Toft intrude on her?'

'She invited him to call. She remembered meeting him when he came here once before. It was perfectly proper. She offered him wine and played the gracious hostess. He was deferential and only stayed a few minutes. I was with them.'

'How surprising! I don't entirely trust the man. He likes to probe into things which don't concern him but if Kate behaved correctly, no harm's done.'

I went to my study and read Thomas's letter offering me accommodation for as long as I wanted and adding, in parenthesis, that he and Grizel now had a second daughter who was called Maud. I hoped this would not prove an inauspicious choice of name for the guiltless infant and set about my preparations to leave Worthwaite within two days.

Next morning I was closeted with Perkin as we agreed arrangements for the manor's upkeep after my departure. He had often acted on behalf of his absent principal and I had no concerns about leaving him in charge but went through the ritual of authorising him to take various necessary actions. His office faced away from the courtyard and the main entrance so I did not hear sounds of hasty arrival and was surprised when a servant announced a visitor was begging to meet me urgently.

I was still more surprised when I recognised the bespattered rider as the elegant Norman, Sir Jacques d'Avranches, to whom I had been introduced at Hartham Manor. He had an ugly cut on his forehead and his cloak was slashed.

'My lord Gaston, Lord Fitzvaughan, has sent me. He begs your help.'

Sir Jacques was panting with the effort of speech and I instructed him to sit down and drink some ale before telling me what had happened. He appeared exhausted.

'Yesterday Hartham Manor was attacked,' he said when he had moistened his throat. 'By a large and well-armed force: some wearing Mowbray colours, others were with their leader, the Earl of Stanwick.'

'Stanwick? He was under duress at Ludlow.'

'It seems the Duke of Norfolk persuaded Richard of York to free him so he could make havoc in these parts; we got the story from a prisoner we took. The Earl is Lord Gaston's enemy. I think you know the history. Stanwick and Mowbray's men stormed the manor-house with overwhelming numbers. We fear a gatekeeper was bribed. They put half a dozen servants to the sword but their main objective was the children's nursery. They raged up the stairs, intent on capturing or killing the Fitzvaughan boys.'

'Dear God!'

Sir Jacques held up his hand at my involuntary exclamation. 'They are safe and Lady Eleanor. We fought the villains off but there were many casualties: on both sides. And some outbuildings were destroyed. Lord Gaston resolved at once his lady and their children must leave Hartham Manor. I have conducted them to Saint Edmundsbury where they are safely lodged for now at the abbey. They are to journey on to Lady Maud's new home at Harrow. A messenger has been sent ahead. They will be secure there but their progress will be slow because Lady Eleanor is poorly with her pregnancy. Lord Gaston implores you to join them at Saint Edmundsbury and accompany them to Harrow, to care for her. He will be forever in your debt. I must return to help him defend the manor-house if it is again attacked but, for the moment, we think this barbarous Earl has withdrawn to Norwich. I have left four men at arms to protect the lady on the road and by good fortune there's a party of merchants leaving Saint Edmundsbury shortly with their own guards. Will you go to her, Doctor?'

I did not hesitate. 'I'll be there by nightfall. Tell Lord Fitzvaughan I'll do all I can to deliver his wife and children safely to Harrow.'

'You have his gratitude and mine.' Sir Jacques went to stand but he swayed and I gripped his shoulders and made him sit.

'As a physician I counsel you to rest an hour and take sustenance. You'll not be much use to Lord Fitzvaughan if you collapse at his feet from exhaustion. I'll get some balm for that cut on your face.'

Within minutes he had fallen asleep and, when he awoke refreshed, I was also ready to leave Worthwaite, earlier than planned but with the full approval of my household. I did not say goodbye to Kate but relied on Judith to tell her, if she enquired, that I had gone to London. I saw Sir Jacques mounted and directed one of the labourers at the manor to go with him. The young Norman repeated his thanks and then bent forward in the saddle as he remembered something confidential.

'In case you have the misfortune to cross paths with him, there is a vile fiend among Earl Stanwick's followers. He screamed he would defile Lord Gaston's little sons before he cut their throats. It was this monster most alarmed Lord Gaston. He is a brutal wretch and has no front teeth in his mouth.'

As we passed through the gate and I turned my horse onto the track to the south, away from Sir Jacques, his last words echoed in my head. There were many men who lacked front teeth and I must not jump to conclusions, but it was Gilbert Iffley's acolyte I recalled with clarity. Under his master's instruction he had helped me when I was injured but he had also been at Blackheath with Jack Cade's rebels, when a small child had been violated and killed. I could not dismiss the coincidence from my mind.

A further coincidence occurred when I reached Saint Edmundsbury for, across the square from the entrance to the abbey, I identified John Toft's wagons standing outside the town's main hostelry. Yet this was not in fact surprising or ominous for Toft was Stephen Boice's haulier and Boice had business interests throughout East Anglia. There was no sign of Toft himself which pleased me but young Georgie Antey waved enthusiastically. I raised my hand to acknowledge him but made a show of presenting myself to the gatekeeper at the abbey in order to secure entry. When the party I was escorting set off next morning the wagons had gone and we saw nothing of them on the road south-west. I told myself I must not invent sinister implications where none existed.

*****

Lady Eleanor was still very young to be enduring her third pregnancy and the drama of recent days would test the stamina of the most robust mother. Nevertheless she was determined not to yield to bodily weakness but to ensure her sons reached a safe refuge with Sir Nicholas and Lady Maud. She was poignantly grateful to me for joining her party and insisted we set out as soon as the merchants were ready to travel, but before long it became clear that riding pillion at their pace exhausted her. Fortunately, the further we moved from Mowbray's territory, the safer we were likely to be from his ruffians, so shortly afterwards we let the others go ahead and adopted a slower pace. Despite this I became anxious about Eleanor's condition and when we reached the town of St. Albans, only a day's journey from Harrow, I declared she must rest for two nights in the great abbey's guesthouse for the sake of her unborn child. It was proof of her weakness that she consented.

While my charges were refreshed in the care of the guest-master at the abbey I wished to make a minor pilgrimage of my own and I entered the monastic church after the service of Sext had concluded. Somewhere, out of sight of the laity, my first patron was buried: Humphrey, Duke of Gloucester, King Henry's youngest uncle, who had died nearly six years previously. I owed much to his favour but had become embroiled in actions which damaged me because of my links with his household. Not least, Gilbert Iffley had been in his service when I first encountered the man who was to plague my life thereafter. Finally, I had been present when Gloucester died in controversial circumstances although I was satisfied his death was due to natural causes. Yet I had been accused of hastening his end. I had many reasons to regret my connections with Duke Humphrey but I owed him enough to pay my respects near to his burial place.

I knelt in front of the great screen which hid the sanctuary from unconsecrated eyes and thought of the cultured Duke who welcomed learned men from other countries to his home; who financed and treasured translations of books containing the wisdom of the ancients; who encouraged lively debates between the savants at his table; who provided for a servant's son to embark on a course of education which led to a physician's cap and gown. Whatever difficulties arose subsequently, how could I not be grateful to Duke Humphrey?

'Are you in trouble, my son?' The wavering voice caused me to open my eyes and look up at an elderly monk regarding me with compassion.

Too many troubles to share with this benign brother, I thought. 'I was just saying a prayer for the soul of Duke Humphrey. I served in his household in my youth.'

'God rest him. He lies near to the shrine of St. Alban behind the high altar. Yet, in humility, he chose to rest at a less exalted level, below the sanctuary. He made generous bequests to the abbey and we honour his memory. But you seem ill at ease yourself. I fancy you have burdens of your own to carry.'

'As do many men. You are perceptive, brother, but I don't seek special consolation.' I rose to my feet, not wishing to prolong our conversation, while the old man continued to peer at me with watery eyes.

'It is given to me sometimes to foresee what will come to pass,' he said. 'It is my blessing and my curse. Our realm faces danger and division. Great men at odds with each other will bring destruction.'

It did not require exceptional prophetic powers to make that pronouncement but his next words were more startling. 'The violence will begin here, outside these walls, and you will minister to the fallen. I know it but I shall not witness it come to pass. I suffer the agony of knowing what I shall not see, of carrying the prophet's grief which I can do nothing to dispel.'

I concluded that the old monk's wits had become obsessed with understandable worry about the risk of warfare within King Henry's realm. I could appreciate his fears; I had often shared them. He lived his life in this enclosed community so there was logic in him imagining that the violence he dreaded would take place in the neighbourhood of the abbey. But I could think of no reason why he identified me with the events he foretold and it made me uncomfortable.

I asked him to excuse me as I had duties to perform but he made me kneel again to receive his blessing and when, he bade me farewell, he asked my name so he might speak it in his prayers.

I hurried back to the guesthouse in considerable distress, anxious to concentrate on the needs of my charges and to forget that disturbing, mind-searing prophecy. By good fortune diversion was at hand.

An impressive company of horsemen was drawn up at the abbey gates and I recognised with delight that they wore the colours of Sir Nicholas Chamberlayne. Then, with even greater pleasure I discerned Sir Nicholas himself speaking to the guest-master. He did not notice me at first but beckoned to his followers on the threshold to bring forward four horses conveying a well-cushioned litter. He had come to protect his step-daughter and convey her in a fitting manner for the remainder of her journey. I greeted him with joy.

I agreed that Lady Eleanor would be well enough to travel in the litter the following morning and Sir Nicholas said he and his men would be billeted in the town overnight. He showered me with thanks for conducting her so far, invited me to stay at Harrow as long as I wished but suggested that, if I was in a hurry to reach my friends in the City, I could go there from St. Albans. I thought it my responsibility to accompany my patient to her step-father's house but said I would then be glad to go on directly to London and this was agreed. At that point he summoned one of his armed guards, suggesting we might remember each other, and a brawny young soldier approached with an unforgettably wicked grin on his face.

'Rendell, how good to see you. Are you part of Sir Nicholas's household now?'

'I still serve the Duke of Somerset but that often involves supporting Sir Nicholas. In fact I won't be with either for much longer. There's a troop of us bound for Gascony, although if it gets much later in the year it won't be good for sailing. We're to reinforce the Earl of Shrewsbury's army. They've made some gains already and in the spring campaign we'll finish off the French resistance, you'll see. I'm to act as sergeant: what do you think of that? All ready for some real fighting.'

He was certainly cheerful at the prospect and he contrasted it favourably with the last few months of escorting the royal progresses round the country, being on ceremonial duty he called it, which he found insufferably boring. I did not enquire whether he had found a new sweetheart and he volunteered no information on the subject. It seemed safe to assume he was formally uncommitted to anyone and that was apt when he was to embark on a dangerous enterprise across the sea. He hoped to visit Grizel and Thomas before setting sail so I should see him again and we agreed to share a jug of ale on that occasion. Rendell rubbed his nose, saying he must go to give instructions to his men, and there was new swagger to his gait as he crossed the square. I watched him go with a mixture of emotions: pride for the little part I had in guiding the young man to gain maturity and win promotion, anxiety for his future on the battlefield.

On arrival at Harrow I satisfied myself that Lady Eleanor and her infants were all in reasonable health after the stresses of the journey. The soldiers, including Rendell, were returning to the City immediately but I must not leave until I had paid a courtesy visit to Lady Maud. Before I could do so, at the entrance to the tower-house, an attendant hurried towards me and handed over a letter which he said had been delivered to await my arrival. I did not recognise the rather unformed handwriting and opened it with curiosity, which only increased as I read it.

I make bold to contact you, Doctor Somers, as I believe you may be travelling to London shortly. I have now left the service of her Grace, Queen Margaret, and am lodged at the house on Tower Hill of which you know. I am unaccompanied, except for servants. If you have been able to discover information on the matter I asked you to look into, I should be humbly grateful if you would call in order to inform me of your conclusions.

Your servant
Ursula Bateby

Half a dozen questions perplexed me. How did she know of my journey? Who had told her of my movements? Had she left the Queen's service because she had abandoned the attempt to find evidence of adultery – or had she found that evidence? How could I contemplate visiting her at the house where I had been assaulted by the Earl of Stanwick? Did the description 'unaccompanied' refer to his absence or Stephen Boice's? Might she suspect I had something to report, however unsubstantiated? If so, on what basis?

Despite all these misgivings, I felt a vague sense of unease about one of the crimes attributed to her brother, now it appeared there might be a different culprit, and I could reasonably share this possibility with her. Meeting her might carry its own risks but the prospect was also provocatively attractive.

Part 4 Harrow and London 1452

Chapter 27

Thrusting aside thoughts of Ursula Bateby, I duly paid my respects to Lady Maud who received me with exaggerated graciousness, giving no sign that she had ever encountered me in different circumstances. I did not begrudge her the satisfaction she clearly felt with her new status and her excitement that she was shortly to accompany Sir Nicholas to the royal court. Nonetheless I was amused when the normally unresponsive Marian, at her mistress's side, gave me the twinkle of a grin and raised one eyebrow to signal her appreciation of Maud's transformational abilities.

Amid a flurry of agitated infants and scurrying nursemaids, Lady Eleanor overcame her exhaustion to give me profound thanks for escorting them safely to Harrow. I urged her to ensure she rested before undertaking any duties in her mother's absence from the house and she promised she would do so. Then I took some hasty refreshment with Sir Nicholas and within the hour I set out alone to ride to the City of London.

Remembering the uneven and sometimes slippery surface of the track down the hill I rode slowly through the village but I nearly came to grief when I jerked the reins on hearing my name called. I leaned forward to pat my startled horse and a bony hand grasped the bridle to steady both rider and mount as a friendly voice greeted me.

'Doctor Somers, I heard you were bringing Lady Eleanor and her children. It may be the last time we meet so I wanted to wish you well.'

'Piers! I didn't know you were here.' In my surprise I did not at first register the significance of his words.

'I came on foot from Hartham Manor, carrying my tools, picking up journeyman's work on my way. I left soon after Lady Maud's marriage.'

'You followed Mistress Willoughby?'

'More than a year has passed now since her husband's death and I thought she might consider my suit favourably. I could have saved myself worn shoe leather and sore feet. She says she must honour Master Robin by waiting another twelvemonth before she could even contemplate taking a second husband. She's fully provided for by Lady Maud and will attend her when she goes to court. What can I offer her to compete with that? She was upset I'd come here. She doesn't want me dogging her footsteps, skulking outside the gates of the manor-house. I'm to go elsewhere until next autumn.'

'But you can return then?'

'She doesn't forbid it but she's given no commitment. I don't doubt she'll meet men at court who can offer far more than me. It'll be painful waiting with no expectation of happiness to come. Maybe I'll return to Dartford to bide my time.'

'Surely it's an optimistic sign that she's left open the possibility of your return?'

Piers gave an uncharacteristically sardonic laugh. 'I no longer look for optimistic interpretations – they're likely to be no more than wishful thinking. I left Dartford in a burst of enthusiasm. Jack Cade brought the hope of righting the wrongs common men suffer. I thought we might get within reach of John Ball's vision. Now, with nobles resorting to violence in their squabbles and brutish disorder left unpunished, we're further than ever from his dream. I no longer nourish hopes.'

It was crass to risk darkening his already despondent mood but I did not stop to think. 'On the way here, at St. Albans Abbey, I met an alarming old monk who prophesied worse to come: actual warfare within King Henry's realm this side of the Narrow Sea. He grieved for England.'

'May the Lord God spare him from seeing his prophecy come to pass. And may He bless you, Doctor Somers, in the work you do to help the afflicted. Although the situation was dire, I still treasure the memory of helping you give relief to the suffering on London Bridge, knowing there is some goodness amidst tribulation. Whatever your responsibility for Robin Willoughby's death, I wish you well, physician, in all you do.'

He released his hand from my bridle ready to let me ride on but I wanted to give him some cheer. 'I'll be lodged with my friends in the City, close to the Tower: Thomas Chope, master carpenter, and his family. Call on me there if you pass through London so we can share a jug of ale.'

'Perhaps. I've a few commissions to complete before I set off. I may well be in the City sometime.'

His failure to commit himself did not augur well for seeing him again and I rode down the hill full of regrets for his disillusionment.

*****

For years I had been accustomed to seek solace in the company of Thomas and Grizel, regarding their boisterous household as a base of stability in a turbulent world. On this occasion I soon realised that, despite Thomas's cordial invitation, I could make no selfish assumption about the support they were able to offer me. Thomas gave a brief welcome and locked my medical instruments and money in his chest but he was apparently preoccupied and quickly excused himself saying he had a meeting of his guild to attend. It was unlike him to treat me with courteous formality but I assumed he had serious matters on his mind.

Grizel looked exhausted and was clearly unwell. She was unusually irritable with her older children while fretting over the small baby who lay swaddled in the cradle. There was a nursemaid in attendance to ease her burdens and she had other assistance in the house but she had lost the resilience which always helped her recover quickly from childbirth. I found this worrying and, although the routine care of infants fell primarily to

333

womenfolk and did not often feature as part of a physician's duties, I offered to examine little Maud. When the swaddling had been replaced, I reported back to Grizel.

'I can see no obvious defect. There's no immediate cause for concern. Weakly babies can prosper with good care. I'm sure you know that better than I do. You must concentrate on recovering your strength.'

Grizel gave me a withering look. 'I've lost one baby after birth, Harry Somers, I know the signs but, with God's help, this one will survive. I don't doubt I will too.'

The note of angry resolution in her voice was troubling. 'What is it, Grizel? There's something else wrong, isn't there? Is it your own health?' She shrugged.

'The weariness will pass, I dare say, and I'll be ready to bear another six or seven over the next ten years, like I did before. That's how it goes.'

I wondered what her irony implied, whether Thomas was inconsiderate in forcing his attentions on her, but did not think I should enquire. I had known them both for well over a decade as a friend but would feel awkward probing their personal lives as a physician. Fortunately for me our conversation was interrupted by the arrival of Rendell, clutching a brace of duck and looking cheerful.

'Got them from the undercook at Somerset's house,' he said, presenting his gift to his sister. 'Did him a favour the other week. And what d'you think? We're to leave as soon as *The Merry Miller* returns to Deptford if the weather holds good. No more than a week to go, then I'm off to fight the French. At last!'

I could not share his enthusiasm for the prospect of renewed fighting against the French but it was pleasing to see him so excited. He made no reference to Grizel's lacklustre condition but he did make one comment about Thomas which I found significant because Rendell was seldom sensitive to the moods of other people.

'Don't know what's got into him,' he said when we were alone and I mentioned his brother-in-law. 'For the last few days he's hardly done more than grunt at me when

I've called. He's got something on his mind. Can't be money problems – his business is flourishing.'

'He may be concerned about Grizel and the baby.'

'I doubt it. I reckon he's having it off with some trollop and he's uncomfortable. He's not cut out for double-dealing. He's always let Griz rule the roost. Maybe now he's puffing out his feathers and snuffling around elsewhere.'

I tried to dissuade Rendell from developing this notion but could not dismiss it from my thoughts. Next morning it was obvious Thomas was trying to avoid me which only bolstered my forebodings. Then, when he disappeared into the workshop, Grizel drew me aside and her words gave substance to my fears

'I shouldn't say this, Harry,' she said, picking up some mending and twisting it in her hands. 'But when you talk to Thomas, man to man, I don't ask you to betray a confidence... but if he tells you...if he suggests...' Abruptly she stood up. 'I'm talking nonsense. It's weakness, I suppose. Forget it.'

'Thomas doesn't seem anxious to speak to me, man to man. Is he concealing something?'

'Forget it,' she repeated and clapped her hands for the children playing in the next room to join us. 'Take Uncle Harry and show him the little chest you made, Hal, with the carving on its door. He's quite the artist, is Hal. Go and see, Harry.'

I duly went with the boys to admire Hal's handiwork and there was no further opportunity to speak to Grizel alone. The atmosphere in the household was becoming oppressive and I could think of only one deeply regrettable explanation.

*****

By the second day I needed to escape from the house and said I should like to wander the streets, looking anew for possible lodgings where I might practise medicine. The passage of time meant my name was no longer an impediment in the City. No one tried to detain me and I spent the morning identifying potential premises for a lone physician, without committing myself to any of them. I dined with no great enjoyment at an inn near the river, doubtful whether any of the accommodation I had viewed would suffice and I was unwilling to explore further until the following day. There were still several hours to pass before I returned to sup with Thomas and Grizel and it was this fact, together with my state of dissatisfaction, which led me to a decision I had otherwise resolved to shun. I knew it was foolhardy and approached Tower Hill with a mixture of curiosity and apprehension.

A courteous retainer whom I had not seen before kept me waiting a few minutes while he reported my presence and then I was conducted to a parlour where Mistress Ursula Bateby was sitting by the fireside. She rose at once to greet me, discarding a heavy wrap which had been draped over her shoulders. There was a yellowing bruise on her jaw.

'I hadn't dared to expect you, Doctor Somers. It seemed presumptuous to invite you. I couldn't even be sure you would receive my letter.'

'I was intrigued that you knew of my movements, disconcerted even. I suppose Stephen Boice has had me tracked?'

She fluttered her hands with affection. 'I haven't seen Stephen for some days. We shan't be disturbed. Will you take wine?'

She had evaded my question and it was not worthwhile pressing for an answer. I accepted a goblet.

'I was nearby with an hour to kill and there is something to tell you, although it can't give you the certainty you'd like.'

'About my brother? What have you discovered?' There was no trace of artifice in her behaviour now.

'Nothing definite. But an unpleasant fellow who was with Gilbert Iffley on Blackheath has made vile threats

336

against small children. It might simply be foul-mouthed bravado but it's a coincidence.'

'Who is this villain?'

'I don't know his name. He lacks front teeth and I've seen him at this house.'

She sank onto the window seat. 'Will Winsford,' she said in a whisper. 'I scarcely know him. He's a ruffian who does the Baron's bidding. Is it possible he could have abused and killed the child on Blackheath?'

'There's not a scrap of evidence but he was in the area. I wouldn't have given the idea a second thought but you seemed so confident of your brother's character that when I heard of this Winsford's perverted menaces, I wanted you to know. There's a faint chance your doubts were justified and, if so, that Baron Glasbury was party to your brother's defamation.'

'I'm touched, Doctor Somers, that you should have such consideration for me. I'm not used to such conduct. You've given me a slender thread of hope. That's more than I believed possible.'

It was as if a mask had been lifted from her face and the pretty young woman smiled at me with natural pleasure. Her charm encouraged me to broach a subject I would have been wise to avoid. 'Is Stephen Boice unkind to you?'

Instinctively she touched the contusion on her jaw. 'I have no complaint. He rarely lays a finger on me. Not like others I know of. I'm his chattel. He's free to do as he will with me. He took me when my mother died. She was a seamstress in his household. I was twelve years old. I had nothing and he's given me a good deal. I dare say without him I'd be earning my keep in the gutter.'

I stared at her, seeing her more clearly than I had done before. 'My mother was a seamstress too.'

She raised her arched eyebrows. 'Is that true? You see how differently fortune favours men from women. You have become a fine physician and I am a whore.'

'I was certainly fortunate. Humphrey of Gloucester acted as patron to me. But you shouldn't belittle yourself. When we first met, you implied you were Boice's mistress. Surely that's more fitting?'

'How sweet you are, Harry Somers, and how innocent. When the fancy takes him Stephen Boice offers my services to his friends – the ultimate hospitality, he calls it. If they are agreeable he watches them fuck me and pleasures himself at the sight. A week ago he gave me to a vicious boor who beat me senseless before he raped me.'

'Dear God!'

'God did not intervene and I serviced the Earl's lust all through the night. I wished myself dead then, physician.'

I was trembling with dread. 'Who was this Earl?'

'I think you know. Roger Egremont, Earl of Stanwick: a lascivious monster. Even Stephen was appalled but he did not choose to protest. It's amusing, don't you think: that I am a Stanlaw by birth and it's a Stanwick who has disgraced me beyond anything I've known?'

'I don't think it amusing at all. He's despicable. Boice too: he's no more than a pimp.'

She rose from her seat and put her hand on my arm, feeling my tremor. 'Your manhood and your profession shelter you from some basic realities. Yet I believe your wife suffers an affliction which must pain you.'

Of course she was bound to know my history and I was overwhelmed by the need to share my heartache. 'It pains me grievously and there's no cure, no hope of relief.'

'I encountered your wife in the past, before she married you. Her huge green eyes would draw any man but she was always devoted to her Uncle Stephen. He took advantage of her devotion to make her do his bidding and earn his praise.'

'So I learned. The hold he has over her has contributed to her turmoil of mind.'

'Yet you've cherished her in spite of the grief she's caused you?'

I could not tell whether her question was freighted with hidden meaning. 'Kate will be my wife while we live but my marriage is over. I've left her with those who give her good care.'

She stared at me and drew breath. 'So we each have a burden. Who would have known? Perhaps the children of seamstresses should comfort each other.' She raised her hands to cup my face and drew it down to hers. I was shocked, astonished, but I did not back away from her kiss.

'I believe you could soothe my battered body with your embrace,' she said, 'but you may recoil from a whore's attentions, befouled by Roger Egremont. Or are you content to purify what he has tainted?'

I did not answer her with words. I was inflamed by carnal desire, so long supressed, but also by the unworthy wish to spite Stephen Boice by making love to the mistress he so casually abused. It was late in the evening when I left Ursula Bateby's bed and by then we had both propitiated the fiendish spirits which drove us to joyful consummation.

*****

Supper had long been cleared when I returned to the Chopes' house. Grizel and the children were asleep but Thomas was waiting for me, sprawled on a bench beside the table with a nearly empty flagon of ale at his elbow. He looked haggard and seemed not to notice my own disorderly appearance, beckoning me to join him.

'Christ in Heaven, Harry. I've got to talk to you.'

I nerved myself to listen to a confession of infidelity, blissfully conscious that I was in no state to offer sage advice.

'Of course.' I flopped onto the chair opposite him.

'I pray to God I'll do no harm. I couldn't bear to hurt Grizel or any of my family. But I can't deceive you any

339

longer. You're my oldest friend. I haven't done what he wanted in any case.' His hand was shaking as he lifted his beaker and set it down again.

'I don't follow you, Thomas. What are you saying?'

'A man you know came to see me a week or more ago. He made me promise something or else Grizel and the children would be harmed. He had a vicious looking thug at his side and I didn't doubt he'd carry out his threats. I'm no weakling, Harry, you know that, but I understood this was unspeakably dangerous.'

The notion that Thomas had been an unfaithful husband dissolved in my mind. 'Who was this man?'

'He said his name was Stephen Boice.'

'Then you were right. He is dangerous. What did he want you to do?'

'He knew you were coming here. He said a letter would be sent for you, to await your arrival, and I must destroy it. If I didn't, my family would reap the consequences. His sidekick sniggered at that. Boice said he'd know whether you'd received the letter so I couldn't try to trick him.'

'And the letter came?'

Thomas nodded. 'A day or two later. But I didn't destroy it. I couldn't bring myself to burn it. Then when you came, I couldn't face you, knowing I was keeping it from you, but panicking about the threats and what I was getting into.' He reached inside his jerkin. 'It's here, Harry: still sealed.'

I knew at once it had come from Perkin at Worthwaite and, when I broke the seal, I saw it had been sent only two days after I left my manor. I stared at it, focusing my eyes, and almost uncomprehending I read the message and then read it again.

Forgive me, Doctor Somers, for conveying this unwelcome news. I have failed in the charge that you gave me but I could do nothing against the armed men who compelled me to obey their dictates. Mistress Somers has gone from the house. She went willingly with the men

340

who came. It seems she was aware they were coming and were to escort her to her uncle, Master Boice. It was her choice and had been planned. The only scrap of solace in this dreadful situation is that Judith has gone with her. The girl insisted. She knew nothing of the scheme but would not let Mistress Somers go without her and, I thank God, Mistress Somers was pleased to take Judith with her. But I do not know where they were bound. I shall enquire throughout the neighbourhood and write if I have further news. I beg you to forgive my negligence which could not prevent this awful mishap.

Thomas watched my face as I read. 'What have I been keeping from you?' he asked.

'Retribution.' I said. 'There's nothing to blame yourself for, Thomas. You had no choice. Everything has been cleverly arranged. God only knows where it will end.'

Chapter 28

I had no sleep that night, lying on my bed with my mind in tumult. At first light one of the apprentices was sent with a message to Somerset's house asking if Rendell could obtain leave to assist us. Meanwhile, with Thomas at my side, I presented myself once again at the house where Ursula Bateby had so recently entertained me. We were kept waiting for several minutes before she appeared, looking as if she had dressed in haste and clutching a wrap thrown over her shoulders. She seemed terrified.

'Doctor Somers, you should not have come here. What do you want?'

'Forgive me, Mistress Bateby. It's imperative that I know where Master Boice has gone. He has taken my wife with him: cajoled her to leave the place where she was safe and cared for by people I trust. I beg you to help me find her. She may be in danger.'

Ursula swallowed and gulped, pulling her shawl tighter. 'He's coming here,' she said in a whisper as if the walls would betray her. 'A message arrived only a few minutes before you came. He will be here by nightfall. But...'

She floundered and I tried to prompt her. 'He's bringing Kate here?'

'I don't think so.' She paused and shook her head. 'No, I'm sure Mistress Somers isn't coming. He would have given instructions for her reception, for rooms to be prepared fit for a lady. The note he sent makes no mention of this.'

'Then I beg you to tell me where he might be coming from. It's a week or more since he abducted Kate.'

She sank onto a stool, running her fingers through the fringe of her wrap. Her brow was furrowed as she concentrated. 'I don't know. He was in East Anglia and I think he was to return to London by sea. But he must be ashore now to have sent the message – and not far away if he's to come tonight. Perhaps he has lodged Mistress

Somers in some house of care but I can't say where or when. Perhaps he's making arrangements today before he comes. I'm sorry, Doctor Somers, I know no more and you mustn't remain here. He would be angry to know I was trying to help you.'

Her eyes were brimming with tears and I did not believe she was dissembling. 'I understand. I'll leave now but I'm bound to seek him out, so I may call here later. Forgive me for troubling you.'

We held each other's eyes for a moment and I was aware of Thomas shuffling his feet beside me so I bowed formally and we left the house.

'You're a dark horse, Harry Somers,' Thomas said as we crossed in front of the Tower. 'If I'm not mistaken, there's something between you and that brazen courtesan. Has Boice carried Kate away to spite you for trespassing on his ground?'

'No!' It came as a shout and I regretted it but Thomas quickly turned his attention to practical matters.

'I'll send a lad to enquire at the wharves what ships have come in over the last few days from East Anglia and who their passengers were. Didn't Boice have Kate incarcerated down in Kent once before?'

'He did but he might think it too obvious to do the same thing twice. Let's get back to your house. That's where people know I'm staying. Perkin might send another message.'

*****

I spent an hour fretting while the daily routine of the Chope household began around me and then Rendell arrived, beaming genially at everyone.

'Got to be on board at Deptford to sail on the noon tide the day after tomorrow. Until then I'm at your service, Doctor S. What's it all about then?'

Briefly I told him what I knew but it seemed an inadequate explanation for calling on his help. There was

343

nothing specific he could do unless I had firm information about Boice's whereabouts.

The apprentice making enquiries at the riverside quays returned with tantalising news of passengers conveyed to the City from Harwich who had landed forty-eight hours earlier. A lady and her attendant could well have been Kate and Judith but they were accompanied by two gentlemen and a group of liveried servants. The master of the vessel had clearly been well paid for giving them passage and he denied any knowledge of their identities or where they were bound. Thomas's resourceful apprentice questioned some layabouts propping up the tavern door near where this party had landed and one of them claimed the travellers made a rapid departure on waiting horses, but that was all which could be established. They could have gone anywhere.

I arranged that the house on Tower Hill would be kept under observation, with Rendell and the apprentices taking turns as anonymous bystanders to report any arrivals or departures. I would present myself at the door as soon as I was alerted to Boice's presence there. Rendell was just setting out to take the first shift when a carthorse clattered into the yard of Thomas's workshop and my soldier friend stopped in his tracks beside it. He shouted back to me as I stood at the kitchen door.

'There's an ill-mounted whippersnapper here wants to see you, Doctor.'

The youthful carter leapt from the horse and hurled himself towards me while Rendell reached out to restrain him. I intervened with assumed calmness.

'It's all right, this is Georgie Antey. I know him. What is it Georgie?'

The lad was flushed from exertion and sweating profusely. 'Thank God,' he panted. 'Didn't know if I'd find you. The wheelwright said you might be here. They need help. At Harrow. Mistress Somers...'

I grasped Georgie's shoulders as he tottered and sat him on the step while Rendell fetched a stoup of ale to refresh him.

'Is my wife at Harrow, Georgie?'

He nodded as he drank deeply. 'They got there yesterday, just before dark. I was helping John Toft when we collected them from some place called Headstone where they'd been lodged the previous night. We had to have a litter for Mistress Somers. She wasn't too well and her maid looked in a sorry state.'

'Judith?' Rendell was listening carefully.

Georgie lowered his eyes. 'I think she'd been assaulted... John Toft reckoned the Earl had had her.'

'The Earl? Dear God, what Earl?'

'By Christ, I'll skewer him!'

Rendell and I exclaimed simultaneously but Georgie concentrated on my question. 'The Earl of Stanwick, they called him. He'd travelled with Master Boice and the rest of them.'

'Is Boice still with them?'

'No. He didn't stay with us after we left Headstone. The Earl was in charge after that, with half a dozen armed men beside him. They took the women and asked for admission to the manor on Harrow Hill. They said Mistress Somers was ailing and needed rest.'

'Sir Nicholas Chamberlayne's manor?' Rendell's exclamation was full of disbelief.

'Sir Nicholas and Lady Maud are away at court,' I said, as the horror of the situation became clearer in my mind. 'They've used my wife's condition to inveigle their way into the house where Lady Eleanor and her children are alone with the servants. We must go at once but they've had all night to wreak havoc on a defenceless family. Stanwick's barbaric and he's sworn to destroy the Fitzvaughans.'

'I'll fetch horses and a troop of men from the Tower. The Governor's a friend of Sir Nicholas. He'll send all the help he can. But, by Christ, that rapist bastard is mine if he's harmed Judith.' Rendell bounded off, red in the face and with clenched fists. I was much too preoccupied to see the irony in him presenting himself as Judith's champion.

'You mentioned the wheelwright,' I said to Georgie. 'This was Piers Ford, I take it. Does he understand what has happened?'

'Yes. He recognised me and called me over to find out what I knew. He sensed something wasn't right when he saw our party going up the hill to the entrance of the manor. Mistress Somers' attendant had her wrists bound together but she mouthed *help* when she caught sight of Master Ford. I was upset by what he told me about the Earl and what the brute might do, so he asked me to ride to the City, gave me directions where you'd be, with Master Chope. But I hadn't got a horse; I couldn't take one of John Toft's without him knowing and Master Ford didn't have one of his own. I ran down the hill and found an inn where they let me hire this old fellow – more use for carting he'd be. I had to find my way in the dark and when I got to the City gates they wouldn't let me in 'til daybreak.'

I realised that Georgie had attracted an audience of Chopes and Grizel came forward with a platter of bread and cheese, mothering the exhausted young messenger.

I patted the lad's shoulder. 'I owe you more than I can say.' Then I turned to Thomas. 'Georgie can't go back to John Toft. He'll be seen as a traitor. Will you make sure he gets proper employment? I'll sponsor him as an apprentice. He's resourceful and intelligent.'

'I can see that,' Thomas said. 'Don't worry, I'll see he's all right but I'm coming with you to Harrow. Grizel will look after Georgie until we're back.'

His expression dared his wife to object to these arrangements but she was a practical woman and knew her husband well. She smiled and put her arm round Georgie. 'Come into the house and have a good meal. Then you can get your strength back.'

'I want to go with them to Harrow,' he protested.

346

'No Georgie, you'd be in danger and we'll have our hands full without trying to defend you. You've done your bit.' I could see how desperately he wanted to join us.

A small boy with eyes shining like azure discs pulled at Georgie's arm. 'Will you tell us the story again? We didn't hear it all. We know you're a hero: a real live hero.'

Georgie beamed and let himself be led away by Hal and his younger brothers while Grizel grinned. 'Thank heaven I've borne one male with common sense,' she said. 'Mind you bring Thomas back in one piece, Harry Somers. He seems himself again now. I pray you'll be in time to help the Fitzvaughans.'

After a few minutes Thomas and I were mounted and ready to depart. Moments later Rendell arrived with a troop of a dozen armed men from the Tower. Together we set off on one of the most hair-raising rides I have ever experienced but I could spare no thought for my discomfort in the saddle or the fear of being flung headlong from my horse. My thoughts were centred on the women and children at Roger Egremont's mercy and the fearful reckoning he intended to exact from them. I dared not contemplate the effect these violent events might have on my wife's shattered wits.

*****

At the lower edge of the village, where the track began to climb more steeply towards the church and manor-house, Piers Ford erupted from the cabin which served as his home and workshop. He waved his long arms wildly when he identified me and I signalled to Thomas and our escort to come to a halt.

'Thanks to the blessed saints and Georgie Antey, you've answered my call. I'm sure there's mischief planned. Though the high constable won't have any of it.'

I dismounted and grasped the flailing arms. 'Is Earl Stanwick still at the manor – with my wife and Judith?'

347

'Yes, I'm sure of it. No one's left. When I rode to Headstone the landlord of the inn kept watch for me. He's a good fellow, believed what I said and lent me a horse. More than the bloody high constable did.'

'Slowly, Piers, I need to understand. You went to find the high constable because you were worried what might happen at the manor?'

'Yes. The landlord knew he was at Headstone taking witness statements about some fracas there'd been there. But the Earl and his party, with Stephen Boice as well, all stayed at Headstone before they came to Harrow. The constable met them and he refused to believe they were villains. Told me to get lost and stop spreading malicious lies or he'd issue a warrant to have me up before the next Sessions. I'd done no better when I tried to alert the gatekeeper at the manor-house. I was too late to stop them getting into the gatehouse but I begged him not to let them through to the courtyard.'

'This was before you went to Headstone?'

Piers looked at me as if I was stupid. 'Of course. I ran up there as soon as I'd seen Judith all battered and trussed up like a criminal or a game-bird for the pot. The gatekeeper knew me, more's the pity. He'd berated me in the past for hanging around to catch sight of Mistress Willoughby. She's not at the manor now – she's away at court with Lady Maud – but the gatekeeper thought I was up to my damned tricks, as he called them. He said I was a trouble-maker and he'd have me thrown out of the village.'

'You've done everything you could, Piers. But there's been no sign of anything wrong at the manor since they were admitted? You say no one's come out?'

Piers grunted. 'Only one thing's not right. I went to have a look again, not long before you came, around noon. The old gatekeeper's not in the lodge. One of the Earl's men is stationed there. He shook his fist at me and warned me to clear off.'

It was the confirmation I needed. 'I shall go there and ask to see my wife. I have every right to do that.

348

Thomas, come with me to the entrance and wait for me if they let me inside. Rendell, keep your troop of soldiers out of sight for now. We'll see how Roger Egremont responds to my request and what happens next. I'll try to find out whether he's holding Lady Fitzvaughan and the children prisoner.'

A few minutes later I approached the gatehouse of the manor with its arched entrance and closed door. I looked carefully along the buildings each side of it, which housed the domestic offices and guest accommodation, and at the outer window above the arch. This belonged to the room where the porter slept, which was furnished with windows facing both ways. I remembered the layout of the manor quite well. It had no moat or drawbridge but an enclosing wall ran round three sides of the courtyard, forming a square with the gatehouse range. Inside the wall and across the courtyard from the entrance stood the old tower where the family lived. I could see no sign of activity through the narrow windows of the frontage.

Controlling my anger and my fear as rigorously as I could, I spoke courteously to the man in Stanwick colours who demanded my business. 'My name is Doctor Somers. I understand my wife is in the manor and I would like to see her. Please present my compliments and ask for me to be admitted.'

The man scowled and with a bang closed the hatch through which I had addressed him. It reminded me of the convent of St. Michael's at Stamford but the occupants of this house were very different from the worthy Prioress.

'He's shut you out, Harry,' Thomas said. 'What do we do now?'

'Wait with assumed patience. I hope he's gone to consult the Earl.'

'A man who's tried to kill you more than once. You're putting yourself at hazard. Rendell's troop could rush the gate.'

'We don't know what's happening inside, whether Stanwick's holding any members of the Fitzvaughan

349

family. He's got as many armed men as we have. There's no guarantee Rendell's troop would succeed in an attack.'

I began to wonder whether I was simply being ignored when the Stanwick retainer reappeared and ordered me to approach the gate with my hands held high.

'Just you, Doctor. Your mate stays where he is. If you lower your hands, you're a dead man.'

I whispered to Thomas. 'If I don't return by the time the sun has moved over the trees to our right, you know what to do.' Then I raised my hands and let myself be dragged through the gap as the outer gate was held ajar.

Before being taken to an adjoining room, I was searched but I had already removed my dagger from inside my gown. The door was bolted behind me and a second door giving access to the courtyard was also locked. The only light came from a small window high above me and I concluded I was in a storage chamber – but it could serve as an occasional cell for an unruly servant or an unwanted guest. I waited. In the distance I caught the sound of high-pitched laughter, unrestrained and deeply disturbing. I knew that it was Kate.

At last there was movement outside the courtyard door and as it opened I flattened myself against the wall behind it. It was not unexpected that the first man to enter held a drawn sword which he quickly pointed at my chest but my stomach lurched when I recognised him as the toothless fellow, whose name I now knew to be Will Winsford, who might be worse than a violent lout. Roger Egremont followed him into the chamber, grinning at my discomfort.

'My dear Doctor,' he said. 'How fortuitous! This is bold indeed. I have business here which mustn't be delayed. What do you want?' It unnerved me that he appeared completely sober and reasonably affable.

'I should like to speak to my wife and remove her and her attendant from this place.'

He made a show of considering the matter. 'Mistress Somers left your home of her own free will, I'm

350

told. But I concede you are her husband. The serving girl is another matter.'

'My wife is seriously afflicted in her mind as I suspect you know. Her attendant is necessary to her care. Lady Eleanor Fitzvaughan is well aware of this.'

'Lady Fitzvaughan has no role in these arrangements. She has not even condescended to greet your wife. It is my business with her ladyship that requires attention.' He sounded annoyed and I came to the conclusion that Lady Eleanor and her children were not yet in his power. That was encouraging.

The Earl gave a forced smile. 'Your wife, Doctor Somers, has served her purpose so far as I'm concerned and is become an embarrassment. Stephen Boice suggested we might win entry to the Chamberlayne manor by pleading her ill health and so it proved but now it will suit me to release her. She is a slut, my dear physician, and has allowed herself to be befouled by those among my followers who are not fastidious. The girl, Judith, tried at first to stab me with a bodkin hidden in her bodice. It was necessary to wrestle it from her and it gave me satisfaction to chastise her for her sauciness. She has been my plaything since then, as I imagine she is yours. I am reluctant to let her go.'

My fists clenched of their own accord and the point of Will Winsford's sword moved to my throat. 'I want them both, Egremont. Name your price.'

He leered at me. 'Ah, Doctor, you tempt me greatly. I have a myriad of prices I should like to extract from you but I must defer the pleasure. If I accede to the whole of your impertinent demand you will owe me whatever I choose to specify next time we meet. Remember that. For now I'll be well rid of that gibbering madwoman you married so you'd better take her and the girl. Get away from Harrow as speedily as you can while I attend to my purpose in coming here.' He opened the inner door and gestured to someone in the courtyard before turning back to face me 'By assisting me in removing your disruptive spouse you make yourself complicit in my plan. Remember that too.'

I did not reply but when the two women were pushed into the room I gasped with horror at their appearance. Kate's dress was filthy and her throat bore bite-marks. Her hands were cupped under her breasts and she was mumbling to herself as if oblivious of her surroundings but, when she saw me, she screamed and screamed again.

Earl Stanwick propelled her towards me. 'This is your lawful mate, Mistress, I bid you joy of him. He may lack the vigour of those with whom you have lately consorted but he may rightfully chastise you for your wanton lewdness.'

Kate stared at the Earl and fell silent but I did not touch her. Judith had been dragged forward, her hair loose, her clothes torn, her wrists tied behind her. Roger Egremont ran his hands over her body and fastened his mouth on hers with lascivious provocation but I knew that rising to that provocation would ruin all I hoped to gain. 'Take her as your subordinate whore, Doctor. The harvest is yours but I have ploughed her virgin field.'

It took all my strength to remain quiescent and allow Stanwick's followers to hustle us through the gate but the effort was so unnatural I feared I would be sick on the threshold. The moment we were outside Kate broke from me and ran but Thomas intercepted her and held her firmly. Judith stared straight ahead, blank-faced and silent; she appeared composed but who could tell what would be the effect of the violent degradation she had suffered? I was suddenly certain that she would not stay in my wife's service: the trauma of what she had personally endured and witnessed was too intimately bound up with Kate's insanity.

My gait was unsteady and I stumbled on the uneven ground, wet now from the rain which had begun to fall. That stumble probably saved my life for the arrow had been well directed and whizzed past my ear as I righted myself. Thomas shouted to me to run and we rounded the corner of the adjacent farm buildings before the second arrow landed harmlessly on the track we had been following a moment before.

I leaned back against the wall, breathing deeply. Thomas had lifted Kate and was carrying her, unresisting, in his arms. Judith continued to trudge ahead as if insensible of what was happening around her. Then I saw Rendell emerge from a doorway and stride towards her. He did not speak but he took her hand and led her into the village. It was a truly thoughtful and considerate action and I was proud of him.

*****

Kate remained peaceful so long as I did not approach her. She and Judith were taken to the inn where the landlord's wife attended them while I held a meeting with Thomas, Rendell and Piers. They were all my friends and I should have felt at ease with them but I was shivering uncontrollably with shame at my impotence in the face of Egremont's vile taunts and in the knowledge of his base activities. I tried to concentrate on what needed to be done next.

'My reading of the situation is that Lady Eleanor and her family are ensconced in the tower. Stanwick was anxious to be rid of us so he could get on with what he called his business. I presume he means his men to storm the tower. We must mount a rescue.'

'The tower's got a good strong door, studded with iron,' Piers said. 'But those fighting men are armed and tough.' He turned to Rendell. 'Your little troop would have to fight their way through the gatehouse before they could even get at the tower.'

'Yeah, it'll be bloody. We need more men. I've sent to the high constable in Headstone for reinforcements. He must have officers he can summon. I've used the name of Lord Scales, Governor of the Tower of London, to demand

353

help. The soldier I've sent won't lose the opportunity to remind the constable that he ignored Piers' request for assistance. Bit of luck that was, them shooting arrows at you, Doctor. Gave us the excuse we needed – proof the Earl ain't a nice friendly guest but bent on murder.'

'Well done, Sergeant Tonks.' Thomas patted his brother-in-law on the back. 'So we just sit tight and hope the studded door holds until they can get here from Headstone. How long do you reckon that'll be?'

'Time for us to have a bite to eat,' said Rendell as the landlord appeared with a platter of cheese and meat and they drew a bench up to the table.

I knew my stomach would rebel if I attempted to feed it so I went outside to sit quietly under the porch. The rain had slackened and there was a slight breeze which seemed to clear my head. It troubled me deeply that the Fitzvaughan family were still in danger and I wandered back towards the manor, peering past the farm to the roofs of the manorial buildings. That was how I came to discern the wafting plume of smoke at the top of the hill, the feeble harbinger of the destruction and grief to follow.

Chapter 29

I burst into the inn in a frenzy of distress. 'They've fired the tower. The bastards are trying to smoke the family out from their sanctuary. We've got to act.'

There were no quibbles and Rendell rallied his soldiers. I suggested Piers take Kate and Judith down the hill to his cabin where they could rest out of sight, well away from what might become a battlefield. I judged it unwise for them to become embroiled in further violence after what they had already experienced and Piers had no appetite to engage in combat.

Thomas and I joined the soldiers and were provided with knives to protect ourselves. Our objectives were obvious: to reach the courtyard and divert the fireraisers from their murderous task, to ensure the Fitzvaughan family remained safe in the tower until the high constable arrived with extra fighting men and the authority of the law. It was a desperate endeavour but we could do nothing else.

The first target was rapidly achieved. Rendell and his troop wasted no time attempting to enter the gatehouse from outside the manor. They ran to the side wall and in moments bunked each other onto the coping. Two men were clutching their bows and they began shooting arrows at the Earl's men. Thomas mounted the wall as easily as the soldiers and, with the help of another fellow, hauled me up by the shoulders, my legs waggling awkwardly in the air before I gained a footing. I squatted on the top of the wall for a moment to take in the scene. In the far corner of the courtyard half a dozen horses were ready saddled and becoming restive as a groom sought to quieten them. Stanwick was prepared for a speedy retreat if necessary.

The arsonists were inevitably side-tracked from their task, as was the intention, but they reacted promptly, swivelling round and racing to hack at their attackers as they jumped to the ground. I saw one of Rendell's colleagues felled and another bludgeoned before Thomas dragged me down and pulled me across the courtyard. 'Fill the bucket at the well,' he shouted. 'I'll cover you.'

At first the combatants ignored us but after we had run across to hurl two bucketsful of water onto the scorching door, we were forced to use our knives in self-defence. I stood little chance against trained fighters so, as Rendell appeared at my elbow to engage with the swordsman confronting me, I slipped sideways and ducked beside the well, trying to assess how serious the situation was. Only then did I appreciate what a grave predicament faced the occupants of the tower.

I should have realised that the column of smoke I had seen originally meant a smouldering fire must have been well established by that point. The flames blistering the heavy entrance door were a secondary distraction. The real danger had been initiated before we scaled the wall, in the place where it could cause most harm: in the tower itself. A ladder remained in place, propped against the stone edifice, reaching within an arm's length of a first-floor window. This opening was no narrow defensive slit but it was graced by an arched frame which had contained leaded lights. Smashed glass lay at the bottom of the ladder and the lead tracery had been twisted by the heat. It was clear that blazing material, probably soaked in grease, had been forced through the broken mullions, creating the billowing smoke and driving anyone in the room to flee. A tell-tale wisp still straggled from the aperture. Then I heard the screams.

I ran with another bucket of water towards the tower door. Hand to hand fighting was in progress all around and no one hindered me. Twice more I made the journey and I gave thanks for the strength of the heavy wood, with its iron studs, which had managed to withstand the worst fury of the flames but now I understood the Earl's heinous design. His enemies, struggling against thick smoke, risked being trapped behind the barrier which should have offered them escape. What their fate would be if they could reach the courtyard was desperately uncertain but this was their only chance to survive.

I was filled with fleeting joy when I heard the clank of the key as it turned in the lock inside the tower. Then the hinges grated as the disfigured door swung open, and I was appalled by the sight of the intended victims pouring from the inferno. They were begrimed and singed; some were choking badly. There were far more people than I expected but of course Lady Eleanor would have summoned all the retainers to share her refuge when she became aware of the danger. And the children... there were at least a dozen of them, from tiny babes to young lads and maidens. The Fitzvaughan sons with their nursemaids, but also servants' children, among whom I recognised one small girl covered in smuts. It was natural that Bess Willoughby had left her children at Harrow when she accompanied Lady Maud to court and little Anne was leading a toddler by the hand, her brother, Rob.

I looked round for Lady Eleanor but did not see her and then I had other preoccupations because a hand seized me by the shoulder and I felt the cold metal of a blade against my throat.

'Drop your weapons, every one of you intruders, or I cut Doctor Somers' gullet. Tie his hands.'

Roger Egremont, Earl of Stanwick, had never sounded so authoritative and his voice echoed against the enclosing walls. Nevertheless the fighting did not slacken immediately and there were confused noises behind me. Some of our soldiers were inclined to disregard the threat but, as the Earl smashed his fist into my face, Rendell shouted at them to obey. My arms were wrenched behind me and bound. Then silence fell over the assembled onlookers while three women staggered from the tower, their clothes blackened: one on each side supporting Lady Eleanor Fitzvaughan who could scarcely stand.

'My Lady has miscarried,' one of the attendants said in a low voice.

'By Christ, my Lady, you've saved me the trouble of eviscerating another brat. It's my issue you should be bearing. You were destined as my bride, and my bride you shall be.' Egremont pulled her forward and fastened his mouth on hers, just as I had seen him assault Judith. 'Which are your sons, madam?'

Eleanor did not reply and wilted as the Earl held her. He pushed her away and she sank to the ground while he strode unerringly to the elder of Gaston's boys who was staring in alarm at his mother.

'I have a fancy to roast this pullet over a brazier.' He turned to his men.' Confine these interfering ruffians in the cellar then light a fire in the courtyard. There's plenty of kindling to hand from the tower. Which is your brother, my pretty manikin?'

The child was speechless with terror and Roger Egremont laughed. 'We'll put every boy infant on the flames then. That way we'll find him: King Herod's method, no less.'

My supporters were manhandled to the gatehouse but I noticed Thomas was not among them and I could see only one of our bowmen. A single body in Lord Scales's livery lay motionless on the beaten earth but he was not a man I recognised. I hoped my two missing colleagues had found a safe place to hide but I did not dare to hope they had escaped.

'King Herod's bloody ploy did not achieve its purpose,' I said but was ignored.

One of Stanwick's men laid a hand on Rob Willoughby but jumped back with a yell when Anne bit his fingers. 'He's not a lord,' she squeaked. 'He's my brother.'

'Then I'll be pleased to dash his brains out, you little vixen.' At the sound of his spluttering, toothless delivery I realised who the man was and shuddered.

Will Winsford pushed the small girl aside and reached for the toddler but at that moment there was a whirr in the air, a cry of pain and shouts. I saw a maid servant whisk the two Willoughby children under her skirts as Winsford turned to the comrade at his shoulder who had sunk to his knees with an arrow protruding from his back.

'The high constable's men are here,' I said boldly, despite my uncertainty as to whether this was true. 'You're outnumbered, Egremont, and facing the full might of the law.'

The Earl twitched as a second arrow landed amidst his men, shot, I now realised, from the inner window of the gatekeeper's room above the archway. Below the hidden archer's post the entrance gate began to creak open. Stanwick pulled Winsford towards him and thrust Gaston's heir into his henchman's hands.

'Take the elder brat and get out. Do your worst. I'll have the woman.'

Winsford ran to the horses with little Walter Fitzvaughan under his arm while Stanwick snatched at the boy's mother. Lady Eleanor had struggled to her knees, supported by her attendants, but she had no strength to resist. I saw her cross herself and the grief on her face was unbearable. Unable to use my pinioned arms I did the only thing I could think of to thwart him and flung myself headlong at the Earl's feet. I caused him to stumble while failing to knock him over but a third arrow whizzed past his ear and this was enough to rattle him. Roger Egremont abandoned his intended prey and made for the horses unencumbered.

The Earl was an expert horseman and as they thundered towards the open gate he was only a length behind Winsford. There were men swarming around the entrance who scattered to each side at the sound of the pounding hooves. I thought at first they must be the high constable's posse. Then I saw Rendell detach himself from the scuffle and hurtle towards our own horses which were tied alongside the farmhouse outside the manor. He flung himself into the saddle and set off in pursuit. There was small chance he could catch them.

Running as best I could with my arms restrained, I reached the gate and Thomas appeared, beaming with pride. I did not stop for him to free my bonds but he followed me in a wordless race to the top of the village street where there was a clear view down the steep hill. The slippery ground had slowed the fugitives' pace and they were still in sight, nearing the cabin which was Piers Ford's home. Rendell was halfway down the hill, standing in the stirrups and brandishing his sword, but once they gained the flatter ground the Earl's fine horses would outpace him.

'Oh, God, no! God in heaven, no!'

I heard the voice but did not know it was mine. I came to a sudden stop, my mouth gaping: then I ran on, skidding and stumbling, faster than I have moved of my own volition, before or since. I ran, aware that my effort was futile, that whatever had transpired was unalterable, that I had come to a point of no return in the labyrinth of my life.

I had seen the flurry of skirts as the figure careered from the cabin and I knew it was Kate. I could not tell why she was driven to this act but I understood exactly what she intended. The horses whinnied, colliding with each other when she flung herself under their hooves, and they fell with feral shrieks of pain at broken fetlocks and shattered pasterns. Their riders had no opportunity to control their mounts. They crashed to the ground and one lay unmoving while the other tried to drag himself away from the stricken animals. Other figures had appeared: Judith, hand to mouth, sinking down beside her mistress, and somehow Piers was carrying a small boy in his arms.

Within an instant Rendell had reached the grisly scene, pulling on the reins and leaping from his saddle, never faltering in his self-appointed task. He lifted his sword and drove it into Earl Stanwick's chest, ignoring the wretched man's scream for mercy. Then he withdrew the blade and plunged it into Egremont's nether regions.

'This is for Mistress Judith,' he yelled as I staggered to a halt beside him and, extracting his sword, he wiped it fussily on a tussock of grass.

I dropped to my knees and Rendell slashed away my bonds so I could cradle Kate's head on my lap. She had a massive wound on her temple, her shoulder was crushed and several bones were broken, but for a moment there was intelligence in her eyes. She looked at me with those luminous green orbs and I thought she gave a slight smile which made me shiver. I leaned down to kiss her. Then she shuddered, moaning feebly, and the breath of life left her, beyond the skill of any physician or lover to help or heal. Thomas and Piers were with me and I glimpsed Rendell holding Judith gently while she sobbed. After that I lost all sense and reason. Perhaps I joined my lost wife in that realm of madness from which I had tried for so long to save her. I do not remember details.

They told me afterwards I was groaning and cursing aloud when I covered Kate's face and crawled across to where Will Winsford lay. His brains were splattered over the stones beside the track which his head had hit when he fell from his horse, but I lifted his shoulders and shook him as if I could resurrect the corpse. 'There's a question you must answer,' I said with all seriousness. 'You know the truth. Answer me, answer me.'

I think it was Thomas who hauled me away from the bodies, forcing me to sit on a bench in the cabin and take a mouthful of ale which I spewed across the floor. I could not rid myself of the spectacle I had witnessed repeating itself over and over before my inward eye: Kate running, leaping, throwing up her arms, crashing to the ground, kicked, trampled, her terrestrial life obliterated. Had she sacrificed herself to save the boy she once tried to kill at Hartham Manor? Or was her intervention to make more certain that the child would die? Or was her only impulse to destroy herself, because her existence had become too great a burden and the opportunity to make an end was presented to her? I would never know and it was

361

possible Kate never knew. I was trying to explain what could not be explained.

I must have sat in blind contemplation for some time before I became aware Piers was beside me. 'It was a miracle I caught the little lad,' he said. 'He was flung in the air by the impact. I just put up my arms instinctively and by God's grace managed to grab him. Mistress Somers martyred herself to save him.'

I grunted, unwilling to confirm or deny his assertion. Other people were coming into the cabin. Rendell set down a flagon of ale and bowed while Judith sank in a curtsey. Piers blew sawdust from the only stool and Thomas wiped it with his sleeve. Then two attendants assisted Lady Eleanor Fitzvaughan to sit and she held out her hand to me as I dragged myself to my feet.

'What can I say, dear Doctor Somers? Gaston's son and heir is safe and you will have our undying gratitude. But at what price? Mistress Somers gave her life for him. You are cruelly bereft. May God and the angels comfort you.'

I bowed my head in acknowledgement. 'My Lady, I cannot comprehend all that has happened. Forgive me.'

'I've had Mistress Somers taken to lie in the church of St. Mary's until you are ready to decide where she should be laid to rest.'

'If the priest is willing to bury her here, I'll be more than content. She could have no better resting place.' My mind was racing with the thought that if she had indeed intended to kill herself, she would be cast out from burial in a sanctified grave. No one else was speculating on her motives, which could never be proved, and I would hold my tongue.

'We'll be honoured to make the arrangements. I know Sir Nicholas will be proud to furnish her tomb in the church and my mother will shed a tear for her sacrifice.'

I jolted myself into alertness. 'My Lady, there are immediate concerns to which I must attend: family matters. I need to go to London. Forgive my departure. I hope to return tomorrow to attend my wife's obsequies but if by chance I'm unable to get here in time, would you please proceed as you consider appropriate. I should like Kate to be buried in a peaceful resting place as soon as possible.'

I needed to say no more; she understood and smiled wearily as if she was humouring a wilful child. 'Of course,' she said without commenting on the oddity of my request.

I remembered the personal loss she had suffered. 'I'm grateful but I beg you to rest, my Lady. You should not exert yourself.'

'It's better for me to be occupied,' she said crisply and I knew she was holding back tears. I think we were both relieved as the sound of horsemen outside the cabin diverted our attention.

Thomas and Piers went to investigate and announced the long overdue arrival of the high constable and his men. I had forgotten all about him but he came to join us and began taking witness statements from all present with punctilious pedantry. He was properly deferential to Lady Eleanor but he treated me as if I was in some way responsible for the disaster which had taken place. He ordered me to stay in the vicinity, suggesting he was minded to have me arrested for breach of the peace, although everyone else tried to disabuse him of the idea. The Fitzvaughan name and the damage to Sir Nicholas Chamberlayne's property carried weight with him but the constable seemed determined to exonerate the Earl of Stanwick and his henchmen from any liability. It crossed my mind that a bribe must have changed hands at the meeting in Headstone the previous evening and I judged the fellow incapable of adjusting his outlook to the changed circumstances.

In truth I did not care. Activity went on round me and I heard the allegations and rebuttals but they had no significance to me. My thoughts were slowly coalescing around one objective which was to become my obsession. I accepted a single commission in the name of my dead wife and set my mind to plan for its accomplishment.

It was near nightfall and Rendell was bound to return to London in order to embark on board ship at noon the following day. The constable made no objection to this: indeed he seemed relieved and suggested that Thomas might wish to accompany him but my old friend would not leave me. We made our farewells to Rendell and I was struck by the mutual respect and dignity which he and Judith showed each other as they parted. It had never occurred to me that underneath the spirited chaffing which went on between them, there might be a deeper appreciation of each other's nature.

I was immensely relieved that Lady Eleanor begged Judith to join her household and that the girl accepted. She would be cared for fondly by the Fitzvaughans and aided to recover from her dreadful ordeal, while I could offer her nothing comparable or so fitting. We were both solemn as we said goodbye but I knew now that I had been mistaken to think she ever had feelings towards me which I could not reciprocate. I was able to voice my genuine regrets at the necessity for her to leave my household without the risk of being misinterpreted. I promised to see her when I visited Hartham Manor and we wished each other God speed.

I was absolutely clear now what I would do and, left alone at last with Thomas and Piers, I explained the obligation I must fulfil.

'Ride back to town with me,' I said to Thomas, 'then go home to Grizel. The constable has dismissed you so he can't complain. I'm going to break my word and leave here despite his orders. I know I may not survive this night. It's nobody's choice but mine. God bless you, Piers, wherever you go and however your future works out. Thanks for your friendship.'

Thomas slapped me on the back. 'Of course I'll ride with you but I'm not going home until you've done what you intend. I'm with you all the way.'

Piers had thrown together a bundle of possessions and he followed us to the door. 'I'm not stopping here any longer, Doctor Somers. There's too much pain in this place. Maybe I'll go on to Dartford but first, if you'll have me, I'll join you on the road to the City.'

I looked from one friend to the other. 'If you wish it. I'm privileged. These may be my last hours but I'll spend them in good company. Come, I have an appointment.'

I have scant recollection of that ride. At Thomas's insistence we followed the City walls round towards the east in order to present ourselves at the Aldgate where he was known as a respected local guildsman. This was a benefit because he talked his way into securing our entry despite the hour of darkness. From there it was a short distance to my destination and I begged both my companions to leave me. They insisted they would wait to see the outcome of my mission but Thomas said he would slip away briefly to tell Grizel where he was. It was a mark of their loyalty that neither he nor Piers tried to dissuade me from my undertaking. Instead they withdrew to the shadows across the square while, for the second time within twenty-four hours, I hammered on the door of that fateful house on Tower Hill.

Honest men rarely have cause to rouse their neighbours in the middle of the night and I feared my insistent knocking would be ignored but I continued to thump the woodwork until I heard a petulant voice inside the hallway.

'Who is disturbing the peace? Be off with you.'

'I need urgently to speak to Master Stephen Boice,' I said as firmly as I could manage. 'I bring news from Harrow.'

I heard exasperated muttering and distinguished the words 'another one', as the bolts were drawn back. It alerted me to the likelihood that Boice already knew something of the events at the Chamberlayne residence. It was perfectly credible that one of Stanwick's men had slipped away from a scene of confusion and carried news of the Earl's death to the City. I never doubted that Boice had helped devise the plot to attack the manor-house and in all probability he had arranged to be informed of the result. It was useful to be forewarned.

The hallway was lit only by the fluttering taper which the servant carried and the staircase beyond him was in darkness. In this house above all other I must be vigilant in case of sudden attack and I fingered the hilt of my dagger.

'Wait in here,' the attendant said, opening a side door, but I hesitated, remembering that this was the room where Roger Egremont and his minions had assaulted me. It was pitch black within.

'I'll wait in the hallway where there's some light,' I said with more assurance than I felt and the man, still mumbling, moved to the stairs. As he did so, a gleam appeared on the landing above and a robed figure holding a candelabrum appeared and stood unmoving, looking down at me.

'Well, well, Doctor Somers, so you have come. Indeed I expected you. Come up. You need not attend us, Mardon.'

The servant shrugged and grunted his acknowledgement as he scuttled towards the back of the house. Slowly, I advanced up the stairs, watching carefully in case Boice drew a weapon and struck me down or underlings joined him from the darkness to tear me apart. Neither of these eventualities occurred. Instead Boice opened the door to an antechamber and proceeded to light the wall-sconces from his candles until we were standing facing each other in pools of flickering illumination. He placed the candelabrum on a side table.

'You were expecting me. How much have you learned of the events at Harrow?'

'That your troublesome wife thwarted Stanwick's designs but you are now free of her lunatic ravings. It was ill luck some cowardly carter's boy deserted us before our enterprise was under way. Toft feared the milksop might have gone running to you. He'll reap the reward of treachery.'

I steadied myself: I must not allow him to rattle me with his offensiveness. 'I'm come for Kate's sake,' I said. 'You are responsible for her death as surely as you are guilty of twisting her fragile wits with your devious

367

provocations. I'm here to seek reparation for all the harm you caused to your niece and the misery she suffered because of it.'

'Dear me, how overemotional you are, Harry. Although I deny any responsibility, in a day or two you'll give me thanks for ridding you of the madwoman. You'll soon find a more accommodating wife. Alas, that French Countess you impregnated years ago is wed to another and out of reach. She was too far above your station. What about that saintly girl who served my niece? I imagine you've been tupping her secretly. Now you can take your pleasure unencumbered by the need to observe discretion under your own roof. Don't be a fool, physician. Fate plays tricks with us all. The prudent man accepts what comes and turns it to his advantage. Look at things dispassionately and you'll agree the world is all the better for the loss of your wretched Mistress Somers and the appalling Roger Egremont.'

'That's vile. With your urge to control and torment, you ruined Kate's life – and mine. I've come to challenge you to fight, until one of us is dead.' I was shouting with frustration at his poise and cynicism.

'What nonsense! I am a merchant and you are a physician; neither of us is a combatant but I suspect I have learned a little more swordplay than you. Why put us both to inconvenience and bring about your own destruction for the sake of a feckless hussy? I refuse to fight. If you wish to do me to death, you'll have to strike first. Kill me in cold blood: do you have the composure to do that? I think not.'

He turned his back on me in a sign of bravado and contempt, knowing I would not attack him while he shunned my challenge.

'You're despicable, Boice. You readily abuse the wits of a helpless woman but you won't accept the consequences. Take up a weapon. I know you'll have the advantage but I'll take that risk.'

368

'Ah, so you want me to end your miserable life and send you after your demented spouse? No, Harry, once and for all, I will not fight you.'

A wide beam of light was cast across the floor as the door opened. 'What is this disturbance, Stephen? Why, Doctor Somers!'

Ursula Bateby had been roused from sleep, pale and dishevelled, the fringed wrap thrown loosely over her shift. When she saw me, she quivered and pulled the garment over her breast. 'What has happened?

'My wife is dead,' I answered quickly. 'Together with the Earl of Stanwick and Will Winsford.'

She gasped and put her hand to her mouth.

'Winsford died in the act of abducting a small boy,' I added, fixing her eyes with mine. 'The Earl directed him to do his worst. Mercifully, the child was rescued unharmed.'

'Dear God!' Her exclamation was whispered but it was one of relief.

The implications of this exchange meant nothing to Boice who looked from one to other of us and his brow darkened. 'What are you speaking of? This does not concern you, Ursula.'

'Oh, but it does. What Harry has just told me concerns me greatly. It's a matter of personal joy to me. He has done me an immense favour.'

'How dare you call him by his given name, you shameless woman? What favour has he done you?'

He paused and I realised he misinterpreted what she had meant but his consternation was gratifying. I grinned brazenly at Mistress Bateby and she returned my smile, lowering her eyes demurely.

'What is this, Ursula? Why are you smirking? Is it possible...? Has this lecherous bastard forced himself on you? Has he dared to usurp my place?'

'No, Stephen, he has taken nothing by force. What he gained was freely given. Harry and I have made the two-headed beast but it was our mutual choice and I am glad of it.'

She stood proudly in front of him and when he struck her across the face she did not flinch. Furiously he aimed another blow at her belly but I yanked him by the shoulder and his fist failed to connect with her body.

'Leave her alone!'

The affront to his self-esteem destroyed his detachment and his fury erupted. 'By Christ, I'll flay the skin from the harlot's cunt after I've dealt with you, you swine. I'll fight you now, with no holds barred.' He whisked a dagger from under his gown and tore towards me. I scarcely had time to draw my own shorter knife but it was in my hand to parry his thrust. His next stroke ripped my sleeve and drew blood. I dodged to the side.

Ursula flattened herself against the wall as we stalked each other around the room, slashing with our blades when we saw an opportunity, evaluating each other's skill. I scratched his wrist with a lunge that owed more to luck than intention and this aggravated his anger. He hurled himself on me, aiming for my throat, and I had to twist and duck to avoid his murderous weapon. I tripped on my gown as I skidded out of range for a moment and I knew I could not evade his blows indefinitely. There could only be one outcome to this conflict but I was so consumed by incoherent grief and hatred that I did not care. Breathing hard, I straightened for his next onslaught.

It came in an instant and was contrived to prove lethal. Holding his dagger aloft to distract me, he seized the candelabrum and brought it down to crash on my arm just above the wrist before thudding to the floor. The pain of the blow was acute; flames singed my hand and scorched my cuff. I had no choice and, in instinctive reflex, I dropped my knife as Boice grasped me by the throat and forced me to my knees. He could not resist a final sneer as he raised the blade to slice my windpipe.

'You stupid interfering vermin: how dare you thwart me?'

That instant of conceited mockery undid him. He was still speaking as the cloth enveloped him, shrouding his head, entangling his arms. He swore while he struggled, jabbing at the material with his weapon, but flames were playing at its edge and spreading to his robe. I wrenched myself free from his clutching fingers and Ursula, now clad only in her shift, held out my little knife which she had retrieved.

'Kill him,' she ordered.

I do not know whether I would have done so in cold blood while he writhed blindly on the floor but his clothes were already ablaze and he was screaming in agony. No physician could repair his shrivelling flesh but I could shorten his anguish. I drove my knife into his chest and twisted it free. My fingers were red-hot.

'Fire! Fire!' Ursula Bateby shouted to alert the servants while she pulled me from the room and down the stairs, out of the house. Behind us I could hear crackling and hissing as the flames took hold of the furnishings in that chamber of atrocity. I felt indifferent to my survival.

*****

Thomas and Piers rushed to our side and a third figure unexpectedly removed her own cloak to throw over Ursula's scanty garment as we hurried into one of the narrow side-streets out of the square. Servants were running from the house we had fled and neighbours were being roused to stop the fire spreading to their properties.

'You're hurt.'

'What's happened?'

'Boice is dead.'

'Come quickly. We can't stay here.'

Over the cacophony of our voices, Grizel's rang out. 'You've got to get away, Harry. The officers are looking for you. They searched our house. I came to warn you. There's

371

a warrant for your arrest. The high constable from Harrow has charged you with absconding, fire-raising and murdering the Earl of Stanwick.'

'But I didn't.' The groundless allegation was more than I could cope with and I gave a sob.

'It'll all be put right,' Piers said. 'Lady Eleanor will attest on your behalf. And Judith and half a dozen other witnesses.'

'Fire-raising? It won't help that the house on Tower Hill has just gone up in flames while you were there.' Thomas sounded worried.

'And I've killed Stephen Boice. I'm innocent of the Earl's death but Boice was burning and my dagger gave him his quietus. Perhaps it's all one.' While declaring my innocence, I experienced a wave of all-consuming guilt.

'Don't talk nonsense.' Thomas gave me a gentle shake. 'You need to leave the City, Harry, at least for a few days. Piers will take you to Dartford until everything is sorted out. One of the lads has gone to rouse a boatman to get you across the river.'

'I'll find a place for you to lie low until it's all cleared up. I'll be with you.' Piers tried to sound cheerful but I was not fooled by his attempt to underplay the danger I faced.

'You'd best come with me, mistress, and I'll find you some clothes. If your things are in that house, they'll not be wearable.' Grizel spoke guardedly to Ursula Bateby, uncertain of the woman's position or her part in the drama of the night.'

Ursula was shivering. 'I'd best make myself scarce. Once they find Stephen's body, the officers will be looking for me too.'

'They'll have no case against you,' I said. 'The servants know I was in the house. I'll carry the blame.'

'But I've lost everything. Stephen provided all I had.'

'Ha!' Grizel now understood the situation perfectly but she was not judgemental. 'There's honest work

372

available to those who will take it. I could find you employment in a decent house.'

'No.' My mind was clearing. 'Ursula's right. She needs sanctuary away from the City. Is young Georgie still with you, Grizel?' She nodded. 'Good. Thomas, get Georgie to take Mistress Bateby to Worthwaite. They'll both be safe there until I can return to the manor. Write a letter to my steward, Perkin, to explain everything. Will you do that?'

Thomas gave his agreement but Ursula was looking at me with widened eyes. 'You are the victor, Doctor Somers. Am I the spoils? I shall not object.'

'I'm offering you a refuge. I make no further commitment. But, if God permits, I shall see you at Worthwaite in due course.'

She bowed her head. 'Then I accept your terms.'

We were now near the Chope house and Thomas went inside to fetch my bundle of physician's instruments and the money I had left in his care.

'I recommend you keep your hand in with your trade, Harry,' he said as he handed over my possessions. 'It'll ease the pain of thinking about everything. Besides you need to put a dressing on that arm of yours. Let's be on our way to the wharves. It'll be light soon. Say your goodbyes.'

I dutifully kissed Grizel with the courteous familiarity of an old friend and then I embraced Ursula Bateby with greater abandon. We had faced peril together, she had saved my life and we were complicit in Boice's demise: these facts seemed more potent bonds than that one night of passion I had spent in her bed. I might never see her again but I would remember her fondly.

*****

Thomas gave instructions to the boatman to take us across to Southwark and waved as we pulled from the riverbank. I waved back while speaking in a low voice to the fellow as he pulled on the oars and I slipped a gold coin onto his lap which he acknowledged with a wink. I resumed my seat facing Piers and noticed he looked uncomfortable.

'What is it?' I asked.

He shuffled on the plank seat. 'It's stupid of me but I've got an awkward feeling about taking you to Dartford. The high constable's officers will find out about me and where I came from. They'll follow us.'

'So it's lucky they won't find me with you. I'm not going to Dartford, Piers. I'm enormously grateful for your help but I must go further away, not just to evade the officers but to have a chance of rebuilding my life. Thomas was right to tell me to practise my trade. It's what I must do to redeem all I've wasted and lost. The boatman is taking us to Deptford. You'll be able to get a horse there to go on to Dartford.'

He stared at me. 'What are you going to do – at Deptford?' He knew the answer as he posed the question. 'Rendell is sailing from Deptford.'

'I think they'll give me passage to Bordeaux. Armies always have need of physicians, perhaps especially one who can turn his hand to surgery when necessary. I had my training on London Bridge. I'm ready to face the savagery of larger battlefields. Wish me well.'

Piers did not hesitate and his face was glowing. 'Take me with you. I also have a life to redeem. I could assist you as I did on London Bridge.' He smiled.

'Do you mean it? We might be going to our deaths.'
'So be it.'

*****

We reached *The Merry Miller* before the tide turned and spoke to the officer in charge of the soldiers already embarked. It quickly became clear that he knew something of the outrage at Harrow and he summoned Sergeant Tonks to join us, inviting him to vouch for our identities and characters.

374

Rendell adopted a deliberative expression, rubbing his nose and pursing his lips, enjoying himself thoroughly. 'Yeah, captain,' he said at length, 'they're who they say they are and Master Ford's an honest man. You'll have to make your own judgement about Doctor Somers. I'm not going to be responsible for taking him with us.'

The officer guffawed. 'Be careful your sense of humour doesn't end up with you on the gibbet one day, Tonks. Fortunately you've told me enough previously about Doctor Somers. Get a cabin freed up for him. We're honoured to have him with us.'

Half an hour later I stood with Rendell and Piers to watch as we sailed past the palace at Greenwich which had once belonged to the late Duke Humphrey of Gloucester, the place where I lived as a lad, where I was given the opportunities I now believed I had squandered. I also remembered that other despairing flight down the Thames which took me to Queenborough Castle and all that ensued from there. So much gained – and lost.

'Him and me we've done this before,' Rendell said to Piers. 'Went to Italy then – fled to exile. Had a rare old time, we did.'

'This is different,' I said, thinking of what I needed to put behind me but would never forget. I was leaving bleakness and danger. Yet on a battlefield I could well encounter greater bleakness and more intense danger. The prospect did not deter me. From the back of my troubled mind came a recollection of the strange old monk at St. Albans who had prophesied warfare within King Henry's realm itself and who grieved for England. Was that really possible? I knew it was. Death in Gascony might be preferable: but who could foresee the future?

I turned my eyes to the river in front of our swaying ship and saw pale autumnal sunlight casting silvery sheen on the turbid water.

HISTORICAL NOTE

Most characters in *The Prophet's Grief* are fictional but many events which provide the background to the story are factual. The fortunes of the uprising led by Jack Cade, also known as Edmund Mortimer, which are detailed in the story, follow the recorded history. Furthermore, Cade did indeed have a squire called Stanlaw who met the fate described but I have seen no account of the crime for which he was executed.

The growing tensions between Richard Plantagenet, Duke of York, and Edmund Beaufort, Duke of Somerset are also well recorded and led to several incidents described in the book. Sir Roger Chamberlayne, Keeper of Queenborough Castle in Kent, is an historical person but I have taken the liberty of giving him a younger brother, Sir Nicholas, for whom there is no record in the annals.

The Prophet's Grief continues the story of the young physician, Harry Somers, which began in *The Devil's Stain,* followed by *The Angel's Wing, The Cherub's Smile* and *The Martyr's Scorn.* Several characters in it (both factual and fictional) appear also in the earlier books.

THE AUTHOR

Pamela Gordon Hoad read history at Oxford University, and the subject has remained of abiding interest to her. She has also always loved the drama and romance of characters and plot in historical fiction. She tried her hand at such creative writing over the years but, due to the exigencies of her career, she mainly wrote committee reports, policy papers and occasional articles for publication. After working for the Greater London Council, she held the positions of Chief Executive of the London Borough of Hackney and then Chief Executive of the City of Sheffield. Later she held public appointments, including that of Electoral Commissioner when the Electoral Commission was established.

Since 'retiring', Pamela has lived in the Scottish Borders and been active in the voluntary sector. For three years she chaired the national board of Relationships Scotland and she continues her involvement with several voluntary sector organisations. Importantly, during the last few years, she has also been able to pursue her aim of writing historical fiction. *The Prophet's Grief* is the fifth book about the young physician, Harry Somers. A sixth book in the series is planned for publication in 2020/21.

Pamela has also published short stories with historical backgrounds in anthologies published by the Borders Writers Forum (which she chaired for three years).

Other books by Silver Quill writers based in the Scottish Borders:

For adults:

The Devil's Stain by Pamela Gordon Hoad: '*A tense fifteenth century English murder mystery, full of twists and turns'*, which introduces Harry Somers, physician and investigator.

The Angel's Wing by Pamela Gordon Hoad: '*The action and drama of the first book continue in this compelling sequel as Harry gains a reputation for his medical skills whilst becoming embroiled in the politics of fifteenth century Italy...'*

The Cherub's Smile by Pamela Gordon Hoad: Harry Somers is torn between allegiances. '*I felt I was there, caught up in the turmoil of fifteenth century England, and the characters were totally "real" – as well as intrigue, there is friendship, passion and disappointment... and pathos.'*

The Martyr's Scorn by Pamela Gordon Hoad: Harry struggles to secure his future. '*A thrilling read. I could not put the book down. With so many strong characters, a real sense of the period and twists and turns that almost take your breath away, the writer has truly excelled herself with this latest addition to the Harry Somers series. Outstandingly good.'*

Crying Through the Wind by Iona Carroll. '*...Sensitively written novel of love, intrigue and hidden family secrets set in post-war Ireland... one of those books you can't put down from the very first paragraph...'*

Familiar Yet Far by Iona Carroll. Second novel in *The Story of Oisin Kelly* trilogy follows the young Irishman in

Crying Through the Wind from Ireland and Edinburgh to Australia. '*The author has a genius, bringing you into whichever country she is writing about. You can smell the rain in Ireland and the dust in the Outback...*'

Homecoming by Iona Carroll: Third novel in the series. '*A deeply moving novel about the struggles facing a wounded soldier on his return to his family*'.

Other People's Lives by Iona Carroll: a collection of stories capturing the lives of ordinary people in often surprising and entertaining ways.

Voices by prize-winning author, Oliver Eade: a tale of murder, family love and child abuse seen through the eyes of a grandfather, father and young girl.

The Parth Path by Oliver Eade: In a post-apocalyptic world ruled by women, one brave young man seeks to recapture the happiness of his childhood.

For young adults:

Golden Jaguar of the Sun by prize-winning author, Oliver Eade: first book of a trilogy, spanning the USA and Mexico: a story of teenage love and its pitfalls and also a tale of adventure, fantasy and the merging of beliefs.

The Merging by Oliver Eade is the second book in his *Beast to God* trilogy and continues the story of the young protagonists in *Golden Jaguar of the Sun.*

Revelation by Oliver Eade completes the *From Beast to God* trilogy. No one could have guessed whom Pepe, Adam's and Maria's son, would find in Xibalba, the land of dead souls.

Number 24 by Oliver Eade: in a story of adventure and young love, four teens from Hawick travel to a land in which humans are dogs' pets.

For details of further books by these and other Silver Quill writers:visit www.silverquillpublishing.com